# ANNE HEREFORD

# MORE WILDSIDE CLASSICS

# ANNE HEREFORD

## MRS. HENRY WOOD

**WILDSIDE PRESS**

# ANNE HEREFORD

This edition published 2005 by Wildside Press, LLC.
www.wildsidepress.com

# CHAPTER 1

## MRS. EDWIN BARLEY

An express train was dashing along a line of rails in the heart of England. On one of the first-class carriages there had been a board, bearing the intimation "For Ladies only," but the guard took it off when the train first started. It had come many miles since. Seated inside, the only passenger in that compartment, was a little girl in deep mourning. All was black about her save the white frills of her drawers which peeped below her short, black, flounced frock. A thoughtful, gentle child, with a smooth, pale forehead, earnest eyes, and long, dark eyelashes that swept her cheek. It was a gloomy September day, foggy, and threatening rain—a sad-looking day; and the child's face seemed to have borrowed the aspect of the weather, pervaded, as it was, by a tinge of sadness. That little girl was myself, Anne Hereford.

The train slackened speed, and glided into an important station, larger than any we had passed. It was striking one, and the guard came up to the carriage. "Now, my little lady," said he, "change lines here, and stop for ten minutes."

I liked that guard. He had a kind, hearty face, and he had come up several times to the carriage-door during the journey, asking how I got on. He told me he had a little girl of his own, about as old as I.

"Are you hungry?" he asked, as he lifted me from the carriage.

"Not very, thank you. I have eaten the biscuits."

"Halloa! Stern!" he called out, stopping a man who was hurrying past. "Are you going with the Nettleby train?"

"Yes. What if I am?" was the man's answer. He was rightly named Stern, for he had a stern, sour face.

"See this little girl. She is in the guard's charge. To be put in the ladies' carriage, and taken on to Nettleby."

The man gave a short nod by way of answer, and hurried away. And the guard took me into a large room, where crowds were pressing round a counter. "Here, Miss Williams," he said, to one of the young women behind it, "give this little lady something to eat and drink, and take care of her till the Nettleby train starts. She's to have what comes to a shilling."

"What will you take, my dear?" asked Miss Williams.

The counter was so full of good things that I did not know what, but fixed at length upon a plum-tart. Miss Williams laughed, and said I had better eat some sandwiches first and the tart afterwards.

She was pouring me out a cup of coffee when the guard came up again. "Your baggage is changed, little lady," said he. "You'll find it all right at the Nettleby Station. Good-day."

"Good-bye, and thank you," I answered, holding out my hand, that he might shake it. I felt sorry to part with him—he seemed like a friend. Soon after, the surly guard put in his head and beckoned to me. He marshalled me to a carriage which had a similar board upon it to the other, "For Ladies only," and shut me in without a word. Two ladies sat opposite to me. They did not speak either; but they stared a great deal. I thought it must be at the two tarts Miss Williams had given me in a paper bag, and I did not like to eat them.

At the next station another lady got in, and she began talking at once.

"Are you travelling all alone, little girl?"

"Yes, ma'am. The guard takes care of me."

"Have you come far?"

I had come from a remote part of Devonshire, the sea-coast. It seemed a long way to me, and I said so.

"Will you tell me your name? I dare say it is a pretty one."

"It is Anne Hereford."

"Devonshire is a very nice part of the country. Have you lived in it all your life?"

"Not quite. I was born in India. Mamma brought me to England when I was three years old."

"You are in deep mourning. Is it for a near relative?"

I did not answer. I turned to look out at the window until the tears should go away again. I could not bear that strangers should see them. The lady asked again, and presently I turned round.

"For mamma."

She was silent for some time, looking at me. "Is your papa dead also?"

"He died a long while before mamma did."

"You say you were born in India: perhaps he was an officer?"

"He was Colonel Hereford."

"How many brothers and sisters have you?"

"Not any."

"Where are you going to live?"

"I don't know. I am going now to my Aunt Selina's."

The train approached a station, and the lady got out, or she probably would have asked me a great deal more. At the station following that, the two silent ladies left, and I was alone again. The first thing I did was to eat my tarts and throw away the paper bag. After that I fell asleep, and remembered no more till the guard's surly voice woke me.

"This is Nettleby, if you are going to get out. He said something about some luggage. How much is it?"

"A large box and a small one, and two carpet-bags. 'Miss Hereford, passenger to Nettleby,' is written on them. Can you please to tell me whether it is far to Mr. Edwin Barley's?"

"I don't know any Mr. Edwin Barley. Jem," added he, to one of the porters, "see after her. I'm going to hand out her things."

"Where do you want to go, miss?" the porter asked.

"To Mr. Edwin Barley's. They told me I must get out at Nettleby Station, and ask to be sent on, unless a carriage met me here."

"You must mean Mr. Edwin Barley of Hallam."

"Yes, that's it. Is it far?"

"Well, Hallam's five miles off, and the house is a mile on this side of it. There's no rail, miss; you must go by the omnibus."

"But you are sure that Mrs. Edwin Barley has not come to meet me?" I asked, feeling a sort of chill creep over me. Not any one had come, and the porter put me into the omnibus with some more passengers. What a long drive it seemed! And the hedges and trees looked very dreary, for the shades of evening were gathering.

At the foot of a hill the omnibus pulled up, and a man who had sat by the driver came round. "Ain't there somebody inside for Mr. Edwin Barley's?"

"Yes; I am."

I got out, and the luggage was put upon the ground. "Two shillings, miss," said the man.

"Two shillings!" I repeated, in great alarm.

"Why, did you expect to come for one—and inside too! It's uncommon cheap, is this omnibus."

"Oh, it is not that. But I have not any money."

"Not got any money!"

"They did not give me any. They gave the guard my fare to Nettleby. Mr. Sterling said I should be sure to be met."

The man went up to the driver. "I say, Bill, this child says she's got no money."

The driver turned round and looked at me. "We can call tomorrow for it; I dare say it's all right. Do you belong to the Barleys, miss?"

"Mrs. Edwin Barley is my aunt. I am come on a visit to her."

"Oh, it's all right. Get up, Joe."

"But please," said I, stopping the man, in an agony of fear—for I could see no house or sign of one, except a small, round, low building that might contain one room—"which is Mr. Edwin Barley's? Am I to stay in the road with the boxes?" The man laughed, said he had supposed I knew, and began shouting out, "Here, missis!" two or three times. "You see that big green gate, miss?" he added to me. "Well, that leads up to Mr. Barley's, and that's his lodge."

A woman came out of the lodge, in answer to the shouts, and opened the gate. The man explained, put the trunks inside the gate, and the omnibus drove on.

"I beg pardon that I can't go up to the house with you, miss, but it's not far, and you can't miss it," said she. "I have got my baby sick in its cradle, and dare not leave it alone. You are little Miss Hereford?"

"Yes."

"It's odd they never sent to meet you at Nettleby, if they knew you were coming! But they have visitors at the house, and perhaps young madam forgot it. Straight on, miss, and you'll soon come to the hall-door; go up the steps, and give a good pull at the bell."

There was no help for it: I had to go up the gloomy avenue alone. It was a broad gravel drive, wide enough for three carriages to pass each other; a thick grove of trees on either side. The road wound round, and I had just got in sight of the house when I was startled considerably by what proved to be a man's head projecting beyond the trees. He appeared to be gazing steadfastly at the house, but turned his face suddenly at my approach. But for that, I might not have observed him. The face looked dark, ugly, menacing; and I started with a spring to the other side of the way.

I did not speak to him, or he to me, but my heart beat with fear, and I was glad enough to see lights from several of the windows in front of me. I thought it a very large house; I found afterwards that it contained eighteen rooms, and some of them small: but then we had lived in a pretty cottage of six. There was no need to ring. At the open door stood a man and a maid-servant, laughing and talking.

"Who are you?" cried the girl.

"I want Mrs. Edwin Barley."

"Then I think want must be your master," she returned. "It is somebody from Hallam, I suppose. Mrs. Edwin Barley cannot possibly see you to-night."

"You just go away, little girl," added the footman. "You must come to-morrow morning, if you want anything."

Their manner was so authoritative that I felt frightened, almost crying as I stood. What if they should really turn me away!

"Why don't you go?" asked the girl, sharply.

"I have nowhere to go to. My boxes are down at the gate."

"Why, who are you?" she inquired, in a quick tone.

"I am Miss Hereford."

"Heart alive!" she whispered to the man. "I beg your pardon, miss. I'll call Charlotte Delves."

"What's that? Who will you call?" broke from an angry voice at the back of the hall. "Call 'Charlotte Delves,' will you? Go in to your work this instant, you insolent girl. Do you hear me, Jemima?"

"I didn't know you were there, Miss Delves," was the half-saucy, half-deprecating answer. "The young lady has come—Miss Hereford."

A tall, slight, good-looking woman of thirty-five or thirty-six came forward. I could not tell whether she was a lady or a smart maid. She wore a small, stylish cap, and a handsome muslin gown with flounces—which were in fashion then. Her eyes were light; long, light curls fell on either side her face and her address was good.

"How do you do, Miss Hereford?" she said, taking my hand. "Come in, my dear. We did not expect you until next week. Mrs. Barley is in the drawing-room."

"Mrs. Barley is in her chamber, dressing for dinner," contended Jemima, from the back of the hall, as if intent on aggravation.

Miss Delves made no reply. She ran upstairs, and opened a door, from whence came a warm glow of firelight. "Wait there a moment," she said, looking round at me. "Mrs. Edwin Barley, the child has come."

"What child?" returned a voice—a young, gay, sweet voice.

"Little Miss Hereford."

"My goodness! Come to-day! And I with no mourning about me, to speak of. Well, let her come in."

I knew my Aunt Selina again in a moment. She had stayed with us in Devonshire for three months two years before, when she was nineteen. The same lovely face, with its laughing blue eyes, and its shining golden hair. She wore an embroidered clear-muslin white dress, with low body and sleeves, and a few black ribbons; jet bracelets, and a long jet chain.

"You darling child! But what made you come in this strange way, without notice?"

"Mr. Sterling said he wrote word to you, Selina, that I should be here on Thursday. You ought to have had the letter yesterday."

"Well, so he did write; but I thought—how stupid I must have been!" she interrupted, with a sudden laugh. "I declare I took it to mean next Thursday. But you are all the more welcome, dear. You have grown prettier, Anne, with those deep eyes of yours."

I stood before her very gravely. I had *dreaded* the meeting, believing it would be one of sobs and lamentation for my mother; not taking into account how careless and light-headed Selina was. I had called her "Selina," since, a little girl of four, I had gone on a visit to Keppe-Carew.

Taking off my bonnet, she kissed me several times, and then held me before her by my hands as she sat on the sofa. Miss Delves went out and closed the door.

"They are not home from shooting yet, Anne, so we can have a little talk to ourselves. When they go to the far covers, there's no knowing when they'll be in: two nights ago they kept me waiting dinner until eight o'clock."

"Who did, Aunt Selina?"

"Mr. Barley, and the rest," she answered, carelessly. "Anne, how very strange it was that your mamma should have died so quickly at the last! It was only two weeks before her death that she wrote to tell me she was ill."

"She had been ill longer than that, Aunt Selina—"

"Call me Selina, child."

"But she did not tell any one until she knew there was danger. She did not tell me."

"It was a renewal of that old complaint she had in India—that inward complaint."

I turned my head and my wet eyes from her. "They told me it was her heart, Selina."

"Yes; in a measure; that had something to do with it. It must have been a sad parting, Anne. Why, child, you are sobbing!"

"Please don't talk of it!"

"But I must talk of it: I like to have my curiosity gratified," she said, in her quick way. "Did the doctors say from the first that there was no hope?"

"Mamma knew there was no hope when she wrote to you. She had told me so the day before."

"I wonder she told you at all."

"Oh, Selina! that fortnight was too short for the leave-taking; for all she had to say to me. It will be years, perhaps, before we meet again."

"Meet again! Meet where?"

"In heaven!"

"You are a strange child!" exclaimed Selina, looking at me very steadfastly. "Ursula has infected you, I see, with her serious notions. I used to tell her there was time enough for it years hence."

"And mamma used to tell you that perhaps, if you put oft and put off, the years hence might never come for you, Selina."

"What! you remember that, do you?" she said, with a smile. "Yes, she used to lecture me; she was fifteen years older than I, and assumed the right to do so."

"Mamma never *lectured;* what she said was always kind and gentle," was my sobbing answer.

"Yes, yes. You think me insensible now, Anne; but my grief is over—that is, the violence of the grief. When the letter came to say Ursula was dead, I cried the whole day, never ceasing."

"Mamma had a warning of her death," I continued; for it was one of the things she had charged me to tell to her sister Selina.

"Had a what, child?"

"A warning. The night before she was taken ill—I mean danger-ously ill—she dreamt she saw papa in a most beautiful place, all light and flowers; no place on earth could ever have been so beautiful except the Garden of Eden. He beckoned her to come to him, and pointed to a vacant place by his side, saying, 'It is ready for you now, Ursula.' Mamma awoke then, and the words were sounding in her ears; she could have felt sure that they were positively spoken."

"And you can tell me this with a grave face, calling it a warning!" exclaimed Selina.

"Mamma charged me to tell it you. She related the dream to us the next morning—"

"*Us!* Whom do you mean, child?"

"Me and our old maid Betty. She was my nurse, you know. Mamma said what a pleasant dream it was, that she was sorry to awake from it; but after she grew ill, she said she knew it was sent as a warning."

Selina laughed. "You have lived boxed up with that stupid old Betty and your mamma, child, until you are like a grave little woman. Ursula was always superstitious. You will say you believe in ghosts next."

"No, I do not believe in ghosts. I do in warnings. Mamma said that never a Keppe-Carew died yet without being warned of it: though few of them had noticed it at the time."

"There, that will do, Anne. I am a Carew, and I don't want to be frightened into watching for a 'warning.' You are a Carew also, on the mother's side. Do you know, my poor child, that you are not left well off?"

"Yes; mamma has told me all. I don't mind."

"Don't mind!" echoed Selina, with another light laugh. "That's because you don't understand, Anne. What little your mamma has left has been sunk in an annuity for your education—eighty or a hundred pounds a year, until you are eighteen. There's something more, I believe, for clothes and incidental expenses."

"I said I did not mind, Selina, because I am not afraid of getting my own living. Mamma said that a young lady, well-educated and of good birth, can always command a good position as governess. She told me not to fear, for God would take care of me."

"Some money might be desirable for all that," returned my aunt, in a tone that sounded full of irreverence to my unaccustomed ears. "The maddest step Colonel Hereford ever took was that of selling out. He thought to better himself, and he spent and lost the money, leaving your mamma with very little when he died."

"I don't think mamma cared much for money, Selina."

"I don't think she did, or she would not have taken matters so quietly. Do you remember, Anne, how she used to go on at me when I said I should marry Edwin Barley?"

"Yes; mamma said how very wrong it would be of you to marry for money."

"Quite true. She used to put her hands to her ears when I said I hated him. Now, what are those earnest eyes of yours searching me for?"

"*Do* you hate him, Selina?"

"I am not dying of love for him, you strange child."

"One day a poor boy had a monkey before the window, and you said Mr. Edwin Barley was as ugly as that. Is he ugly?"

Selina burst into a peal of laughter. "Oh, he is very handsome, Anne; as handsome as the day: when you see him you shall tell me if you don't think so. I—What is the matter? What are you looking at?"

As I stood before my aunt, the door behind her seemed to be pushed gently open. I had thought some one was coming in; and said so.

"The fire-light must have deceived you, Anne. That door is kept bolted; it leads to a passage communicating with my bedroom, but we do not use it."

"I am certain that I saw it open," was my answer; and an unpleasant, fanciful thought came over me that it might be the man I saw in the avenue. "It is shut now; it shut again when I spoke."

She rose, walked to the door, and tried to open it, but it was fast.

"You see, Anne. Don't you get fanciful, my dear; that is what your mamma was." But I shook my head in answer.

"Selina, did not Mr. Edwin Barley want me to go to Mrs. Hemson's instead of coming here?"

"Who told you that?"

"I heard Mr. Sterling talking of it with mamma."

"Mr. Edwin Barley did, little woman. Did you hear why he wished it?"

"No."

"You should have heard that, it was so flattering to me. He thought I was too giddy to take charge of a young lady."

"Did he?"

"But Ursula would not accept the objection. It could not matter for a few weeks, she wrote to Mr. Edwin Barley, whether I were giddy or serious, and she could not think of consigning you, even temporarily, to Mrs. Hemson. Ah! my cousin Frances Carew and I took exactly opposite courses, Anne; I married for money, she for love. She met an attractive stranger at a watering-place, and married him."

"And it was not right?"

"It was all wrong. He was a tradesman. A good-looking, educated man—I grant that; but a tradesman. Never was such a thing heard of, as for a Carew to stoop to that. You see, Anne, she had learnt to like him before she knew anything of his position, or who he was. He was a visitor at the place, just as she was. Of course she ought to have given him up. Not she; she gave herself and her money to him, and a very pretty little fortune she had."

"Did she marry in disobedience?"

"That cannot be charged upon her, for she was alone in the world, and her own mistress. But a Carew of Keppe-Carew ought to have known better."

"She was not of Keppe-Carew, Selina."

"She was. Don't you know that, Anne? Her father was Carew of Keppe-Carew; and when he died without a son, his brother, your mamma's father and mine, succeeded to KeppeCarew. He died in his turn, leaving no son, and Keppe-Carew and its broad lands went to a distant relative, the male heir. We three Carews have all married badly, in one way or another."

Mrs. Edwin Barley was speaking dreamily then, as if forgetting any one heard her.

"She, Frances, married Hemson the tradesman, placing a barrier between herself and her family; Ursula married Colonel Hereford, to wear out a few of her best years in India, and then to die in poverty, and leave a child unprovided for; and I have married Edwin Barley. Which is the worst, I wonder?"

I thought over what she said in my busy brain. Few children had so active a one.

"Selina, you say you married Mr. Edwin Barley because he is rich."

"Well?"

"Why did you, when you were rich yourself?"

"*I* rich? You will count riches differently when you are older. Why, Anne, do you know what my fortune was? Four thousand pounds. Ursula had the same, and she and Colonel Hereford spent it. That put a notion into my father's head, and he tied mine up tight enough, securing it to my absolute use until I die."

"Will it be Mr. Barley's when you die, Selina?"

"Were I to die before next Monday, it would be yours, pussy, for it is so settled. After that, if I die without a will, it would go to Mr. Edwin Barley; but I shall be of age next Monday, and then can make one. I think it must be my first care—a will," she laughed. "So munificent a sum to dispose of! Shall I leave it to you?"

The room-door was pushed open, and some one entered. A shortish man, of nearly forty years, in a velveteen shooting-coat and gaiters, and with a dark face: the same dark face that had looked out from the trees in the avenue. I shrank round Selina with a sudden fear. Not that the features were particularly ill-favoured in themselves, but so dark and stern. And the remembrance of the fright was on me still.

"Where are you coming to, child?" she said. "This is Mr. Edwin Barley."

# CHAPTER 2

## IN THE WOOD

That Mr. Edwin Barley! My imagination had been setting the face down for a robber's at least; and the thought flashed over me—How could Selina have married him? Another thought came with it—Had he been the intruder at the door?

"Who is that, Selina?" he asked in a very strong, determined voice, but not an unpleasing one.

"Anne Hereford. Fancy my making so stupid a mistake as to conclude it was next Thursday the lawyer meant. And she has had to find her way from Nettleby in the best way she could."

He looked at me with his black eyes, the blackest eyes I had ever seen. Either they wore a warning expression, or I fancied so, and I took it to mean I was not to say I saw him watching the house from the avenue. No fear, after that, that I should speak of it.

"Did you walk from Nettleby, little one?"

"No, sir. I came in the omnibus to the gate."

"She has been asking me if you were very handsome; and I told her to wait and see," observed Selina, with a laugh, and somehow it grated on my ears. He made no reply in words, but his brow contracted a little. I noticed one thing—that he had very pretty teeth, white and even.

"How is it you are home before the others?" she resumed. "And where are they lingering? Charlotte Delves says the dinner is spoiling."

"They cannot be far behind," was Mr. Edwin Barley's answer. "I'll go and dress."

As he went out of the room we heard sounds of voices and laughter. Selina opened the window, and I stood by her. The night had grown clearer, the moon was bright. Three gentlemen, dressed something like Mr. Edwin Barley, were approaching the house with game, guns, and dogs.

"Can you see them by this light, Anne?"

"I can see that two are young, and one looks old. He has grey hair."

"Not very old, not more than fifty—but he is so stout. It is the parson, Mr. Martin."

"Do parsons go out shooting, Selina?"

"Only when they can get the chance," she laughed. "That young one is Philip King, a ward of Mr. Edwin Barley's. He and I are not friends at all, and I do what I can to vex him. He is terribly ill-tempered."

"Is he?"

"He fell in love with me at Easter, the silly boy! Fancy that! One can't think it was in earnest, you know, but it really seemed like it. I asked him if he would like his ears boxed, and Mr. Edwin Barley gave us both a sharp talking-to, saying we ought to be sent to school again."

"Both! But if it was not your fault?"

"Mr. Edwin Barley said it was my fault," she returned, with a laugh. "Perhaps it was. He has not, as I believe, loved Philip King since."

"Who is the other one with them, Selina?" I asked, as the gentlemen below disappeared.

"The other is George Heneage—a great friend of mine. Hush! he is coming up."

George Heneage entered. A young man, tall, slender, active; with a pale, pleasant face, and dark wavy hair. He had a merry smile, and I thought I had never seen any one so nice-looking. Mrs. Edwin Barley moved to the fire, and he took her hand in greeting.

"Well! And how have you been all day? Dull?"

It was the pleasantest voice in the world! Quite a contrast to that of Mr. Edwin Barley.

"Much any of you care whether I am dull or gay," she returned in answer, half laughing, half pouting. "The partridges get all your time, just now. I might be dead and buried before any of you came home to see after me."

"We must shoot, you know, Selina. One of us, at any rate, came home a couple of hours ago—Barley."

"Not to me. He has only just come in. You must be mistaken."

"Look here. I was away for a short time from the party, seeing after the horse I lamed the other day, and when I got back, Barley had vanished: they thought he had gone to look after me. Perhaps he had in one sense, the great simpleton—Halloa! who's that?" he broke off, seeing me for the first time, as I stood partly within the shade of the window-curtain.

"It is little Anne Hereford. She has arrived a week before I expected her. Anne, come forward, and let Mr. Heneage make love to you. It is a pastime he favours."

He lifted me up by the waist, looked at me, and put me down again.

"A pretty little face to make love to. How old are you?"

"Eleven, sir."

"Eleven!" he echoed, in surprise. "I should have taken you for nine at the very most. Eleven!"

"And eleveneen in sober sense," interposed Selina, in her lightest and most careless manner. "I suppose children are so who never live with brothers and sisters. You should hear her talk, George! I tell her her mamma and nurse have made an old woman of her."

"Dare I venture to your presence in this trim, Mrs. Edwin Barley?"

The speaker was the Reverend Mr. Martin, who came slowly in, pointing to his attire.

"It is Barley's fault, and you must blame him, not me," he continued. "Barley invited me to say grace at your table today, and then disappeared, keeping us waiting for him until now, and giving me no time to go home and make myself presentable."

"Never mind, Mr. Martin, there are worse misfortunes at sea," she said, in that charmingly attractive manner that she could sometimes use. "I have sat down with gentlemen in sheeting-coats before to-day, and enjoyed my dinner none the worse for it. Is that you, Miss Delves?"

Footsteps were passing the open door, and Miss Delves came in.

"Did you speak, Mrs. Edwin Barley?"

"Yes. Take this child, please: she must have some tea. Anne dear, ask for anything to eat that you best fancy. You shall come up again after dinner."

We went to a small parlour on the ground floor—Miss Delves said it was her own sitting-room—and she rang the bell. The maid who had been gossiping at the front-door came in to answer it.

"Are you at tea still, Jemima?"

"Yes, Miss Delves."

"I thought so. There's no regularity here unless I'm everywhere about myself. Bring in a cup for Miss Hereford, and some bread and butter."

They both left the room. I supposed that Miss Delves was going to dine presently, for a cloth was spread over one end of the table, with a knife and silver forks, the cruet-stand and salt-cellar, glasses, and a decanter of wine. Presently Jemima came back with a small tray, that had my tea upon it. She seemed a free-and-easy sort of girl, sat down in a chair, and began chattering. Another servant came in with a small jar of preserves. They called her Sarah.

"Miss Delves has sent some jam for the young lady, if she'd like it. Or will she take a slice of cold meat first, she says?"

"I'll have the jam, please."

"That's right, miss," laughed Jemima. "Sweets is good."

"Aren't you coming to your tea, Jemima? There'll be a fuss if she comes in and finds you have not begun it."

"Bother the tea! We are not obliged to swallow it down just at the minute she pleases," was the answer of Jemima.

"I say," exclaimed the other suddenly, "what do you think I saw? Young King—"

Jemima gave a warning shake of the head, and pointed to me. The conversation was continued in a whisper, in which I once caught the words, "that handsome George Heneage." Presently steps were heard approaching, and the two maids disturbed themselves. Sarah caught up the plate of bread and butter, and stood as if she were handing it to me, and Jemima stirred the fire vigorously. It had been warm in the day, but the bit of lighted fire in the grate looked pleasant in the autumn evening. The footsteps passed on.

"How stupid you are, Sarah! startling one for nothing!" exclaimed Jemima.

"I thought it was Charlotte Delves. It sounded just like her foot."

"She's in the kitchen, and won't come out of it till the dinner's gone in. She's in one of her tempers to-day."

"Is Charlotte Delves the mistress?" I could not help asking.

Both the maids burst out laughing. "She would like to be, miss; and she is, too, in many things," answered Jemima. "When young madam came home first—"

"Hush, Jemima! she may go and repeat it again."

Jemima looked at me. "No: she does not look like it. You won't go and repeat in the drawing-room the nonsense we foolish servants talk, will you, Miss Hereford?"

"Of course I will not. Mamma taught me never to carry tales; she said it made mischief."

"And so it does, miss," cried Jemima. "Your mamma was a nice lady, I'm sure! Was she not Mrs. Edwin Barley's sister?"

Before I had time to answer, Charlotte Delves came in. We had not heard her, and I thought she must have crept up on tiptoe. Sarah made her escape. Jemima took up the jam-pot.

"What are you waiting for?" she demanded, with asperity.

"I came in to see if the young lady wanted anything, ma'am."

"When Miss Hereford wants anything, she will ring." Jemima retired. I went on with my tea, and Miss Delves began asking me questions about home and mamma. We were interrupted by a footman. He was bringing the fish out of the dining-room, and he laid the dish down on the table. Miss Delves turned her chair towards it, and began her dinner. I found that this was her usual manner of dining, but I thought it a curious one. The dishes, as they came out of the dining-room, were placed before her, and she helped herself. Her other meals she took when she pleased, Jemima generally waiting upon her. I did wonder who she could be.

It seemed that I had to sit there a long time. I was then taken upstairs by Jemima, and my hair brushed. It hung down in curls all round, and Jemima pleased me by saying it was the loveliest brown hair she had ever seen. Then I was marshalled to the drawing-room. Jemima opened the door quietly, and I went in, seen, I believe, by no one. It was a large room, three-cornered in shape, quite full of bright furniture. Selina's grand piano was in one of the angles.

Standing before the fire, talking, were the clergyman and Mr. Edwin Barley. A stranger might have taken one for the other, for the clergyman was in his sporting clothes, and Mr. Barley was all in black, with a white neckcloth. On a distant sofa, apparently reading a newspaper, sat Philip King; his features were handsome, but they had a very cross, disagreeable expression. He held the newspaper nearly level with his face, and I saw that his eyes, instead of being on it, were watching the movements of Mrs. Edwin Barley. She was at the piano, not so much singing or playing, as trying scraps of songs and pieces. Mr. Heneage was standing by and talking to her. I went quietly round by the chairs at the back, and sat down on the low footstool at the corner of the hearth. The clergyman saw me and smiled. Mr. Barley did not; he stood with his back to me. He also seemed to be watching the piano, or those at it, while he spoke in low, confidential tones with the clergyman.

"I disagree with you entirely, Barley," Mr. Martin was saying. "Rely upon it, he will be all the better and happier for following a profession. Why! at Easter he made up his mind to read for the Bar!"

"Young men are changeable as the wind, especially those whom fortune has placed at ease in the world," replied Mr. Barley. "Philip was red-hot for the Bar at Easter, as you observe; but something appears to have set him against it now."

"You, as his guardian and trustee, should urge him to take it up; or, if not that, something else. A life of idleness plays the very ruin with some natures; and it strikes me that Philip King has no great resources within him to counteract the mischief of no occupation. What is the amount of his property?" resumed Mr. Martin, after a pause.

"The estate brings in about eighteen hundred a year." "Nonsense! I thought it was only ten or twelve."

"Eighteen, full. Reginald's was a long minority, you know."

"Well, if it brought in eight-and-twenty, I should still say give him a profession. Let him have some legitimate work; occupy his hands and his head, and they won't get into mischief. That's sound advice, mind, Barley."

"Quite sound," rejoined Mr. Barley; but there was a tone in his voice throughout that to me seemed to tell either of want of sincerity or else of a knowledge that to urge a profession on Philip King would be wrong and useless. At this period of my life people used to reproach me with taking up prejudices, likes and dislikes; as I grew older, I knew that God had gifted me in an eminent degree with the faculty of reading human countenances and human tones.

"I have no power to force a profession upon him," resumed Mr.

Edwin Barley; "and I should not exercise it if I had. Shall I tell you why?"

"Well?"

"I don't think his lungs are sound. In my opinion, he is likely to go off as his brother did."

"Of consumption!" hastily muttered the clergyman: and Mr. Edwin Barley nodded.

"Therefore, why urge him to fag at acquiring a profession that he may not live to exercise?" continued Mr. Barley. "He looks anything but well; he is nothing like as robust as he was at Easter."

Mr. Martin turned his head and attentively scanned the face of Philip King. "I don't see anything the matter with him, Barley, except that he looks uncommonly cross. I hope you are mistaken."

"I hope I am. I saw a whole row of medicine phials in his room yesterday: when I inquired what they did there, he told me they contained steel medicine-tonics—the physician at Oxford had ordered them. Did you ever notice him at dinner—what he eats?"

"Not particularly."

"Do so, then, the next opportunity. He takes scarcely anything. The commencement of Reginald's malady was loss of appetite: the doctors prescribed tonics for him. But they did not succeed in saving him."

Once more Mr. Martin turned his eyes on Philip King. "How old was Reginald King when he died?"

"Twenty-three. Three years older than Philip is now."

"Well, poor fellow, I hope he will outlive his weakness, whatever may cause it, and get strong again. That money of his would be a nice windfall for some one to drop into," added the clergyman, after a pause. "Who is heir-at-law?"

"I am."

"You!"

"Of course I am," was the quiet reply of Mr. Edwin Barley.

"Nurse him up, nurse him up, then," said the clergyman, jokingly. "Lest, if anything did happen, the world should say you had not done your best to prevent it; for you know you are a dear lover of money, Barley."

There may have been a great deal more said, but I did not hear. My head had sought the wall for its resting-place, and sleep stole over me.

What I felt most glad of, the next morning, was to get my purse. There were twenty-seven shillings in it; and old Betty had caused it to be put in one of the boxes, vexing me. "People in the train might rob me of it," she said.

Jemima waited on me at dressing, and I had breakfast in Miss Delves's parlour. Afterwards I went up to Mrs. Edwin Barley in the drawing-room. She was in mourning, deep as mine.

"I had been tempted to put it off for a cool dress yesterday evening," she said to me. "What with dinner, and the fire they *will* have, though I am sure it is not weather for it, I feel melted in black. The fire is kept large to please Philip King. So Miss Delves informed me when I remonstrated against it the other day. He must be of a chilly nature."

Remembering what I had heard said the previous night, I thought he might be. But the words had afforded the opportunity for a question that I was longing, in my curiosity, to put.

"Selina, who is Miss Delves? Is she a lady or a servant?"

"You had better not call her a servant, Anne; she would never forgive it," answered Selina, with a laugh. "She is a relative of Mr. Edwin Barley's."

"Then, why does she not sit with you, and dine at table?"

"Because I do not choose that she shall sit with me, and dine at table," was the resentful, haughty retort; and I could see that there had been some past unpleasantness in regard to Miss Delves. "When Mr. Edwin Barley's mother died, who used to live with him, Charlotte Delves came here as mistress of the house. That was all very well so long as there was no legitimate mistress, but ages went on, and I came to it. She assumed a great deal. I found she was planted down at table with us, and made herself my companion in the drawing-room at will. I did not like it; and one day I told my husband so in her presence. I said that I must be sole mistress in my own house, and quitted the room, leaving them to settle it. Since then she has taken the parlour for her sitting-room, and looks to the household, as she did before. In short, Miss Delves is housekeeper. I have no objection to that; it saves me trouble, and I know nothing of domestic management. Now and then I invite her to take tea with us, or to a drive with me in the pony carriage, and we are vastly polite to each other always."

"But if you do not like her—"

"Like her!" interrupted Selina. "My dear child, we hate each other like poison. It was not in human nature, you know, for her not to feel my entrance to the house as a *wrong*, displacing her from her post, and from the influence she had contrived to acquire over Mr. Edwin Barley. They were as intimate as brother and sister; and I believe he is the only living being she cares for in the whole world. When I took a high tone with her, it exasperated her all the more against me, there's no doubt of it; and she repays it by carrying petty tales of me to Mr. Edwin Barley."

"And whose part did he take, Selina!"

"Mine, of course—always!" she returned, with a forcible emphasis on the first word. "But it has never been open warfare between me and Miss Delves, Anne; you must understand that.

Should anything of the sort arise, she would have to quit the house. A bitter pill that would be, for she has no money, and would have to go out as housekeeper in reality, or something of the kind. My occupation would be gone then."

"What occupation?"

"That of saying and doing all sorts of wild things to make her think ill of me. She goes and whispers them to Mr. Edwin Barley. He listens to her—I know he does, and that provokes me. Well, little pet, what are those honest brown eyes of yours longing to say?"

"Why did you marry him, Selina?"

"People say for money, Anne. I say it was fate."

"He persuaded you, perhaps?"

"He did. Persuaded, pressed, worried me. He was two years talking me into it. Better, perhaps, that he had given his great love elsewhere! Better for him, possibly, that he had married Charlotte Delves!"

"But did he want to marry Charlotte Delves?"

"Never. I don't believe that even the thought ever entered his head. The servants say she used to hope it; but they rattle nonsense at random. Edwin Barley never cared but for two things in the world: myself and money."

"Money?"

"Money, Anne. Pretty little pieces of gold and silver; new, crisp bank-notes; yellow old deeds of parchment, representing houses and lands. He cares for money almost as much as for me; and he will care for it more than for me in time. Who's this?"

It was Philip King. He came in, looking more cross, if possible, than he did the previous night. His face shone out pale and sickly, too, in the bright morning sun. Selina spoke, but did not offer her hand.

"Good-morning, Mr. King; I hope you feel better to-day. You did not get down to breakfast, I understand. Neither did I."

"I did get down to breakfast," he answered, speaking as if something had very much put him out. "I took it with Mr. Edwin Barley in his study."

"Leaving George Heneage to breakfast alone. You two polite men! Had I known that, I would have come down and breakfasted with him."

That she said this in a spirit of mischief, in a manner most especially calculated to provoke him, I saw by the saucy look that shot from her bright blue eyes.

"I think you and Heneage breakfast together quite often enough as it is, Mrs. Edwin Barley."

"You do? Then, if I were you, sir, I would have the grace to keep such thoughts to myself: or tell them to Mr. Edwin Barley, if you like. He might offer you a premium for them—who knows?"

Philip King was getting into an angry heat.

"I hope you have tolerably strong shoulders," she resumed, as if struck with some sudden thought.

"Why so?"

"George Heneage intends to try his cane upon them on the next convenient day."

His lips turned white.

"Mrs. Barley, what do you mean?"

"Just what I say. You have taken to peep and pry after me—whether set on by any one, or from some worthy motive of your own, you best know. It will not serve you, Philip King. If there is one thing more detestable than another, it is that of spying. I happened to mention this new pastime of yours before Mr. Heneage, and he observed that he had a cane somewhere. That's all."

The intense aggravation with which she said it was enough to rouse the ire of one less excitable than Philip King. He was breaking out in abuse of Mr. Heneage, when the latter happened to come in. A few menacing words, a dark look or two from either side, and then came the quarrel.

A quarrel that terrified me. I ran out of the room; I ran back again; I don't know what I did. Mrs. Edwin Barley seemed almost as excited as they were: it was not the first time I had seen her in a passion. She called out (taking the words from the old ballad, "Lord Thomas"), that she cared more for the little finger of George Heneage than for the whole body of ill-conditioned Philip King. I knew it was only one of her wild sayings: when in a passion she did not mind what she said, or whom she offended. I knew that this present quarrel was altogether Selina's fault—that her love of provocation had brought it on. Mr. Edwin Barley had gone over to his brother's; and it was well, perhaps, that it was so.

Jemima appeared on the stairs, carrying up a pail—there was no second staircase to the house. "What is the matter, Miss Hereford?" she asked. "Goodness me! how you are trembling!"

"They are quarrelling in there—Mr. Heneage and Mr. King. I am afraid they will fight."

"Oh, it has come to that, has it?" said Jemima, carelessly. "I thought it would. Never mind them, Miss Hereford; they'll not hurt you."

She tripped upstairs with the pail, as if a quarrel were the most natural event in the world, and I looked into the room again. Mr. Heneage held Philip King by the collar of the coat.

"Mark me!" he was saying. "If I catch you dodging my movements again, if I hear of your being insolent to this lady, I'll shoot you with as little compunction as I would a partridge. There!"

"What is Mrs. Edwin Barley to you, that you should interfere?"

retorted Philip King, his voice raised to a shriek. "And she! Why does she set herself to provoke me every hour of my life?"

"I interfere of right: by my long friendship with her, and by the respect I bear for her mother's memory. Now you know."

Mr. Heneage gave a shake to the collar as he spoke, and I ran up to my room, there to sob out my terror. My heart was beating, my breath catching itself in gasps. In my own peaceful home I had never seen or heard the faintest shadow of a quarrel.

By-and-by Jemima came in search of me. Mrs. Edwin Barley was waiting for me to go out in the pony-carriage. I bathed my face and my red eyes, was dressed, and went down. At the door stood a low open basket-chaise, large and wide, drawn by a pony. Mrs. Edwin Barley was already in it, and Mr. Heneage stood waiting for me. He drove, and I sat on a stool at their feet. We went through green lanes, and over a pleasant common. Not a word was said about the recent quarrel; but part of the time they spoke together in an undertone, and I did not try to hear. We were away about two hours.

"You can run about the grounds until your dinner's ready, if you like, Anne," Mrs. Barley said to me when we alighted. "I dare say you feel cramped, sitting so long on that low seat."

She went in with Mr. Heneage, the footman saying that some ladies were waiting. I ran away amidst the trees, and presently lost myself. As I stood, wondering which way to take, Mr. Edwin Barley and Philip King came through, arm-in-arm, on their way home, talking together eagerly. I thought Philip King was telling about the quarrel.

It was no doubt unfortunate that my acquaintance with Mr. Edwin Barley should have begun with a fright. I was a most impressionable child, and *could not* get over that first fear. Every time I met him, my heart, as the saying runs, leaped into my mouth. He saw me and spoke.

"So you have got back, Anne Hereford?"

"Yes, sir," I answered, my lips feeling as if they were glued together.

"Where's Mrs. Barley?"

"She has gone indoors, sir."

"And George Heneage. Where's he?"

"He went in also, sir. John said some visitors were waiting to see Mrs. Barley."

And to that he made no rejoinder, but went on with Philip King.

Nothing more occurred that day to disturb the peace of the house. A gentleman, who called in the afternoon, was invited to dine, and stayed. Mrs. Edwin Barley rang for me as soon as she went up to the drawing-room. I thought how lovely she looked in her black net dress, and with the silver ornaments on her neck and arms.

"What did you think of Mr. Philip King's temper this morning, Anne?" she asked, as she stood near the fire and sipped the cup of coffee that John had brought in.

"Oh, Selina! I never was so alarmed before."

"You little goose! But it was a specimen, was it not, of gentlemanly bearing?"

"I think—I mean I thought—that it was not Mr. King who was in fault," I said; not, however, liking to say it.

"You thought it was George Heneage, I suppose. Ah! but you don't know all, Anne; the scenes behind the curtain are hidden from you. Philip King has wanted a chastisement this fortnight past; and he got it. Unless he alters his policy, he will get one of a different nature. Mr. Heneage will as surely cane him as that I stand here."

"Why do you like Mr. Heneage so much, Selina?"

"I like him better than any one I know, Anne. Not with the sort of liking, however, that Mr. Philip King would insinuate, the worthy youth! Though it is great fun," she added, with a merry laugh, "to let the young gentleman think I do. I have known George Heneage a long time: he used to visit at Keppe-Carew, and be as one of ourselves. I could not like a brother, if I had one, more than I do George Heneage. And Mr. Philip King and his ally, Charlotte Delves, tell tales of me to my husband! It is as good as a comedy."

A comedy! If she could only have foreseen the comedy's ending!

On the following morning, Saturday, they all went out shooting again. Mrs. Edwin Barley had visitors in the forenoon, and afterwards she drove over to Hallam in the pony carriage, with the little boy-groom Tom, not taking me. I was anywhere: with Charlotte Delves; with Jemima; reading a fairytale I found; playing "Poor Mary Anne" on the piano. As it grew towards dusk, and no one came home, I went strolling down the avenue, and met the pony carriage. Only Tom was in it.

"Where is Mrs. Edwin Barley?"

"She is coming on, miss, with Mr. Heneage. He came up to the lodge-gate just as we got back."

I went to the end of the avenue, but did not see her. The woman at the lodge said they had taken the path on the left, which would equally bring them to the house, though by a greater round. I ran along it, and came to the pretty summerhouse that stood where the ornamental grounds were railed off from the pasture at the back and the wood beyond. At the foot of the summer-house steps my aunt stood, straining her eyes on a letter, in the fading light; George Heneage was looking over her shoulder, a gun in his hand.

"You see what they say," he observed. "Rather peremptory, is it not?"

"George, you must go by the first train that starts from Nettleby," she returned. "You should not lose a minute; the pony carriage will take you. Is that you, Anne?"

"I would give something to know what's up, and why I am called away in this fashion," was his rejoinder, spoken angrily. "They might let me alone until the term I was invited for here is at an end."

Mrs. Edwin Barley laughed. "Perhaps our friend, Philip King, has favoured Heneage Grange with a communication, telling of your fancied misdoings."

No doubt she spoke it lightly, neither believing her own words nor heeding the fashion of them. But George Heneage took them seriously; and it unfortunately happened that she ran up the steps at the same moment. A stir was heard in the summer-house. Mr. Heneage dashed in in time to see Philip King escaping by the opposite door.

The notion that he had been "spying" was, of course, taken up by Mr. Heneage. With a passionate word, he was speeding after him; but Mrs. Edwin Barley caught his arm.

"George, you shall not go. There might be murder done between you."

"I'll pay him off; I'll make him remember it! Pray release me. I beg your pardon, Selina."

For he had flung her hand away with rather too much force, in his storm of passion; and was crashing through the opposite door and down the steps, in pursuit of Philip King. Both of them made straight for the wood; but Philip King had a good start, and nothing in his hand; George Heneage had his gun. Selina alluded to it.

"I hope it is not loaded! Flying along with that rate, he might strike it against a tree, and be shot before he knows it. Anne, look here! You are fleeter than I. Run crosswise over that grass to the corner entrance; it will take you to a path in the wood where you will just meet them. Tell Mr. Heneage, from me, that I *command* him to come back, and to let Philip King alone. I command it, in his mother's name."

I did not dare to refuse, and yet scarcely dared to go. I ran along, my heart beating. Arrived at the entrance indicated I plunged in, and went on down many turns and windings amidst the trees. They were not very dense, and were intersected by narrow paths. But no one could I see.

And now arrived a small calamity. I had lost my way. How to trace an exit from the wood I knew not, and felt really frightened. Down I sat on an old stump, and cried. What if I should have to stay there until morning!

Not so. A slight noise made me look up. Who should be standing near, his back against a tree, smoking a cigar and smiling at me, but Philip King.

"What is the grief, Miss Anne? Have you met a wolf?"

"I can't find my way out, sir."

"Oh, I'll soon show you that. We are almost close to the south border. You—"

He stopped suddenly, turned his head, and looked attentively in a direction to the left. At that moment there came a report, something seemed to whizz through the air, and strike Philip King. He leaped up, and then fell to the ground with a scream. This was followed, so instantly that it seemed to be part and parcel of the scream, by a distant exclamation of dismay or of warning. From whom did it come?

Though not perfectly understanding what had occurred, or that Philip King had received a fatal shot, I screamed also, and fell on my knees; not fainting, but with a horrible sensation of fear, such as perhaps no child ever before experienced. And the next thing I saw was Mr. Edwin Barley, coming towards us with his gun, not quite from the same direction as the shot, but very near it. I had been thinking that George Heneage must have done it, but another question arose now to my terrified heart: Could it have been Mr. Edwin Barley?

"Philip, what is it?" he asked, as he came up. "Has any one fired at you?"

"George Heneage," was the faint rejoinder. "I saw him. He stood there."

With a motion of the eyes, rather than with aught else, poor Philip King pointed to the left, and Mr. Edwin Barley turned and looked, laying his gun against a tree. Nothing was to be seen.

"Are you sure, Philip?"

"I tell it you with my dying lips. I saw him."

Not another word. Mr. Edwin Barley raised his head, hut the face had grown still, and had an awful shade upon it—the same shade that mamma's first wore after she was dead. Mr. Barley put the head gently down, and stood looking at him. All in a moment he caught sight of me, and I think it startled him.

"Are you there, you little imp?"

But the word, ugly though it sounds, was spoken in rough surprise, not in unkindness. I cried and shook, too terrified to give any answer. Mr. Barley stood up before Philip King, so that I no longer saw him.

"What were you doing in the wood?"

"I lost my way, and could not get out, sir," I sobbed, trembling lest he should press for further details. "That gentleman saw me, and was saying he would show me the way out, when he fell."

"Had he been here long?"

"I don't know. I was crying a good while, and not looking up. It was only a minute ago that I saw him standing there."

"Did you see Mr. Heneage fire?"

"Oh no, sir. I did not see Mr. Heneage at all."

He took my hand, walked with me a few steps, and showed me a path that was rather wider than the others.

"Go straight down here until you come to a cross-path, running right and left: it is not far. Take the one to the right, and it will bring you out in front of the house. Do you understand, little one?"

"Yes, sir," I answered, though in truth too agitated to understand distinctly, and only anxious to get away from him. Suppose he should shoot me! was running through my foolish thoughts.

"Make speed to the house, then," he resumed, "and see Charlotte Delves. Tell her what has occurred: that Philip King has been shot, and that she must send help to convey him home. She must also send at once for the doctor, and for the police. Can you remember all that?"

"Oh yes, sir. Is he much hurt?"

"He is dead, child. Now be as quick as you can. Do not tell your aunt what has happened: it would alarm her."

I sped along quicker than any child ever sped before, and soon came to the cross-path. But there I made a mistake: I went blindly on to the left, instead of to the right, and I came suddenly upon Mr. Heneage. He was standing quite still, leaning on his gun, his finger on his lip to impose silence and caution on me, and his face looked as I had never seen it look before, white as death.

"Whose voice was that I heard talking to you?" he asked, in a whisper.

"Mr. Edwin Barley's. Oh, sir, don't stop me; Mr. King is dead!"

"Dead! Mr. King dead?"

"Yes, sir. Mr. Edwin Barley says so, and I am on my way to the house to tell Miss Delves to send for the police. Mr. Heneage, did you do it?"

"I! You silly child!" he returned, in accents of rebuke. "What in the world put that in your head? I have been looking for Philip King—waiting here in the hope that he might pass. There, go along, child, and don't tremble so. That way: you are coming from the home, this."

Back I went, my fears increasing. To an imaginative, excitable and timid nature, such as mine, all this was simply terrible. I did gain the house, but only to rush into the arms of Jemima, who happened to be in the hall, and fall into a fit of hysterical, nervous sobbing, clinging to her tightly, as if I could never let her go again.

A pretty messenger, truly, in time of need!

# CHAPTER 3

## GOING OUT IN THE FOG

Philip had arrived from another quarter. A knot of labourers on the estate, going home from work, happened to choose the road through the wood, and Mr. Edwin Barley heard them.

One of them, a young man they called Duff, was at the house almost as soon as I. He came into the hall, and saw me clinging to Jemima. Nothing could have stopped my threatened fit of hysterics so effectually as an interruption. Duff told his tale. The young heir had been shot in the wood, he said. "Shot dead!"

"The young heir!" cried Jemima, with a cry. She was at no loss to understand who was meant: it was what Philip King had been mostly styled since his brother's death. Charlotte Delves came forward as Duff was speaking. Duff took off his felt hat in deference to her, and explained.

She turned as white as a sheet—white as George Heneage had looked—and sat down on a chair. Duff had not mentioned George Heneage's name, only Mr. Edwin Barley's: perhaps she thought it was the latter who had fired the shot.

"It must have been an accident, Duff. They are so careless with their guns!"

"No, ma'am, it was murder! Leastways, that's what they are saying."

"He cannot be dead."

"He's as dead as a door-nail!" affirmed Duff, with decision. "I can't be mistaken in a dead man. I've seen enough of 'em, father being the grave-digger. They are bringing him on, ma'am, now."

Even as Duff spoke, sounds of the approach stole on the air from the distance—the measured tread of feet that bear a burden. It came nearer and nearer; and Philip King, or what was left of him, was laid on the large table in the hall. As is the case in some country-houses, the hall was furnished like a plain room. Duff, making ready, had pushed the table close to the window, between the wall and the entrance-door, shutting me into a corner. I sank down on the matting, not daring to move.

"Light the lamp," said Mr. Edwin Barley.

The news had spread; the servants crowded in; some of the women began to shriek. It became one indescribable scene of confusion, exclamations, and alarm. Mr. Edwin Barley turned round, in anger.

"Clear out, all of you!" he said, roughly. "What do you mean by making this uproar? You men can stay in the barn; you may be wanted," he added, to the out-door labourers.

They crowded out at the hall-door; the servants disappeared through the opposite one. Mr. Edwin Barley was one who brooked no delay in being obeyed. Miss Delves remained, and she drew near.

"How did it happen?" she asked, in a low voice, that did not sound much like hers.

"Get me some brandy, and a teaspoon!" was Mr. Edwin Barley's rejoinder. "He is certainly dead, as I believe; but we must try restoratives, for all that. Make haste; bring it in a wine-glass."

She ran into the dining-room, and in the same moment Mrs. Edwin Barley came lightly down the stairs. She had on her dinner-dress, black silk trimmed with crape, no ornaments yet, and her lovely light hair was falling down over her bare neck. The noise, as it appeared, had disturbed her in the midst of dressing.

"What is all this disturbance?" she began, as she tripped across the hall; and it was the first intimation Mr. Edwin Barley had of her presence. He might have arrested her, had there been time; but she was bending over the table too soon. Believing, as she said afterwards, that it was a load of game lying there, it must have been a great shock; the grey-and-brown woollen plaid they had flung over him, from the neck downwards, looking not unlike the colour of partridge feathers in the dim light. There was no gas in the house; oil was burnt in the hall and passages—wax candles in the sitting-rooms.

"It is Philip King!" she cried, with a sort of shriek. "What is the matter? What is amiss with him?"

"Don't you see what it is?" returned Mr. Edwin Barley, who was all this while chafing the poor cold hands. "He has been shot in the chest; marked out in the wood, and shot down like a dog."

A cry of dread—of fear—broke from her. She began to tremble violently. "How was it done, Edwin? Who did it?"

"You."

"*I!*" came from her ashy lips. "Are you going mad, Edwin Barley?"

"Selina, this is as surely the result of your work as though you had actually drawn the trigger. I hope you are satisfied with it!"

"How can you be so cruel?" she asked, her bosom heaving, her breath coming from her in gasps.

He had spoken to her in a low, calm tone—not an angry one. It changed to sorrow now.

"I thought harm would come of it; I have thought so these two days; not, however, such harm as this. You have been urging that fellow a little too much against this defenceless ward and relative of mine; but I could not have supposed he would carry it on to murder. Philip King would have died quite soon enough without that, Selina; he was following Reginald with galloping strides."

Charlotte Delves returned with a teaspoon and the brandy in a wine-glass. As is sure to be the case in an emergency, there had been an unavoidable delay. The spirit-stand was not in its place, and for a minute or two she had been unable to find it. Mr. Edwin Barley took up a teaspoonful. His wife drew away.

"Was it an accident, or—or—done deliberately?" inquired Charlotte Delves, as she stood there, holding the glass.

"It was deliberate murder."

"Duff said so. But who did it?"

"It is of no use, Charlotte," was all the reply Mr. Barley made, as he gave her back the tea-spoon. "He is quite dead."

Hasty footsteps were heard coming along the avenue, and up the steps to the door. They proved to be those of Mr. Lowe, the surgeon, from Hallam.

"I was walking over to Smith's to dinner, Mr. Edwin Barley, and met one of your labourers coming for me," he exclaimed in a loud tone, as he entered. "He said some accident had happened to young King."

"Accident enough," said Mr. Edwin Barley. "Here he lies." For a few moments nothing more was said. Mr. Lowe was stooping over the table.

"I was trying to give him some brandy when you came in."

"He'll never take brandy or anything else again," was the reply of Mr. Lowe. "He is dead."

"As I feared. Was as sure of it, in fact, as a non-professional man can well be. I believe that he died in the wood, a minute after the shot struck him."

"How did it happen?" asked the surgeon. "These young fellows are so careless!"

"I'll tell you all I know," said Mr. Barley. "We had been out shooting—he, I, and Heneage, with the two keepers. He and Heneage were not upon good terms; they were sour with each other as could be; had been cross and crabbed all day. Coming home, Heneage dropped us; whether to go forward, or to lag behind, I am unable to say. After that, we met Smith—as he can tell you, if you are going to his house. He stopped me about that right-of-common business, and began discussing what would be our better mode of proceeding against the fellows. Philip King, whom it did not interest, said he should go on, and Smith and I sat down on the bench outside the beer shop, and called for a pint of cider. Half-an-hour we may have sat there, and then I started for home through the wood, which cuts off the corner—"

"Philip King having gone forward, did you say?" interrupted the surgeon.

"Yes. I was nearly through the wood, when I heard a slight movement near me, and then a gun was fired. A terrible scream—the scream of a man, Lowe—succeeded in an opposite direction. I pushed through the trees, and saw Philip King. He had leaped up with the shot, and was then falling to the ground. I went to his succour, and asked who had done it. 'George Heneage,' was his answer. He had seen him raise his gun, take aim, and fire upon him."

Crouching down there on the matting, trembling though I was, an impulse prompted me to interrupt: to say that Mr. Edwin Barley's words went beyond the truth. All that Philip King had said was, that he saw George Heneage, saw him stand there. But fear was more powerful than impulse, and I remained silent. How could I dare contradict Mr. Edwin Barley?

"It must have been an accident," said Mr. Lowe. "Heneage must have aimed at a bird."

"There's no doubt that it was deliberate murder!" replied Mr. Edwin Barley. "My ward affirmed it to me with his dying lips. They were his own words. I expressed a doubt, as you are doing. 'It was Heneage,' he said; 'I tell it you with my dying lips.' A bad man!—a villain!" Mr. Barley emphatically added. "Another day or two, and I should have kicked him out of my house; I waited but a decent pretext."

"If he is that, why did you have him in it?" asked the surgeon.

"Because it is only recently that my eyes have been opened to him and his ways. This poor fellow," pointing to the dead, "lifted their scales for me in the first instance. Pity the other is not the one to be lying here!"

Sounds of hysterical emotion were heard on the stairs: they came from Mrs. Edwin Barley. It appeared that she had been sitting on the lowest step all this time, her face bent on her knees, and must have heard what passed. Mr. Barley, as if wishing to offer an apology for her, said she had just looked on Philip King's face, and it had frightened her much.

Mr. Lowe tried to persuade her to retire from the scene; but she would not, and there she sat on, growing calm by degrees.

The surgeon measured something with a teaspoon into a wine-glass, filled it up with cold water, and made her drink it. He then took his leave, saying that he would call again in the course of the evening. Not a minute had he been gone, when Mr. Martin burst into the hall.

"What is this report?" he cried, in agitation. "People are saying that Philip King is killed."

"They might have said murdered," said Mr. Edwin Barley. "Heneage shot him in the wood."

"Heneage!"

"Heneage. Took aim, and fired at him, and killed him. There never was a case of more deliberate murder."

That Mr. Edwin Barley was actuated by intense animus as he said this, the tone proved.

"Poor fellow!" said the clergyman, gently, as he leaned over him and touched his face. "I have seen for some days they were not cordial with each other. What ill-blood could have been between them?"

"Heneage had better explain that when he makes his defence," said Mr. Edwin Barley, grimly.

"It is only a night or two ago that we were speculating on his health, upon his taking a profession; we might have spared ourselves the pains, poor lad. I asked you, who was his heir-at-law, little thinking another would so soon inherit."

Mr. Edwin Barley made no reply.

"Why—good heavens!—is that Mrs. Barley sitting there?" he inquired in a low tone, as his eyes fell on the distant stairs.

"She won't move away. These things do terrify women. Don't notice her, Martin: she will be better left to herself."

"Upon my word, this is a startling and sudden blow," resumed the clergyman, again recurring to the death. "But you must surely be mistaken in calling it murder."

"There's no mistake about it: it was wilful murder. I am as sure of it as though I had seen the aim taken," persisted Mr. Barley. "And I will pursue Heneage to the death."

"Have you secured him? If it really is murder, he must answer for it. Where is he?"

Mr. Barley spoke a passionate word. It was a positive fact—account for it, any one who can—that until that moment he had never given a thought to the securing of George Heneage. "What a fool I have been!" he exclaimed, "what an idiot! He has had time to escape."

"He cannot have escaped far."

"Stay here, will you, Martin. I'll send the labourers after him; he may be hiding in the wood until the night grows darker."

Mr. Edwin Barley hastened from the hall, and the clergyman bent over the table again. I had my face turned to him, and was scarcely conscious, until it had passed, of something dark that glided from the back of the hall, and followed Mr. Barley out. With him gone, to whom I had taken so unaccountable a dislike and dread, it was my favourable moment for escape; I seemed to fear him more than poor Philip King on the table. But nervous terror held possession of me still, and in moving I cried out in spite of myself. The clergyman looked round.

"I declare it is little Miss Hereford!" he said, very kindly, as he took my hand. "What brought you there, my dear?"

I sobbed out the explanation. That I had been pushed into the corner by the table, and was afraid to move. "Don't tell, sir, please!

Mr. Edwin Barley might be angry with me. Don't tell him I was there."

"He would not be angry at a little girl's very natural fears," answered Mr. Martin, stroking my hair. "But I will not tell him. Will you stay by your aunt, Mrs. Edwin Barley?"

"Yes, please, sir."

"But where *is* Mrs. Barley?" he resumed, as he led me towards the stairs.

"I was wondering, too," interposed Charlotte Delves, who stood at the dining-room door. "A minute ago she was still sitting there. I turned into the room for a moment, and when I came back she was gone."

"She must have gone upstairs, Miss Delves."

"I suppose she has, Mr. Martin," was Miss Delves's reply. But a thought came over me that it must have been Mrs. Edwin Barley who had glided out at the hall-door.

And, in point of fact, it was. She was sought for upstairs, and could not be found; she was sought for downstairs, all in vain. Whither had she gone? On what errand was she bent? One of those raw, damp fogs, prevalent in the autumn months, had come on, making the air wet as if with rain, and she had no out-door things on, no bonnet, and her black silk dress had a low body and short sleeves. Was she with her husband, searching the wood for George Heneage?

The dark oak-door that shut out the passage leading to the domains of the servants was pushed open, and Jemima's head appeared at it. I ran and laid hold of her.

"Oh, Jemima, let me stay by you!"

"Hark!" she whispered, putting her arm round me. "There are horses galloping up to the house."

Two police-officers, mounted. They gave their horses in charge to one of the men-servants, and came into the hall, the scabbards of their swords clanking against the steps.

"I don't like the look of them," whispered Jemima. "Let us go away."

She took me to the kitchen. Sarah, Mary, and the cook were in it; the latter a tall, stout woman, with a rosy colour and black eyes. Her chief concern seemed to be about the dinner.

"Look here," she exclaimed to Jemima, as she stood over her saucepans, "everything's a-spiling. Who's to know whether they'll have it served in one hour or in two?"

"I should think they wouldn't have it served at all," returned Jemima: "that sight in the hall's enough dinner for them today, one would suppose. The police are come now."

"Ah, it is bad, I know," said the cook. "And the going to look at it took everything else out of my head, worse luck to me! I forgot my soles were on the fire, and when I got back they were burnt to the pan. I've had to scrape 'em now, and put 'em into wine sauce. Who's this coming in?"

It was Miss Delves. The cook appealed to her about the dinner.

"It won't be eatable, ma'am, if it's kept much longer. Some of the dishes is half cold, and some's dried up to a scratchin'."

"There's no help for it, cook; you must manage it in the best way you can," was Miss Delves's reply. "It is a dreadful thing to have happened, but I suppose dinner must be served all the same for the master and Mrs. Edwin Barley."

"Miss Delves, is it true what they are saying—that it was Mr. Heneage who did it?" inquired Sarah.

"Suppose you trouble yourself with your own affairs, and let alone what does not concern you," was Miss Delves's reprimand.

She left the kitchen. Jemima made a motion of contempt after her, and gave the door a bang.

"She'll put in *her* word against Mr. Heneage, I know; for she didn't like him. But I am confident it was never he that did it—unless his gun went off accidental."

For full an hour by the clock we stayed in the kitchen, uninterrupted, the cook reducing herself to a state of despair over the delayed dinner. The men-servants had been sent out, some to one place, some to another. The cook served us some coffee and bread-and-butter, but I don't think any one of us touched the latter. I thought by that time my aunt must surely have come in, and asked Jemima to take me upstairs to her. A policeman was in the hall as we passed across the back of it, and Charlotte Delves and Mr. Martin were sitting in the dining-room, the door open. Mrs. Edwin Barley was nowhere to be found, and we went back to the kitchen. I began to cry; a dreadful fear came upon me that she might have gone away for ever, and left me to the companionship of Mr. Edwin Barley.

"Come and sit down here, child," said the cook, in a motherly way, as she placed a low stool near the fire. "It's enough to frighten her, poor little stranger, to have this happen, just as she comes into the house."

"I say, though, where can the mistress be?" Jemima said to her, in a low tone, as I drew the stool into the shade and sat down, leaning my head against the wall.

Presently Miss Delves's bell rang. The servants said they always knew her ring—it came with a jerk. Jemima went to answer it. It was for some hot water, which she took up. Some one was going to have brandy-and-water, she said; perhaps Mr. Martin—she did not know. Her master was in the hall then, and Mr. Barley, of the Oaks, was with him.

"Who's Mr. Barley of the Oaks, Jemima?" I asked.

"He is master's elder brother, miss. He lives at the Oaks, about three miles from here. Such a nice place it is—ten times better than this. When the old gentleman died, Mr. Barley came into the Oaks, and Mr. Edwin into this."

Then there was silence again for another half-hour. I sat with my eyes closed, and heard them say I was asleep. The young farm labourer, Duff, came in at last.

"Well," said he, "it have been a useless chase. I wonder whether I am wanted for anything else."

"Where have you been?" asked Jemima.

"Scouring the wood, seven of us, in search of Mr. Heneage: and them two mounted police is a-dashing about the roads. We haven't found him."

"Duff, Mr. Heneage no more did it than you did."

"That's all you know about it," was Duff's answer. "Master says he did."

"Have a cup of coffee, Duff?" asked the cook.

"Thank ye," said Duff. "I'd be glad on't."

She was placing the cup before him, when he suddenly leaned forward from the chair he had taken, speaking in a covert whisper.

"I say, who do you think was in the wood, a-scouring it, up one path and down another, as much as ever we was?"

"Who?" asked the servants in a breath.

"The young missis. She hadn't an earthly thing on her but just what she sits in, indoors. Her hair was down, and her neck and arms was bare; and there she was, a-racing up and down like one demented."

"Tush!" said the cook. "You must have seen double. What should bring young madam dancing about the wood, Duff, at this time o' night?"

"I tell ye I see her. I see her three times over. Maybe she was looking for Mr. Heneage, too. At any rate, there she was, and with nothing on, as if she'd started out in a hurry, and had forgot to dress herself. And if she don't catch a cold, it's odd to me," added Duff. "The fog's as thick as pea-soup, and wets you worse than rain. 'Twas enough to give her her death."

Duff's report was true. As he spoke, a bell called Jemima up again. She came back, laid hold of me without speaking, and took me to the drawing-room. Mrs. Edwin Barley stood there, just come in; she was shaking like a leaf, with the damp and cold, her hair dripping wet. When she had seen her husband leave the hall in search of George Heneage, an impulse came over her to follow and interpose between the anger of the two, should they meet. At least, partly this, partly to look after George Heneage herself, and warn him to escape. She gave me this explanation openly.

"I could not find him," she said, kneeling down before the fire, and holding out her shivering arms to the blaze. "I hope and trust he has escaped. One man's life is enough for me to have upon my hands, without having two."

"Oh, Aunt Selina! *you* did not take Philip King's life!"

"No, I did not take it. And I have been guilty of no intentional wrong. But I did set the one against the other, Anne—in my vanity and wilfulness."

Looking back to the child's eyes with which I saw things then, and judging of these same things with my woman's experience now, I can but hold Selina Barley entirely to blame. An indulged daughter, born when her sister Ursula was nearly grown up, she had been suffered to have her own way at Keppe-Carew, and grew up to think the world was made for her. Dangerously attractive, fond to excess of admiration, she had probably encouraged Philip King's boyish fancy, and then turned round upon him for it. At the previous Easter, on his former visit, she had been all smiles and sweetness; this time she had done nothing but turn him into ridicule. "What is sport to you may be death to me," said the fly to the spider. It might not have mattered so much from *her*, this ridicule; but she pressed George Heneage into the service: and Philip King was not of a disposition to bear it tamely. His weak health made him appear somewhat of a coward; he was not strong enough to take the law into his own hands, and repay Mr. Heneage with personal chastisement. Selina's liking for George Heneage was no doubt great; but it was not an improper liking, although the world—the little world at Mr. Edwin Barley's—might have wished to deem it so. Before she married Mr. Edwin Barley, she refused George Heneage, and laughed at him for proposing to her. She should wed a rich man, she told him, or none at all. It was Mr. Edwin Barley himself who invited Heneage to his house, and also Philip King, as it most unfortunately happened. His wife, in her wilful folly—I had almost written her wilful wickedness—played them off one upon another. The first day they met, Philip King took umbrage at some remark of Mr. Heneage's, and Selina, liking the one and disliking the other, forthwith began. A few days further on, and young King so far forgot his good manners as to tell her she "liked that Coxcomb Heneage too much." The reproach made her laugh; but she, nevertheless, out of pure mischief, did what she could to confirm Philip King in the impression. He, Philip King, took to talking of this to Miss Delves; he took to watching Selina and George Heneage; there could be little doubt that he carried tales of his observation to Mr. Edwin Barley, which only incited Selina to persevere; the whole thing amused her immensely. What passed between Mr. and Mrs. Edwin Barley in private about it, whether anything or nothing, was never known. At the moment of the accident he was exceedingly vexed with her; *incensed* may be the proper word.

And poor Philip King! Perhaps, after all, his death may have been a mistake—if it was in truth George Heneage that it proceeded from. Circumstances, as they came out, seemed to say that he had not been "spying," but only taking the short cut through the summer-house on his way home from shooting; an unusual route, it's true, but not an impossible one. Seeing them on the other side when he entered it, he waited until they should proceed onwards; but Mrs. Barley's sudden run up the steps sent him away. Not that he would avoid them; only make his escape, without their seeing him, lest he should be accused of the very thing they did accuse him of—spying. But he was too late; the creaking of the outer door betrayed him. At least this was the opinion taken up by Mr. Martin, later, when Selina told the whole truth to him, under the seal of secrecy.

But Mrs. Edwin Barley was kneeling before the fire in the drawing-room, with her dripping hair; and I standing by her looking on; and that first terrible night was not over.

"Selina, why did you stay out in the wet fog?"

"I was looking for him, I tell you, Anne."

"But you had nothing on. You might have caught your death, Duff said."

"And what if I had?" she sharply interrupted. "I would as soon die as live."

It was one of her customary random retorts, meaning nothing. Before more was said, strange footsteps and voices were heard on the stairs. Selina started up, and looked at herself in the glass.

"I can't let them see me like this," she muttered, clutching her drooping hair. "You wait here, Anne."

Darting to the side-door she had spoken of as leading to her bed-room, she pulled it open with a wrench, as if a bolt had given way, and disappeared, leaving me standing on the hearthrug.

# CHAPTER 4

## ILLNESS

He who first entered the room was a gentleman of middle age and size. His complexion was healthy and ruddy; his short dark hair, sprinkled with grey, was combed down upon the forehead: his countenance was good-natured and simple. This was Mr. Barley of the Oaks. Not the least resemblance did he bear to his brother. Following him was one in an official dress, who was probably superior to a common policeman, for his manners were good, and Mr. Barley called him "Sir." It was not the same who had been in the hall.

"Oh, this—this must be the little girl," observed Mr. Barley. "Are you Mrs. Edwin's niece, my dear—Miss Hereford?"

"Yes, sir."

"Do you knew where she is?"

"In her bedroom, I think, sir."

It had transpired that a quarrel had taken place the previous Friday between Mr. Heneage and Philip King; and the officer had now been in the kitchen to question Jemima. Jemima disclaimed all knowledge of the affair, beyond the fact that she had heard of it from little Miss Hereford, whom she saw on the stairs, crying and frightened. He had now come to question me.

"Now, my little maid, try and recollect," said the officer, drawing me to him. "What did they quarrel about?"

"I don't know, sir," I answered. And I spoke the literal truth, for I had not understood at the time.

"Can you not recollect?"

"I can recollect," I said, looking at him, and feeling that I did not shrink from him, though he was a policeman. "Mr. King seemed to have done something wrong, for Mr. Heneage was angry with him, and called him a spy; but I did not know what it was that he had done. I was too frightened to listen; I ran out of the room."

"Then you did not hear what the quarrel was about?"

"I did not understand, sir. Except that they said that Mr. King was mean, and a spy."

"They!" he repeated, catching me up quickly; "who else was in the room?"

"My Aunt Selina."

"Then she took Mr. Heneage's part?"

"Yes, sir."

"How did the quarrel end? Amicably, or in ill-feeling?"

"I don't know, sir. I went away, and stayed in my bedroom."

"My sister-in-law, Mrs. Edwin, may be able to tell you more

about it, as she was present," interposed Mr. Barley.

"I dare say she can," was the officer's reply. "It seems a curious thing altogether—that two gentlemen should be visiting at a house, and one should shoot the other. How long had they been staying here?"

"Let's see," said Mr. Barley, rubbing his forefinger upon his forehead. "It must be a month, I fancy, sir, since they came. Heneage was here first: some days before Philip."

"Were they previously acquainted?"

"I—think—not," said Mr. Barley, speaking with hesitation. "Heneage was here on a short visit in the middle of the summer, but not Philip: whereas Philip was here at Easter, and the other was not. No, sir, I believe they were not acquainted before, but my brother can tell you."

"Who is this Mr. Heneage?"

"Don't you know? He is the son of the member for Wexborough. Oh, he is of very good family—very. A sad blow it will be for them, if things turn out as black as they look. Will he get clear off, think you?"

"You may depend upon it, he would not have got off far, but for this confounded fog that has come on," warmly replied the police-officer. "We shall have him to-morrow, no doubt."

"I hardly ever saw such a fog at this time of year," observed Mr. Barley. "I couldn't see a yard before me as I came along. Upon my word, it almost seems as if it had come on purpose to screen him."

"Was he a pleasant man, this Heneage?"

"One of the nicest fellows you ever met, sir," was Mr. Barley's impulsive reply. "The last week or two Edwin seems to have taken some spite against him; I don't know what was up between them, for my part: but I liked Heneage, what I saw of him, and thought him an uncommon good fellow. Mrs. Edwin Barley has known him a long time; my brother only recently. They all met in London last spring."

"Heneage derives no benefit in any way, by property or otherwise, from his death?" observed the policeman, speaking half as a question, half as a soliloquy.

"It's not likely, sir. The only person to benefit is my brother. He comes in for it all."

The officer raised his eyes. "Your brother comes in for young King's fortune, Mr. Barley?"

"Yes, he does. And I'll be bound he never gave a thought to inheriting it. How should he, from a young and hearty lad like Philip? Edwin has croaked about Philip's health of late, said he was consumptive, and going the way of his brother Reginald; but I saw nothing amiss with Philip."

"May I ask why you don't inherit, Mr. Barley, being the elder brother?"

"He was no blood relation to me. My father married twice, I was the son of the first wife; Edwin of the second; and Philip King's father and Edwin's mother were cousins. Philip had no male relative living except my brother, therefore he comes in for the estate."

Mrs. Edwin Barley appeared at the door, and paused here, as if listening to the conclusion of the last sentence. Mr. Barley turned and saw her, and she came forward. She had twisted up her damp hair, and thrown on a shawl of white China crape. Her eyes were brilliant, her cheeks carmine—beautiful she looked altogether.

The officer questioned her as to the cause of the quarrel which she had been present at, but she would give him no satisfactory answer. She "could not remember;" "Philip King was in the wrong, she knew that;" "the officer must excuse her talking, for her head ached, and her brain felt confused." Such was the substance—all, in fact, that he could get from her. He bowed and withdrew, and Mr. Barley followed him downstairs, Selina bolting the door after them.

"Now, Anne, I must have a little conversation with you," she said, drawing me to her as she sat on the low ottoman. And I could see that she shivered still. She proceeded to question me of what had occurred after I left her at the summerhouse. I told her; and had got to where Philip King was shot, when she interrupted.

"Good Heavens, child! you *saw* him shot?"

"I heard the noise, and saw him fall. It seemed to come from the spot where he had been gazing."

"Did you see who did it?" she asked, scarcely above her breath.

"No."

"Then you saw no one about except Philip King?"

"I saw Mr. Edwin Barley. He was near the spot from whence the shot seemed to come, looking through the trees and standing still, as if he wondered what could be amiss. For, oh, Selina! Philip King's scream was dreadful, and must have been heard a long way."

My aunt caught hold of my arm in a sort of fright. "Anne! what do you say? You saw *Edwin Barley* at that spot! Not Mr. Heneage?"

"I did not see Mr. Heneage at all then. I saw only Mr. Edwin Barley. He came up to Philip King, asking what was the matter."

"Had he his gun with him—Edwin Barley?"

"Yes, he was carrying it."

She dropped my arm, and sat quite still, shrinking as if some blow had struck her. Two or three minutes passed before she spoke again.

"Go on, Anne. What next? Tell me all that passed, for I suppose you heard." And I related what I knew, word for word.

"You have not told me all, Anne."

"Yes, I have."

"Did not Philip King say that Mr. Heneage had raised his gun, aimed at him, and fired? that he saw him do it?"

"He did not, aunt. He only said what I have told you."

"Lie the first!" she exclaimed, lifting her hand and letting it fall passionately. "Then you never saw Mr. Heneage?"

"I saw him later." And I went on to tell her of meeting him through my taking the wrong turning. I told her all: how he looked as one in mortal fright; what he said; and of my asking him whether he had done it.

"Well?" she feverishly interrupted. "Well?"

"He quite denied it," I answered, repeating to her exactly the words Mr. Heneage had said.

"You say he looked scared—confused?"

"Yes, very much so."

"And Mr. Edwin Barley—did he?"

"Not at all. He looked just as he always looks. He seemed to be surprised, and very sorry; his voice, when he spoke to Philip King, was kinder than I ever heard it."

Another pause. She seemed to be thinking.

"I can hardly understand where it was you saw George Heneage, Anne: you must show me to-morrow. Was it on the same side from which the shot came?"

"Yes; I think near to the place. Or how could he have heard Mr. Barley speak to me?"

"How long had you been in the wood when the shot was fired?"

"About ten minutes or a quarter-of-an-hour."

"Little girls compute time differently from grown-up people, Anne. A few minutes might seem like a quarter-of-an-hour to you."

"Mamma taught me how differently time appears to pass, according to what we may be doing, Aunt Selina. That when we are pleasantly occupied, it seems to fly; and when we are impatient for it to go on, or in any suspense or fear, it does not seem to move. I think I have learnt to be pretty exact, and I do believe that I was in the wood nearly a quarter-of-an-hour. I was running about for some time, looking for Mr. Heneage, as you told me, before I found I had lost myself. And then I was some minutes getting over the fright. I had said my prayers, and—"

"You had—WHAT?"

"I was much alarmed; I thought I might have to stay in the wood until morning, and I could only pray to God to protect me: I knew that harm would not come to me then. It must have been a quarter-of-an-hour in all: so you see Mr. Heneage did not do it in the heat of passion, in running after him: he must have done it deliberately."

"I don't care," she repeated to herself, in a sort of defiant voice; "I know George Heneage did not wilfully shoot Philip King. If he did do it, it was an accident; but I don't believe he did."

"If he did not, why did he hide in the wood, and look as if he had done something wrong, Selina? Why did he not go boldly up, and see what was amiss with Philip King, as Mr. Edwin Barley did?"

"There is no accounting for what people do in these moments of confusion and terror: some act in one way, some in another," she said, slowly. "Anne, I don't like to speak out openly to you—what I fear and what I don't fear, It was imperative upon George Heneage to hasten home—and he may not have believed that Philip King was really dead."

"But, Selina—"

"Go! go! lie down there," she said, drawing me to the distant sofa, and pushing me on it, with the pillow over my head. "You are asleep, mind! He might think I had been tutoring you."

So sudden and unexpected was the movement, I could only obey, and lie still. Selina unbolted the door, and was back in her seat before Mr. Edwin Barley entered the room.

"Are you coming down to dinner, Selina?"

"Dinner! It is well for you that you can eat any," was her answer. "You must dine without me to-day—those who dine at all. Now, don't disturb that sleeping child, Mr. Barley! I was just going to send her to bed."

"It might do you more good to eat dinner than to roam about in a night-fog," was Mr. Edwin Barley's rejoinder. "It is rather curious you should choose such a night as this to be out in, half-naked."

"Not curious," she said, coldly: "very natural."

"Very! Especially that you should be tearing up and down the wood paths, like a mad woman. Others saw you as well as myself, and are speaking of it."

"Let them speak."

"But for what purpose were you there?"

"I was looking for George Heneage. There! you may make the most of it."

"Did you find him?"

"No. I wish I had: *I wish I had*. I should have learnt from him the truth of this night's business; for the truth, as I believe, has not come to light yet."

"What do you suppose to be the truth?" he returned, in a tone of surprise; whether natural, or assumed, who could say?

"No matter—no matter now: it is something that I scarcely dare to glance at. Better, even, that Heneage had done it, than—than—what I am thinking of. My head is confused to-night," she broke off; "my mind unhinged—hardly sane. You had better leave me, Mr. Barley."

"You had better come and eat a bit of dinner" he said roughly, but not unkindly. "None of us can touch much, I dare say, but we are going to sit down. William is staying, and so is Martin. Won't you come and try to take a bit? Or shall I send you something up?"

"It would be of no use."

Mr. Edwin Barley looked at her: she was shivering outwardly and inwardly. I could just see out under the corner of the cushion.

"You have caught a violent cold, Selina. How could you think of going out?"

"I will tell you," she added, in a more conciliating spirit. "I went out because you went. To prevent any encounter between you and George Heneage,—I mean any violence. After that, I stayed looking for him."

"You need not have feared violence from me. I should have handed him over to the police, nothing more."

There was a mocking sound in his voice as he spoke. Selina sat down and put her feet on the fender.

"I hate to dine without some one at the head of the table," Mr. Edwin Barley said, turning to the door. "If you will not come, I shall ask Charlotte Delves to sit down."

"It is nothing to me who sits down when I am not there."

He departed with the ungracious reply ringing in his ears: and ungracious I felt it to be. She bolted the door again, and pulled the blue velvet cushion off my head.

"Are you smothered, child? Get up. Now, mark me: you must not say a word to Mr. Edwin Barley of what happened at the summer-house. Do not mention it at all—to him, or to any one else."

"But suppose I am asked, Selina?"

"How can you be asked? Philip King is gone, poor fellow; George Heneage is not here, and who else is there to ask you? You surely have not spoken of it already?" she continued, in a tone of alarm.

I had not spoken of it to any one, and told her so. Jemima had questioned me as to the cause of my terror, when I ran in from the wood, and I said I had heard a shot and a scream; I had not courage to say more.

"That's well," said Selina.

She sent me to rest, ordering Jemima to stay by me until I was asleep. "The child may feel nervous," she remarked to her, in an undertone, but the words reached me. And I suppose Jemima felt nervous, for one of the other maids came also.

The night passed; morning came; Sunday; and with it illness for Mrs. Edwin Barley. I gathered from Jemima's conversation, while she was dressing me, that Selina had slept alone: Mr. Edwin Barley, with his brother and some more gentlemen, had been out a great part of the night looking for George Heneage. It was so near morning when they returned, that he would not go to his wife's room for fear of disturbing her.

I ran in when I went downstairs. She lay in bed, and her voice, as she spoke to me, did not sound like her own. "Are you ill, Selina? Why do you speak so hoarsely?"

"I feel very ill, Anne. My throat is bad—or my chest, I can scarcely tell which: perhaps it is both. Go downstairs, and send Miss Delves to me."

I have said that I was an imaginative, thoughtful, excitable child, and as I hastened to obey her, one sole recollection (I could have said fear) kept running through my brain. It was the oracular observation made by Duff, relating to his mistress and the fog: "It's enough to give her her death!" Suppose she *had* caught her death? My fingers, fastening my narrow waistband, trembled at the thought.

The first thing I saw when I went down was a large high screen of many folds, raised across the hall, shutting out part of it from view. It seemed to strike me back with fear. Sarah was coming out of the dining-room with a duster in her hand: it was early yet. I caught hold of her gown.

"Sarah, what is behind there?"

"The same that was last night, miss," she answered. "Nothing is to be moved until the coroner has come."

"Have they taken Mr. Heneage?"

"Not that I have heard of, miss. One of the police was in just now, and he told Miss Delves there was no news."

"I want to find Miss Delves. Where is she?"

"In master's study. You can go in. Don't you know which it is? It's that room built out at the back, half-way up the first flight of stairs. You can see the door from here."

In the study sat Mr. Barley and Mr. Edwin Barley at breakfast, Charlotte Delves serving them. I gave her my aunt's message, but was nearly scared out of my senses at being laid hold of by Mr. Edwin Barley.

"Go up at once, Charlotte, and see what it is," he said. "How do you say, little one—that her throat is bad?"

"Yes, sir; she cannot speak well."

"No wonder; she has only herself to thank," he muttered, as Charlotte Delves left the room. "The wonder would be if she were not ill."

"Why?" asked Mr. Barley, curiously, lifting his head.

"Oh, she got frightened last night when poor Philip was brought in, and ran out in the fog after me with nothing on."

He released my arm, and Mr. Barley put a chair for me beside him, and gave me some breakfast. I had taken quite a liking to him, he was so simple and kind. He told me he had no little girls or boys of his own, and his wife was always ill, unable to go out.

"Mrs. Edwin Barley appears exceedingly poorly," said Charlotte Delves, when she returned. "Lowe said he should be here this morning; he shall see her when he comes. She must have taken cold."

Scarcely had she spoken when the surgeon arrived. Mr. Edwin Barley went upstairs with him. Mr. Lowe came down alone afterwards, and I caught a moment to speak to him when no one was listening.

"Will my Aunt Selina get well, sir?"

"I do not know, my dear," he answered, turning upon me his grave face. "I fear she is going to be very ill."

Sunday came to an end; oh, such a dull day it had seemed!—and Monday morning dawned. It was Selina's birthday: she was twenty-one.

Nothing could be heard of George Heneage. The police scoured the country; handbills were printed, offering a reward for his apprehension; no effort was left untried, but he was not found. Opinions were fiercely bandied about: some said he must have escaped in the fog, and got off by the railway from Nettleby, or by the other line beyond Hallam; others thought he was lying concealed near the spot still. Mr. Edwin Barley was in great anger at his escape, and vowed he would pursue him to the death.

Not on this day, but the following, Tuesday, Mr. Heneage's father came to the house—a fine old gentleman, with white hair. Mr. Lowe corrected me for calling him old, and said he could not be much more than fifty. I had not then the experience to know that whilst young people call fifty old, those past that age are apt to style it young. I saw him twice as he went along the passages, but was not close to him. He was a courteous, gentlemanly man, but seemed bowed down with grief. It was said he could not understand the calamity at all, and decidedly refused to believe in his son's guilt. If the shot had in truth proceeded from him, the gun must have gone off by accident.

"Then why should he run away?" argued Mr. Edwin Barley.

He stayed in the house altogether but about two hours, and had an interview with Mrs. Edwin Barley in her bedroom before his departure. Refreshments were laid for him, but he declined to touch anything: I heard the servants commenting on it.

In the afternoon the coroner's inquest sat. It was held in the dining-room. The chief witness was Mr. Edwin Barley. I was not called upon, and Selina said it was a proof that he had not mentioned I was present at the time. You may be sure I took care not to mention it; neither did she. Nothing transpired touching the encounter at the summer-house; therefore the affair appeared to the public involved in mystery. Mr. Edwin Barley protested that it was a mystery to him. He could not conceive what motive Heneage could have had in taking Philip King's life. Mr. Edwin Barley testified that Philip King, in dying, had asserted he saw George Heneage take aim and fire at him, and there was no one to contradict the assertion. I knew Philip

King had not said so much; but no one else knew it, except Mrs. Edwin Barley, and she only from me. They did not require her to appear at the inquest; it was assumed that she knew nothing whatever about the transaction.

Charlotte Delves was called, at the request of the jury, because Philip King had sat with her in her parlour for half-an-hour the morning of his death; but she proved that he had not touched upon anything unpleasant, or spoken then of George Heneage. The feeling between them had not been good, she testified, and there used to be bickerings and disputes. "What about?" asked the jury; but Miss Delves only answered that she "could not say." The fact was, Mr. Edwin Barley in his stern way had ordered her not to bring in his wife's name.

Whilst the inquest was sitting I stayed in Selina's room. She seemed very restless, turning about in bed continually, and telling me to listen how it was "going on." But I could hear nothing, though I went often on the stairs to try.

"What was that stir just now, Anne?" she asked, when it was late.

"They called from the dining-room to have the chandelier lighted. John went in and did it."

"Is it dark, Anne?"

"Not dark. It is getting dark."

Dark it appeared to be in the chamber, for the crimson silk curtains were drawn before the large, deep bay-window, and also partially round the bed. You could distinguish the outline of objects, and that was all. I went close up to the bed and looked at her; she was buried in the pillows: that she was very ill I knew, for a physician from Nettleby had come that morning with Mr. Lowe.

"I think it must be over." she said, as a bustle was heard below. "Go and see, dear."

I went half-way down the stairs in the dark. No one had thought to light the hall-lamp. Sure enough, they were pouring out of the room, a crowd of dark figures, talking as they came, and slowly making for the hall-door. Suddenly I distinguished Mr. Edwin Barley coming towards the stairs.

To his study, as I thought, and back went I, not caring to encounter him. Added to my childish dislike and fear of Mr. Edwin Barley, since Saturday night another impulse to avoid him had been added: a dread, which I could not divest myself of, that he might question me as to that meeting at the summer-house, and to the subsequent interview with George Heneage. Selina had ordered me to be silent; but if he found anything out and questioned me, what could I do? I know that the fear was upon me then and for a long time afterwards.

I crept swiftly back again up the stairs, and into my aunt's room.

Surely he was not coming to it! Those were his footsteps, and they drew nearer: he could not have turned into his study! No, they came on. In the impulse of the moment, I pushed behind the heavy window-curtain. It was drawn straight across from wall to wall, leaving a space between it and the bow of the window nearly as large as a small room. There were three chairs there, one in the middle of the window and at the two sides. I sat down on one of them, and, pulling the white blind slightly aside, looked out at the dark figures who were then sauntering down the avenue.

"Well, it's over," said Mr. Edwin Barley to his wife, as he came in and shut the door. "And now all the work will be to find him."

"How has it ended?" she asked.

"Wilful murder. The coroner was about to clear the room, but the jury intimated that they required no deliberation, and returned their verdict at once."

"Wilful murder against whom?"

"Against George Heneage. Did you suppose it was against you or me?"

There was a pause. I felt in miserable indecision, knowing that I ought, in honour, to go out and show myself, but not daring to do it. Selina resumed, speaking as emphatically as her inflamed throat permitted.

"I cannot believe—I never will believe—that George Heneage was capable of committing murder. His whole nature would rise up against it: as his father said in this room a few hours ago. If the shot did come from his gun, it must have been fired inadvertently."

"The shot did come from his gun," returned Mr. Edwin Barley. "There's no 'if' in the question."

"I am aware you say so; but it was passing strange that you, also with your gun, should have been upon the spot. Now, stay!—don't put yourself in a passion. I cannot help saying it. I think all this suspense and uncertainty is killing me!"

Mr. Edwin Barley dragged a chair to the side of the bed, anger in the very sound. I felt ready to drop, lest he should see me through the slit in the curtain.

"We will have this out, Selina. It is not the first time you have given utterance to hints that you ought to be ashamed of. Do you suspect that I shot Philip King?"

His tone was so stern that, perhaps, she did not like to say "yes" outright, and tampered with the question.

"Not exactly that. But there's only your word to prove that it was George Heneage. And you know how incensed you have latterly been against him."

"Who caused me to be incensed? Why, you."

"There was no real cause. Were it the last words I had to speak,

Edwin"—and she burst into tears—"were I dying I would assert it. I never cared for George Heneage in the way you fancy."

"*I* fancy! Had I fancied that, I should have flung George Heneage out of my house long ago," was his rejoinder, spoken calmly. "But now hear me, Selina. It has been your pleasure to declare so much to me. On my part, I declare to you that Heneage, and Heneage only, killed Philip King. Dispossess your mind of all dark folly. You must be insane, I think, to take it up against your husband."

"Did you see Heneage fire?" she asked, after a silence.

"No. I should have known pretty surely that it could only be Heneage, had there been no proof against him; but there were Philip's dying words. Still, I did not see Heneage at the place, and I have never said I did. I was pushing home through the wood, and halted a second, thinking I heard voices: it must have been Philip talking to the child: at that very moment a shot was fired close to me—close, mind you—not two yards off; but the trees are thick just there, and whoever fired it was hid from my view. I was turning to search, when Philip King's awful scream rang out, and I pushed my head beyond the trees and saw him in the act of falling to the ground. I hastened to him, and the other escaped. This is the entire truth, so far as I am cognizant of it."

It might have been the truth; and, again, it might not. It was just one of those things that depend upon the credibility of the utterer. What little corroboration there was, certainly was on Mr. Edwin Barley's side: *only* that he had asserted more than was true of the dying words of Philip King. If these were the simple facts, the truth, why have added falsehood to them?

"Heneage could have had no motive for taking the life of Philip King," argued Mrs. Edwin Barley. "That he would have caned him, or given him some other sound chastisement, I grant you—and richly he deserved it, for he was the cause of all the ill-feeling that had arisen in the house—but, to kill him! No, no!"

"And yet you would deem me capable of it!"

"I am not accusing you. But when you come to speak of motives, I cannot help seeing that George Heneage could have had none."

"You have just observed that the author of the mischief, the bad feeling which had sprung up in the house, was Philip King; but you are wrong. The author was you, Selina."

No answer. She put up one of her hot hands, and shaded her eyes.

"I forgive you," he continued. "I am willing to bury the past in silence: never to recur to it—never henceforth to allude to it, though the boy was my relative and ward, and I liked him. But I would recommend you to bear this tragical ending in mind, as a warning for the future. I will not tolerate further folly in my wife; and your own sense ought to tell you that had I been ambitious of putting some one out of the world, it would have been Heneage, not Philip. Heneage has killed him, and upon his head be the consequences. I will never cease my endeavours to bring it home to him. I will spare no pains, or energy, or cost, until it is accomplished. So help me, Heaven!"

He rose with the last solemn word, and put the chair back in its place. On his way to the door he turned, speaking in a softer voice.

"Are you better this evening, Selina?"

"No. It seems to me that I grow worse with every hour."

"I'll send Lowe up to you. He is somewhere about."

"Oh, aunt, aunt!" I said, going forward with lifted hands and streaming eyes, as he left the chamber, "I was here all the time! I saw Mr. Edwin Barley coming in, and I hid behind the window-curtain. I never meant to be a listener: I was afraid to come out."

She looked at me without speaking, and her face, hot with fever, grew more flushed. She seemed to be considering; perhaps remembering what had passed.

"I—I—don't think there was anything very particular said, that you need care; or, rather, that I need," she said at length. "Was there?"

"No, Selina. Only—"

"Only what, child? Why do you hesitate?"

"You think it might have been Mr. Edwin Barley. I wish I had not heard that."

"I said, or implied, it was as likely to have been he as the other. Anne," she suddenly added, "you possess thought and sense beyond your years: what do you think?"

"I think it was Mr. Heneage. I think so because he has run away, and because he looked so strangely when he was hiding. And I do not think it was Mr. Edwin Barley. When he told you how it occurred just now, and that it was not he, his voice sounded as though he were speaking the truth."

"Oh, dear!" she moaned, "I hope it was so! What a mercy if that Philip King had never come near the house!"

"But, Selina, you are sorry that he is dead?"

"Sorry that he is dead? Of course I am sorry. What a curious child you are! He was no favourite of mine; but," she cried, passionately clasping her hands, "I would give all I am worth to call him back to life."

But I could not be reconciled to what I had done, and sobbed on heavily, until lights and Mr. Lowe came in together.

# CHAPTER 5

## ANOTHER DREAM

"If ever I heard the like of that! one won't be able to open one's lips next before you, Miss Hereford. Did I say anything about her dying, pray? Or about your dying? Or my dying? Time enough to snap me up when I do."

Thus spoke Jemima, with a volubility that nearly took her breath away. She had come to my room in the morning with the news that Mrs. Edwin Barley was worse. I burst into tears, and asked if she were going to die: which brought forth the above rebuke.

"My thoughts were running upon whether we servants should have mourning given us for young Mr. King," resumed Jemima, as if she were bent upon removing unpleasant impressions from my mind. "Now just you make haste and dress yourself, Miss Hereford—Mrs. Edwin Barley has been asking for you."

I made haste; Jemima helped; and she ushered me to the door of the sick-room, halting to whisper a parting word.

"Don't you begin crying again, miss. Your aunt is no more going to die than I am."

The first words spoken by Mrs. Edwin Barley were a contradiction to this, curious coincident though it may seem. She was lying very high on the frilled white pillows, no cap on, her cheeks hectic, and her lovely golden hair falling around her head. A large bright fire burned in the grate, and a small tray, with a white cloth and cup on it, stood on the table near.

"Child," she began, holding out her hand to me, "I fear I am about to be taken from you."

I did not answer; I did not cry; all tears seemed scared away then. It was a confirmation of my secret, inward fears, and my face turned white.

"What was that you said to me about the Keppe-Carews never dying without a warning? And I laughed at you! Do you remember? Anne, I think the warning came to me last night."

I glanced timidly round the room. It was a luxurious bed-chamber, costly furniture and pretty toilette trifles everywhere. The crimson silk curtains were drawn closely before the bay-window, and I could see Selina clearly in the semi-light.

"Your mamma told you she had a dream, Anne. Well, I have had a dream. And yet I feel sure it was not a dream, but reality; reality. She appeared to me last night."

"Who? Mamma?"

"Your mamma. The Keppe-Carew superstition is, that when one

is going to die, the last relative, whether near or distant, who has been taken from them by death, comes again to give them notice that their own departure is near. Ursula was the last who went, and she came to me in the night."

"It can't be true," I sobbed, shivering from head to foot.

"She stood there, in the faint rays of the shaded lamp," pursued Selina, not so much as listening to me. "I have not really slept all night; I have been in that semi-conscious, dozing state when the mind is awake both to dreams and to reality, knowing not which is which. Just before the clock struck two, I awoke partially from one of these semi-dreams, and I saw your mamma at the foot of the bed—a shadowy sort of figure and face, but I knew it for Ursula's. She just looked at me, and said 'Selina!' Then I woke up thoroughly—the name, the sound of her well-remembered voice ringing in my ears."

"And seeing her?" I eagerly asked.

"No. Seeing nothing but the opening between the curtains at the foot of the bed, and the door beyond it; nothing more than is to be seen now."

"Then, Selina, it was a dream after all?"

"In one sense, yes. The world would call it so. To me it was some-thing more. A minute afterwards the clock struck two, and I was as wide awake as I am now."

The reaction came, and I burst into tears. "Selina! it was a dream; it could only have been a dream!"

"I should no doubt think so, Anne, but for what you told me of your mamma's warning. But for hearing that, I might never have remembered that such a thing is said to follow the Keppe-Carews."

What with remorse for having told her, though charged by my mother to do it, and what with my own fears, I could not speak for hysterical sobbing.

"You stupid little sensitive thing!" exclaimed Selina, with a touch of her old lightness; "perhaps in a week's time I shall be well, and run-ning about out of doors with you. Go down to Charlotte Delves's parlour, and get your breakfast, and then come to me again. I want you to go on an errand for me; but don't say so. Mind that, Anne."

"No, no; I won't say it, Selina."

"Tell them to give you some honey."

They brought the honey and set out other good things for me in Miss Delves's parlour, but I could not eat. Charlotte Delves was very kind. Both the doctors came up the avenue. I watched them into the house; I heard them come downstairs again. The physician from Nettleby went straight out: Mr. Lowe came to the parlour.

"My dear," he said to me, "you are to go up to Mrs. Edwin Barley."

"Is she much worse, sir?" I lingered to ask.

"I can hardly say how she is," was his answer. "We must hope for the best."

He stayed in the room himself, and shut the door while he talked to Miss Delves. The hall-clock struck ten as I passed under it, making me start. The hall was clear to-day, and the window and door stood a little open. Jemima told me that Philip King was in a sitting-room at the back, one that was rarely used. I ran quickly up to Selina's chamber. Mr. Edwin Barley was in it, to my dismay. He turned to leave it when I went in, and put his hand kindly enough upon my hair.

"You look pale, little one; you should run out of doors for a while."

His wife watched him from the room with her strangely altered eyes, and then beckoned to me.

"Shut the door, and bolt it, Anne." And very glad I felt to do it. It was impossible to overcome my fear of Mr. Edwin Barley.

"Do you think you could find your way to Hallam?"

"I dare say 1 could, aunt."

"Selina, call me Selina," she impatiently interposed. "Call it me to the last."

To the last!

"You remember the way you came from Nettleby, Anne? In going out at the gates by the lodge, Nettleby lies on your left hand, Hallam on your right. You understand?"

"Oh, quite."

"You have only to turn to the right, and keep straight along the high road; in a short time you come to Hallam village. The way is not at all lonely; cottages and houses are scattered all along it."

"I am sure I could go quite easily, Selina."

"Then put your things on, and take this note," she said, giving me a little piece of paper twisted up, that she took from under the pillow. "In going down Hallam Street, you will see on the left hand a house standing by itself, with 'Mr. Gregg, Attorney-at-Law,'on a plate on the door. Go in, ask to see Mr. Gregg alone, and give him that note. But mind, Anne, you are not to speak of this to any one. Should Mr. Edwin Barley or any one else meet you, and inquire where you are going, say only that you are walking out. Do you fully understand?"

"Yes."

"Hide the note, so that no one sees it, and give it into Mr. Gregg's hands. Tell him I hope he will comprehend it, but that I was too ill to write more elaborately."

No one noticed me as I left the house, and I pursued the road to Hallam, my head and thoughts full. Suppose Mr. Edwin Barley should meet and question me! I knew that I should make a poor hand at deception: besides being naturally open, mamma had brought me up to be so very candid and truthful. I had crushed the note inside my glove, having no better place of concealment—suppose he should seize my hand and find it! And if the gentleman I was going to see should not be at home, what was I to do then? Bring the note back to Selina, or leave it? I ought to have asked her.

"Well, my little maid, and where are you off to?"

The salutation proceeded from Mr. Martin, who had come right upon me at a turning of the road. My face grew hot as I answered him.

"I am out for a walk, sir."

"But this is rather far to come alone. You are close upon Hallam."

"My Aunt Selina knows it, sir," I said, trembling lest he should stop me, or order me to walk back with him.

"Oh, very well," he answered, good-naturedly. "How is she to-day?"

"She is not any better, sir," I replied. And he left me, telling me I was not to lose myself.

I came to the houses, straggling at first, but soon contiguous to each other, as they are in most streets. Mr. Gregg's stood alone, its plate on the door. A young man came running out of it as I stood hesitating whether to knock or ring.

"If you please, is Mr. Gregg at home?"

"Yes," answered he. "He is in the office. You can go in if you want him."

Opening an inner door, he showed me into a room where there seemed to be a confused mass of faces. In reality there might have been three or four, but they multiplied themselves to my timid eyes.

"A little girl wants to see Mr. Gregg," said the young man.

A tall gentleman came forward, with a pale face and grey whiskers. He said he was Mr. Gregg, and asked what my business was.

"I want to see you by yourself, if you please, sir."

He led the way to another room, and I took the note out of my glove and gave it to him. He read it over—to me it appeared a long one—looked at me, and then read it again.

"Are you Anne Hereford?"

"Yes," I said, wondering how he knew my name. "My aunt, Mrs. Edwin Barley, bade me say she was too ill to write it better, but she hoped you would understand it."

"Is she so ill as to be in danger?"

"I am afraid so."

He still looked at me, and twirled the note in his fingers. I could see that it was written with a pencil.

"Do you know the purport of this?" he inquired, pointing to the note.

"No, sir."

"Did you not read it coming along? It was not sealed."

"Oh, no. I did not take it out of my glove."

"Well—tell Mrs. Edwin Barley that I perfectly understand, and shall immediately obey her: tell her all will be ready by the time she sends to me. And—stay a bit. Have you any Christian name besides Anne?"

"My name is Anne Ursula."

"And what was your father's name? And what your mother's?"

"Papa's was Thomas, and mamma's Ursula," I answered; wondering very much.

He wrote down the names, asked a few more questions, and then showed me out at the street-door, giving a parting injunction that I was not to forget the words of his message to Mrs. Edwin Barley, and not to mention abroad that I had been to his office.

Reaching home without hindrance, I was about to enter the sickroom, when Miss Delves softly called to me from the upper stairs: Mrs. Edwin Barley was sleeping, and must not be disturbed. So I went higher up to take my things off, and Charlotte Delves asked me into her chamber—a very nice one, immediately over Mrs. Edwin Barley's.

"Tread softly, my dear. If she can only sleep, it will do her good."

I would not tread at all, though the carpet was thick and soft, but sat down on the first chair. Miss Delves was changing her cap. She wore very nice ones always.

"Miss Delves, I wish you'd please to tell me. Do you think my aunt will get well?"

"It is to be hoped so," was the answer. "But Mr. Edwin Barley is fretting himself to fiddle-strings over it."

"Do *you* think she will?"

Miss Delves was combing out her long flaxen curls; bright thick curls they were; very smooth, and of an exceedingly light shade. She twirled two round her finger before she answered.

"Yes, I think she will. It is true that she is very ill—very; but, on the other hand, she has youth in her favour."

"Is she dangerously ill?"

"No doubt. But how many people are there, lying in danger daily, who recover! The worst of it is, she is so excited, so restless: the doctors don't like that. It is not to be wondered at, with this trouble in the house; she could not have fallen ill at a more unfortunate time. I think she has a good constitution."

"Mamma used to say that all the Carews had that. They were in general long-lived."

Charlotte Delves looked round at me. "Your mamma was not long-lived. She died young—so to say."

"But mamma's illness came on first from an accident. She was hurt in India. Oh, Miss Delves! can't anything be done to cure my Aunt Selina?"

"My dear, everything will be done that it is possible to do. The doctors talk of the shock to the system; but, as I say, she is young. You must not be too anxious; it would answer no end. Had you a nice walk this morning?"

"Yes."

She finished her hair, and put on the pretty cap, its rich lace lappets falling behind the curls. Then she took up her watch and chain, and looked out at the window as she put them round her neck.

"Here's a policeman coming to the house! I wonder what he wants?"

"Has there been any news yet of George Heneage?"

"None," she answered. "Heneage Grange is being watched."

"Is that where he lives?"

"It is his father's place."

"And is it near to here?"

"Oh no. More than a hundred miles away. The police think it not improbable that he escaped there at once. The Grange has been searched for him, we hear, unsuccessfully. But the police are by no means sure that he is not concealed there, and they have set a watch."

"Oh dear! I hope they will not find him!" I said it with a shudder. The finding of George Heneage seemed to promise I knew not what renewal of horror. Charlotte Delves turned her eyes upon me in astonishment and reproof.

"You hope they will not find him! You cannot know what you are saying, Miss Hereford. I think I would give half the good that is left in my life to have him found—and hung. What right had he to take that poor young man's life? or to bring this shocking trouble into a gentleman's family?"

Very true. Of course he had none.

"Mr. Edwin Barley has taken a vow to track him out; and he will be sure to do it, sooner or later. We will go down, Miss Hereford."

The policeman had not come upon the business, at all, but about some poaching matter. Mr. Edwin Barley came out of his wife's room as we were creeping by it. Charlotte Delves asked if Mrs. Edwin was awake.

"Awake? Yes! and in a most excitable state," he answered, irritably. "She does not sleep three minutes together. It is giving herself no chance of recovery. She has got it in her head now that she's going to die, and is sending for Martin."

He strode down to the waiting policeman. Charlotte Delves went into Mrs. Edwin Barley's room, and took me. Selina's cheeks were still hectic with fever; her blue eyes bright and wild.

"If you would only try to calm yourself, Mrs. Edwin Barley!"

"I am as calm as I can expect to be," was her answer, given with some petulance. "My husband need not talk; he's worse than I am.

He says now the doctors are treating me wrongly, and that he shall call in a fresh one. I suppose I shall die between them."

"I wish I knew what would soothe you," spoke Charlotte Delves, in a kind, pleasant voice.

"I'm very thirsty, and have taken all the lemonade; you can fetch me up some more. Anne, do you stay here."

Charlotte Delves took down the lemonade waiter, and Selina drew me to her. "The message, Anne!—the message! Did you see Mr. Gregg?"

I gave her the message as I had received it. It was well, she said, and turned away from me in her restlessness. Mr. Martin came in the afternoon: and from that time he seemed to be a great deal with Selina. A day or two passed on, bringing no change: she continued very ill, and George Heneage was not found.

I had another walk to Hallam on the Friday. Philip King's funeral was to be on the Saturday, and the walk appeared to have some connexion with that event. Selina sent no note this time, but a mysterious message.

"See Mr. Gregg alone as before, Anne," were the orders she gave me. "Tell him that the funeral is fixed for eleven o'clock to-morrow morning, and he must be at hand, and watch his time. You can mention that I am now too ill to write."

"Tell him—what do you say, Selina?"

"Tell him exactly what I have told you; he will understand, though you do not. Why do you make me speak?" she added, irritably. "I send you in preference to a servant on this private business."

I discharged the commission; and, with the exception of about one minute on my return, did not see Selina again that day. It was said in the household that she was a trifle better. Mr. Edwin Barley had been as good as his word, and a third doctor attended now, a solemn old gentleman in black dress clothes and gold spectacles. It transpired, no one but Miss Delves knowing with what truth, that he agreed with his two brethren in the treatment they had pursued.

Saturday morning. The house woke up to a quiet bustle. People were going and coming, servants were moving about and preparing, all in a subdued decorous manner. The servants had been put into mourning—Mr. Edwin Barley was all in black, and Charlotte Delves rustled from room to room in rich black silk. Philip King had been related to her in a very distant degree. Mrs. Edwin Barley was no worse; better, if anything, the doctors said. From what could be gathered by us, who were not doctors, the throat was a trifle better; she herself weaker.

The funeral was late. The clocks were striking eleven as it wound down the avenue on its way to the church, an old-fashioned little structure, situated at right angles between the house and Hallam. In the first black chariot sat the clergyman, Mr. Martin; then followed the hearse; then two mourning-coaches. In the first were Mr. Edwin Barley, his brother, and two gentlemen whom I did not know—they were the mourners; in the other were the six pall-bearers. Some men walked in hatbands, and the carriages were drawn by four horses, bearing plumes.

"Is it out of sight, Anne?"

The questioner was my aunt, for it was at her window I stood, peeping inside the blind. It had been out of sight some minutes, I told her, and must have passed the lodge.

"Then go downstairs, Anne, and open the hall-door. Stand there until Mr. Gregg comes; he will have a clerk with him: bring them up here. Do all this quietly, child."

In five minutes Mr. Gregg arrived, a young man accompanying him. I shut the hall-door and took them upstairs. They trod so softly just as though they would avoid being heard. Selina held out her hand to Mr. Gregg.

"How are you to-day, Mrs. Edwin Barley?"

"They say I am better," she replied; "I hope I am. Is it quite ready?"

"Quite," said he, taking a parchment from one of his pockets. "You will hear it read?"

"Yes; that I may see whether you understood my imperfect letter. I hope it is not long. The church, you know, is not so far off; they will be back soon."

"It is quite short," Mr. Gregg replied, having bent his ear to catch her speech, for she spoke low and imperfectly. "Where shall my clerk wait whilst I read it?"

She sent us into her dressing-room, the clerk and I, whence we could hear Mr. Gregg's voice slowly reading something, but could not distinguish words or sense; once I caught the name "Anne Ursula Hereford." And then we were called in again.

"Anne, go downstairs and find Jemima," were the next orders. "Bring her up here."

"Is it to give her her medicine?" asked Jemima, as she followed me upstairs.

"I don't know."

"My girl;" began the attorney to Jemima, "can you be discreet, and hold your tongue?"

Jemima stared very much: first at seeing them there, next at the question. She gave no answer in her surprise, and Mrs. Edwin Barley made a sign that she should come close to her.

"Jemima, I am sure you know that I have been a good mistress to you, and I ask you to render me a slight service in return. In my present state of health, I have thought it necessary to make my will; to devise away the trifle of property I possess of my own. I am about to sign it, and you and Mr. Gregg's clerk will witness my signature. The service I require of you is, that you will not speak of this to any one. Can I rely upon you?"

"Yes, ma'am, certainly you may," replied the servant, speaking in earnest tones; and she evidently meant to keep her word honestly.

"And my clerk I have answered to you for," put in Mr. Gregg, as he raised Mrs. Edwin Barley and placed the open parchment before her.

She signed her name, "Selina Barley;" the clerk signed his, "William Dixon;" and Jemima hers, "Jemima Lea." Mr. Gregg remarked that Jemima's writing *might* be read, and it was as much as could be said of it. She quitted the room, and soon afterwards Mr. Gregg and his clerk took their departure in the same quiet manner that they had come. I was closing the hall-door after them, when the sound of silk, rustling up, fell on my startled ears, and Charlotte Delves stepped into the hall from one of the passages. She had been shut up in her parlour.

"Who is it that has gone out?"

But I was already half-way up to Selina's room, and would not hear. Miss Delves opened the door and looked after them.

And at that moment Jemima appeared. Charlotte Delves laid hold of her, and no doubt turned her inside out.

"Anne, my dear, if I die you are now provided for. At least—"

"Oh, Selina! Selina! You cannot be going to die!"

"Perhaps not. I hope not. Yes, I do hope it, Anne, in spite of my fancied warning—which, I suppose, was only a dream, after all. My mind must have dwelt on what you said about Ursula. If you ever relate to me anything of the sort again, Anne, I'll beat you."

I stood conscience-stricken. But in telling her what I did, I had only obeyed my mother. I like to repeat this over and over again.

"At least, as well provided for as I have it in my power to provide," she continued, just as though there had been no interruption. "I have left you my four thousand pounds. It is out at good interest—five per cent.; and I have directed it to accumulate until you are eighteen. Then it goes to you. This will just keep you; just be enough to keep you from going out as a governess. If I live, you will have your home with me after leaving school. Of course, that governess scheme was all a farce; Ursula could only have meant it so. The world would stare to see a governess in a granddaughter of Carew of Keppe-Carew."

The will lay on the bed. She told me to lock it up in the opposite cabinet, taking the keys from underneath the pillow, and I obeyed her. By her directions, I took the cabinet key off the bunch, locked it up alone in a drawer, and she returned the bunch underneath her pillow. By that time she could not speak at all. Charlotte Delves, happening to come in, asked what she had been doing to reduce her strength like that.

It was a miserable day after they came in from the funeral. Mr. Edwin Barley did not seem to know what to do with himself, and the other people had gone home. Mr. Martin was alone with Selina for a great portion of the afternoon. At first I did not know he was there, and looked in. The clergyman was kneeling down by the bed, praying aloud. I shut the door again, hoping they had not heard it open. In the evening Selina appeared considerably better. She sat up in bed, and took a few spoonfuls of arrowroot. Mr. Edwin Barley, who was in the arm-chair near the fire, said it was poor stuff, and she ought to take either brandy or wine, or both.

"Let me give you some in that, Selina," he cried. And indeed he had been wanting to give it her all along.

"I should be afraid to take it; don't tease me," she feebly answered, and it was astonishing how low her voice was getting. "You know what the doctors say, Edwin. When once the inflammation (or whatever it is) in the throat has passed, then I may be fed up every hour. Perhaps they will let me begin to-morrow."

"If they don't mind, they'll keep you so low that—that we shall have to give you a bottle of brandy a day." I think the concluding words, after the pause, had been quite changed from what he had been going to say, and he spoke half-jokingly. "I know that the proper treatment for you would have been stimulants. I told Lowe so again to-day, but he would not have it. But for one thing, I'd take the case into my own hands, and give you a wine-glass of brandy now."

"And that one thing?" she asked, in her scarcely perceptible voice.

"The doubt that I *might* do wrong."

Jemima appeared at the door with a candle: it was my signal. Selina kissed me twice, and said she should hope to get up on the morrow. I went round to Mr. Edwin Barley.

"Good-night, sir."

"Is it your bed-time, child? Good-night."

# CHAPTER 6

## DEAD!

Eight o'clock the next morning, and the church-bells ringing out on the sunshiny air! Everything looked joyous as I drew up the blind—kept down for a week previously. I dressed myself, without waiting for Jemima, in my Sunday frock with its deep crape trimmings. The house would be open again to-day; Selina be sitting up.

I scrambled over my dressing; I fear I scrambled over my prayers. Everything was so still below I thought they had forgotten me. Going down, I knocked at Selina's door, and was waiting to hear her answer, when one of the maids came running up the stairs in a flurry. It was Sarah.

"You cannot go in there, Miss Hereford."

"I want to see how my aunt is."

"Oh, she—she—you must not go in, miss, I say. Your aunt cannot see you just now; you must please go down into Miss Delves's parlour."

Dropping the handle of the door in obedience, I went down a few steps. Sarah ascended to the upper flights. But the girl's manner had alarmed me; and, without any thought of doing wrong, I turned back, and softly opened the door. The curtains were drawn closely round the bed.

"Are you worse, Selina?"

No reply came, and I feared she was worse. Perhaps lying with leeches to her throat. I had seen leeches to a throat once, and had never forgotten the sight. At that moment the appearance of the room struck me as strange. *It seemed to have been put to rights.* I pulled open the curtain in full dread of the leeches.

Alas! it was not leeches I saw; but a still, white face. The face of my Aunt Selina, it is true, but—dead. I shrieked out, in my terror, and flew into the arms of Sarah, who came running in.

"What is the matter?" exclaimed Charlotte Delves, flying up to the landing where we stood.

"Why, Miss Hereford has been in there; and I told her not to go!" said Sarah, hushing my face to her as she spoke. "Why couldn't you listen to me, miss?"

"I didn't know Miss Hereford was up; she should have waited for Jemima," said Charlotte Delves, as she laid hold of me, and led me down to her parlour.

"Oh, Miss Delves, Miss Delves, what is it?" I sobbed. "Is she really dead?"

"She is dead, all too certain, my dear. But I am very sorry you should have gone in. It is just like Jemima's carelessness."

"What's that?—that's like my carelessness, Miss Delves?" resentfully inquired Jemima, who had come forward on hearing the noise.

"Why, your suffering this child to dress herself alone, and go about the house at large. One would think you might have been attentive this morning, of all others."

"I went up just before eight, and she was asleep," answered Jemima, with as pert an accent as she dared to use. "Who was to imagine she'd awake and be down so soon?"

"Why did she die? what killed her?" I asked, my sobs choking me. "Dead! *dead!* My Aunt Selina dead!"

"She was taken worse at eleven o'clock last night, and Mr. Lowe was sent for," explained Charlotte Delves. "He could do nothing, and she died at two."

"Where was Mr. Edwin Barley?"

"He was with her."

"Not when she was taken worse," interposed Jemima. "I was with her alone. It was my turn to sit up, and she had spoken quite cheerfully to me. Before settling myself in the arm-chair, I went to see if she had dropped asleep. My patience!—my heart went pit-a-pat at the change in her. I ran for Mr. Edwin Barley, and he came in. Mr. Lowe was sent for: everything was done, but she could not be saved."

I turned to Charlotte Delves in my sad distress. "She was so much better last night," I said, imploringly. "She was getting well."

"It was a deceitful improvement," replied Charlotte Delves—and she seemed really sad and grieved. "Lowe said he could have told us so had he been here. Mr. Edwin Barley quite flew out at him, avowing his belief that it was the medical treatment that had killed her."

"And was it?" I eagerly asked, as if, the point ascertained, it could bring her back to life. "Do they know what she died of?"

"As to knowing, I don't think any of them know too much," answered Charlotte Delves. "The doctors say the disorder, together with the shock her system had received, could not be subdued. Mr. Edwin Barley says it could have been, under a different treatment. Lowe tells me now he had little hope from the first."

"And couldn't open his lips to say so!" interposed Jemima. "It's just like those doctors. The master is dreadfully cut up."

They tried to make me take some breakfast, but I could neither eat nor drink. Jemima said they had had theirs "ages ago." None of the household had been to bed since the alarm.

"All I know is, that if blame lies anywhere it is with the doctors," observed Charlotte Delves, as she pressed me to eat. "Every direction they gave was minutely followed."

"Why did no one fetch me down to see her?"

"Child, she never asked for you; she was past thinking of things.

And to you it would only have been a painful sight."

"That's true," added Jemima. "When I looked at her, all unconcerned, I saw death in her face. It frightened me, I can tell you. I ran to call the master, thinking—"

"Thinking what?" spoke Charlotte Delves, for Jemima had made a sudden pause.

"Nothing particular, Miss Delves. Only that something which had happened in the day was odd," added Jemima, glancing significantly at me. "The master was in his room half undressed, and he came rushing after me, just as he was. The minute he looked on her he murmured that she was dying, and sent off a man for Mr. Lowe, and another for the old doctor from Nettleby. Lowe came at once, but the other did not get here till it was over. She died at two."

Jemima would have enlarged on the details for ever. I felt sick as I listened. Even now, as I write, a sort of sickness comes over me with the remembrance. I wandered into the hall, and was sobbing with my head against the dining-room door-post, not knowing any one was there, when Mr. Edwin Barley gently unlatched the door and looked out.

He had been weeping, as was easy to be seen. His eyes were red—his air and manner subdued; but my acquired fear of him was in full force, and I would rather have gone away than been drawn in.

"Child, don't cry so."

"I never took leave of her, sir. I did not see her before she died."

"If weeping tears of blood would bring her back to life, she'd be here again," he responded, almost fiercely. "They have killed her between them; they have, Anne; and, by Heavens! if there was any law to touch them, they should feel it."

"Who, sir?"

"The doctors. And precious doctors they have proved themselves! Why do you tremble so, child? They have not understood the disorder from the first: it is one requiring the utmost possible help from stimulants; otherwise the system cannot battle with it. They gave her none; they kept her upon water, and—she is lying there. Oh I that I had done as it perpetually crossed my mind to do!" he continued, clasping his hands together in anguish. "That I had taken her treatment upon myself, risking the responsibility! She would have been living now!"

If ever a man spoke the genuine sentiments of his heart, Mr. Edwin Barley appeared to do so then, and a little bit of my dislike of him subsided—just a shade of it.

"I am sorry you should have come into the house at this time, my poor child; some spell seems to have been upon it ever since. Go now to Charlotte Delves; tell her I say she is to take good care of you."

He shut himself in again as I went away. Oh, the restless day! the miserable day! That, and the one of mamma's death, remain still upon my memory as the two sad epochs of my life, standing out conspicuously in their bitterness.

Moving about the house restlessly; shedding tears by turns; leaning my head on the sofa in Miss Delves's parlour! She was very kind to me but what was any kindness to me then? It seemed to me that I could never, never be happy again. I had so loved Selina! I wanted to see her again. It was almost as if I had *not* seen her in the morning, for the shock of surprise had startled away my senses. I had looked upon mamma so many times after death, that the customary dread of childhood at such sights lingered but little with me. And I began to watch for an opportunity to go in.

It came at twilight. In passing the room I saw the door open, and supposed some of the maids might be there. In I went bravely; and passed round to the far side of the bed, nearest to the window and the fading light.

But I had not courage to draw aside the curtain quite at first, and sat down for a moment in the low chair by the bed-head, to wait until courage came. Some one else came first; and that was Mr. Edwin Barley.

He walked slowly in, carrying a candle, startling me almost to sickness. His slippers were light, and I had not heard his approach. It must have been he who had left the door open, probably having been to fetch the very candle in his hand. He did not come near the bed, at least on the side where I was, but seemed to be searching for something; looking about, opening two or three drawers. I sat cowering, feeling I had no business to be there; my heart was in my mouth, when he went to the door and called Charlotte Delves.

"Where are my wife's keys?" he inquired, as she came up.

"I do not know," was her answer; and she began to look about the room as he had previously done. "They must be somewhere."

"Not know! But it was your place to take possession of them, Charlotte. I want to examine her desk; there may be directions left in it, for all I can tell."

"I really forgot all about the keys," Charlotte Delves said deprecatingly. "I will ask the women who were here. Why! here they are; in this china basket on the mantelpiece," she suddenly exclaimed. "I knew they could not be far off."

Mr. Edwin Barley took the keys, and went out, the desk under his arm. Charlotte followed him, and closed the door. But I was too much scared to attempt to remain; I softly opened it, and stole out after them, waiting against the wall in the shade. They had halted at the turning to Mr. Barley's study, half-way down the stairs, and were talking in subdued tones. Charlotte Delves was telling him of the lawyer's visit on the previous day.

"I did not mention it before," she observed. "Of course, while poor Mrs. Edwin was here, it was not my business to report to you on anything she might do, and to-day has had too much trouble in it. But there's no doubt that Gregg was here, and a clerk with him. Little Miss Hereford showed them out, and I suppose admitted them. It was an odd time to choose for the visit—the hour of the funeral."

Can you imagine how terrified I felt as Charlotte Delves related this? I had done no wrong; I had simply obeyed the orders of Mrs. Edwin Barley; but it was uncertain what amount of blame her husband might lay to my share, and how he would punish it.

"It is strange what Gregg could be doing here at that time with a clerk; and in private, as you appear to assume," said Mr. Edwin Barley. "Could he have come by appointment, to transact any legal business for my wife?"

"But, if so, why should she wish it kept from you?" And Charlotte Delves's voice had a jealous ring in it: jealous for the rights of her cousin, Edwin Barley.

"I don't know. The little girl may be able to explain. Call her up."

Another fright for me. But the next moment his voice countermanded the order.

"Never mind, Charlotte; let it be. When I want information of Anne Hereford, I'll question her myself. And if my wife did anything, made a will, or gave Gregg any other directions, we shall soon know of it."

"Made a will!" exclaimed Charlotte Delves.

"I should not think it likely that she would without speaking to me, but she could do it: she was of age," replied Mr. Barley.

He went into his study with the desk, and Charlotte Delves passed downstairs. I got into her parlour as soon as she did, never having seen my dear Aunt Selina.

They took me to see her the next day, when she was in her first coffin. She looked very calm and peaceful; but I think the dead, generally speaking, do look peaceful; whether they have died a happy death or not. A few autumn flowers were strewed upon her flannel shroud.

In coming out of the room, my face streaming with tears, there stood Mr. Lowe.

"Oh, sir!" I cried, in my burst of grief, "what made her die? Could you not have saved her?"

"My little girl, what she really died of was exhaustion," he answered. "The disease took hold of her, and she could not rally from it. As to saving her—God alone could have done that."

There was no inquest this time. The doctors certified to some cause of death. The house was more closely shut up than before; the servants went about speaking in whispers; deeper mourning was prepared for them. In Selina's desk a paper had been found by Mr. Edwin Barley—a few pencilled directions on it, should she "unhappily die." Therefore the prevision of death had been really upon her. She named two or three persons whom she should wish to attend her funeral, Mr. Gregg being one of them.

Saturday again, and another funeral! Ever since, even to this hour, Saturdays and funerals have been connected together in my impressionable mind. I had a pleasant dream early that morning. I saw Selina in bright white robes, looking peacefully happy, saying that her sins had been washed away by Jesus Christ, the Redeemer. I had previously sobbed myself to sleep, hoping that they had.

It was fixed for twelve o'clock this time. The long procession, longer than the other one had been, wound down the avenue. Mr. Edwin Barley went in a coach by himself; perhaps he did not like to be seen grieving; three or four coaches followed it, and some private carriages, Mr. Barley's taking the lead. There was not a dry eye amidst the household—us, who were left at home—with the exception of Charlotte Delves. I did not see her weep at all, then or previously. The narrow crape tucks on her gown were exchanged for wide ones, and some black love-ribbon mingled with her hair. I sobbed till they came back, sitting by myself in the dining-room.

It was the very room they filed into, those who entered. A formidable array, in their sweeping scarves and hatbands; too formidable for me to pass, and I shrank into the far corner, between the sideboard and the dumb-waiter. But they began to leave again, only just saying good-day in a low tone to Mr. Edwin Barley, and got into the coaches that waited. Mr. Gregg the lawyer remained, and Mr. Barley.

"Pardon me that I stay," observed the lawyer to Mr. Edwin Barley; "I am but obeying the request of your late wife. She charged me, in the event of her death, to stay and read the will after the funeral."

"The will!" echoed Mr. Edwin Barley.

"She made a will just before she died. She gave me instructions for it privately; though what her motives were for keeping it a secret, she did not state. It was executed on the day previous to her death."

"This is news to me," observed Mr. Edwin Barley. "Do you hold the will?"

"No, I left it with her. You had better remain, my little girl," the lawyer added to me, touching my arm with his black glove as I was essaying to quit the room. "The will concerns you. I asked your wife if I should take possession of it, but she preferred to keep it herself."

"I do not know where it can have been put, then," returned Mr. Edwin Barley, whilst his brother lifted his head in interest. "I have examined her desk and one or two of her drawers where she kept papers; but I have found no will."

"Perhaps you did not look particularly for a will, not knowing she had made one, and so it may have escaped your notice, sir," suggested the lawyer.

"Pardon me; it was the precise thing I looked for. I heard of your visit to my wife: not, however, until after her death; and it struck me that your coming might have reference to something of the sort. But I found no will: only a few pencilled words on a half-sheet of paper in her desk. Do you know where it was put?"

The lawyer turned to me. "Perhaps this little lady may know," he said. "She made one in the room when I was with Mrs. Edwin Barley, and may have seen afterwards where the will was placed."

Again I felt sick with apprehension: few children at my age have ever been so shy and sensitive. It seemed to me that all was coming out; at any rate, my share in it. But I spoke pretty bravely.

"You mean the paper that you left on my Aunt Selina's bed, sir? I put it in the cabinet; she directed me to do so."

"In the cabinet?" repeated Mr. Edwin Barley to me.

"Yes, sir. Just inside as you open it."

"Will you go with me to search for it?" said Mr. Edwin Barley to the lawyer. "And you can go into Miss Delves's parlour, Anne; little girls are better out of these affairs."

"Pardon me," dissented Mr. Gregg. "Miss Hereford, as the only interested party, had better remain. And if she can show us where the will is, it will save time."

Mr. Edwin Barley looked as if he meant to object, but did not. "The child's nerves have been unhinged," he said to the lawyer, as they went upstairs, I and Mr. Barley following.

The key of the cabinet lay in the corner of the drawer where I had placed it. Mr. Edwin Barley took it from me and opened the cabinet. But no will was to be seen.

"I did not think of looking here," he observed; "my wife never used the cabinet to my knowledge. There is no will here."

There was no will anywhere, apparently. Drawers were opened; her desk, standing now on the drawers, was searched; all without effect.

"It is very extraordinary," said Mr. Gregg to him.

"I can only come to one conclusion—that my wife must have destroyed it herself. It is true the keys were lying about for several hours subsequent to her death, at any one's command; but who would steal a will?"

"I do not suppose Mrs. Edwin Barley would destroy it," dissented Mr. Gregg. "Nothing can be more improbable. She expressed her happiness at having been able to make a will; her great satisfaction. Who left the keys about, sir?"

"The blame of that lies with Charlotte Delves. It escaped her memory to secure them, she tells me: and in the confusion of the sudden blow, it is not to be wondered at. But, and if the keys were left about? I have honest people in my house, Mr. Gregg."

"Who benefited by the will?" asked Mr. Barley of the Oaks. He had helped in the search, and was now looking on with a face of puzzled concern. "Who comes into the money, Gregg?"

"Ay, who?" put in Mr. Edwin Barley.

"This little girl, Anne Ursula Hereford. Mrs. Edwin Barley bequeathed to her the whole of her money, and also her trinkets, except the trinkets that had been your own gift to her, Mr. Edwin Barley." And he proceeded to detail the provisions of the short will. "In fact, she left to Miss Hereford everything of value she had to leave; money, clothes, trinkets. It is most strange where the will can be."

"It is more than strange," observed Mr. Edwin Barley. "Why did she wish to make the will in secret?"

"I have told you, sir, that she did not say why."

"But can you not form an idea why?"

"It occurred to me that she thought you might not like her leaving all she had away from you, and might have feared you would interfere."

"No," he quietly said, "I should not have done that. Every wish that she confided to me should have been scrupulously carried out."

"Oh, but come, you know! a big sheet of parchment, sealed and inscribed, can't vanish in this way," exclaimed Mr. Barley. "It must be somewhere in the room."

It might be, but no one could find it. Mr. Barley grew quite excited and angry: Mr. Edwin was calm throughout. Mr. Barley went to the door, calling for Miss Delves.

"Charlotte, come up here. Do you hear, Charlotte?"

She ran up quickly, evidently wondering.

"Look here," cried Mr. Barley: "Mrs. Edwin's will can't be found. It was left in this cabinet, my brother is told."

"Oh, then, Mrs. Edwin did make a will?" was the response of Charlotte Delves.

"Yes; but it is gone," repeated Mr. Barley of the Oaks.

"It cannot be gone," said Charlotte. "If the will was left in the cabinet, there it would be now."

The old story was gone over again; nothing more. The will had been made, and as certainly placed there. The servants were honest, not capable of meddling with that or anything else. But there was no sign or symptom of a will left.

"It is very strange," exclaimed Mr. Edwin Barley, looking furtively from the corner of his black eyes at most of us in succession, as if we were in league against him or against the will. "I will have the house searched throughout."

The search took place that same evening. Himself, his brother, Mr. Gregg, and Charlotte Delves took part in it. Entirely without success.

And in my busy heart there was running a conviction all the time, that Mr. Edwin Barley had himself made away with the will.

"Will you not act in accordance with its provisions, sir?" Mr. Gregg asked him as he was leaving.

"I do not think I shall," said Mr. Edwin Barley. "Produce the will, and every behest in it shall be fulfilled. Failing a will, my wife's property becomes mine, and I shall act as I please by it."

The days went by; ten unhappy days. I spent most of my time with Miss Delves, seeing scarcely anything of Mr. Edwin Barley. Part of the time he was staying at his brother's, but now and then I met him in the passages or the hall. He would give me a nod, and pass by. I cannot describe my state of feeling, or how miserable the house appeared to me: I was as one unsettled in it, as one who lived in constant discomfort, fear, and dread; though of what, I could not define. Jemima remarked one day that "Miss Hereford went about moithered, like a fish out of water."

The will did not turn up, and probably never would: neither was any clue given to the mystery of its disappearance. Meanwhile rumours of its loss grew rife in the household and in the neighbourhood. Whether the lawyer talked, or Mr. Barley of the Oaks, and thus set them afloat, was uncertain, but it was thought to have been one or the other. I know I had said nothing; Charlotte Delves said she had not; neither, beyond doubt, had Mr. Edwin Barley. When an acquaintance once asked him whether the report was true, he answered, Yes, it was true so far as that Mr. Gregg said his late wife had made a will, and it could not be found; but his own belief was that she must have destroyed it again; he could not suspect that any of the household would tamper with its mistress's private affairs.

One day Mr. Edwin Barley called me to him. I was standing by the large Michaelmas-daisy shrub, and he passed along the path.

"Are you quite sure," he asked in his sternest tone, but perhaps it was only a serious one, "that you did not reopen the cabinet yourself, and do something with the parchment?"

"I never opened it again, sir. If I had, my aunt must have seen me. And I could not have done so," I added, recollecting myself, "for she kept the bunch of keys under her pillow."

"She was the only one, though, who knew where it was placed," muttered Mr. Edwin Barley to himself, alluding to me, as he walked on.

"It's a queer start about that will!" Jemima resentfully remarked that same night when she was undressing me. "And I don't half like it;

I can tell you that, Miss Hereford. They may turn round on me next, and say I made away with it."

"That's not likely, Jemima. The will would not do you any good. Do you think it will ever be found?"

"It's to be hoped it will—with all this unpleasantness! I wish I had never come within hearing of it, for my part. The day old Gregg and the young man were here, Charlotte Delves got hold of me, pumping me on this side, pumping me on that. Had they been up to Mrs. Edwin Barley? she asked: and what had their business been with her? She didn't get much out of me, but it made me as cross as two sticks. It *is* droll where the will can have gone! One can't suspect Mr. Edwin Barley of touching it; and I don't; but the loss makes him all the richer. That's the way of the world," concluded Jemima: "the more money one has, the more one gets added to it. It is said that he comes into possession of forty thousand pounds by the death of Philip King."

The ten days' sojourn in the desolate house ended, and then Charlotte Delves told me I was going to leave it. In consequence of the death of Selina, the trustees had assigned to Mrs. Hemson the task of choosing a school for me. Mrs. Hemson had fixed on one near to the town where she resided, Dashleigh; and I was to pass a week at Mrs. Hemson's house before entering it. On the evening previous to my departure, a message came from Mr. Edwin Barley that I was to go to him in the dining-room. Charlotte Delves smoothed my hair with her fingers, and sent me in. He was at dessert: fruit and wine were on the table; and John set a chair for me. Mr. Edwin Barley put some walnuts that he cracked and a bunch of grapes on my plate.

"Will you take some wine, little girl?"

"No, thank you, sir. I have just had tea."

Presently he put a small box into my hands. I remembered having seen it on Selina's dressing-table.

"It contains a few of your Aunt Selina's trinkets," he said. "All she brought here, except a necklace, which is of value, and will be forwarded, with some of her more costly clothes, to Mrs. Hemson for you. Do you think you can take care of these until you are of an age to wear them?"

"I will take great care of them, sir. I will lock them up in the little desk mamma gave me, and I wear the key of it round my neck."

"Mind you do take care of them," he rejoined, with suppressed emotion. "If I thought you would not, I would never give them to you. You must treasure them always. And these things, recollect, are of value," he added, touching the box. "They are not child's toys. Take them upstairs, and put them in your trunk."

"If you please, sir, has the will been found?" I waited to ask.

"It has not. Why?"

"Because, sir, you asked me if I had taken it; you said I was the only one who knew where it had been put. Indeed, I would not have touched it for anything."

"Be easy, little girl. I believe my wife herself destroyed the will; but I live in hope of coming to the bottom of the mystery yet. As you have introduced the subject, you shall hear a word upon it from me. Busybodies have given me hints that I ought to carry out its substance in spite of the loss. I do not think so. The will, and what I hear connected with its making, has angered me, look you, Anne Hereford. Had my wife only breathed half a word to me that she wished you to have her money, every shilling should be yours. But I don't like the underhand work that went on in regard to it, and shall hold it precisely as though it had never existed. If I ever relent in your favour, it will not be yet awhile."

"I did not know she was going to leave me anything, indeed, sir."

"Just so. But it was you who undertook the communications to Gregg, it seems, and admitted him when he came. You all acted as though I were a common enemy; and it has vexed me in no measured degree. That's all, child. Take another bunch of grapes with you."

I went away, carrying the casket and the grapes. Jemima was packing my trunks when I went upstairs, and she shared the grapes and the delight of looking at the contents of the casket: Selina's thin gold chain, and her beautiful little French watch, two or three bracelets, some rings, brooches, and a smelling-bottle encased in filigree gold. All these treasures were mine. At first I gazed at them with a mixed feeling, in which awe and sorrow held their share; Jemima the same: it seemed a profanation to rejoice over what had been so recently *hers:* but the sorrow soon lost itself in the moment's seduction. Jemima hung the chain and watch round her own neck, put on all the bracelets, thrust the largest of the rings on her little finger, and figured off before the glass; whilst I knelt on a chair looking on in mute admiration, anticipating the time when they would be adorning me. Ah, my readers! when we indeed become of an age to wear ornaments, how poor is the pleasure they afford then, compared with that other early anticipation!

A stern voice shouting out "Anne Hereford!" broke the charm, startling us excessively. Jemima tore off the ornaments, I jumped from the chair.

"Anne, I want you," came the reiterated call. It was from Mr. Edwin Barley. He stood at the foot of the stairs as I ran down, my heart beating, expecting nothing but that the precious treasures were going to be wrested from me. Taking my hand, he led me into the dining-room, sat down, and held me before him.

"Anne, you are a sensible little girl," he began, "and will understand what I say to you. The events, the tragedies which have happened in this house since you came to it, are not pleasant; they do not bring honour either to the living or the dead. Were everything that occurred to be rigidly investigated, a large share of blame might be cast on my wife, your Aunt Selina. It is a reflection I would have striven to shield her from had she lived. I would doubly shield her now that she is dead. Will you do the same?"

"Yes, sir; I should like to do so."

"That is right. Henceforth, when strangers question you, you must know nothing. The better plan will be to be wholly silent. Remember, child, I urge this for Selina's sake. We know how innocent of deliberate wrong she was, but she was careless, and people might put a different construction on things. They might be capable of saying that she urged Heneage to revenge. You were present at that scene by the summer-house, from which Heneage ran off, and shot King. Do not ever speak of it."

I think my breath went away from me in my consternation. How had Mr. Edwin Barley learnt that? It could only have been from Selina.

"She sent me after Mr. Heneage, sir, to tell him to let Philip King alone—to command it in his mother's name."

"I know. Instead of that he went and shot him. I would keep my wife's name out of all this; you must do the same. But that you are a child of right feeling and of understanding beyond your years, I should not say this to you. Good-bye. I shall not see you in the morning."

"Good-bye, sir," I answered. "Thank you for letting them all be kind to me."

And he shook hands with me for the first time.

# CHAPTER 7

## AT MISS FENTON'S

I must have been a very impressionable child; easily swayed by the opinions of those about me. The idea conveyed to my mind by what I had heard of Mrs. Hemson was, that she was something of an ogre with claws; and I can truthfully say, I would almost as soon have been consigned to the care of an ogre as to hers. I felt so all the time I was going to her.

Charlotte Delves placed me in the ladies' carriage at Nettleby Station under charge of the guard—just as it had been in coming. And once more I, poor lonely little girl, was being whirled on a railroad journey. But ah! with what a sad amount of experience added to my young life!

Two o'clock was striking as the train steamed into Dashleigh Station. I was not sure at first that it was Dashleigh, and in the uncertainty did not get out. Several people were on the platform, waiting for the passengers the train might bring. One lady in particular attracted my notice, a tall, fair, graceful woman, with a sweet countenance. There was something in her face that put me in mind of mamma. She was looking attentively at the carriages, one after another, when her eyes caught mine, and she came to the door.

"I think you must be Anne," she said, with a bright smile, and sweet voice of kindness. "Did you not know I should be here? I am Mrs. Hemson."

That Mrs. Hemson! that the ogre with claws my imagination had painted! In my astonishment I never spoke or stirred. The guard came up.

"This is Dashleigh," said he to me. "Are you come to receive this young lady, ma'am?"

Mrs. Hemson did receive me, with a warm embrace. She saw to my luggage, and then put me in a fly to proceed to her house. A thorough gentlewoman was she in all ways; a *lady* in appearance, mind, and manners. But it seemed to me a great puzzle how she could be so; or, being so, that she could have married a retail tradesman.

Mr. Hemson was a silk-mercer and linendraper. It appeared to me a large, handsome shop, containing many shopmen and customers. The fly passed it and stopped at the private door. We went through a wide passage and up a handsome staircase, into large and well-furnished sitting-rooms. My impression had been that Mrs. Hemson lived in a hovel, or, at the best, in some little dark sitting-room behind a shop. Mrs. Jones, who kept the little shop where mamma used to buy her things, had only a kitchen behind. Upstairs again were the nursery and bedrooms, a very large house altogether. There were six children, two girls who went to school by day, two boys at a boarding-school, and two little ones in the nursery. In the yard behind were other rooms, occupied by the young men engaged in the business, with whom Mrs. Hemson appeared to have nothing whatever to do.

"This is where you will sleep, Anne," she said, opening the door of a chamber which had two beds in it. "Frances and Mary sleep here, but they can occupy the same bed whilst you stay. Make haste and take your things off, my dear, for dinner is ready."

I soon went down. There was no one in the drawing-room then, and I was looking at some of the books on the centre table, when a gentleman entered: he was tall, bright, handsome; a far more gentlemanly man than any I had seen at Mr. Edwin Barley's; more so than even George Heneage. I wondered who he could be.

"My dear little girl, I am glad you have arrived safely," he said, cordially taking my hand. "It was a long way for them to send you alone."

It was Mr. Hemson. How could they have prejudiced me against him, was the first thought that struck me. I had yet to learn that people in our Keppe-Carew class of life estimate tradespeople not by themselves but by their callings. The appearance of Mrs. Hemson had surprised me; how much more, then, did that of her husband! Mrs. Jones's husband was a little mean man, who carried out the parcels, and was given, people said, to cheating. Since Selina mentioned Mr. Hemson's trade to me, I had associated the two in my mind. Well-educated, good and kind, respected in his native town, and making money fast by fair dealing, Mr. Hemson, to my ignorance, was a world's wonder.

"Is she not like Ursula, Frederick!" exclaimed Mrs. Hemson, holding up my chin. "You remember her?"

He looked at me with a smile. "I scarcely remember her. I don't think Ursula ever had eyes like these. They are worth a king's ransom; and they are honest and true."

We went into the other room to dinner—a plain dinner of roast veal and ham, and a damson tart, all admirably cooked and served, with a well-dressed maid-servant to wait upon us. Altogether the house seemed thoroughly well conducted; a pleasant, plentiful home, and where they certainly lived as quiet gentlepeople, not for show, but for comfort. Mr. Hemson went downstairs after dinner, and we returned to the drawing-room.

"Anne," Mrs. Hemson said, smiling at me, "you have appeared all amazed since you came into the house. What is the reason?"

I coloured very much; but she pressed the question.

"It is—a better house than I expected, ma'am."

"What! did they prejudice you against me?" she laughed. "Did your mamma do that?"

"Mamma told me nothing. It was my Aunt Selina. She said you had raised a barrier between—between—"

"Between myself and the Carews," she interrupted, filling up the pause. "They say I lost caste in marrying Mr. Hemson. And so I did. But—do you like him, Anne?"

"Very, very much. He seems quite a gentleman."

"He is a gentleman in all respects except one; but that is one which people cannot get over, rendering it impossible for them to meet him as an equal. Anne, when I became acquainted with Mr. Hemson, I did not know he was in trade. Not that he intentionally deceived me, you must understand; he is a man of nice honour, incapable of deceit; but it fell out so. We were in a strange place, both far away from home, and what our relative positions might be at home never happened to be alluded to by either of us. By the time I heard who and what he was, a silk-mercer and linendraper, I had learnt to value him above all else in the world. After that, he asked me to be his wife."

"And you agreed?"

"My dear, I first of all sat down and counted the cost. Before giving my answer, I calculated which I could best give up, my position in society as a gentlewoman and a gentleman's daughter of long pedigree, or Frederick Hemson. I knew that constant slights—not intentional ones, but what I should feel as such—would be my portion if I married him; that I should descend for ever in the scale of society—must leap the great gulf which separates the gentlewoman from the tradesman's wife. But I believed that I should find my compensation in him: and I tried it. I have never repented the step; I find more certainly, year by year, that if I threw away the shadow, I grasped the substance."

"Oh, but surely you are still a gentlewoman!"

"My dear, such is not my position: I have placed myself beyond the pale of what the world calls society. But I counted all that beforehand, I tell you, and I put it from me bravely. I weighed the cost well; it has not been more than I bargained for."

"But indeed you are a gentlewoman," I said, earnestly, the tears rising to my eyes at what I thought injustice; "I can see you are."

"Granted, Anne. But what if others do not accord me the place? I cannot visit gentlepeople or be visited by them. I am the wife of Mr. Hemson, a retail trader. This is a cathedral town, too; and, in such, the distinctions of society are bowed to in an ultra degree."

"But is it right?"

"Quite right; perfectly right; as you will find when you are older. If you have been gathering from my words that I rebel at existing things, you are in error. The world would not get along without its social distinctions, though France once had a try at it."

"Yes, I know."

"I repeat, that I sat down and counted *the cost*; and I grow more willing to pay it year by year. But, Anne dear," and she laid her hand impressively on my arm, "I would not recommend my plan of action to others. It has answered in my case, for Mr. Hemson is a man in a thousand; and I have dug a grave and buried my pride; but in nine cases out of ten it would bring unhappiness and repentance. Nothing can be more productive of misery generally, than an unequal marriage."

I did not quite understand. She had said that she was paying off the cost year by year.

"Yes, Anne. One part of the cost must always remain—a weighty incubus. It is not only that I have placed myself beyond the pale of my own sphere, but I have entailed it on my children. My girls must grow up in the state to which they are born: let them be ever so refined, ever so well educated, a barrier lies across their path. In visiting, they must be confined to their father's class; they can never expect to be sought in marriage by gentlemen. Wealthy tradespeople, professional men, they may stand a chance of; but gentlemen, in the strict sense of the term, never."

"Will they feel it?"

"No; oh no. That part of the cost is alone mine. I have taken care not to bring them up to views above their father's station. There are moments when I wish I had never had children. We cannot put away our prejudices entirely, we Keppe-Carews, you see, Anne," she added, with a light laugh.

"I don't think any one can," I said, with a wise shake of the head.

"And now, Anne—to change the subject—what were the details of that dreadful tragedy at Mr. Edwin Barley's?"

"I cannot tell them," I answered, with a rushing colour, remembering Mr. Edwin Barley's caution as to secrecy. Mrs. Hemson misunderstood the refusal.

"Poor child! I suppose they kept particulars from you: and it was right to do so. Could they not save Selina?"

"No—for she died. Mr. Edwin Barley says he knows she was treated wrongly."

"Ill-fated Selina! Were you with her when she died, Anne?"

"I was with her the night before. We thought she was getting better, and she thought it. She had forgotten all about the warning, saying it must be a dream."

"About the what?" interrupted Mrs. Hemson.

"While Selina was ill, she saw mamma. She said the Keppe-Carews always had these warnings."

"Child, be silent!" imperatively spoke Mrs. Hemson. "How could they think of imbuing you with their superstitions. It is all fancy."

"Mamma had the same warning, Mrs. Hemson. She said papa called her."

"Be quiet, I say, child!" she repeated, in a tone of emotion. "These subjects are totally unfit for you. Mind, Anne, that you do not allude to them before my little girls; and forget them yourself."

"They do not frighten me. But I should not speak of them to any one but you, Mrs. Hemson."

"Frances and Mary will be home from school at five, and be delighted to make acquaintance with you. You are going to school yourself next week. Have you heard that?"

"To a school in Dashleigh?"

"In the suburbs. The trustees have at length decided it, and I shall be at hand, in case of illness, or anything of that sort. Had your Aunt Selina lived, you would have been placed at Nettleby."

"Where am I to spend the holidays?"

"At school. It is to Miss Fenton's that you are going."

"Is that where Frances and Mary go?"

"No," she answered, a smile crossing her lips. "They would not be admitted to Miss Fenton's"

"But why?"

"Because she professes to take none but gentlemen's daughters. My daughters, especially with their father living in the same town, would not do at any price. It will be a condescension," she laughed, "that Miss Fenton allows you to dine with us once in a way"

"Perhaps she will not take me," I breathlessly said.

"My dear, she will be only too glad to do so. You are the daughter of Colonel Hereford, the granddaughter of Carew of Keppe-Carew."

And in spite of the lost caste of Mrs. Hemson, in spite of the shop below, I never spent a happier week than the one I spent with her.

And now came school life; school life that was to continue without intermission, and did continue, until I was eighteen years of age. Part of these coming years were spent at Miss Fenton's; the rest (as I found afterwards) at a school in France. It is very much the custom to cry down French scholastic establishments, to contrast them unfavourably with English ones. They may deserve the censure; I do not know; but I can truthfully say that so far as my experience goes, the balance is on the other side.

Miss Fenton's was a "Select Establishment," styling itself a first-class one. I have often wondered whether those less select, less expensive, were not more liberal in their arrangements. Fourteen was the number of girls professed to be taken, but never once, during my stay, was the school quite full. It had a name; and there lay the secret of its success. The teaching was good; the girls were brought on well: but for the comforts! You shall hear of them. And I declare that I transcribe each account faithfully.

There were nine pupils at the time I entered: I made the tenth. Miss Fenton, an English teacher, a French teacher who taught German also, and several day-masters, instructed us. Miss Fenton herself took nothing, that I saw, but the music; she was about five-and-thirty, tall, thin, and very prim.

"You will be well off there, my dear, in regard to living," Mrs. Hemson had said to me. "Miss Fenton tells me her pupils are treated most liberally; and that she keeps an excellent table. Indeed, she ought to do so, considering her terms."

Of course I thought I *should* be treated liberally, and enjoy the benefits of the excellent table.

We arrived there just before tea-time, six o'clock. Mrs. Hemson, acting for my trustees, had made the negotiations with Miss Fenton; of course she took me to school, stayed a few minutes with Miss Fenton, and then left me. When my things were off, and I was back in the drawing-room, Miss Fenton rang the bell.

"You shall join the young ladies at once," she said to me; "they are about to take tea. You have never been to school before, I think."

"No, ma'am. Mamma instructed me."

"Have the young ladies gone into the refectory?" Miss Fenton inquired, when a maid-servant appeared.

"I suppose so, ma'am," was the answer. "The bell has been rung for them."

"Desire Miss Linthorn to step hither."

Miss Linthorn appeared, a scholar of fifteen or sixteen, very upright. She made a deep curtsy as she entered.

"Take this young lady and introduce her," said Miss Fenton. "Her name is Hereford."

We went through some spacious, well-carpeted passages; the corners displaying a chaste statue, or a large plant in beautiful bloom; and thence into some shabby passages, uncarpeted. Nothing could be more magnificent (from a moderate middle-class point of view) than the show part, the *company* part of Miss Fenton's house; nothing much more meagre than the rest.

A long, bare deal table, with the tea-tray at one end; two plates of thick bread-and-butter, and one plate of thinner; the English teacher pouring out the tea, the French one seated by her side, and eight girls lower down, that was what I saw on entering a room that looked cold and comfortless.

Miss Linthorn, leaving me just inside the door, walked up to the teachers and spoke.

"Miss Hereford."

"I heard there was a new girl coming in to-day," interrupted a young lady, lifting her head, and speaking in a rude, free tone. "What's the name, Linthorn?"

"Will you have the goodness to behave as a lady—if you can, Miss Glynn?" interrupted the English teacher, whose name was Dale. "That will be your place, Miss Hereford," she added, to me, indicating the end of the form on the left side, below the rest. "Have you taken tea?"

"No, ma'am."

"Qu'elles sont impolies, ces filles Anglaises!" said Mademoiselle Leduc, the French teacher, with a frowning glance at Miss Glynn for her especial benefit.

"It is the nature of school-girls to be so, mademoiselle," pertly responded Miss Glynn. "And I beg to remind you that we are not under your charge when we are out of school in the evening; therefore, whether we are 'impolies' or 'polies,' it is no affair of yours."

Mademoiselle Leduc only half comprehended the words; it was as well she did not. Miss Dale administered a sharp reprimand, and passed me my tea. I stirred it, tasted it, and stirred it again.

"Don't you like it?" asked a laughing girl next to me; Clara Webb, they called her.

I did not like it at all, and would rather have had milk and water. So far as flavour went, it might have been hot water coloured, was sweetened with brown sugar, and contained about a teaspoonful of milk. I never had any better tea, night or morning, as long as I remained; but school-girls grow used to these things. The teachers had a little black teapot to themselves, and their tea looked good. The plate of thin bread-and-butter was for them.

A very handsome girl of seventeen, with haughty eyes and still more haughty tones, craned her neck forward and stared at me. Some of the rest followed her example.

"That child has nothing to eat," she observed. "Why don't you hand the bread-and-butter to her, Webb?"

Clara Webb presented the plate to me. It was so thick, the bread, that I hesitated to take it, and the butter was scraped upon it in a sparing fashion; but for my experience at Miss Fenton's I should never have thought it possible for butter to have been spread so thin. The others were eating it with all the appetite of hunger. The slice was too thick to bite conveniently, so I had to manage as well as I could, listening—how could I avoid it?—to a conversation the girls began amongst themselves in an undertone. To hear them call each other by the surname alone had a strange sound. It was the custom of the school. The teachers were talking together, taking no notice of the girls.

"Hereford? Hereford?" debated the handsome girl, and I found her name was Tayler. "I wonder where she comes from?"

"I know who I saw her with last Sunday, when I was spending the day at home. The Hemsons."

"What Hemsons? Who are they?"

"Hemsons the linendrapcrs."

"Hemsons the linendrapcrs!" echoed an indignant voice, whilst I felt my own face turn to a glowing crimson. "What absurd nonsense you are talking, Glynn!"

"I tell you I did. I knew her face again the moment Linthorn brought her in. She came to church with them, and sat in their pew."

"I don't believe it," coldly exclaimed an exceedingly ugly girl, with a prominent mouth. "As if Miss Fenton would admit that class of people! Glynn is playing upon our credulity; just as she did, do you remember, about that affair of the prizes. We want some more bread-and-butter, Miss Dale—may we ring?"

"Yes, if you do want it," replied Miss Dale, turning her face from mademoiselle to speak.

"Betsey, stop a moment, I have something to ask you!" suddenly called out one dressed in mourning, leaping over the form and darting after the maid, who had come in and was departing with the plate in her hand. A whispered colloquy ensued at the door, half in, half out of it; close to me, who was seated near it.

"I say, Betsey! Do you know who the new pupil is?"

"Not exactly, miss. Mrs. Hemson brought her."

"Mrs. Hemson! There! Glynn said so! Are you sure?"

"I am quite sure, Miss Thorpe. Mrs. Hemson has been here several times this last week or two; I knew it was about a new pupil. And when she brought her to-night, she gave me half-a-crown, and told me to be kind to her. A nice lady is Mrs. Hemson as ever I spoke to."

"I dare say she may be, for her station," spoke Miss Thorpe, going back to her seat with a stalk.

"I say, girls—I have been asking Betsey—come close." And they all drew their heads together. "I thought I'd ask Betsey: she says she does come from the Hemsons. Did you ever know such a shame?"

"It *can't be*, you know," cried the one with the large mouth. "Miss Fenton would not dare to do it. Would my papa, a prebendary of the cathedral, allow me to be placed where I could be associated with tradespeople?"

"Ask Betsey for yourselves," retorted Miss Thorpe. "She says it was Mrs. Hemson who brought her to school."

"Nonsense about asking Betsey," said Nancy Tayler; "ask herself. Come here, child," she added, in a louder tone, beckoning to me.

I went humbly up, behind the form, feeling very humble indeed just then. They were nearly all older than I, and I began again to think it must be something sadly lowering to be connected with the Hemsons.

"Are you related to Hemsons, the shopkeepers?"

"Yes. To Mrs. Hemson. Mamma was—"

"Oh, there, that will do," she unceremoniously interposed, with a scornful gesture. "Go back to your seat, and don't sit too close to Miss Webb; she's a gentleman's daughter."

My readers, you may be slow to believe this, but I can only say that it occurred exactly as written. I returned to my seat, a terrible feeling of mortification having passed over my young life.

They never spoke to me again that evening. There was no supper, and at half-past eight we went up to bed; three smallish beds were in the room where I was to sleep, and one large one with curtains round it. The large one was Miss Dale's, and two of us, I found, shared each of the smaller ones; my bedfellow was Clara Webb. She was a good-humoured girl, more careless upon the point of "family" than most of the rest seemed to be, and did not openly rebel at having to sleep with me. Miss Dale came up for the candle after we were in bed.

The bell rang at half-past six in the morning, our signal for getting up: we had to be down by seven. There were studies till eight, and then breakfast—the same wretched tea, and the same coarse bread-and-butter. At half-past eight Miss Fenton read prayers; and at nine the school business commenced.

At ten, mademoiselle was assembling her German class. Seven only of the pupils learnt it. I rose and went up with them: and was rewarded with a stare.

"What will be the use of German to *her*?" rudely cried Miss Peacock, a tall, stout girl, directing to me all the scorn of which a look is capable. "I should not fancy Miss Hereford is to learn German, Mademoiselle Leduc. It may be as well to inquire."

Mademoiselle Leduc looked at me, hesitated, and then put the question to Miss Fenton, her imperfect English sounding through the room.

"Dis new young lady, is she to learn de German, madam?"

Miss Fenton directed her eyes towards us.

"Miss Hereford? Yes. Miss Hereford is to learn everything taught in my establishment."

"Oh!" said Nancy Tayler, *sotto voce*. "Are you to be a governess, pray, Miss Hereford?"

A moment's hesitation between pride and truth, and then, with a blush of shame in my cheeks for the hesitation, came the brave answer.

"I am to be a governess; mamma gave the directions in her will. What fortune she left is to be expended upon my education, and she said there might be no better path of life open to me."

"That's candid, at any rate," cried Miss Peacock. And so I began German.

We dined at two; and I don't suppose but that every girl was terribly hungry. I know I was. With a scanty eight o'clock breakfast, children ought not to wait until two for the next meal. We had to dress for dinner, which was laid in Miss Fenton's dining-room, not in the bare place called the refectory; Miss Fenton dining with us and carving. It was handsomely laid. A good deal of silver was on the table, with napkins and finger-glasses; indeed, the style and serving were irreproachable. Two servants waited: Betsey and another. The meat was roast beef—a part of beef I had never seen; it seemed a large lump of meat and no bone. Very acceptable looked it to us hungry schoolgirls. We shall have plenty now, I thought.

My plate came to me at last; *such* a little mite of meat, and three large potatoes! I could well have put the whole piece of meat in my mouth at once. Did Miss Fenton fancy I disliked meat? But upon looking at the other plates, I saw they were no better supplied than mine was; plenty of potatoes, but an apology for meat.

"Would we take more?" Miss Fenton asked, when we had despatched it. And the question was invariably put by her every day; we as invariably answered "Yes." The servants took our plates up, and brought them back. I do not believe that the whole meat combined, supplied to all the plates in that second serving, would have weighed two ounces. Potatoes again we had, as much as we liked, and then came a baked rice pudding.

Miss Fenton boasted of her plentiful table. That there was a plentiful dinner always placed on the table was indisputable, *but we did not have enough of it*; we were starved in the sight of plenty. I have seen a leg of mutton leave the table (nay, the joints always so left the table), when two hearty eaters might well have eaten all that had been cut out of it, and upon that the whole thirteen had dined! I, a woman now, have seen much of this stingy, deceitful habit of carving, not only in schools, but in some private families. "We keep a plentiful table," many, who have to do with the young will say. "Yes," I think to myself, "but are those you profess to feed helped to enough of it?" Sometimes, often indeed, two dishes were on the table; we were asked which we would take, but never partook of both. The scanty breakfast, this dinner, and the tea I have described, were all the meals we had; and this was a "select," "first-class" establishment, where the terms charged were high. Miss Fenton took her supper at eight, alone, and the teachers supped at nine in the refectory. Rumours were abroad in the school, that these suppers, or at least Miss Fenton's, were sumptuous meals. I know we often smelt savoury cooking at bedtime. Sometimes we had pudding before meat, often we had cold meat, sometimes hashed; often meat pies, with a very thick crust over and under. I do not fancy Miss Fenton's butcher's bill could have been a heavy one. Altogether, it recurs to me now as a fraud: a fraud upon the parents, a cruel wrong upon the children. A child who is not well nourished, will not possess too much of rude health and strength in after-life.

That was an unhappy day to me! How I was despised, slighted, scorned, I cannot adequately describe. It became so palpable as to attract the attention of the teachers, and in the evening they inquired into the cause. Mademoiselle Leduc could not by any force of reasoning be brought to comprehend it; she was unable to understand why I was not as good as the rest, and why they should not deem me so; things are estimated so differently in France from what they are in England.

"Bah!" said she, slightingly, giving up as useless the trying to comprehend, "elles sont folles, ces demoiselles."

Miss Dale held a colloquy with one or two of the elder girls, and then called me up. She began asking me questions about my studies, what mamma had taught me, how far I was advanced, all in a kind, gentle way; and she parted my hair on my forehead, and looked into my eyes.

"Your mamma was Mrs. Hemson's sister," she said, presently.

"Not her sister, ma'am; her cousin."

"Her cousin, was it?" she resumed, after a pause. "What was your papa? I heard Miss Fenton say you were an orphan."

"Papa?"

"I mean, in what position?—was he in trade?"

"He was an officer in Her Majesty's service. Colonel Hereford."

"Colonel Hereford?" she returned, looking at me as though she wondered whether I was in error. "Are you sure?"

"Quite sure, Miss Dale. Mamma was Miss Carew of Keppe-Carew."

"Miss Carew of Keppe-Carew!" she exclaimed, with a little scream of surprise; for the Keppe-Carews were of note in the world.

"Mrs. Hemson was a Keppe-Carew also," I continued. "She forfeited her position to marry Mr. Hemson; and she says she has not repented it."

Miss Dale paused; said she remembered to have heard the noise it made when a Miss Carew of Keppe-Carew quitted her home for a tradesman's; but had never known that it related to Mrs. Hemson.

"I was a stranger to Dashleigh until I came here as teacher," she observed, beckoning up the two young ladies, Miss Tayler and Miss Peacock.

"When next you young ladies take a prejudice against a new pupil, it may be as well to make sure first of all of your grounds," she said to them, her tones sarcastic. "You have been sending this child to 'Coventry' on the score of her not being your equal in point of family; let me tell you there's not one of you in the whole school whose family is fit to tie the shoes of hers. She is the daughter of Colonel Hereford, and of Miss Carew of Keppe-Carew."

They looked very blank. Some of the other girls raised their heads to listen. Miss Peacock and one or two more—as I found afterwards—were only the daughters of merchants; others of professional men.

"She is related to the Hemsons," spoke Miss Peacock, defiantly. "She has acknowledged that she is."

"If she were related to a chimney-sweeper, that does not take her from her own proper position," returned Miss Dale, angrily. "Because a member of the Keppe-Carew family chose to forfeit her rank and sacrifice herself for Mr. Hemson, is Miss Hereford to be made answerable for it? Go away, you silly girls, and don't expose yourselves again."

The explanation had its weight in the school, and the tide set in for me as strenuously as it had been against me. The avowal that I was to be a governess appeared to be ignored or disbelieved, and the elder girls began a system of patronage.

"How much money have you brought, little Anne Hereford?"

I exhibited my purse and its three half-crowns, all the money Mrs. Hemson had allowed me to bring.

"Seven and sixpence! That's not much. I suppose you would wish to act in accordance with the custom of the school?"

I intimated that I of course should—if I knew what that was.

"Well, the rule is for a new girl to give a feast to the rest. We have it in the bedroom after Dale has been for the candle. Ten shillings has been the sum usually spent—but I suppose your three half-crowns must be made sufficient; you are only a little one."

I wished to myself that they had left me one of the half-crowns, but could not for the world have said it. I wrote out a list of the articles suggested, and gave the money to one of the servants, Betsey, to procure them; doing all this according to directions. Cold beef and ham, rolls and butter, penny pork pies, small German sausages, jam tarts, and a bottle of raisin wine comprised the list.

Betsey smuggled the things in, and conveyed them to the play-room. Strict orders meanwhile being given to me to say that I brought them to school in my box, should the affair, by mischance, be found out. It would be so cruel to get Betsey turned out of her place, they observed; but they had held many such treats, and never been found out yet.

Miss Dale came as usual for the candle that night, and took it. For a few minutes we lay still as mice, and then sprang up and admitted the rest from their bedroom. Half-a-dozen wax tapers were lighted, abstracted from the girls' private writing-desks, and half-a-dozen more were in readiness to be lighted, should the first not hold out.

And the feast began.

"Now, Anne Hereford, it's your treat, so of course you are the one to wait upon us. You must go to the decanter for water when we want it, and listen at the door against eavesdroppers, and deal out the rolls. By the way, how many knives have come up? Look, Peacock."

"There's only one. One knife and two plates. Well, we'll make the counterpane or our hands do for plates."

"Our hands will be best, and then we can lick up the crumbs. Is the corkscrew there? Who'll draw the cork of the wine?"

"Hush! don't talk so loud; they are hardly at supper yet downstairs," interposed Miss Tayler, who was the oldest girl in the school. "Now, mind! we'll have no disputing about what shall be eaten first, as we had last time; it shall be served regularly. Beef and ham to begin with: pork pies and sausages next; jam tarts last; rolls and butter ad libitum; water with the feast, and the wine to finish up with. That's the order of the day, and if any girl's not satisfied with it, she can retire to bed, which will leave the more for us who are. You see that washhand-stand, little Hereford? Take the water-bottles there, and pour out as we want it; and put a taper near, or you may be giving yourself a bath. Now then, I'll be carver."

She cut the ham into ten portions, the beef likewise, and told me to give round a roll. Then the rolls were cut open and buttered, various devices being improvised for the latter necessity, by those who could not wait their turn for the knife; tooth-brush handles prevailing, and fingers not being altogether absent. Next came the delightful business of eating.

"Some water, little Hereford."

I obeyed, though it was just as I was about to take the first mouthful of the feast. Laying down my share on the counterpane, I brought the tumbler of water.

"And now, Hereford, you must listen at the door."

"If you please, may I take this with me?" for I had once more caught up the tantalizing supper.

"Of course you can, little stupid!"

I went to the door, the beef and ham doubled up in one hand, the buttered roll in the other, and there ate and listened. The scene would have made a good picture. The distant bed on which the eatables were flung, and on which the tapers in their little bronze stands rested, and the girls in their night-gowns gathered round, half lounging on it, talking eagerly, eating ravenously, enjoying themselves thoroughly; I shivering at the door, delighted with the feast, but half-terrified lest interruption should come from below. That unlucky door had no fastening to it, so that any one could come, as the girls expressed it, bolt in. Some time previously there had been a disturbance, because the girls one night locked out Miss Dale, upon which

Miss Fenton had carried away the key.

"Our beef and ham's gone, Anne Hereford. Is yours?"

It was Georgina Digges who spoke, and she half-turned round to do so, for she was leaning forward on the bed with her back to me. I was about to answer, when there came a shrill scream from one of the others; a scream of terror. It was followed by another and another, until they were all screaming together, and I darted in alarm to the bed. Georgina Digges, in turning round, had let her night-gown sleeve touch one of the wax tapers, and set it on fire.

Confusion ensued! the shrieks rising and the flames with them. With a presence of mind perfectly astonishing in one so young, Nancy Tayler tore up the bedside carpet and flung it round her.

"Throw her down, throw her down! it is the only chance!" Nancy screamed to the rest, and there she was on the ground by the time those downstairs had rushed up. Some smothered more carpet on her, some threw a blanket, and the cook further poured out all the water from the washing jugs.

"Who is it?" demanded Miss Fenton, speaking and looking more dead than alive.

None of us answered; we were too terrified; but Miss Dale, who had been taking hurried note of our faces, said it must be Georgina Digges: her face was the only one missing.

I wonder what Miss Fenton thought when she saw the items of the feast as they lay on the bed! The scanty remains of the beef and ham, the buttered rolls half eaten, others ready to be buttered, the pork pies, the German sausages, the jam tarts, and the bottle of wine. Did a thought cross her that if the girls had been allowed better dinners, they might have been less eager for stolen suppers? *She* had probably been disturbed at her excellent supper, for a table napkin was tucked before her, underneath the string of her silk apron.

"You deceitful, rebellious girls!" exclaimed Miss Fenton. "Who has been the ringleader in this?"

A pause, and then a voice spoke from amidst the huddled group of girls—whose voice I did not know then and have never known to this day.

"The new girl, Anne Hereford. She brought the things to school in her box."

Miss Fenton looked round for me: I was standing quite at the back. I had not courage to contradict the words. But just then a commotion arose from the group which stood round the burnt girl, and Miss Fenton turned to it in her sickening fear.

The doctors came, and we were consigned to bed, Georgina Digges being taken into another room. Happily, she was found not to be dangerously burnt, badly on the arm and shoulder, but no further.

Of course there was great trouble in the morning. Mrs. Hemson was sent for, and to her I told the truth, which I had not dared to tell to Miss Fenton. The two ladies had afterwards an interview alone, in which I felt sure Mrs. Hemson repeated every word I had spoken. Nothing more was said to me. Miss Fenton made a speech in the school, beginning with a reproach at their taking a young child's money from her, and going on to the enormity of our offence in "sitting up at night to gormandize" (apologizing for the broad word), which she forbade absolutely for the future.

Thus the affair ended. Georgina Digges recovered, and joined us in the schoolroom: and she was not taken away, though we had thought she would be. But, in spite of the accident and Miss Fenton's prohibition, the feasts at night did go on, as often as a new girl came to be made to furnish one, or when the school subscribed a shilling each, and constituted it a joint affair. *One* little wax taper did duty in future, and that was placed on the mantelpiece, out of harm's way.

And that is all I shall have to say of my school-life in England.

# CHAPTER 8

## EMILY CHANDOS

In the grey dawn of an August morning, I stood on a steamer that was about to clear out from alongside one of the wharves near London Bridge. It was bound for a seaport town in France. Scarcely down yet, the night-clouds still hung upon the earth, but light was breaking in the eastern horizon. The passengers were coming on board—not many; it did not appear that the boat would have much of a freight that day. I heard one of the seamen say so; *I* knew nothing about it; and the scene was as new to me as the world is to a bird, flying for the first time from a cage where it has been hatched and reared.

I was fifteen, and had left Miss Fenton's for good; thoroughly well-educated, so far. And now they were sending me to a school in France to finish.

I will not say precisely where this school was situated: there are reasons against it; but what little record I give of the establishment shall be true and faithful. It was not at Boulogne or at Calais, those renowned seaports, inundated with Anglo-French schools; neither was it in Paris or Brussels, or at Dieppe. We will call the town Nulle, and that's near enough. It was kept by two ladies, sisters, the Demoiselles Barlieu. The negotiations had been made by my trustees, and Mrs. Hemson had brought me to London, down to the steamer on this early morning, and was now consigning me to the care of Miss Barlieu's English governess, whom we had met there by appointment. She was a very plain young person, carrying no authority in appearance, and looking not much like a lady. Authority, as I found, she would have little in the school; she was engaged to teach English, and there her duties ended.

"You had better secure a berth and lie down," she said to me. "The night has been cold, and it is scarcely light enough yet to be on deck."

"Any ladies for shore?" cried a rough voice at the cabin door.

"Shore!" echoed Miss Johnstone, in what seemed alarm. "You are surely not going to start yet! I am waiting for another young lady."

"It won't be more than five minutes now, mum."

"A pupil?" I asked her.

"I believe so. Mademoiselle Barlieu wrote to me that two—"

"Any lady here of the name of Johnstone?"

The inquiry came from a middle-aged, quiet-looking person, who was glancing in at the cabin door. By her side stood a most elegant girl of seventeen, perhaps eighteen, her eyes blue, her face brilliantly fair, her dress handsome.

"I am Miss Johnstone," said the teacher, advancing.

"What a relief! The steward thought no governess had come on board, and I must not have dared to send Miss Chandos alone. My lady—"

"You would, Hill; so don't talk nonsense," interrupted the young lady, with a laugh, as she threw up her white veil, and brought her beauty right underneath the cabin lamp. "Would the fishes have swallowed me up any the quicker for not being in some one's charge? Unfasten my cloak, Hill."

"This young lady is Miss Chandos, ma'am," said the person addressed as Hill, presenting the beautiful girl to Miss Johnstone. "Please take every care of her in going across."

The young lady wheeled round. "Are you our new English teacher?"

"I am engaged as English governess at Mademoiselle Barlieu's," replied Miss Johnstone, who had not at all a pleasant manner of speaking. "She wrote me word that I might expect Miss Chandos and Miss Hereford on board."

"Miss Hereford!" was the quick response. "Who is she?" But by that time I was lying down in the berth, and the rough voice again interrupted.

"Any lady as is for shore had better look sharp, unless they'd like to be took off to t'other side the Channel."

"What fun, Hill, if they should take you off," laughed Miss Chandos, as the former started up with trepidation. "Now, don't stumble overboard in your haste to get off the boat."

"Good-bye to you, Miss Emily, and a pleasant journey! You won't fail to write as soon as you arrive: my lady will be anxious."

"Oh, I will gladden mamma's heart with a letter, or she may be thinking the bottom of the steamer has come out," lightly returned Miss Chandos. "Mind, Hill, that you give my love to Mr. Harry when he gets home."

Those who were for shore went on shore, and soon we were in all the bustle and noise of departure. Miss Chandos stood by the small round table, looking in the hanging-glass, and turning her gleaming golden ringlets round her fingers. On one of those fingers was a ring, its fine large stones forming a heart's-ease: two were yellow topaz, the other three dark amethyst: the whole beautiful.

"May I suggest that you should lie down, Miss Chandos?" said our governess for the time being. "You will find the benefit of doing so."

"Have you crossed the Channel many times?" was the reply of Miss Chandos, as she coolly proceeded with her hair: and her tone to Miss Johnstone was a patronizing one.

"Only twice; to France and home again."

"And I have crossed it a dozen times at least, between school and Continental voyages with mamma, so you cannot teach me much in that respect. I can assure you there's nothing more disagreeable than to be stewed in one of these suffocating berths. When we leave the river, should it prove a rough sea, well and good, but I don't put myself into a berth until then."

"Have you been long with the Miss Barlieus?" inquired Miss Johnstone of her.

"Two dismal years. But I have outlived the dismality now—if you will allow me to coin a word. Mamma has known the Barlieus all her life: an aunt of theirs was her governess when she was young; and when we were returning home from Italy, mamma went to the place and left me there, instead of taking me on to England. Was I not rebellious over it! for three months I planned, every day, to run away on the next."

"But you did not?" I spoke up from my berth, greatly interested.

Miss Chandos turned round and looked at me. "No," she laughed, "it was never accomplished. I believe the chief impediment was, not knowing where to run to. Are you Miss Hereford?"

"Yes."

"What a bit of a child you seem! You won't like a French school, if this is your first entrance into one. Home comforts and French schools are as far apart as the two poles."

"But I am not accustomed to home comforts; I have no home. I have been for some years at an English school, where there was little comfort of any sort. Do your friends live in England? Have you a home there?"

"A home in England!" she answered, with some surprise at the question, or at my ignorance. "Of course: I am Miss Chandos. Chandos is mamma's present residence; though strictly speaking, it belongs to Sir Thomas."

All this was so much Greek to me. Perhaps Miss Chandos saw that it was, for she laughed gaily.

"Sir Thomas Chandos is my brother. Harry is the other one. We thought Tom would have retired from the army and come home when papa died, two or three years ago; but he still remains in India. Mamma writes him word that he should come home and marry, and so make himself into a respectable man; he sends word back that he is respectable enough as it is."

"Your papa was—?"

"Sir Thomas Chandos. Ah, dear! if he had only lived! He was so kind to us! Mamma is in widow's weeds yet, and always will be."

"And who was she who brought you on board?"

"Hill. She is the housekeeper at Chandos. Some one has always taken me over until this time, generally Harry. But Harry is away, and Miss Barlieu wrote word to mamma that the English governess could bring me, so Hill was despatched with me to town."

"What a beautiful ring!" I exclaimed, as the stones flashed in the lamp-light.

Her eyes fell upon it, and a blush and a smile rose to her face. She sat down on the edge of my berth, and twirled it over with the fingers of her other hand.

"Yes, it is a nice ring. Let any one attempt to give me a ring that is not a nice one; they would get it flung back at them."

"Is Mademoiselle Barlieu's a large school?"

"Middling. There were seventy-five last trimestre."

"Seventy-five!" I repeated, amazed at the number.

"That includes the externes—nearly fifty of them—with whom we have nothing to do. There are three class-rooms: one for the elder girls, one for the younger, and the third (the size almost of the large hall at the Tribunal of Commerce) for the externes."

"Are there many teachers?"

"Six, including the English governess and the two Miss Barlieus; and six masters, who are in almost constant attendance."

"Altogether, do you like being there?"

"Yes," she said, laughing significantly; "I like it very well *now*. I am going on deck to watch the day break; so adieu for the present."

We had a rough passage; of which I cannot think to this day without—without wishing not to think of it; and late in the afternoon the steamer was made fast to the port it was bound for. In the midst of the bustle preparatory to landing, a gentleman, young, vain, and good-looking, leaped on board, braving the douaniers, who were too late to prevent him, and warmly greeted Miss Chandos.

"My dear Emily!"

"Speak in French, Alfred," she said, taking the initiative and addressing him in that language—her damask cheeks, her dimples, and her dancing eyes all lovely. "I have not come alone, as I thought I should. A duenna, in the shape of the English governess, has charge of me."

"Miss Chandos, the men are calling out that we must land."

The interruption came from Miss Johnstone, who had approached, looking keenly at the gentleman. The latter, with scant courtesy to the governess, made no reply: he was too much occupied in assisting Miss Chandos up the landing-steps. Miss Chandos turned her head when she reached the top.

"Be so good as to look in the cabin, Miss Johnstone; I have left a hundred things there, odds and ends. My warm cloak is somewhere."

Miss Johnstone appeared anything but pleased. It is not usual for pupils to order their teachers to look after their things; and Miss

Chandos was somewhat imperious in manner: not purposely: it was her nature to be so. I turned with Miss Johnstone, and we collected together the items left by Miss Chandos. By the time we reached the custom-house, she had disappeared. Twenty minutes after, when we and our luggage had been examined, we found her outside, walking to and fro with the gentleman.

"Where are your boxes, Miss Chandos?" asked Miss Johnstone.

"My boxes? I don't know anything about them. I gave my keys to one of the commissionaires; he will see to them. Or you can, if you like."

"I do not imagine that it is my business to do so," was Miss Johnstone's offended reply. But Miss Chandos was again walking with her companion, and paid no heed to her.

"Halloa, de Mellissie! have you been to England?" inquired a passing Englishman of Miss Chandos's friend.

"Not I," he replied. "I stepped on board the boat when it came in, so they took their revenge by making me go through the custom-house and turning my pockets inside out. Much good it did them."

An omnibus was waiting round the corner, in which we were finally to be conveyed to our destination, Mademoiselle Barlieu's. Seated in it was a little, stout, good-tempered dame of fifty, Mademoiselle Caroline, the senior teacher. She received Miss Chandos with open arms, and a kiss on each cheek. The gentleman politely handed us by turn into the omnibus, and stood bowing to us, bareheaded, as we drove away.

"Do you think him handsome?" Miss Chandos whispered to me, the glow on her face fading.

"Pretty well. What is his name?"

"Alfred de Mellissie. You can be good-natured, can't you?" she added.

"I can, if I like."

"Then be so now, and don't preach it out to the whole school that he met me. He—"

"Is that gentleman a relative of yours, Miss Chandos?" interrupted Miss Johnstone from the end of the omnibus.

Miss Chandos did not like the tone or the question: the one savoured of acrimony, the other she resented as impertinent. She fixed her haughty blue eyes on Miss Johnstone before she answered: they said very plainly: "By what right do you presume to inquire of me?" And Miss Johnstone bit her lips at the look.

"They are not related to us. Madame de Mellissie is an intimate friend of my mother, Lady Chandos." And that was all she condescended to say, for she turned her back and began laughing and chattering in French with Mademoiselle Caroline.

The Miss Barlieus received us graciously, giving us all the same friendly greeting that the old teacher had given only to Miss Chandos. Two pleasant, kind-hearted maiden ladies were they, not very young. Miss Annette confessed to having passed thirty-five. We were their visitors that evening, and were regaled with nice things in their own parlour.

I said I would relate the mode of treatment in that school. It was a superior establishment, the terms high *for France*; but they were not much more than half the amount of Miss Fenton's. Here they included the month's holiday in autumn. At Miss Fenton's the holidays were three months in the year; and if you stayed (as I did), extra fees had to be paid.

The dormitories were spacious and airy, a small, separate bed being given to each pupil. No French school can be overcrowded, for they are under the close inspection of the Government; and the number of pupils to be taken is registered. A large airy room is set apart as an infirmary, should any fall ill.

Clang! clang! clang! went the great bell in the morning, waking us out of our sleep at six. Dressing, practising, lessons, and prayers, occupied the time until eight. Miss Johnstone read prayers to the English pupils, all Protestants; Mademoiselle Caroline read them to the French, who were Roman Catholics. For breakfast there was as much bread-and-butter as we liked to eat, and a small basin each of rich milk. Some of the English girls chose tea in preference, which they were at liberty to do. On Sunday mornings, breakfast was a treat: coffee and *petit pains*, a sort of roll. We had them hot, two each, and a small pat of butter. Such coffee as that we never get in England: one-third coffee, two-thirds hot milk, and strong even then. Breakfast over (to go back to the week days), we played until nine, and then came studies until twelve.

The professed dinner-hour was half-past twelve, but the cook rarely sent it in before a quarter to one. We all dined together with Miss Barlieu and Miss Annette, at two long tables. I remember the dinner, that first day, as well as though I had eaten it yesterday. A plateful of soup first, very poor, as all French soup is; after that the bouilli, the meat that the soup is made of. The English at first never like this bouilli, but in time they learn to know how good it is, eaten with the French piquante mustard. Sometimes carrots were served with the bouilli, sometimes small pickled cucumbers: this day we had cucumbers. Remembering Miss Fenton's, I wondered if that comprised the dinner. And, talking of Miss Fenton's, I have never mentioned that in her house we were not allowed bread at dinner; here, if we could have eaten a whole loaf, we might have had it.

It did not comprise the dinner. There came on some delicious roast veal and potatoes; and afterwards fried pancakes, with sugar. On Sundays we sometimes had poultry, always a second dish of vegetables, and a fruit or cream tart. The beverage was the same as at Miss Fenton's—beer or water, as might be preferred. Four or five of the girls had wine; but it was either supplied by the parents, or paid for as an extra. It was commonly reported that in some other schools, in the colleges especially, the soup, the bouilli, bread and potatoes, comprised the dinner *every day*, with a roast joint in addition on Sundays.

At two o'clock came school again until four, when we were released for half-an-hour, and each had a slice of bread-and-butter, called collation. Then school again until six, and supper at seven. The suppers varied; meat was never served, but vegetables were often: sometimes bread-and-cheese and salad; or bread-and-butter, with an egg, or with shrimps, or fried potatoes; and tea. I think this was a more sensible mode of living than Miss Fenton's. Altogether I can truly say that we experienced liberality and kindness at Miss Barlieu's; it was a far better home than the other.

But I have not got over the first day yet. In assorting her clothes after unpacking, Miss Chandos missed a new velvet mantle; there was some commotion about it, and she was told that she ought to have watched more narrowly the examination of her trunks in the custom-house. Miss Chandos took the loss equably, as she appeared to do most things. "Oh, if it's lost, mamma must send me over another," was her careless comment.

We were at our studies in the afternoon when Mademoiselle Annette entered. The mode of sitting was different here from what it had been at Miss Fenton's. There, we sat on a hard form for hours together without any support for the arms or back: stooping was the inevitable consequence, and many of the girls contracted a curve of the spine; or, as the saying ran, "grew aside." In France we sat at a sloping desk, on which our arms rested, so that the spine could not grow fatigued. I never once, the whole period I stayed at Miss Barlieu's, saw a crooked girl. Mademoiselle Annette entered and accosted Miss Chandos.

"I understand, Miss Chandos, that you did not take any care of your boxes yourself at the custom-house; merely gave up your keys?"

A slight accession of colour, and Miss Chandos turned round her fair bright face, acknowledging that it was so.

"But, my dear, that was evincing great carelessness."

"I don't see it, Mademoiselle Annette," was Miss Chandos's smiling dissent. "What are the commissionaires for, but to take charge of keys and examine baggage?"

"Well; they have been up from the customs to say that the mantle was not left there. The commissionaire himself is here now; he says everything taken out of your boxes was safely put in again."

"It was a beautiful mantle, Mademoiselle Annette, and I dare say some one caught it up and ran off with it when the man's attention was turned the other way. It can't be helped: there are worse misfortunes at sea."

"What gentleman was it that you were walking about with?" resumed Mademoiselle Annette.

"Gentleman?" returned Miss Chandos, in questioning tones, as if she could not understand, or did not remember. "Gentleman, Mademoiselle Annette?"

"A gentleman who came on board to speak to you; and who assisted you to land: and with whom you were walking about afterwards, whilst the other ladies were in the custom-house?"

"Oh, I recollect; yes. There was a gentleman who came on board: it was Monsieur de Mellissie." Very brilliant had Miss Chandos's cheeks become; but she turned her face to the desk as if anxious to continue her studies, and Mademoiselle Barlieu saw it not.

"What took him on board?" resumed Mademoiselle Annette.

"As if I knew, Mademoiselle Annette!" lightly replied the young lady. "He may have wanted to speak to the captain—or to some of the sailors—or to me. He did not tell me."

"But you were promenading with him afterwards!"

"And very polite of him it was to give up his time to me, whilst I was waiting for them to come out," replied Miss Chandos. "I returned him my thanks for it, Mademoiselle Annette. If the new English teacher had had a thousand boxes to clear, she could not have been much longer over it. I thought she was never coming."

"Well, my dear, do not promenade again with Monsieur de Mellissie. It is not the right thing for a young lady to do; and Miladi Chandos might not be pleased that you should."

"On the contrary, Mademoiselle Annette, mamma charged me with twenty messages to give him, in trust for his mother," replied the undaunted girl. "I was glad of an opportunity of delivering them."

Mademoiselle Annette said no more. She charged the girls as she quitted the room to prepare their geography books, for she should return for that class in five minutes.

"I say, Emily Chandos, whatever is all that about?" asked a young lady, Ellen Roper.

"I don't care! It's that new English teacher who has been reporting! Alfred jumped on board as soon as we touched the side, and I stayed with him until the omnibus was ready—or until we were ready for the omnibus. Where was the harm? *You* did not tell, Anne Hereford?"

"I have not spoken of it to any one."

"No; I was sure of that: it's that precious teacher. I did not like her before, but for this I'll give her all the trouble I can at my English lessons. Such folly for Mademoiselle Barlieu to engage a girl as governess; and she's no better. I could teach her. She's not nice, either;

you can't like or respect her."

"I think the Miss Barlieus were surprised when they saw her," observed Ellen Roper. "Mademoiselle Annette asked her this morning if she were really twenty-one. So that is the age she must have represented herself to be in writing to them."

In the course of a day or two Emily Chandos received a letter from home. Lady Chandos had discovered that the velvet mantle, by some unaccountable mischance, had not been put into the boxes. She would forward it to Nulle.

The De Mellissies were staying in the town. Madame de Mellissie, the mother, an English lady by birth, had been intimate with Lady Chandos in early life; they were good friends still. Her son, and only child, Monsieur Alfred de Mellissie, chief of the family now, in place of his dead father, appeared to make it the whole business of his life to admire Emily Chandos. The school commented on it.

"It can never lead to anything," they said. "He is only a Frenchman of comme-ça family, and she is Miss Chandos of Chandos."

And—being Miss Chandos of Chandos—it occurred to me to wonder that she should be at that French school. Not but that it was one of the first to be found in France; but scarcely the place for Miss Chandos. I

I said as much—talking one day with Mademoiselle Annette, when I was by her, drawing.

"My dear, Emily Chandos, though one of the most charming and lovable girls ever seen, is inclined to be wild; and Miladi Chandos thinks the discipline of a school good for her," was the answer. "They do not care to have a governess residing at Chandos."

"But why, mademoiselle?"

Mademoiselle Annette shook her head mysteriously. "I know not. Miladi said it to me. She is altered terribly. There is always a cloud hanging over Chandos. Go on with your sketch, my dear: young ladies should not be curious."

One of the first questions put to me by the girls was—were any names given in for my visiting. I did not understand the question. We elder ones were seated at the table, doing German exercises—or pretending to do them. Miss Barlieu had found me so well advanced, that I was put in the first classes for every study. Ellen Roper saw I looked puzzled, and explained.

"When a pupil is placed at school in France, her friends give in the names of the families where she may visit, and the governess writes them down. It is not a bad custom."

"It is a miserable custom, Ellen Roper," retorted Miss Chandos. "When the Stapletons were passing through Nulle last spring, they invited me to the hotel for a day, and Mademoiselle Barlieu put her veto upon it, because their name had not been given in by mamma. Lady Stapleton came and expostulated; said her husband, Sir Gregory, was the oldest friend possible of the late Sir Thomas Chandos, had been for years, and that they would take every imaginable care of me, and she knew Lady Chandos would wish me to go. Not a bit of it; you might as well have tried to move the house as to move Mademoiselle Barlieu. Miladi Chandos had not given her the name, she said, and she could not depart from the usual custom. Don't you remember what a passion I was in? Cried my eyes out, and would not do a single devoir. Anne Hereford, you can write home and ask them to give in some names to Miss Barlieu."

Home! What home had I to write to?

# CHAPTER 9

## AN IRREVOCABLE STEP

There was war between the English governess and Emily Chandos. Emily was excessively popular; with her beauty, her gaiety, and her generous wilfulness; she did nearly what she liked in the school—except of course with the Miss Barlieus. For myself, I had learnt to love her. She had her faults—what girl is without them? She was vain, petulant, haughty when displeased, and a little selfish. But she possessed one great gift of attraction—that of taking hearts by storm. Miss Johnstone began with a mistake: striving to put down Miss Chandos. She was over-strict besides with her lessons and exercises; and more than once reported her to Miss Annette for some trifling fault, magnified by her into a grave one. The girls espoused Emily's cause; and Miss Johnstone grew to be regarded, and also treated, with contempt. It vexed her greatly; and there were other things.

Her name was Margaret. But she had incautiously left an open letter about, in which she was repeatedly called "Peg." Of course that was quite enough for the girls, and they took to calling her Peg, almost in her hearing. A new English pupil, who entered as weekly boarder, went up at the English dictation and addressed her as "Miss Pegg," believing it to be her real name. You should have seen Miss Johnstone's dark and angry face, and the dancing eyes of Emily Chandos.

Madame de Mellissie had left for Paris; but her son, Monsieur Alfred, remained at Nulle—his attraction being, as the girls said openly, Emily Chandos. Emily laughed as she listened: but denial she made none. They said another thing—that the beautiful heart's-ease ring she wore had been his love-gift: and still there was no express denial. "Have it so, if you like," was all Emily said.

"She cannot think *seriously* of him, you know," Ellen Roper observed one day. "It is a match that could never be allowed by her family. He is quite a second-rate sort of Frenchman, and she is Miss Chandos of Chandos. He is a bit of a jackanapes too, vain and silly."

"Ellen Roper, I am within hearing, I beg to inform you," said Miss Chandos, from half-way up the desk, her face in a lovely glow.

"That is just why I said it," returned Ellen Roper, who, however, had not known Emily was near, and started at the sound of her voice. "I dare say he has not above a thousand pounds or two a-year; a very fair patrimony for a Frenchman, you know; but only fancy it for one in the position of Miss Chandos."

"Go on, Ellen Roper! I'll tell something of you by-and-by."

"And, setting aside everything else, there's another great barrier," went on Ellen Roper, making very strong objections in her spirit of mischief. "The De Mellissies are Roman Catholics; cela va, you know; while the Chandoses are staunch Conservative Protestants. Lady Chandos would almost as soon give Emily to the Grand Turk as to Alfred de Mellissie."

A sort of movement at the desk, and we looked round. Quietly seated on the low chair in the corner, her ears drinking in all, for we had been speaking in English, was Miss Johnstone. Had she been there all the time? Emily Chandos' bright check paled a little, as if there had fallen upon her a foreshadowing of evil.

I do not know that it would have come, but that circumstances worked for it. On this afternoon, this very same afternoon as we sat there, Emily was called out of the room by one of the maids, who said Mrs. Trehern had called to see her.

"Trehern?—Trehern?" cried Emily, as she went. "I don't know the name from Adam."

Back she soon came with a radiant face, and presented herself to Mademoiselle Annette, who was in class.

"Oh, mademoiselle, some friends are here, and they wish me to go out with them. Will you give me permission? It is Mr. and Mrs. Trehern."

"Trehern? Trehern?" repeated Mademoiselle Annette. "I don't remember that name on your visiting list."

Emily knew quite well it was not there, since this was the first time she had seen either of the parties: but she had trusted to the good luck of Mademoiselle Annette's believing that it was.

"Mamma will be so vexed if I do not go. She is very intimate with the Treherns. They have only just arrived in the town, mademoiselle, and have descended at the Hotel du Lion d'Or."

Which concluding words gave us the clue to Emily's eagerness for the visit. For it was at that renowned hotel that Mr. Alfred de Mellissie had been sojourning since his mother's departure. Mademoiselle Annette was firm.

"You know the rules of the school, my dear. We have heard nothing of these gentlepeople from your mamma, and it is impossible that you can be allowed to go."

Emily Chandos carried back her excuses to the salon, and after school gave vent to her mortification in a private outburst to us.

"Such a dreadful shame, these horrid French rules! As if the Treherns would have poisoned me! But I despatch a letter to mamma to-night to get permission. They are going to stay a month at Nulle. It is the bridal tour."

"Have they just come from England?"

"Not at all. She is French, and never was in England in her life.

She is a friend"—dropping her voice still lower—"of the De Mellissies; at least her mother is: it was through Alfred they called upon me to-day."

"Then does Lady Chandos not know them?"

"She knows him. It is a Cornish family. This one, young Trehern, fell in love with a French girl, and has married her. They were married last Thursday, she told me. She had the most ravishing toilette on to-day: a white and blue robe: you might have taken it for silver. She's nearly as young as I am."

The letter despatched to Lady Chandos by Emily set forth the praises of Mrs. Trehern, and especially dwelt upon the fact that her mother was a "dear friend" of Madame de Mellissie. Not a word said it, though, that Mr. Alfred de Mellissie was sojourning at the Lion d'Or, or at Nulle. And there came back permission from Lady Chandos for Emily to visit them: she wrote herself to Miss Barlieu, desiring that it might be so. Emily was in her glory.

A great apparent friendship sprang up between her and young Mrs. Trehern, who was something like herself, inexperienced and thoughtless. She was of good family, pleasing in manners, and quite won the hearts of the Miss Barlieus. Relatives of hers, the De Rosnys, lived in their château near Nulle—the cause of her passing sojourn there. We school-girls remembered how Maximilian de Bethune, the young Baron de Rosny, had been the envoy despatched by Henri le Grand to solicit assistance of Queen Elizabeth, in the years subsequent to the great slaughter of the Huguenots. We assumed that Mrs. Trehern might be of the same family; but did not know it.

Often and often she arrived at the school to take out Emily Chandos. At length the Miss Barlieus began to grumble: Mademoiselle Chandos went out too frequently, and her studies were getting in arrear. Emily protested it was her mamma's wish and pleasure that she should take advantage of the sojourn of Mrs. Trehern to go out, and exhibited part of a letter from Lady Chandos, in which the same appeared to be intimated. Mademoiselle Annette shook her head, and said it was a good thing the month of Mrs. Trehern's stay was drawing to its close.

Now it happened about this time that an uncle of Miss Johnstone's passed through Nulle on his way to Paris, staying for a day at the Hotel du Lion d'Or. He invited his niece to go to see him, saying she might bring any one of the young ladies with her. She chose me, to my own surprise: perhaps the reason was that I had never taken an active part in annoying her as some of the rest had. The Miss Barlieus allowed me to go; for they looked upon it, not that I was about to pay an indiscriminate visit, but going out with one of the governesses, under her safe convoy and companionship.

"Where are you off to, little Hereford?" demanded Emily

Chandos, who was attiring herself before the one glass in the bed-room when I went up, for she was to spend the afternoon with the Treherns.

"Miss Johnstone's uncle is at the Lion d'Or, and she has asked me to dinner there. We are to dine at the table d'hôte."

"The Lion d'Or!" cried Emily, turning round. "What a chance! to have that sharp-sighted duenna, Peg, dining at table with us!"

"What, do you—do the Treherns dine at the table d'hôte?"

"Where else should they dine? The hotel is too full, just now, to admit of private dinners."

Mr. Johnstone came for us, and we walked about, looking at the old town, until six o'clock, the dinner hour. A novel scene to me was that crowded dining-room, with its array of company, of waiters, and of good cheer; so novel that for some time I did not notice four seats, immediately opposite to us, quite vacant.

All eyes were raised at the four who came in to fill them. Mr. and Mrs. Trehern; she dressed elaborately, perfectly; not a fold of her robe out of place, not a hair of her many braids; Alfred de Mellissie, with his airs of a petit maître, but good-looking enough; and Emily Chandos, with her gay and sparkling beauty.

"Just look there, Miss Hereford! Do you see that?"

Miss Johnstone's words were spoken in a low tone of consterna-tion. I *would not* understand to whom she alluded.

"See what, Miss Johnstone?"

"Miss Chandos," she answered, devouring Emily with her eyes. "I wonder if the Demoiselles Barlieu know that while she has been pretending to visit the Treherns, it has been a cloak for her meeting that Frenchman?"

"Oh, Miss Johnstone! She *has* visited the Treherns."

"I can see through a mill-stone," was Miss Johnstone's cold answer.

Never were more defiant looks cast upon a governess than Emily Chandos threw over the table at Miss Johnstone. That the latter pro-voked them by her manner there was no doubt. I think—I always had thought—that she was envious of Miss Chandos, though whence or why the feeling should have arisen I cannot say. They were the most distinguished group at table, Mr. Trehern—a fine, big, burly Cornishman—and his wife, Monsieur de Mellissie and Emily: and the waiters treated them with marked distinction. Even the appurte-nances of their dinner were superior, for none others within the range of my view ventured upon sparkling Moselle and ice. They rose from table earlier than many, Emily throwing me a laughing nod, as she took Mr. Trehern's arm, Alfred de Mellissie following with Mrs. Trehern; but not vouchsafing the slightest notice of Miss Johnstone.

"She may take her leave of it," I heard the latter whisper to herself.

Mr. Johnstone did not mend the matter, or his niece's temper. "What a lovely girl that is!" he exclaimed. "She is English."

"Yes," answered Miss Johnstone, her lips parting with acrimony. "She is one of my pupils."

"One of your pupils! How is it she took no notice of you?" Miss Johnstone made no reply, but the acrimony on her lips grew sharper: very sharp indeed when she saw Emily escorted home by Monsieur de Mellissie, with Mrs. Trehern's maid in attendance.

The explosion came next day. Miss Johnstone lodged a formal complaint in private before the Miss Barlieus. Miss Chandos, she felt perfectly certain, was being made clandestine love to by Monsieur Alfred de Mellissie!

"Seated at the table d'hôte with the young man!—accompanied by him home afterwards!" cried Mademoiselle Annette. "It is not to be believed."

Miss Johnstone said it was, and called me as a witness. Emily Chandos was commanded to the salon, and questioned.

She could not deny it; she did not attempt it: rather braved it out.

"Where was the harm of it, Mademoiselle Annette? Monsieur de Mellissie did not attempt to eat me."

"You know that the customs and ideas of our country are against this kind of thing," emphatically pronounced Miss Barlieu. "I am surprised at you, Mademoiselle Emily; you have deceived us. I shall write to miladi your mother to-day. If she sanctions this public visiting, I cannot. I cannot possibly allow any young lady in my establishment to run the risk of being talked of as imprudent. You will not go to Mrs. Trehern again; she has shown herself little capable of taking care of you."

"Do you mean, mademoiselle, that I am not to go out in future when invited?" asked Emily, her heart beating visibly.

"I shall very unmistakably point out to your mamma the desirability of your not again going out to visit; certainly you will not while Monsieur de Mellissie remains at Nulle," was the pointed reply of Miss Barlieu.

And Emily Chandos knew that her liberty was over. But for this, would she have taken the irrevocable step she did take? Alas! it was soon too late to speculate.

An immediate reply came from Lady Chandos, interdicting all indiscriminate visiting for Emily; and saying that she must make good use of her time in study, as she would leave school early in the spring.

Did the arrival of that letter expedite the catastrophe? I cannot tell. It was known that Madame de Mellissie, the mother, was at Nulle again, and a very short time went on.

We were doing English with Miss Johnstone one afternoon,

when Mrs. Trehern called. Emily was allowed to see her, but Mademoiselle Barlieu accompanied her to the salon. Some sort of explanation took place, and Mrs. Trehern was informed that Miss Chandos could not visit her again. She left, and Emily returned to the class, but the English lesson was over then. Over in disgrace, for none of us had done well; at least, Miss Johnstone said we had not. By way of punishment, she protested she should make us finish it after supper.

We had bread-and-butter and shrimps for supper that night—I shall always remember it; and we prolonged it as much as we could, drinking three cups of tea each, and eating as many shrimps as we could get. Emily Chandos did not appear, and Mademoiselle Caroline—who had viewed the scandal touching Alfred de Mellissie with shocked displeasure—would not allow her to be called, saying she was "sulking." But the supper, spin it out as we would, could not last all night, and Miss Johnstone, as good as her word, called us up with our English books.

"Go and find Miss Chandos," she said to me. "She has chosen to go without her supper, but she shall not escape her lesson."

Emily was not to be found. Amidst a search of commotion, the like of which I had never seen, it was discovered that she had quitted the house. The De Mellissies, the next inquired for, had quitted the town. A telegraphic message went to Chandos, and Mademoiselle Barlieu took to her bed with chagrin.

The despatch brought back Mr. Chandos, Emily's brother. About the same hour that he arrived, a letter was received from London from Monsieur Alfred de Mellissie, saying that he and Miss Chandos had just been married by special licence, and also by the rites of the Romish Church. That his English mother had aided and abetted the step, although she did not accompany them in their flight to England, there was no question of.

Miss Barlieu saw Mr. Chandos in her chamber; the affair had made her really ill. Afterwards, as I was passing down the stairs, he came forth from the drawing-room from an interview with Miss Annette. She was talking very fast, her eyes streaming with grief, and Mr. Chandos strove to soothe her.

"It all comes of that indiscriminate visiting, sir, that was allowed to Mademoiselle Chandos," she said, with bitter tears. "I told my sister ten times that Miladi Chandos was wrong to permit it. Ah! sir, we shall not ever get over the blow. Nothing of the kind has ever happened to us."

"Do not distress yourself," Mr. Chandos answered. "I can see that no shadow of blame rests with you. That lies with Emily and the De Mellissies: my sister's fortune is a great prize to a Frenchman."

What made me gather myself into a nook of the wall, and gaze upon Mr. Chandos, as he passed out in the dusk of the evening? Not the deep, mellow tones—not the sweet accent of voice in which his words were spoken. That they were all that, my ear told me; but something else had struck upon me—his face and form. Where had I seen him?

Somewhere, I felt certain. The contour of the pale face, with its fine and delicate features; something in the tall, slim figure, even in the manner of turning his head as he spoke: all seemed to touch on a chord of my memory. Where, where could I have seen Mr. Chandos?

The question was not solved, and time went steadily on again.

# CHAPTER 10

## AT MRS. PALER'S

Nineteen years of age. Nineteen! For the last twelvemonth, since the completion of my education, I had helped in the school as one of the governesses. The Miss Barlieus, whose connection was extensive among the English as well as the French, had undertaken the responsibility of "placing me out," as my trustees phrased it. When I was eighteen their task, as trustees, was over, and the annuity I had enjoyed ceased. Henceforth I had no friends in the world but the Miss Barlieus: and truly kind and good those ladies were to me.

I was attacked with an illness soon after my eighteenth birthday: not a severe one, but lasting tolerably long; and that had caused me to remain the additional twelvemonth, for which I received a slight salary. They liked me, and I liked them.

So I was to be a governess after all! The last descendant of the Herefords and the Keppe-Carews had no home in the world, no means of living, and must work for them. My pride rebelled against it now, as it never had when I was a child; and I made a resolution never to talk of my family. I was an orphan; I had no relatives living: that would be quite sufficient answer when asked about it. Keppe-Carew had again changed masters: a little lad of eight, whose dead father I had never seen, and who perhaps had never heard of me, was its owner now.

I had never heard a syllable of Mr. Edwin Barley since I left him, or of any of his household, or of the events that had taken place there. That George Heneage had never been traced, I knew; that Mr. Edwin Barley was still seeking him, I was quite sure: the lapse of years could not abate the anger of a man like him. Mrs. Hemson was dead now, a twelvemonth past; so that I was entirely alone in the world. As to the will, it had not been found, as was to be supposed, or the money would have been mine. My growth in years, the passing from the little girl into the woman, and the new ties and interests of my foreign school life, had in a degree obliterated those unhappy events, and I scarcely ever gave even a thought to the past.

Mr. and Mrs. Paler were staying temporarily at Nulle; well-connected English people, about to fix their residence in Paris. They were strangers to me personally, but the Miss Barlieus knew something of their family, and we heard that Mrs. Paler was inquiring for a governess; one who spoke thoroughly English, French, and German. Mademoiselle Annette thought it might suit me, and proposed to take me to call on them at the Lion d'Or Hotel.

I seized upon the idea eagerly. The word Paris had wrought its own charm. To be conveyed to that city of delight appeared only secondary to entering within the precincts of a modern Elysium.

"Oh, Mademoiselle Annette, pray let us go! I might perhaps do for them."

Mademoiselle Annette laughed at the eagerness so unequivocally betrayed. But she set off with me the same day.

The Lion d'Or was full. Mr. and Mrs. Paler had no private sitting-room (there were only two salons in the whole house), and we were ushered into their chamber, French fashion. Mr. Paler was a stout man in gold spectacles, shy and silent; his wife, a tall handsome woman, with large eyes and dark hair, talked enough for both. Some conversation ensued, chiefly taken up by Mrs. Paler explaining the sort of governess she wished for, Mr. Paler having quitted us.

"If you require a completely well-educated young lady—a gentlewoman in every sense of the term—you cannot do better than engage Miss Hereford," said Mademoiselle Annette.

"But what's her religion?" abruptly asked Mrs. Paler. "I would not admit a Roman Catholic into the bosom of my family; no, not though she paid me to come. Designing Jesuits, as a great many of them are!"

Which, considering she was speaking to a Roman Catholic, and that a moment's consideration might have told her she was, evinced anything but courtesy on the lady's part, to say nothing of good feeling. Mademoiselle Annette's brown cheek deepened, and so did mine.

"I belong to the Church of England, madam," I answered.

"And with regard to singing?" resumed Mrs. Paler, passing to another qualification unceremoniously. "Have you a fine voice?—a good style?—can you teach it well?"

"I sing little, and should not like to teach it. Neither am I a very brilliant player. I have no great forte for music. What I do play I play well, and I can teach it well."

"There it is! Was there ever anything so tiresome?" grumbled Mrs. Paler. "I declare you cannot have everything, try as you will. Our last governess was first-rate in music—quite a divine voice she had—and her style perfect; but of all the barbarous accents in French and German (not to speak of her wretched grammar), hers were the worst. Now, you are a good linguist, but no hand at music! What a worry it is!"

"May I ask what age your children are?" interposed Mademoiselle Annette, who could speak sufficient English to understand and join in the conversation.

"The eldest is twelve."

"Then I can assure you Miss Hereford is quite sufficient musician for what you will want at present, madam. It is not always the most brilliant players who are the best instructors; our experience has taught us the contrary is the case."

Mrs. Paler mused. "Does Miss Hereford draw?"

"Excellently well," replied Mademoiselle Annette.

"I have a great mind to try her," debated Mrs. Paler, as if soliloquizing with herself. "But I must just pay my husband the compliment of asking what he thinks: though I never allow any opinion of his to influence me. He is the shyest man possible! he went out, you saw, as you came in. I am not sure but he will think Miss Hereford too good-looking; but she has a very dignified air with her, though her manners are charmingly simple."

"When you have considered the matter, madam, we shall be glad to receive your answer," observed Mademoiselle Annette, as she rose. And Mrs. Paler acquiesced.

"Anne," began Mademoiselle Annette, as we walked home, "I do not think that situation will suit you. You will not be comfortable in it."

"But why?" I asked, feeling my golden visions of Paris dimmed by the words. "I think it would perfectly suit me, mademoiselle."

"Madame Paler is not a nice lady; she is not a gentlewoman. I question, too, if she would make you comfortable."

"I am willing to risk it. You and Mademoiselle Barlieu have told me all along that I cannot expect everything."

"That is true, my child. Go where you will, you must look out for disagreeables and crosses. The lives of all of us are made up of trials; none, save ourselves, can feel them; few, save ourselves, can see, or will believe in them. Many a governess, tossed and turned about in the world's tempest, weary of her daily task, sick of its monotony, is tempted, no doubt, to say, 'Oh that I were established as the Demoiselles Barlieu are, with a home and school of my own!' But I can tell you, Anne, that often and often I and my sister envy the lot of the poorest governess out on her own account, because she is free from anxiety."

She spoke truly. Every individual lot has its peculiar trials, and none can mitigate them. "The heart knoweth its own bitterness." I walked on by her side then, in my young inexperience, wondering whether *all* people had these trials, whether they would come to me. It was my morning of life, when the unseen future looks as a bright and flowery dream. Mademoiselle Annette broke the silence.

"You will never forget, my dear, that you have a friend in us. Should you meet with any trouble, should you be at any time, out of a situation, come to us; our house is open to you."

"Thank you, thank you, dear Mademoiselle Annette," I replied, grasping her hand. "I will try and do brave battle with the world's cares; I have not forgotten my mother's lessons."

"Anne," she gravely responded, "do not *battle:* rather welcome them."

Well, I was engaged. And, as the Demoiselles Barlieu observed, it was not altogether like my entering the house of people entirely strange, for they were acquainted with the family of Mr. Paler: himself they had never before seen, but two of his sisters had been educated in their establishment.

A week or two after the Palers had settled themselves in Paris, I was escorted thither by a friend of the Miss Barlieus. The address given me was Avenue de St. Cloud, Commune de Passy. We found it a good-looking, commodious house, and my travelling protector, Madame Bernadotte, left me at the door. A young girl came forward as I was shown into a room.

"Are you Miss Hereford, the new governess?"

"Yes. I think I have had the pleasure of seeing you at Nulle," I answered, holding out my hand to her.

"That I'm sure you've not. I never was at Nulle. It was Kate and Harriet who went there with papa and mamma. I and Fanny and Grace came straight here last week from England, with nurse."

Now, strange to say, it had never occurred to me or to the Miss Barlieus to ask Mrs. Paler, during the negotiations, how many pupils I should have. Two children were with them at Nulle, Kate and Harriet, and I never supposed that there were others; I believed these would be my only pupils.

"How many are you, my dear?"

"Oh, we are five."

"Am I to teach you all?"

"Of course. There's nobody else to teach us. And we have two little brothers, but they are quite in the nursery."

Had Mrs. Paler purposely concealed the number? or had it been the result of inadvertence? The thought that came over me was, that were I engaging a governess for five pupils, I should take care to mention that there were five. They came flocking round me now, every one of them, high-spirited, romping girls, impatient of control, their ages varying from six to twelve.

"Mamma and papa are out, but I don't suppose they'll be long. Do you want to see mamma?"

"I shall be glad to see her."

"Do you wish for anything to eat?" inquired Miss Paler. "You can have what you like: dinner or tea; you have only to ring and order it. We have dined and had tea also. Mamma has not; but you don't take your meals with her."

As she spoke, some noise was heard in the house, and they all ran out. It proved to be Mrs. Paler. She went up to her own sitting-room, and thither I was summoned.

"So you have got here safely, Miss Hereford?" was her salutation, spoken cordially enough. But she did not offer to shake hands with me.

"I have been making acquaintance with my pupils, madam. I did not know there were so many."

"Did you not? Oh, you forget; I have no doubt I mentioned it."

"I think not. I believed that the two Miss Palers I saw at Nulle were your only children."

"My only children! Good gracious, Miss Hereford, what an idea! Why, I have seven and have lost two, which made nine. You will take the five girls; five are as easily taught as two."

I did not dispute the words. I had come, intending and hoping to do my duty to the very utmost extent, whether it might be much or little Though certainly the five pupils did look formidable in prospective, considering that I should have to teach them everything, singing excepted.

"I hope you will suit me," went on Mrs. Paler. "I have had many qualms of doubt since I engaged you. But I can't beat them into Mr. Paler; he turns round, and politely tells me they are 'rubbish,' as any heathen might."

"Qualms of doubt as to my being only nineteen, or about my skill in music?" I asked.

"Neither; your age I never made an objection, and I dare say your music will do very well for the present. Here's Mr. Paler."

He came in, the same apparently shy, silent, portly man as at Nulle, in his gold spectacles. But he came up kindly to me, and shook hands.

"My doubts turn upon serious points, Miss Hereford," pursued Mrs. Paler. "If I thought you would undermine the faith of my children and imbue them with Roman Catholic doctrines—"

"Mrs. Paler!" I interrupted, in surprise. "I told you I was a Protestant, brought up strictly in the tenets of the Church of England. Your children are of the same faith: there is little fear, then, that I should seek to undermine it. I know of none better in the world."

"You must excuse my anxiety, Miss Hereford. Can you conscientiously assure me that you hate all Roman Catholics?"

I looked at her in amazement. And she looked at me, waiting for my answer. A smile, unless I mistook, crossed the lips of Mr. Paler.

"Oh, Mrs. Paler, what would my own religion be worth if I could hate? Believe me there are excellent Christians amongst the Roman Catholics, as there are amongst ourselves. People who are striving to do their duty in this world, living and working on for the next. Look at the Miss Barlieus! I love them dearly; every one respects them: but I would not change my religion for theirs."

"It is the fact of your having spent four years in their house that makes me doubtful. But I think I can trust you; you look so sincere and true. The alarming number of converts to Romanism which we have of late years been obliged to witness, must make us all fearful."

"Perverts, if you please," interrupted Mr. Paler. "When I hear of our folk going over to the Romish faith, I always suspect they are those who have not done their duty in their own. A man may find all he wants in his own religion, if he only looks out for it."

"Oh, that's very true," I exclaimed, my eyes sparkling, glad, somehow, to hear him say it. "It is what I have been trying to express to Mrs. Paler."

"She has her head full of some nonsensical fear that her children should be turned into Roman Catholics.—I suppose because we are in a Catholic country" he resumed, looking at his wife through his glasses. "She'll talk about it till she turns into one herself, if she doesn't mind; that's the way the mania begins. There's no more fear of sensible people turning Catholics than there is of my turning Dutchman: as to the children, the notion is simply absurd. And what sort of weather have you had at Nulle, Miss Hereford, since we left it?"

"Not very fine. Yesterday it poured with rain all day."

"Ah. That would make it pleasant for travelling, though."

"Yes: it laid the dust."

"Did you travel alone?"

"Oh no; the Miss Barlieus would not have allowed it. It is not etiquette in France for a young lady to go out even for a walk alone. An acquaintance of the Miss Barlieus, Madame Bernadotte, who was journeying to Paris, accompanied me."

"Well, I hope you will be comfortable here," he concluded.

"Thank you; I hope so."

"And look here, I'll give you a hint. Just you get the upper hand of those children at once, or you'll never do it. They are like so many untrained colts."

Nothing more was said. I had not been asked to sit, and supposed the silence was a hint that I must quit the room. Before I had gone far, a servant came and said I was to go back to it. Mrs. Paler was alone then, looking very solemn and dark.

"Miss Hereford, you have been reared in seclusion, mostly in school, and probably know little of the convenances—the exactions of social life. Do not be offended if I set you right upon a point—I have no doubt you have erred, not from want of respect, but from lack of knowledge."

What had I done? of course I said I should be obliged to her to set me right in anything when found wrong.

"You are a governess; you hold a dependent situation in my house. Is it not so?"

"Certainly it is," I answered, wondering much.

"Then never forget that a certain amount of respect in manner is due to myself and to Mr. Paler. I do not, of course, wish to exact the deference a servant would give—you must understand that; but there's a medium: a medium, Miss Hereford. To you, I and Mr. Paler are 'madam' and 'sir,' and I beg that we may be always addressed as such."

I curtsied and turned away, the burning colour dyeing my face. It was my first lesson in dependence. But Mrs. Paler was right; and I felt vexed to have forgotten that I was only a governess. Misplaced rebellion rose in my heart, whispering that I was a lady born; that my family was far higher in the social world than Mr. or Mrs. Paler's; whispering, moreover, that that lady was not a gentlewoman, and never could be one. But after a few minutes spent in sober reflection, common sense chased away my foolish thoughts, leaving in place a firm resolution never so to transgress again. From that hour, I took up my position bravely—the yielding, dependent, submissive governess.

But what a life of toil I entered upon! and—where were my dreams of Paris? Have you forgotten that they had visited me, in all their beautiful delusion? I had not. Delusive hopes are always the sweetest.

When I had stayed three months at Mrs. Paler's I had never once been into Paris further than the Champs Elysées. Except that we went every Sunday morning in a closed carriage to the Ambassador's chapel, I saw nothing of Paris. The streets may have been of crystal, the fountains of malachite marble, the houses of burnished gold, for all I witnessed of them—and I believe my warm imagination had pictured something of the like resplendence. There was no pleasure for me; no going out; my days were one lasting scene of toil.

I am not going to complain unjustly of Mrs. Paler's situation, or make it out worse than it was. It has become much the fashion of late years—I may say a mania—to set forth the sorrows and ill-treatment that governesses have to endure: were the other side of the question to be taken up, it might be seen that ladies have as much to bear from governesses. There are good situations and there are bad ones; and there are admirable governesses, as well as undesirable and most incapable ones; perhaps the good and bad on both sides are about balanced. I was well treated at Mr. Paler's; I had a generous diet, and a maid to wait upon me in conjunction with the two elder girls. When they had visitors in an evening, I was admitted on an equality (at any rate to appearance); I had respect paid me by the servants; and I was not found fault with by Mr. and Mrs. Paler. Could I desire better than this? No. But I was overworked.

Put it to yourselves what it was, if you have any experience in teaching. Five girls, all in different stages of advancement, to learn everything, from German and good English down to needlework. The worst task was the music; the drawing lessons I could give conjointly. All five learnt it, piano and harp, and two of them, the second and the youngest but one, were so wild and unsteady that they could not be trusted to practise one instant alone. I rose every morning at half-past six to begin the music lessons, and I was usually up until twelve or one o'clock the next morning correcting exercises, for I could not find time to do them during the day. "Make time," says some one. I could only have made it by neglecting the children.

"Our last governess never did a thing after six in the evening," Kate said to me one day. "You should not be so particular, Miss Hereford."

"But she did not get you on to your mamma's satisfaction."

"No, indeed: mamma sent her away because of that. She did not care whether we advanced or not. All she cared for was to get the studies over anyhow."

Just so: it had been eye-service, as I could have told by their ignorance when I took the girls in hand. My dear mother had instructed me differently: "Whatever you undertake, Anne, let it be done to the very best of your ability: do it as to God; as though His eye and ear were ever present with you."

I appealed to Mrs. Paler: telling her I could not continue to work as I was doing, and asking what could be done.

"Oh, nonsense, Miss Hereford, you must be a bad economizer of time," she answered. "The other governesses I have had did not complain of being overworked."

"But, madam, did they do their duty?"

"Middling for that—but then they were incorrigibly lazy. We are *quite* satisfied with you, Miss Hereford, and you must manage your time so as to afford yourself more leisure."

I suggested to Mrs. Paler that she should have help for part of the music lessons, but she would not hear of it; so I had to go on doing my best; but to do that best overtaxed my strength sadly. Mrs. Paler might have had more consideration: she saw that I rarely went out; one hurried walk in the week, perhaps, and the drive to church on Sunday. My pupils walked out every day, taken by one or other of the servants; but they did not go together: two or three stayed with me while the rest went, and when they came back to me these went. Mrs. Paler insisted upon my giving an hour of music to each child daily, which made five hours a day for music alone. The confinement and the hard work, perhaps the broken spirits, began to tell upon me; nervous headaches came on, and I wrote to the Miss Barlieus, asking what I should do. I wrote the letter on a Sunday, I am sorry to say, failing time on a week-day. None of us went abroad on a Sunday afternoon. Mrs. Paler protested that nothing but sin and gallivanting was to be seen out of doors on a French Sunday; and once home from church we were shut up for the rest of the day. She did not go out herself, or suffer any one else to go; Mr. Paler excepted. He took the reins into his own hands.

The Miss Barlieus answered me sensibly; it was Miss Annette who wrote. "Put up with it to the close of your year from the time of entrance," she said. "It is never well for a governess to leave her situation before the year is up, if it can be avoided, and were you to do so, some ladies might urge it as an objection to making another engagement with you. You are very young still. Give Mrs. Paler ample notice, three months, we believe, is the English usage—and endeavour to part with her amicably. She must see that her situation is beyond your strength."

I took the advice, and in June gave Mrs. Paler warning to leave, having entered her house in September. She was angry, and affected to believe I would not go. I respectfully asked her to put herself in idea in my place, and candidly say whether or not the work was too hard. She muttered something about "over-conscientiousness;" that I should get along better without it. Nothing more was said; nothing satisfactory decided, and the time went on again to the approach of September. I wondered how I must set about looking out for another asylum; I had no time to look out, no opportunity to go abroad. Mr. Paler was in England.

"Miss Hereford, mamma told me to say that we shall be expected in the drawing-room to-night; you, and I, and Harriet," observed Kate Paler to me one hot summer's day. "The Gordons are coming and the de Mellissies."

"What de Mellissies are those?" I inquired, the name striking upon my ear with a thrill of remembrance.

"What de Mellissies are those? why, *the* de Mellissies," returned Kate, girl-fashion. "She is young and very pretty; I saw her when I was out with mamma in the carriage the other day."

"Is she English or French?"

"English, I'll vow. No French tongue could speak English as she does."

"When you answer in that free, abrupt manner, Kate, you greatly displease me," I interposed. "It is most unladylike."

Kate laughed; said she was free-spoken by nature, and it was of no use trying to be otherwise. By habit more than by nature, I told her: and I waited with impatience for the evening.

It was Emily. I knew her at once. Gay-mannered, laughing, lovely as ever, she came into the room on her husband's arm, wearing a pink silk dress and wreath of roses. Alfred de Mellissie looked ill; at least he was paler and thinner than in the old days at Nulle. She either did not or would not remember me; as the evening drew on, I felt sure that she did not, for she spoke cordially enough to me, though as to an utter stranger. It happened that we were quite alone once, in the recess of a window, and I interrupted what she was saying about a song.

"Have you quite forgotten me, Madame de Mellissie?"

"Forgotten you!" she returned, with a quick glance. "I never knew you, did I?"

"In the years gone by, when you were Miss Chandos. I am Anne Hereford."

A puzzled gaze at me, and then she hid her face in her hands, its penitent expression mixed with laughter. "Never say a word about that naughty time, if you love me! Every one says it should be buried five fathoms deep. I ought to have known you, though, for it is the same gentle face; the sweet and steady eyes, with the long eyelashes, and the honest good sense and the pretty smile. But you have grown out of all knowledge. Not that you are much of a size now. What an escapade that was! The staid Demoiselles Barlieu will never get over it. I shall go and beg their pardon in person some day. Were you shocked at it?"

"Yes. But has it brought you happiness?"

"Who talks of happiness at soirées? You must be as unsophisticated as ever, Anne Hereford. Has that Johnstone left?"

"A long, long while ago. She was dismissed at the end of a few months. The Miss Barlieus did not like her."

"I don't know who could like her. And so you are a governess?"

"Yes," I bravely avowed. "I have been nearly a year with the Miss Palers."

"You must get leave to come and see me. Alfred, here's an old schoolfellow of mine. I dare say you will remember her."

Monsieur de Mellissie came at the call, and was talking to me for the rest of the evening.

The great things that a night may bring forth! The sadness that the rising of another sun may be bearing to us on its hot wings!

It was the morning following the soirée. I was in the schoolroom with the girls, but quitted it for a minute to read a letter in peace that arrived by the early post. It was written by Miss Barlieu. A very kind letter, telling me to go back to them whilst I looked out for a fresh situation, should I not get one before leaving Mrs. Paler. Suddenly the door opened, and Mrs. Paler came in without any ceremony of knocking, her face white, and an open letter in her hand. She looked scared, fierce; agitation impeding her free utterance.

"Here's news!" she brought out at length, her voice rising to a scream; "here's news to come upon me like a thunderbolt! Does he expect me to live through it?"

"Oh, Mrs. Paler, what has happened? You look ill and terrified.

You have had bad tidings! Will you not tell them to me?"

"What else have I come for but to tell you?" she retorted, speaking in tones that betrayed as much anger as distress. "I went to the study after you, and frightened the girls; they were for following me here, so I locked them in. I must tell some one, or my feelings will burst bounds; they always were of a demonstrative nature. Not like *his*, the sly, quiet fox!"

My fears flew to Mr. Paler. He had been in England some time now, ever since the middle of May. Though I did not understand her anger, or the last words.

"You have heard from Mr. Paler, madam!" I uttered. "Some harm has happened to him!"

"Harm! yes, it has. Harm to me and my children, though, more than to him. Miss Hereford, he has just gone and ruined himself."

"How?" I asked, feeling grieved and puzzled.

"It was always his mania, that turf-gambling, and as a young man he got out of thousands at it. I thought how it would be—I declare I did—when he became restless here in Paris just before the Epsom Meeting, and at last went off to it. 'You'll drop some hundreds over it, if you do go,' I said to him. 'Not I,' was his retort, 'since I have had children to drop hundreds over, I don't spare them for race-horses.' A wicked, reckless man!"

"And has he—dropped the hundreds, madam?"

"Hundreds!" she shrieked; and then, looking covertly around the room, as if fearful others might be listening, she sank her voice to a whisper: "He has lost thirty thousand pounds."

"Oh!" I exclaimed, in my horror. Mrs. Paler wrung her hands.

"Thirty thousand pounds, every pound of it—and I hope remorse will haunt him to his dying day! Epsom, Ascot, Good-wood—I know not how many other courses he has visited this summer, and has betted frantically at all. The mania was upon him again, and he could not stop himself. He is lying ill now at Doncaster, at one of the inns there, and his brother writes; he tells me they dare not conceal the facts from me any longer."

"Shall you not go over to him, madam?"

"I go over to him!" she retorted; "I would not go to him if he were dying. But that my children are his, I would never live with him again; I would never notice him: I would get a divorce, if practicable, but for their sakes. You look shocked, Miss Hereford; but you, an unmarried girl, cannot realize the blow in all its extent. Do you think a man has any *right* wilfully to bring disgrace and misery upon his wife and children?"

"Oh, madam—no!"

"It is my punishment come home to me," she wildly exclaimed. "They told me how it would be, sooner or later, if I persisted in marrying James Paler: but I would not listen to them. My mother and sisters will say it serves me right."

I heard the children squealing and kicking at the schoolroom door, and did not dare to go to them.

"It is next door to ruin," said Mrs. Paler; "it will take from us more than half our income; and present debt and embarrassment it must bring. Ah! see how some things—trifles—happen sometimes for the best! I thought it a great misfortune to lose you, but I am glad of it now, for I am sure I can no longer afford an expensive governess. Nor many servants, either. Oh, woe's me!"

I stood looking at her distress with great pity, feeling that Mr. Paler must be next kin to a madman. And yet I had liked him: he was most affectionate to his children, and solicitous for the comfort of his household. Mrs. Paler seemed to become suddenly awake to the uproar. She darted to the schoolroom, scolded one, boxed another, locked the door upon them again, and came back to me.

"I had better settle things with you at once, Miss Hereford. If I take it into my head, I may go off to my family in England at a minute's notice; there's no knowing. Your time here will expire in a fortnight?"

"Yes."

"I had intended to offer an increased salary, if you would stay on—but that's all out of the question now. I suppose you have no settled plans; no fresh situation to go to?"

"Madam, it has not been in my power to look out for one."

"True. Yet it is better that you should go. I don't know what may become of us in future: where we shall live, or what we shall do—perhaps go to some obscure place in Germany, or Scotland, or Wales, and economize: anywhere, so that it's cheap. I wonder that such men, who deliberately bring ruin on their families, are permitted to live! But now we must try and find you another situation."

"Perhaps Madame de Mellissie may know of something: and I think she would interest herself for me, if I knew how to see her."

"You can go and see her," replied Mrs. Paler, "you can go to-day, and call upon her. My maid shall take you. Never mind the studies: I feel as if I should not care if the girls never learnt anything again—with this blow upon them."

I did not wait for a second permission: the thought that Emily de Mellissie might help me to a fresh situation had been floating in my mind all night. She was well-connected in England; she was in the best society in Paris; and she was good-natured.

In the afternoon I proceeded to the hotel (as it was called) of old Madame de Mellissie, for it was her house, and her son and daughter-in-law lived with her. Emily was at home, surrounded by morning callers, quite a crowd of them. She looked intensely surprised at seeing me; was, or I fancied it, rather distant and haughty in manner; and, pointing to a chair, desired me to wait. Did she deem I had presumptuously intruded as one of those morning callers? Very humbly I waited until the last had gone: schooling myself to remember that I was only a poor governess, whilst she was Madame Alfred de Mellissie, *née* Miss Chandos of Chandos.

"And so you have soon come to pay me a visit, Miss Hereford!"

"I have come as a petitioner, rather than a visitor, Madame de Mellissie. Can you spare me five minutes?"

"I can spare you ten if you like, now those loungers are gone."

I forthwith told my tale. That I was leaving Mrs. Paler's, where I was overworked: that I had thought it possible she might know of some situation: if so, would she kindly recommend me?

"The idea, Anne Hereford, of your coming to me upon such an errand!" was her laughing answer. "As if I troubled myself about vacant situations! There is a rumour current in Paris this morning that James Paler has been idiot enough to go and ruin himself on the turf. That he has lost a great deal of money is certain, for the newspapers allude to it in a manner not to be mistaken. Thank goodness, Alfred has no weakness that way, though he is empty-headed enough. Is it not a dreadful life, that of a governess?"

"At Mrs. Paler's it has been one of incessant toil. I hope to go where the duties will be lighter. It is not the life I like, or would have chosen; but I must bend to circumstances."

"That's true enough. I will ask all my friends in Paris if they—By the way," she abruptly broke off, speaking with deliberation, "I wonder whether—if you should be found suitable—whether you would like something else?"

I made no reply; only waited for her to explain herself.

"The case is this, Miss Hereford," she resumed, assuming a light manner. "I thought of going to Chandos on a visit; my husband was to have conducted me thither, but Madame de Melissie has been ailing, and Alfred says it would not do for him to leave her. This morning we had a dispute over it. 'There's nothing much amiss with her,' I said; 'were she in danger, it would be a different matter, but it's quite unreasonable to keep me away from Chandos for nothing but this.' Monsieur Alfred grew vexed, said he should not quit her, and moreover, did not himself feel well enough to travel—for he has a sort of French fever hanging about him. They are always getting it, you know. I am sick of hearing one say to another, *'J'ai la fièvre aujourd'hui!'* Then I said I should go without him: 'With great pleasure,' he complacently replied, provided I would engage a lady as companion, but he should not trust me alone. Complimentary to my discretion, was it not?"

I could not deny it—in a certain sense.

"But the bargain was made; it was indeed. I am to look out for a companion, and then I may be off the next hour to England; destination Chandos. Would you like to take the place?"

A thousand thoughts flew over me at the abrupt question, crowding my mind, dyeing my cheeks. The prospect, at the first glance, appeared like a haven of rest after Mrs. Paler's. But—what would be my duties?—and was *I*, a comparative child, fit for the post? Should I be deemed so by Monsieur de Melissie?

"What should I have to do?" I asked.

"Anything I please," she answered. "You must amuse me when I am tired, read to me when I feel inclined to listen, play to me when I wish, be ready to go out when I want you, give orders to my maid for me, write my letters when I am too idle to do it, and post yourself at my side to play propriety between this and Chandos. Those are the onerous duties of a dame de compagnie, are they not? but I have no experience in the matter. Could you undertake them?"

She spoke all this curiously, in haughty tones, but with a smile on her face. I did not know how to take it. "Are you speaking seriously, Madame de Melissie?"

"Of course I am. Stay, though. About the payment? I could not afford to give much, for my purse has a hole at both ends of it, and I am dreadfully poor. I suppose you have had a high salary at Mrs. Paler's?"

"Sixty guineas."

"Oh, don't talk of it!" she exclaimed, stopping her ears. "I wish I could give it; but I never could squeeze out more than twenty. Anne, I will make a bargain with you: go with me to Chandos, stay with me during my visit there; it will not last above a week or two; and when we return here, I will find you a more lucrative situation. For the time you are with me, I will give you what I can afford, and of course pay your travelling expenses!"

With the word "Anne," she had gone back to the old familiar manner of our school-days. I accepted the offer willingly, subject, of course, to the approval of Monsieur de Mellissie; and feeling very doubtful in my own mind whether it would be carried out. As to the payment—what she said seemed reasonable enough, and money wore but little value in my eyes: I had not then found out its uses. Provided I had enough for my ordinary wants of dress, it was all I cared for; and a large sum was due to me from Mrs. Paler.

Somewhat to my surprise, Monsieur de Mellissie approved of me as his wife's companion, paying me a compliment on the occasion. "You are young, Mademoiselle Hereford, but I can see you are one fully to be trusted: I confide my wife to you."

"I will do what I can, sir."

"You laugh at my saying that thing," he said, speaking in his sometimes rather odd English. "You think my wife can better take care of you, than you of her."

"I am younger than she is."

"That goes without saying, mademoiselle. You look it. The case is this," he added, in a confidential tone. "It is not that my wife wants protection on her journey; she has her femme de chambre; but because I do not think they would like to see her arriving alone at Chandos. My lady is difficile."

The permission to depart accorded, Madame de Mellissie was all impatience to set off. I bought a dress or two, but she would not allow me time to get them made, and I had to take them unmade. Though I was going to Chandos as a humble companion, I could not forget that my birth would have entitled me to go as a visitor, and wished to dress accordingly.

The foolish girl that I was! I spent my money down to one napoleon and some silver; it was not very much I had by me; and then Mrs. Paler, to my intense consternation, told me it was not convenient to pay me my salary.

She owed me thirty guineas. I had received the first thirty at the termination of the half-year: it was all spent, including what I had laid out now. I appealed to Mrs. Paler's good feeling, showing my needy state. In return she appealed to mine.

"My dear Miss Hereford, I have not got it. Until remittances shall reach me from Mr. Paler, I am very short. You do not require money for your journey, Madame Alfred de Mellissie pays all that, and I will remit it to you ere you have been many days at Chandos. You will not, I am sure, object so far to oblige a poor distressed woman."

What answer could I give?

On a lovely September morning we started for Boulogne-sur-Mer, Madame Alfred de Mellissie, I, and her maid Pauline. Monsieur de Mellissie saw us off at the station.

"I would have run down to Boulogne to put you on board the boat, but that I do not feel well enough; my fever is very bad to-day," he said to me and his wife. She took no notice of the words, but I saw they were true: his pale thin face had a hectic flush upon it, his hand, meeting mine in the adieu, burnt me through my glove.

"Madame de Mellissie, your husband certainly has an attack of fever," I said, as the train started.

"Ah, yes, no doubt; the French, as I previously observed, are subject to it. But it never comes to anything."

# CHAPTER 11

## CHANDOS

The station of Hetton, some fifty miles' journey from London on the Great Western line, and two from Chandos, lay hot and bright in the September sun. It was afternoon when we reached it. Madame de Mellissie had preferred to stay a night in London, and go on the next day at leisure. A handsome close carriage was in waiting outside the station, its three attendants wearing the Chandos livery, its panels bearing the arms of the Chandos family, surmounted by the badge of England's baronetage, the bloody hand. The servants lifted their hands to their hats, and respectfully welcomed Madame de Mellissie.

"Is mamma well?" she inquired of them.

"Quite well, madam."

"And my brother? Why is he not here?"

"Mr. Chandos, madam, was obliged to attend a county meeting."

"Those ponderous county meetings!" she retorted. "And they never do any good. Step in, Miss Hereford."

We were soon driving along. Pauline sat behind with one of the footmen, the other remained to bring on the luggage. Madame de Mellissie looked out at the points of road as we passed, with all the glee of a child.

"This is my second visit only to Chandos since my marriage. For two years mamma was implacable, and would not see me; but last year she relented, and I came here for a little while. I don't believe, though, mamma will ever forgive me in her heart. I am sorry for it now."

"Sorry for having—having married as you did?"

"Ay, I am. Those rebellious marriages never bring luck. They can't, you know; only, girls are so thoughtless and stupid. I made my own bed, and must lie on it; it is not so bad as it might have been: but—of course, all that's left is to make the best of it. Alfred says we should get on better if we had children. I say we should not. And there, in the distance, you see the chimneys of Chandos. Look, Anne—"

She was wayward in her moods; wayward to me as to others. Sometimes, during our past journey, she would be distantly polite, calling me "Miss Hereford:" the next moment open and cordial as ever she had been at school. That she had thrown herself away in a worldly point of view, marrying as she did, was indisputable, and Emily Chandos was not one to forget it.

Chandos was a long, low, red-brick house, with gables and turrets to its two wings, and a small turret in the middle, which gave it a somewhat Gothic appearance. It was only two storeys high, and struck me as looking low, not elevated, perhaps partly from its length. No steps ascended to the house, the lower rooms were on a level with the ground outside. It was a sort of double house; the servants' rooms, kitchens, and chambers, all looking to the back, where there was a separate entrance. Extensive grounds lay around it, but they were so crowded with trees, except just close to the house, as to impart a weird-like, gloomy appearance; they completely shut Chandos House from the view of the world beyond, and the world beyond from the view of Chandos. A pretty trellised portico was at the entrance; jessamine, roses, and clematis entwined themselves round it, extending even to the windows on either hand. Before the carriage had well stopped, a gentleman rode up on horse-back, followed by a groom. He threw himself from his horse, and came to the carriage-door.

"Back just in time to receive you, Emily. How are you, my dear?"

She jumped lightly from the carriage, and he was turning away with her when he saw me. His look of intense surprise was curious to behold, and he stopped in hesitation. Emily spoke: her tone a slighting one, almost disparaging.

"It is only my companion. Would you believe it, Harry, Alfred took a prudent fit, and would not suffer me to travel alone? So I engaged Miss Hereford: she was in quest of a situation; and we knew each other in days gone by."

He assisted me from the carriage. It was the same fine man I had seen some years before at Mademoiselle Barlieu's; the same pale countenance, with its delicate features and rather sad expression; the same sweet voice. He then gave his arm to his sister, and I followed them to the sitting-room. They called it the oak-parlour; a large, square room, somewhat dark, its colours harmoniously blending, and its windows shaded with the trained clematis and jessamine. It was the favourite sitting-room at Chandos. Other reception-rooms there were: a gorgeous double drawing-room, a well-stored library, a spacious dining-room; but the oak-parlour was the favourite. And none could wonder at it; for it was one of those seductive apartments that speak to the feelings of repose.

"Where's mamma?" exclaimed Emily, as we entered.

"Not far; she will be here directly, you may be sure," replied Mr. Chandos. "Is this your first visit to our part of the country, Miss Hereford?"

"Yes; I never was here before."

Now what was there in this reply to offend Madame de Mellissie? or did she resent his speaking to me at all? She turned round, haughty pride stamped on every line of her countenance, rebuke on her tongue: though the rebuke lay in the tone, rather than in the words.

"Miss Hereford! the gentleman to whom you speak is Mr. Chandos."

Had I again omitted the sign of my dependent situation, the "sir?" I, who had resolved, with my then burning face (burning again now), never so to offend for the future—I supposed that that was the meaning of Madame de Mellissie; I suppose so still, to this hour. I had spoken as though I were the equal of Mr. Chandos: I must not—I *would* not—so offend again.

"Emily, my love, you are welcome."

A little woman had entered the room, and was holding Madame de Mellissie in her arms. It was Lady Chandos. She wore a small and pretty widow's cap of net, a rich but soft black silk dress, and black lace mittens. Her nose was sharp, and her small face had a permanent redness, the result of disturbed health. She was not like her daughter, not half so beautiful; and she was not like her handsome son, unless it was in the subdued, sad expression. She quite started back when her eyes fell on me, evidently not prepared to see a stranger.

"Miss Hereford, mamma; a young lady whom I have engaged as companion. Alfred would not suffer me to travel alone."

Lady Chandos turned to me with a pleasant smile, but it struck me as being a forced one.

"I think you look more fit to take care of Miss Hereford, Emily, than Miss Hereford of you," she said.

"I am the elder by some two or three years, if you mean that, mamma. Oh! it was just a whim of my husband's."

More questioning on either side; just the information sought for when relatives meet after a long absence. Emily answered carelessly and lightly; and I sat behind, unnoticed.

Hill was called. Hill was still at Chandos, lady's-maid and house-keeper, a confidential servant. She came forward, wearing a dark-brown gown and handsome black silk apron, her grey hair banded under her close white lace cap. Lady Chandos spoke with her in an undertone, most likely consulting what chamber I should be placed in, for Hill turned her eyes upon me and looked cross.

A wide staircase, its balustrades of carved oak, gilded in places, wound up to the rooms above. A gallery, lighted from above, ran along this upper floor, from wing to wing, paintings lining it. It seemed as if the wings had some time been added to the house, for they were of a different style of architecture. A green-baize door shut them out from the gallery. Beyond this was a narrow corridor, and then a double door of stout oak, which formed the real entrance to the wings: the same on both sides. What rooms might be within them, I did not yet know. Each wing had a staircase of communication between its upper and lower floors, and also a small door of exit to the grounds on the sides of the house, where the trees grew very thick. In the east wing (the house, you must understand, facing the south), this lower outer door was kept locked and barred—to all intents and purposes, closed up; in the west wing, which was inhabited exclusively by Lady Chandos, the door was simply locked, and could be opened inside at will; though no one ever made use of it but herself, and she very rarely. Several rooms opened from the gallery to the front—all of them bed-chambers, except one: that was the library. The library was the room next to the east wing. Opposite to it was a door opening to a room that looked back, level with the north rooms in the east wing. A similar room opened from the gallery at the other end. In fact, the house was built in uniform—one end the same as the other. Between the doors of these two rooms the wall of the gallery ran unbroken; there was, in fact, no communication whatever, as regards the upper rooms between the back portion of the house and the front.

And now for the ground-floor. The portico was not in the middle of the house, but near to the east wing; one room only, the large dining-room, that seemed to be never used, lying between. The hall was rather small, dark, and shut in, the oak parlour being on the left hand as you entered. Two doors at the back of the hall led, the one to the handsome staircase, the other to the kitchens and other domestic rooms belonging to the household. A spacious corridor, underneath the gallery above, branched off from the hall by means of an open archway behind the oak parlour, and ran along the house; and the various reception rooms, all looking front, including Mr. Chandos's private sitting-room, opened from it. A passage at the other end of the corridor led to the rooms at the back, but it had been closed up; and there was no communication whatever on this lower floor with the wings. The doors in the hall, leading to the stairs and to the servants' offices, as often as not stood open during the day. Lady Chandos sat much in the west wing; she seemed to like being alone. And I think that is all that need be said at present with regard to the indoor features of the house. The description has not been given unnecessarily.

Hill marshalled me up the staircase. It had been decided that I was to have the "blue room." The stairs terminated in a wide landing. The library and the east wing lay to the right, as we ascended; the long gallery on the left. Hill passed two chamber-doors, and opened a third, that of the blue room. It was as little calculated for immediate occupation as any room can well be; the whole of the furniture being covered up with clean sheets of linen, except the blue silk window-hangings. Madame de Mellissie had the room next to it, and I could hear her talking in it with her mother. Hill surveyed matters, and gave a sort of grunt.

"Ugh! I thought the maids had uncovered this room yesterday: as I've just told my lady. They must have hurried over their cleaning pretty quick. Please to step this way, miss. If you'll wait here a few minutes, I'll have things arranged."

She went back along the gallery, opened the door of the first bedroom on this side the staircase, and showed me in. It was a very pretty room, not large; its hangings and curtains of delicate chintz, lined with pale rose-colour, and its furniture *not* covered up, but as evidently not in occupation. I wondered why they could not put me in that. The window was wide open. I untied my bonnet and stood there, Hill closing the door and going downstairs, no doubt to call up the housemaids.

With the exception of the gravel drive below, and the green lawn in front of it, its velvet softness dotted with the brightest flowers, the place seemed to look upon nothing but trees, intersected with gloomy walks. Trees of all sorts—low as dwarf shrubs, high as towering poplars, dark green, light green, bright green. The walks branched everywhere—one in particular, just opposite my window, looked very gloomy, shaded as it was by dark pine-trees. I found afterwards that it was called the Pine Walk. Why the place should have struck upon me with a gloom, I can hardly tell; other people might have seen nothing to justify the impression. "Chandos has need to live in a world of its own," I thought, "for assuredly it is shut in from all view of the outer world."

There arose a sound as of some one softly whistling. It came from the adjacent window, one in the gallery, which must have been open the same as mine. I did not like to lean forward and look. Another moment, and the whistling ceased; some one else appeared to have come up, and voices in conversation supervened. They were those of Lady Chandos and her son, and I became an involuntary hearer of what troubled me much.

"This is one of Emily's wild actions," said Lady Chandos. "She knows quite enough of our unhappy secrets to be sure that a stranger is not wanted at Chandos."

"Look for the most improbable thing in the world, mother, before you look for discretion or thought in Emily," was the reply of Mr. Chandos. "But this is only a young girl, unsuspicious naturally from her age and sex: Emily might have introduced a more dangerous inmate. And it may happen that—"

"I know what you would urge, Harry," interrupted the voice of Lady Chandos. "But there's no certainty. There cannot be: and it is most unfortunate that Emily should have brought her here. Every night, night by night as they come round, I lie awake shivering; if the wind does but move the trees, I start; if an owl shrieks forth its dreary note, I almost shriek with it. You know what we have cause to fear. And for a stranger to be sleeping in the house!"

"Yes, it is certainly unfortunate."

"It is more than that; it is dangerous. Harry, I have never, I hope, done a discourteous thing, but it did occur to me to put this young girl to sleep on the servants' side of the house. I think her being so lady-like in appearance saved her from it, not my good manners. I don't know what to do."

Mr. Chandos made no reply.

"I wish I had done it!" resumed Lady Chandos. "But there's another thing—Emily might object: and to have any fuss would be worse than all. Still, look at the risk—the stake! Is it too late, do you think, Harry? Would it do to change her room now?"

"My dear mother, you are the best judge," observed Mr. Chandos. "I should not change the room if I could possibly avoid it; the young lady might consider it in the light of an indignity. Emily introduced her in a slighting sort of manner; but her looks are refined, her manners those of a gentlewoman."

"Yes, that's true."

"How long does Emily think of remaining?"

"She says two weeks. But she is as uncertain as the wind. How *could* she think of bringing a stranger with her?"

"Have you told her all?—why it is just now particularly undesirable?"

"No. She never has been told. And I hope and trust she may be gone again before—before trouble comes."

"Quite right; I should not tell her. Well, mother, as you ask my opinion, I say things had better remain as arranged; let the young lady occupy the blue room. How cross Hill looked over it!"

"Not without cause. I cannot think how Emily can have been so senseless. It is just as though she had planned the annoyance—bringing her here without writing! Had she written, I should have forbidden it."

"Let us hope that nothing will happen."

"Harry, we cannot answer for it. Again, on Ethel's account, a stranger in the house is not desirable. Emily might have thought of that."

The voices ceased; I suppose the speakers quitted the place; and down I sat, overwhelmed with shame and consternation. To be introduced in this unwelcome manner into a house, bringing annoyance and discomfort to its inmates, seemed to me little less than a crime; I could scarcely have felt more guilty had I committed one.

And what was the mystery? That something or other was amiss in the family was all too evident. "Have they a ghost here?" I said to myself, in peevishness. Involuntarily the long-past words of Annette Barlieu flashed into my mind: and I had never thought of them since they were spoken. "There is always a cloud hanging over Chandos. They do not care to have a governess residing there: Miladi said it to me." Then what was the cloud?—what was the fear?

Hill came in again, saying I was to keep the chintz-room. Lady Chandos, in passing just now along the gallery to her own apartments in the west wing, saw for the first time that the blue room was not ready. So it was decided between her and Hill that I should occupy the chintz one.

The luggage was brought up, and I began to dress for dinner. A question occurred to me—are companions expected to dress, in the wider sense of the term? I really did not know, in my inexperience. My birth entitled me to do so; but did my position? A minute's hesitation told me I was a guest at Chandos, treated and regarded as one, and might appear accordingly. So I put on a pretty low blue silk, with my necklace of real pearls, that had once been mamma's, and the pale-blue enamelled bracelets with the pearl clasps. I had been obliged to dress a good deal at Mrs. Paler's in the evening; and—to confess the truth—I liked it.

I stood at the door, hesitating whether to go down, as one is apt to do in a house, the ways of which are unfamiliar, when Mr. Chandos, ready for dinner, came suddenly out of the room opposite to the library, nearly opposite to mine, the one that I spoke of as looking to the back of the house, and adjoining the back rooms of the east wing. I concluded that it was his bed-chamber. He smiled at me as he crossed to the stairs, but did not say anything. Directly after, Emily de Mellissie appeared in the gallery, radiant in white silk, with an apple-blush rose in her hair, and a diamond aigrette embedded in it. They said she was full of whims—as I knew for myself. How ardently I hoped that some whim would send her speedily away from Chandos!

We went into the first drawing-room, one of the most beautiful rooms I had ever seen, its fittings violet and gold. Lady Chandos was there, and did not appear to have changed her dress. The dinner was served in the oak-parlour; not once in a year did they use the great dining-room. Lady Chandos kindly passed her arm through mine; and Mr. Chandos brought in his sister.

It was a pleasant dinner, and a pleasant evening. Emily was on her best behaviour, telling all manner of amusing anecdotes of Paris life to her mother and brother, ignoring me. I listened, and was spoken to by the others now and then. We did not quit the oak-parlour. When dessert was taken, Hickens, the butler, removed it and brought in tea. "After my snug sitting-room upstairs, the drawing-room is so large," observed Lady Chandos to me, as if in apology; "I like this parlour best."

Upon retiring to rest a neat-looking servant with light hair, whose name I found was Harriet, came to the chintz-room, and asked whether she should do anything for me. She said she was one of the housemaids—there were two besides herself, Lizzy Dene and

Emma. Altogether, including the coachman, a helper in the stables, and two gardeners—all four of whom were out of doors, living half-a-mile away—there were seventeen servants at Chandos. A large number, as it seemed to me, considering the very little attendance that was required of them. I told Harriet I had been accustomed to wait upon myself, and she retired.

But I could not get to sleep. The conversation I had overheard kept haunting me. I wondered what the mystery could be; I wondered whether I should be disturbed in the night by noises, or anything else. What uncanny doings could there be in the house?—what unseemly inmates, rendering it inexpedient that a stranger should share its hospitality? Was it really tenanted by ghosts?—or by something worse? At any rate, they did not molest me, and my sleep at last was tranquil.

We went down the following morning at half-past eight; Emily in a white dimity robe of no shape, but tied round the waist with a scarlet cord, the effect altogether rather untidy; I in a mauve-coloured muslin, with ribbons of the same shade; and found Lady and Mr. Chandos waiting breakfast in the oak-parlour. The panels of this room were of alternate white and carved oak, with a great deal of gilding about both; it had a most unusual appearance; I had never seen anything like it before. The ceiling was white, with gilt scrolls round it, and cornices. The large chimney-glass was in a carved oak frame, gilded in places to match the walls; the slanting girandole opposite the window, reflecting the green grass and the waving trees in its convex mirrored surface, had a similar frame. The chandelier for the wax lights was of gilt, also the branches on the mantelpiece, and those of the girandole. It was a pleasant room to enter—as I thought that morning. The oak-brown silk curtains, with their golden satin-wrought flowers, were drawn quite back from the windows, which were thrown open to the lovely morning air; a bright fire burnt in the grate opposite the door; the breakfast-table with its snow-white linen, its painted Worcester china, and its glittering silver, was in the centre. Easy-chairs stood about the room, a sofa against the wall—all covered to match the curtains—brown and gold: a piano was there, a sideboard stood at the back, underneath the reflecting mirror; other chairs, tables, ornaments; and the dark carpet was soft as the softest moss. Out of all order though cavillers for severe taste might have called the room, I know that it possessed an indescribable charm.

Lady Chandos, dressed just as she had been the previous day—and I found it was her usual dress at all times—sat with her back to the window, her son facing her, I and Emily on either side. Breakfast was about half over when Hickens brought in some letters on a small silver waiter, presenting them to Mr. Chandos. I was soon to learn that all letters coming to the house, whether for servants or others, were invariably handed first of all to Mr. Chandos. One of these was directed to "Lady Chandos;" two to "Harry Chandos, Esquire;" the fourth to "Mrs. Chandos." Mr. Chandos put his mother's letter on the waiter again, and Hickens handed it to her. He then came back with the waiter to his master, who placed the other letter upon it.

"For Mrs. Chandos." And Hickens went out with it.

Who was Mrs. Chandos? I should have liked to ask, but dared not.

"Do you mean to say that there is no letter for me, Harry?" exclaimed Madame de Mellissie. "That's my punctual husband! He said he should be quite certain to send me a letter to-day."

"The French mail often comes in later, Emily," remarked her brother.

He and Lady Chandos read their letters, Emily talked and laughed, and the meal came to an end. At its conclusion Mr. Chandos offered to go round the grounds with his sister.

"Yes, I'll go," she answered. "You can go also, Miss Hereford, if you like. But we must get our bonnets and parasols, first, Harry."

My bonnet and parasol were soon found, and I stood at my bed-room door, waiting for Emily. As she came down the gallery, the green-baize door on my right, leading to the east wing, opened, and a middle-aged lady appeared at it. Madame de Mellissie advanced and cordially saluted her.

"I should have paid you a visit yesterday, Mrs. Freeman, but that I heard Mrs. Chandos was ill."

"You are very kind, madam," was the lady's reply. "Mrs. Chandos was exceedingly unwell yesterday, but she is better to-day. She—"

Mrs. Freeman was interrupted. A lovely-looking girl—girl she looked, though she may have been seven or eight-and-twenty—appeared at the door of one of the rooms in the wing. Her dress was white; she wore a beautiful little head-dress of lace and lavender ribbons, and she came forward, smiling.

"I heard you had arrived, Emily dear, and should have joined you all yesterday, but I was so poorly," she said, clasping Madame de Mellissie's hand. "How well you look!"

"And you look well also," replied Emily. "We must never judge you by your looks, Mrs. Chandos."

"No, that you must not: I always look in rude health, in spite of my ailments," answered Mrs. Chandos. "Will you not come and sit with me for half-an-hour?"

"Of course I will," was Madame de Mellissie's reply, as she untied her bonnet and threw it to me carelessly, speaking as careless words.

"Have the goodness to tell Mr. Chandos that I am not going out yet." Mrs. Chandos, who had not noticed me before, turned in surprise, and looked at me; but Madame de Mellissie did not, I suppose, deem me worth an introduction.

I went downstairs to deliver her message. Mr. Chandos was waiting in the oak-parlour, talking to his mother.

"Madame de Mellissie has desired me to say that she will not go out yet, sir."

"I did not expect she would," he answered, with a slight laugh, "for she is as changeable as the wind. Tell her so from me, will you, Miss Hereford?"

He bent his dark blue eyes upon me with a half-saucy glance, as if intimating that he meant what he said.

"Very well, sir."

I returned to my own room, took off my things, and sat down to think.

Who was Mrs. Chandos?

# CHAPTER 12

## OUT OF DOORS AT CHANDOS

That day was a dull one. I did not feel at home, and could not make myself feel so. Madame de Mellissie went out in the carriage with Lady Chandos, and I was alone. I strolled out a little in the afternoon, just to see what the place outside was like. The entrance-gates were on the left, the gravel drive leading straight to them; but there were so many paths and walks, and trees and rocks, and banks and flower-beds on either side, that you might almost lose yourself, and quite lose sight of the broad drive. The most curious-looking feature about Chandos was the little upper turret: but for the narrow Gothic window in it, it might have been taken for a pigeon-house.

I came back, and crossed to the Pine Walk; that again was inter-sected by paths, conducting it was hard to say whither. The trees tow-ered aloft, the lower shrubs were high and thick. In three minutes after quitting the house, not a vestige even of its chimneys was to be seen; and I retraced my steps, not caring to lose myself. But for the beautiful order in which everything was kept, the place might have been called a wilderness.

I noticed one thing: that the front windows in each of the wings had their inside shutters closed; strong oak shutters: both the lower and the upper rooms were shut in from the light of day. I never saw them opened while I stayed at Chandos. The lower windows, looking to the sides of the house, were also kept dark; but the rooms above and those looking to the back were open. A narrow gravel path, shut in by laurels, led round the wings to the back of the house. The ser-vants used that by the east wing, the one inhabited by Mrs. Chandos. No one used the other, except Lady Chandos. For a servant or any one else to be seen there would have been high treason, involving probably dismissal. It was an understood law of the house, and never rebelled against. The shrubs on Lady Chandos's side had grown thick as a very grove, affording just space for one person to pass to the small door that gave entrance to the wing. I knew nothing of the prohibi-tion in strolling there that day. On learning it afterwards, I felt thankful not to have been seen.

I was indoors, and sitting in my bed-chamber, the chintz room, when the carriage returned. Emily, in high spirits, saw me as she ran upstairs, and came in.

"All alone, Anne! We have had a charming drive. To-morrow, if you are good, you shall have one; we'll take the large carriage."

She stood with her foot on a small low chair, tilting it about, and looking out at the servants, who were turning the horses to drive round to the stables at the back.

"What a nice place this seems to be, Madame de Mellissie! But I think, if I were Lady Chandos, I should have the trees and shrubs thinned a little."

"It is mamma's pleasure that they shall be thick. She only lives in retirement. Were my brother, Sir Thomas, to come home, he might effect a change. As long as he is away, mamma's will is paramount at Chandos."

"How many brothers have you?"

"Two. Sir Thomas and Harry."

"Have you lost any?"

"Any brothers? A little one: Greville. He died when he was six years old. Why do you ask?"

"I was only wondering who Mrs. Chandos was. It has been crossing my mind that she is perhaps a daughter-in-law."

Madame de Mellissie turned on me a haughty face of reproof. "It certainly is no affair of yours, Miss Hereford. Mrs. Chandos is Mrs. Chandos; she is no impostor."

"I beg your pardon, madam," I meekly answered, feeling I had deserved it. What right had I, Anne Hereford, to be curious, and to show it?

It effectually silenced me for the rest of the day. We dined together; herself, Lady Chandos, and I. Mrs. Chandos I saw no more of, and Mr. Chandos was dining at Marden, a town some few miles off.

We were at breakfast the following morning, when the letters, as before, were brought in. Two or three for the servants, which Mr. Chandos returned to Hickens, one for Mr. Chandos, and one for Madame Alfred de Mellissie.

"I thought he would be writing," Emily observed, in a tone of apathy, carelessly holding out her hand for the letter. "Though I know he hates it like poison, Frenchman like."

"It is not your husband's hand, Emily," said Mr. Chandos.

"No? Why—I declare it is old Madame de Mellissie's! What can be amiss?" she cried.

"There! was ever anything like that?" she exclaimed, glancing down the letter. "Alfred's taken ill: his fancied gastric-fever has turned into a real one. And I must go back without delay, the old mère writes."

"Is he very ill?" inquired Lady Chandos.

"So *she* says—in danger. But she is timid and fanciful. I shall not go."

"Will you allow me to see the letter, Emily?" asked Lady Chandos, in a grave tone.

"See it and welcome; read it out for the public benefit, if you will, mamma. Look at Harry, staring at me with his blue eyes! He deems me, no doubt, the very model of a loving wife."

"Emily! can you have read this letter?" asked Lady Chandos.

"Yes, I've read it."

"Then how can you hesitate? Your husband is in danger! he may not survive: he will not, they say, unless a change takes place. You must hasten away by the first train."

"Mamma, you need not take the half of it for gospel. Madame de Mellissie is so wrapped up in her son, that if his finger aches she sends for a doctor, and asks whether it will mortify."

"Child! I must recommend you to go," was the impressive response of Lady Chandos.

"Of course I shall go; I never meant to hesitate," came the peevish answer. "But it is excessively tiresome."

It appeared that the letter to Mr. Chandos was also from Madame de Mellissie, asking him to urge his sister's instant departure. She finished her breakfast, and was leaving the room to prepare, when she saw me following.

"I do not want you just now, Miss Hereford. Pauline will see to my things."

"But I have my own to pack."

"Your own! What for? Alfred de Mellissie is not your husband, that you should hasten to him."

"But—am I not to go with you, madam?"

"Certainly not," was her emphatic answer. "It would be a needless expense and trouble."

I felt dumbfounded. "But, Madame de Mellissie, what am I to do?"

"Do! Why, stay here till my return. What else should you do? I shall be back in a few days at most. I know what Monsieur Alfred's danger is! Only, if I did not make the journey, madame la mère would hold me forth to all Paris as a model of barbarity. Mamma," she quickly added, turning to Lady Chandos, "I shall return here to finish my visit as soon as I can get away. It will not be a week before you will see me again. You can let Miss Hereford wait here for me, can't you? Can't you, Harry?"

"Provided Miss Hereford will make herself at home with us, which I fancy she has not yet done," was the reply of Mr. Chandos, looking at me with a smile. Lady Chandos simply bowed her head.

"Oh, she is one who always gives you the notion of being shy," carelessly replied Emily, as she ran up the staircase.

What was I to do? I could not say to her, "You shall take me;" but, after the conversation I had overheard, it was most unpleasant to me to stay. I ran after Emily. I told her that my remaining might not be really agreeable to Lady and Mr. Chandos. Her reply was, that they must make it agreeable, for there was no accommodation for me at Madame de Mellissie's.

"Look here, Anne; don't be shy and stupid. I cannot drop you in the street like a waif, en route, and I cannot take you home. Suppose Alfred's illness should turn to typhus-fever? Would it be well for you to be there? But there's no room for you, and that's the fact."

I disclosed to her my penniless condition, for some of my poor twenty-five shillings had melted on the journey from Paris, and I had only fifteen left. I begged her to lend me some money, and I would find my way alone to Nulle. Emily laughed heartily, but she did not give me any.

"I shall be back next week, child. Make yourself easy."

By midday she was gone, Pauline attending her, and Mr. Chandos escorting her to the station. I was left, with the words I had heard spoken, as to my unwelcome presence in the house, beating their refrain on my brain, Whether Lady Chandos remonstrated privately with her daughter against leaving me, or whether she recognized it as a sort of necessity, and tacitly acquiesced in the arrangement, I had no means of knowing.

What was I to do with myself? Put on my things and go out? There was nothing else to do. As I came down with them on, Lady Chandos met me in the hall.

"Are you going out, Miss Hereford?"

"If you have no objection, madam. But I was only going because I felt at a loss for something to occupy myself with. Perhaps you can give me something to do, Lady Chandos?"

"I cannot aid you, I believe. It is a pity Madame de Mellissie should have left you here, for I fear you will find it dull; but I suppose there was no help for it, I speak for your sake, my dear," she kindly added.

"I should be so glad to do anything for you. I can sew."

"My maids do the sewing," she said. "You will find some pleasant walks in the vicinity. There is one to the left, as you leave the gates, exceedingly rural and quiet. You will be quite safe; it is an honest neighbourhood."

I found the walk she spoke of and stayed out for nearly two hours. Not a single house, except one, did I pass. I found afterwards that what few houses there were lay to the right. This one stood in view of the entrance-gates, nearly opposite to the lodge; a substantial, moderate-sized house, closed at present, and displaying a board—"To Let." I had half a mind to open its front-gate and explore the garden, but I had been out long enough, and turned to Chandos.

I was not to go home without an adventure. In passing through the small iron gate, by the side of the large ones, an awfully fierce great dog sprang forward, savagely barking. Back I flew, and shut the gate between us: why he did not leap over the gate, I don't know; he stood there barking, and rattling part of a chain that was attached to his collar. Never having been brought into contact with dogs, I was terribly afraid of fierce ones, and cowered there in an agony of fear, not daring to run away, lest the angry animal should leap the gate and spring upon me.

Footsteps came behind me, and I looked round, hoping for protection. It was Mr. Chandos. He saw what was the matter, and seemed to make but one bound to the gate.

"Stay there, Miss Hereford!"

He passed quietly through, and confronted the dog; the dog confronted him, barking still.

"Nero!"

The voice allayed the angry passions, and the dog stepped up. Mr. Chandos seized the end of the chain.

"You and I must have a settling for this, Nero. Will you come here, Miss Hereford, and I will teach him to know you, so that he does not alarm you again, should he get loose. He must have broken his chain."

"Oh, sir! Pray do not make me come near him!"

Mr. Chandos turned his face quickly towards me. "Are you afraid of dogs?"

"Rather, sir. I am of that one."

At this juncture, a groom came running up, in search of the dog. Mr. Chandos spoke sharply to him, and the man answered, in a tone of deprecation, that it was no fault of his; that the dog sometimes, in his fits of effort to get loose was as a "born devil," and in one of those fits had, a quarter-of-an-hour before, snapped his chain, and burst through the stable window.

"He has run the fit off, then," said Mr. Chandos, "for he is quiet enough now. Take him back, and mind you secure him well."

The man took the chain in his hand, and went off, leading the dog. Mr. Chandos opened the gate for me. I had not overcome the fright yet, and my face felt ashy pale.

"My poor child! It has indeed frightened you. Do you feel faint?"

"I shall not faint, sir. I never fainted in my life."

Without the least ceremony, he placed my hand within his arm, and walked on. A little to the right, underneath some thick cypress trees, there was a bench. He bade me sit down, and seated himself beside me.

"You will be all the better for resting here a minute or two. How did it happen? Where did you and Mr. Nero encounter each other?"

"I had been out walking, sir. Lady Chandos told me of a pretty walk there is to the left, outside the gates. In coming back, I was just inside the gate, when the dog came up, leaping and barking."

"And you were frightened?"

"Very much frightened. Had I not occasion, sir? One moment later, and he might have torn me to pieces."

"It is my dog," he resumed, "and I am exceedingly sorry he should have given you alarm. Will you return good for evil?"

"Good for evil! In what manner, sir?" I asked.

"By not mentioning this to my mother," he replied. "She has a great dislike to dogs being kept on the premises. Some few months ago, when a friend of mine was dying, he asked me to take his dog—this one which has just frightened you—but Lady Chandos would only consent to its coming here on condition that it should be kept tied up. It is a valuable dog though fierce on occasions, the confinement to which it is for the most part condemned making it more fierce. I will take care it does not break bounds again, and I would prefer that my mother should not know of this."

"I will not tell her, sir. I suppose Lady Chandos dislike dogs as much as I do?"

"She does not dislike dogs: she rather likes them. But she objects—at least, she has objected latterly—to having them loose about the premises."

"She fears their going mad, perhaps?"

Mr. Chandos laughed. "No, she does not fear that. I must make you and Nero friends, Miss Hereford; you will then find how little he is to be dreaded. You shall come to the stable with me when he is chained up fast. How long have you known my sister?" he resumed, changing the subject.

"I knew her a little at Mademoiselle Barlieu's. I entered the school just before she left it."

"Then you must have known—have known—the circumstances under which she quitted it?"

He had begun the sentence rapidly, as if impelled to it by impulse, but after the hesitation, continued it more slowly.

"Yes, sir. They could not be kept from the school."

"A mad act—a mad act!" he murmured; "and—if I may read signs—heartily repented of. It is, I fancy, an exemplification of the old saying, Miss Hereford, 'Marry in haste, and repent at leisure.' Poor Emily has leisure enough for it before her: she is only beginning life. I went over at the time to Mademoiselle Barlieu's."

"Yes, sir; I saw you when you were going away, and I hid myself in a niche of the hall while you passed. I knew you again as soon as I met you here."

"You must have a good memory for faces, then," he said, laughing.

"I think a circumstance made me recollect you, sir. It was, that your face struck upon me at Mademoiselle Barlieu's as being familiar to my memory; I felt sure that if I had not seen you before, I had seen some one very like you."

He turned and looked at me a full minute ere he spoke.

"Who was it, Miss Hereford?"

"I cannot tell, sir. I wish I could tell. The resemblance in your face haunts me still."

"It's not much of a face to remember," he slightingly said, as a stout gentleman came through the entrance-gates. He carried a roll of paper, or parchment, and was wiping his brows, his hat off.

"You look warm, Dexter," called out Mr. Chandos.

"It's a close day for autumn, sir, and I walked over," was the response of the new-comer, as he turned out of the great drive and came up. "I'm glad to catch you at home, Mr. Chandos. I have had an offer for this house."

Mr. Chandos made room for him to sit down. "I have been turning myself into a knight-errant, Dexter; delivering a lady from the fangs of a ferocious dog."

Mr. Dexter looked as if he did not know whether to take the words in jest or earnest.

"That dog of mine got loose, and terrified this young lady nearly out of her life. I really do not know but he would have attacked her, had I not come home at the very moment. She is sitting here to gain breath and courage. About the house? which house do you mean?"

"I speak of the house opposite your lodge-gates, sir," resumed Mr. Dexter, after giving me a polite nod. "Haines came over to me this morning, saying a gentleman wished to take it, and required to enter immediately."

"What gentleman? Who is he?"

"Nobody belonging to this neighbourhood, sir: a stranger. Haines spoke of a Mr. Freshfield; but was not clear upon the point whether it was for Mr. Freshfield himself, or for a friend of Mr. Freshfield's. It's all perfectly right, Haines says; he will be answerable for that; rent as safe as if it were paid beforehand."

"Well, I shall be glad to let the house," returned Mr. Chandos. "You need not rise, Miss Hereford; we are not discussing secrets. It has been empty these nine months, you know, Dexter; and empty houses bring no good to themselves."

"Very true, sir. I had an offer for it some days back, and did not trouble you with it, for I know you would not have accepted the tenant. It was that Major Mann, and his rough lot," added Mr. Dexter, dropping his voice.

"Oh," shortly replied Mr. Chandos, his lip curling. "I should be sorry to have them within hail of my gates."

"I was sure of that. He pressed hard, though; seemed to have taken a fancy for the place. I put him off as civilly as I could: it's no use to make enemies of people, where it can be helped. 'My Lady Chandos will only let it to a quiet tenant,' I told him. 'Wants a Darby and Joan, perhaps?' said he, turning up his nose. 'Something of that sort, major,' I answered; and so the thing dropped through. Haines assures me the present applicant is most respectable; all that could be desired."

"Very well, Dexter, I give you power to treat. You know who would be acceptable and who not, just as well as I do."

"Haines wants the bargain to be concluded to-day, sir," said Mr. Dexter, rising. "He has orders to furnish at once."

"Is Haines going to furnish?"

"As it appears. I should fancy it may be for some one arriving from abroad. There's plenty of money, Haines says. I had better put a man or two on to the garden at once, had I not, sir?"

"Yes. And don't have those complaints about the locks, Dexter, as we had, you may remember, when the last house on the estate was let. Let them be examined throughout."

"I'm off, then," said Mr. Dexter. "Good-day, sir. My respects to my lady. Good-day, ma'am."

"Good-day," I answered.

"Possessions bring trouble, Miss Hereford," cried Mr. Chandos, as Mr. Dexter moved away. "There are several houses on this estate, and they are almost as much plague as profit. One tenant finds fault and grumbles; another must have this, that, and the other done; a third runs away, leaving no rent behind him, and his premises dilapidated. Our last agent was not a desirable one; accepted tenants who were not eligible, and did not look after details. He died some months back, and a pretty game we found he had been carrying on; grinding the tenants down, and cheating us. Dexter, recently appointed, appears to be a keen man of business, and straightforward: that is, as agents go: they are none of them too honest."

"I think I should let the houses for myself, sir, on my own estate, and not employ an agent."

"Do you mean that as a piece of advice to me, Miss Hereford?" be returned, smiling. "What I might do on my own estate, I cannot answer for: but this one is not mine. It belongs to my brother, Sir Thomas Chandos. The mistress of it for the time being is my mother; but I take the trouble off her hands. Here's Dexter coming back again!"

"It is not often I go away and leave half my errand undone, though I have this time," Mr. Dexter called out as he came up, and extended the roll of paper he held. "This is the plan of the proposed alteration in the stables at the farm, sir, which you wished to look over. Shall I carry it to the house?"

"By no means. I'll carry it myself, if you will give it me," replied

Mr. Chandos. And the agent finally departed.

"Are you sufficiently rested, Miss Hereford?"

My answer was to rise and proceed towards the house. Mr. Chandos, walking by my side, seemed absorbed in the roll, which he had partially opened. On the right the drive leading to the stables branched off. I was glad that Mr. Chandos passed on, and did not propose to go to Nero then. Lady Chandos came forward as we were entering the portico.

"What is this—about the dog attacking you, Miss Hereford?" she exclaimed.

I was so taken aback, after the wish expressed by Mr. Chandos, and the promise I had given him, that I remained like a stupid mute. He answered.

"Nero got loose, mother. Miss Hereford was in the act of entering the gate—or had just entered, was it not, Miss Hereford?—and he like a castle's zealous watch-dog, prevented her advancing further."

"Did he touch you, Miss Hereford?" Lady Chandos asked, turning to me.

"He was not quick enough, madam: I ran back beyond the gate. My fear was, that he would leap over; but he did not. Perhaps it was too high."

"But he would have attacked you had you not gone back?"

"I think he would. He seemed very savage."

"Harry, this is just what I have feared," Lady Chandos observed to her son, in a peculiarly significant tone. "A fierce, powerful dog like that *is* liable to break his chain and get loose; and I have said so to you over and over again. He would attack a stranger—any one he did not know, and might cause a fearful disturbance. You know why I have feared this."

"The stables are safely closed at night, mother," was the somewhat curious reply of Mr. Chandos.

"Robin says the dog sprang through the window; dashed through the glass. There can be no security against that, day or night."

"My opinion is, that some of the men must have been teasing him, and so worked him into a fury. I shall inquire into it, and if I find it to be the fact, whoever did it shall go. Better precaution shall be observed for the future."

"Yes," said Lady Chandos, in decisive tones, "and that precaution must be sending away the dog."

"But really, mother, there is no necessity."

"Harry, I am surprised at you. You know why I urge it: why I ought to urge it."

The conversation did not make me feel very comfortable, and I interposed. "I do beg that no change may be made on my account, Lady Chandos. No harm is done. I am not hurt."

"It is not on your account I am speaking, Miss Hereford. And—as you are not hurt—I am pleased that the thing has happened, because it must prove to Mr. Chandos the necessity for sending away the dog. He could not see it previously."

"I should see it equally with you, mother, were the dog to be insecurely fastened. But if we make him secure—"

"You deemed him secure now," she interrupted. "I will not risk it. Good Heavens, Harry! have you forgotten the stake?"

"What stake?" I thought, as I went up to my room. Certainly the words savoured of something that I could not comprehend.

Standing at the window at the head of the stairs was the young lady whom they called Mrs. Chandos. She wore a bonnet and shawl, and spoke as I approached.

"I do believe it is raining!"

"Yes," I replied; "some drops were falling when I came in." But it appeared that Mrs. Chandos, when she spoke, had not thought she was addressing me, for she turned round in astonishment at the sound of my voice.

"Oh—I beg your pardon," she coldly said. And then I saw that she had a white kitten in her arms. I went into my room but did not close the door, and in a minute I heard the approach of Mrs. Freeman.

"Did you ever know anything so tiresome?" exclaimed Mrs. Chandos to her. "It is raining fast. I am sure it is not once in a month, hardly, that I make up my mind to walk in the grounds, but so sure as I do, I am prevented. It rains; or it snows; or it's too hot; or there's thunder in the air! It comes on purpose, I know."

"Perhaps it will not be much," replied Mrs. Freeman; who, by the sound of her voice, appeared to be also now looking out at the window.

"It will: look at those clouds, gathering fast into one thick mass. O—oh!" she added, with a shiver, "I don't like to hear the dripping of the rain on the trees: it puts me in mind of—of—"

"Of what, my dear?" asked Mrs. Freeman.

"Of the night I first heard those awful tidings. It was raining then, a steady, soaking rain, and I had been listening to its falling on the leaves till the monotony of the sound worried me, and I began wishing *he* was at home. Not on these trees, you know; we were at the other place. Drop, drop, drop; as the rain never sounds but where there are trees for it to fall on. The opening of the room-door interrupted me, and my lady came in. Ah! I shall never forget her; her face was white, her eyes looked wild, her hands were lifted; I saw there was something dreadful to be told. She sat down, and drawing me to her, said—"

"Hush—sh—sh!" interposed Mrs. Freeman, with quick caution. "You may be speaking for other ears than mine."

"I was not going to allude to facts," was the retort of Mrs. Chandos, her tone peevish at the interruption. "My lady asked me if I could bear trouble; fiery trouble, such as had rarely overtaken one in my rank of life before; and my answer was to fall into a fainting-fit at her feet. Never, since then, have I liked to hear the rain pattering down on the leaves where the trees are thick."

I would have shut my door, but feared it might look ungracious to do so. They had eyes, and could see that it was open, if they pleased to look; therefore they might choose their subjects accordingly. Mrs. Chandos resumed.

"Who *is* that young lady? She came up the stairs, and I spoke without looking round, thinking it was you."

"I don't know who. A Miss Hereford. She came here with Madame de Mellissie as travelling companion."

"But she is a stranger to Lady Chandos?"

"Entirely so."

"Then why does Lady Chandos permit her to be here? Is it well, in this house of misfortune? Is it prudent?"

"Scarcely so. Of course Lady Chandos can only hope—how you are squeezing that kitten, my dear!"

"Pretty little thing! it likes to be squeezed," responded Mrs. Chandos. "It is hiding itself from you; from that ugly bonnet. You do wear frightful bonnets, Mrs. Freeman; as ugly as the black ones of Lady Chandos."

"I do not think widows' bonnets ugly," was the reply of Mrs. Freeman. "To some faces they are particularly becoming."

"They are so ugly, so disfiguring, that I hope it will be long before I am called upon to wear them," returned Mrs. Chandos, speaking impulsively. "Were my husband to die—but there! I know what you want to say; why do I dwell upon trifles such as bonnets, when heavy calamities are on the house?"

"Suppose you walk about the gallery, my dear?" suggested Mrs. Freeman. "I see no chance of the rain leaving off."

"No, I'll go back and take my things off, and play with pussy. Poor pussy wanted a walk in the grounds as much as. I did. Oh,"—with a shriek—"it's gone!"

For the kitten, allured, perhaps, by the attractions of a promenade in the grounds, had leaped from the arms of Mrs. Chandos on to a shrub below. I saw it from my window. The shriek brought out Mr. Chandos from the house; he looked up.

"My kitten, Harry," she said. "It has flown away from me. Get it, will you? But I am sorry to give you the trouble."

Mr. Chandos took the kitten from the bush and once more looked up; at my window as well as at theirs.

"Who will come for it? Will you, Miss Hereford?—and oblige

my—oblige Mrs. Chandos."

Oblige my *what?* Was he going to say "sister-in-law" when he suddenly stopped himself? But, if so, why should he have stopped himself? And how could she be his sister-in-law? Were she the wife of Sir Thomas, she would be Lady Chandos; and Emily had said her brother Thomas was not married. She had said she had only two brothers, Thomas and Harry; who, then, was this young Mrs. Chandos? That she had a husband living was apparent, from the conversation I had just heard; and I had imagined all along that she must be the daughter-in-law of Lady Chandos.

These thoughts passed through my head as I ran down for the kitten. Mr. Chandos handed it to me, and turned away, for he was called to by some one at a distance. At the same moment the kitten was taken from my hands. It was by Mrs. Freeman, who had also come down.

"I hope it is not hurt, poor thing," she said, looking at it. "It seems lively enough."

"Mr. Chandos said it was not hurt, when he gave it to me."

"Oh, that's right. Had it been hurt, Mrs. Chandos would have grieved over it. She is fond of this kitten; and she has so few pleasures, poor child!"

"Who *is* Mrs. Chandos?" I asked, in a low tone.

"Madam?" returned Mrs. Freeman.

The tone—cold, haughty, reserved—struck me as conveying the keenest reproach for my unjustifiable curiosity; unjustifiable so far as that I had betrayed it. I faltered forth the question again—for she seemed looking at me and waiting; and it might be that she had not heard it.

"Who is Mrs. Chandos?"

"Mrs. Chandos?" was the answer. "Who should she be? She is Mrs. Chandos." And Mrs. Freeman stalked away.

That same evening at dusk, the dog Nero was taken away. A few words spoken by Hickens to his master enlightened me as to the exit.

"Is he going to be shot?" I asked, impulsively, of Mr. Chandos.

"Oh no. A farmer living near has promised to take care of him."

But the tone was not quite so free as usual, and I said no more.

# CHAPTER 13

## A SHOCK

The time passed monotonously. Always looking upon myself as an intruder, I could not feel at home at Chandos. A letter arrived in course of post from Emily de Mellissie, saying she had found her husband certainly ill, but not as much so as "la mère" had been willing to lead them to expect. In a few days she should write and fix the date of her return. I was at a loss what to do in more senses than one. Not liking to sit down to the piano uninvited—and no one did invite me—it remained closed. Now and then, when I knew that neither Lady Chandos nor her son was at home, I would play quietly for a few minutes—stealthily might be the better term. Twice Lady Chandos took me for a drive; she went herself every day; generally taking Mrs. Chandos. The latter I very rarely saw at any time.

And so I was reduced to walking and reading. Newspapers, books, and reviews lay about the room. Had I been anything of a dressmaker, I should have made up the dresses bought in Paris, failing the money to give them out; as it was, they lay in my large trunk, unmade. Mr. Chandos had told me the books in the library were at my service, and I chose some of them.

One morning, when I had gone there to get a book, Lady Chandos, passing the door, saw me and came in. I was standing before a book-case in the darkest part of the room; before which the inner curtains had always been drawn. They were undrawn now, but the doors were locked as usual.

"Are you searching for a book, Miss Hereford?"

"Yes, madam. Amidst so many—"

The sight of Lady Chandos's face caused my sentence to fail. The evident astonishment with which she gazed on the bookcase; the displeased, nay, the dismayed, expression of her countenance, was something curious. In my timidity, I feared she might think I had undrawn the curtains. There appeared to be books of all kinds, shapes, and sizes, inside; pamphlets and loose papers. Mr. Chandos happened to come out of his room, and she called him.

"Harry," she began, in sharp, authoritative tones, "who has been at this book-case, and left the curtains undrawn?"

"It must have been Mrs. Chandos," he replied, advancing to his mother's side. "The doors are locked, I see; there's no great harm done."

"No harm!" repeated Lady Chandos; "look here."

She pointed to a name written on the white paper cover of one of the books. Mr. Chandos knitted his brow as he bent closer.

"Very thoughtless of her; very negligent," murmured Lady Chandos. "I have said before the keys ought not to be entrusted to Ethel."

As I quitted the room quietly, not liking to remain in it, I saw Mr. Chandos take a bunch of keys from his pocket; and, subsequently, heard the silk curtains drawn close, and the doors relocked. Never should I feel free to go to the bookcase again. I had one volume of Shakespeare out, and must make the most of it.

We were having lovely days, and this was one of them. I strolled out, the book in my hand. But, before settling to read, I went to the gates to see how they were getting on with the opposite house. They had been busy furnishing it for two or three days, and I—for want of something better to do—had taken an interest in it, and watched the things going in. It appeared all in order this morning; there was no bustle, no litter; curtains were up, blinds were half-drawn, and smoke was ascending from more than one chimney. The tenant or tenants must have arrived and taken possession.

As I stood leaning over the small side-gate, there came out of that house a man; a gentleman, to appearance; short, and with a dark face. But of the latter I caught only a passing glimpse, for he turned his back immediately to look up at the front of the house. Calling to a man-servant, he appeared to be pointing out something that he wished done, or finding fault with something that had been left undone. I could not hear the words, but I could the tones; they were authoritative, as was his manner. He was evidently the master.

I thought I had seen him before, for there was something in his figure, and even in the passing sight of his face, which struck upon me as being familiar. I waited for him to turn again, that I might obtain a better view; but he did not, and soon went in. I walked back to a shady bench, and began reading. It was underneath the trees that shaded the side of the broad open walk. Presently the sound of two people, apparently encountering each other, reached me from behind the shrubs.

"Are you here alone, Ethel?" was asked by Mr. Chandos.

"Yes, I took a fancy to come; I and my kitten. Mrs. Freeman said wait an hour or two, and perhaps she could come with me. She is ill."

"What ails her?"

"I don't know. She often complains now; pains come in her head."

"Did you unlock the book-case in the library and leave the curtains undrawn?"

"What book-case?" returned Mrs. Chandos.

"*That* book-case."

"What next, Harry! As if I should do anything of the sort!"

"You had the keys last night. And no one opens that bookcase but yourself."

"I did open that book-case, I remember, and undraw the curtains; I thought they were dusty, but I'm sure I thought I drew them again. I'm very sorry."

"Be more cautious for the future, Ethel. Lady Chandos is vexed. You see, while this young lady is in the house—"

"But I cannot see what business she has in the library," interrupted Mrs. Chandos, in a quick, complaining tone. "A stranger has no right to the run of the house. I think you must all be out of your minds to have her here at all."

"In regard to the library, Ethel, I told her—"

They were the last words that reached me. Mrs. Chandos, ever changeable, was walking rapidly to the house again.

Presently Mr. Chandos came down the broad walk, saw me, and approached.

"Are you fond of Shakespeare's works?" he asked, when he knew what I was reading.

"I have never read them, sir."

"Never read them!" he cried, in surprise. "You cannot mean that, Miss Hereford."

"But, sir, I have always been at school. And school-girls have no opportunity for obtaining such works. At my English school, Miss Fenton's, there were some volumes of Shakespeare in the governess's private parlour; but I never saw anything of them but their backs."

"Have you never read Byron?"

"Oh no."

"Nor any novels?"

"Not any books of that kind."

He looked at me with a half-smile, standing with his back against a tree. "I think I understood from my sister that you are an orphan?"

"Yes, sir."

"Have you no home?"

"I have neither home nor relatives. The place that seems more like a home to me than any other is Mademoiselle Barlieu's, at Nulle. I was there four years."

"Did you never get any French novels there?"

"Indeed no."

"My sister told me she did."

"I don't see how that could have been, sir, unless she read them when she was out. Miss Chandos visited a great deal."

"Yes, to her cost."

He drew in his lips when he spoke, as one in pain, and his blue eyes—they were so dark as to be purple in some lights—went out far away, as if looking into the past.

"We were too closely superintended to admit of our reading any books, unless by permission; as to novels, the Miss Barlieus would have been in fits at the thought. And since I left them I have been too fully occupied to read for recreation. This is the first leisure time I have had for nearly as long as I can remember."

"Indeed! It must seem strange to you."

"So strange, sir, that I am not sure whether I like it or not." Mr. Chandos laughed. "Did you visit much, when you were at Nulle?"

"No, sir. I had not a friend in the town. Towards the last, Miss Annette would sometimes take me when she went out to spend the evening."

"Will you allow me to direct your reading, Miss Hereford?" he returned, after a pause.

"Oh, sir, if you would!" I answered eagerly. "For, in truth, that library seems to me like a wild sea, with its multitude of books."

"Yes; and a young lady might fall amidst shoals; for all the books are not equally worthy!"

"Perhaps, sir, you will look out a few and give to me."

"I will, with pleasure."

"Thank you. Meanwhile, may I go on with this, as I have begun it?"

He left the tree, took the book from my hand and looked at it. "'Othello;' yes, you may read that."

As he returned the book to me and resumed his position against the tree, some one approached from the outer gate. I thought it was a visitor. He came strolling on in the very middle of the broad avenue, his arms underneath his coat-tails; and soon I perceived it was the gentleman I had seen at the newly-occupied house, giving his directions to the servant. But ah! as he neared us, remembrance, with its cold chill of terror, struck upon my heart. I knew him instantly. It was Mr. Edwin Barley. Mr. Edwin Barley, and not in the least altered.

"Do you want anything, sir?" demanded Mr. Chandos. For the intruder was passing us without ceremony, and turning his head about from side to side as curiously and freely as he might have done on the public road.

"I don't want anything," was the independent answer, and Mr. Edwin Barley stood and faced Mr. Chandos as he spoke it, looking at him keenly. "The open air is free to walk in, I believe."

"Quite so—when you are without those boundaries. But these are private property."

"I am aware that they are the grounds belonging to Chandos House; but I did not know a stranger might not be permitted to walk in them."

"Lady Chandos prefers privacy. Strangers are not in the habit of entering here; nor can their doing so be sanctioned."

"I presume that I am speaking to Mr. Harry Chandos?"

Mr. Chandos bowed his head, very coldly. Mr. Edwin Barley bowed in his turn; it might have been called an introduction.

"I will retreat," he said, "and I suppose I must beg your pardon for intruding. It did not occur to me that my strolling in might be unwelcome."

Mr. Chandos said nothing to detain him, and Mr. Edwin Barley raised his hat and departed. Mr. Chandos returned the courtesy, and looked after him.

"Who can he be, I wonder? I don't much like his face."

"I think it is the new tenant, sir. I saw him at the house just now."

"*He* the tenant!" returned Mr. Chandos. "Miss Hereford, what is the matter with you? You are as white as that statue."

I turned it off, giving no explanation; and Mr. Chandos walked towards the gate. I dare say I did look white, for the sight of Mr. Edwin Barley brought back all the old horror of the events that had occurred during my sojourn in his house. Not that it was so much the recollection that drove the colour from my cheeks, as the dread fear that he should recognize me; though why I should have feared it, I did not know. Little chance was there of that—had I been calm enough to judge the matter sensibly. While Mr. Edwin Barley had remained stationary in appearance, I had changed from a child into a woman.

But what had led to Mr. Edwin Barley entering as the tenant of that small and inferior house? he, with his fine fortune and his fine estates! There seemed to be mystery enough at Chandos! was this going to be another mystery?

"I believe you must be right, Miss Hereford; he has entered the house," said Mr. Chandos, returning. "If he is really the new tenant—as I suppose he is—he appears by no means a prepossessing one. I wonder what his name may be?"

I could not, for the whole world, have told Mr. Chandos that I knew his name; I could not have told that I knew him. All my hope was that it would never be betrayed that I had known him, that he was any connection of mine, or that he would ever recognize me. What, what could have brought Edwin Barley to Chandos?

# CHAPTER 14

## THE NEW TENANT BY THE LODGE-GATES

The new tenant by the lodge-gates! And it was Edwin Barley! What could have brought him to Chandos?

Was it to look after me?

The conviction that it was so, fixed itself in my mind with startling force, and I grew nearly as sick with fear as I had been when I was a little child. That he was personally unknown to the Chandos family was evident: it seemed a strange thing that he should come and plant himself down at their very gates as soon as I became an inmate of the house. Had he in some crafty manner made himself acquainted with my entrance to it the very hour it took place? Surely it must have been so. And he had lost no time in following.

When once suspicion connected with fear arises in man's mind, or in woman's, the most trifling circumstances are allowed to confirm it. Events, however unconnected with it in reality, accidental coincidences that have no rapport (I'm afraid that's a French word, but I can't help it) with it whatever, are converted by the suggestive imagination into suspicious proofs, and looked upon as links in the chain. It might have occurred to my mind—it did occur to it—that it was just within the range of possibility that Mr. Edwin Barley's advent had nothing whatever to do with me or my presence at Chandos, that it might be wholly unconnected with it, and he ignorant of it and of who I was; but I threw this view away at once in my fear, and did not glance at it a second time. Edwin Barley had come to Chandos because I was there, and no power of reasoning could have removed this impression from me. All these years, and he had never (so far as appeared) sought to put himself in personal connection with the family: why should he have done it now, save for my presence in it?

Thought is quick. Before Mr. Chandos returned to me from watching Edwin Barley out at the lodge-gates and across the road, I had gone over it all in my mind, and arrived at my unpleasant conviction. Some dim idea of putting as great a space of ground between me and him as was practicable, caused me to rise hastily from the garden-chair and turn to go indoors. Mr. Chandos walked by my side, talking of various things—the leaves that were beginning to fall, the fineness of the early autumn day, the discontent of Mr. Nero in his new home at the farmer's—having apparently forgotten already the episode of the intrusion. I answered in monosyllables, scarcely knowing what, my mind full of its new trouble.

I had done no harm during my short sojourn at Mr. Edwin Barley's, in those long past days; I had never heard of or from him since; he had never, so far as I knew, inquired after me; so why should I fear him now? I cannot answer this: I have never been able to answer it—no, not even since things, dark and mysterious then, have been made clear. The fear had taken possession of me, and probably seemed all the worse because it was vague and inexplicable.

Luncheon was on the table when we turned into the oak-parlour, and Lady Chandos ready for it. Hickens was opening a bottle of claret.

"Harry, Hickens says that our new tenant has arrived," observed Lady Chandos.

We were sitting down then, and Mr. Chandos did not immediately reply. Perhaps Hickens thought the news required confirmation, for he turned round from the sideboard.

"The gentleman took possession last night, sir; so Brooks tells me: himself and four or five servants. It is only a single gentleman; there's no family. Immensely rich, they say."

"Do you know who he is, Harry?" pursued Lady Chandos.

"I don't know who he is, but I have just seen himself," replied Mr. Chandos. "He came in at our gates, deeming Chandos public property. I had to warn him off by telling him it was private."

"What did he want?" asked Lady Chandos.

"Nothing, except to look about him. Had I known he was your new tenant, I might not have been in so great a hurry to eject him."

"Oh, but, Harry, it was as well to do it. Better to let him understand from the first that we cannot have strangers entering here at will. It would not suit me, you know; I like privacy."

"That is what I told him."

"I suppose you were civil?"

"Quite civil, both of us—on the surface, at any rate. I did not take to him at first sight; that is, to his looks; and I don't fancy he took to me. There was something peculiar in the tone of his voice, and he eyed me as though he wished to take my photograph."

"He did not know you, I dare say."

"He said he supposed he was speaking to Mr. Harry Chandos. Perhaps he thought it discourteous to be warned off in that manner. Not that he looks like one to go in for much courtesy himself: there was an air of independence about him *alrnost* bordering upon insolence. This young lady, I fancy, was not prepossessed in his favour."

I had sat with my head bent on my plate, trying to seem unconcerned, as if the matter were no business of mine. The sudden address of Mr. Chandos turned my face crimson. Lady Chandos looked at me.

"He—is very ugly," I stammered in my perplexity.

"Is he?" she cried, turning to her son.

"He is rather ill-favoured, mother; a short, dark man. There is one redeeming feature in his face; his teeth. They are small, white, and regular: very beautiful."

"What is his name?"

"I don't know," said Mr. Chandos.

"Not know his name!" repeated Lady Chandos, laughing slightly; "and yet you accepted him as tenant!"

"Oh, well, Dexter made all the arrangements. I did not interfere personally."

"I think, before I accepted a man as tenant, I should make myself acquainted with his name," spoke Lady Chandos, in a half-joking tone, evidently attaching no importance to the matter. "Do you happen to have heard it, Hickens?"

"No, my lady."

"We shall learn it soon enough," carelessly observed Mr. Chandos. "A man may not make a less desirable tenant because he happens not to have a handsome face. Tastes differ, you know, Miss Hereford. Were we all bought and sold by our looks, what a squabbling of opinions there'd be!"

The meal was nearly over, when a startling interruption occurred. Mrs. Chandos burst wildly into the room, agitated, trembling; her hands raised, her face ashy white. Mr. Chandos threw down his knife and fork, and rose in consternation.

"Oh, Lady Chandos! Oh, Harry!" came the words, almost in a shriek. "Do come! She has fallen on the carpet in a fit—or something of the sort. I think she may be dying!"

"Excited again, Ethel!" observed Lady Chandos, the perfect calmness of her tone presenting a curious contrast to the other. "When will you learn to take trifles quietly and rationally? Who has fallen? The white kitten?"

Mrs. Chandos did not like the reproach. "There's nothing to blame me for this time," she said, with a sob of vehemence. "It is Mrs. Freeman. She is lying there on the floor, looking frightful. I am not sure but she's dead."

"Take care of her, Harry," said Lady Chandos. "I will see what it is."

"Shall I go?" he asked. "It may be better. You can stay with Ethel."

Lady Chandos only answered by waving him back, as she quitted the room. Mrs. Chandos trembled excessively, and Mr. Chandos placed her in an easy-chair.

"Calm yourself, Ethel—as my mother says."

"What nonsense you talk, Harry! As if every one could have their feelings under control as she has—as you have! Time was when I was calm and heedless enough, Heaven knows, but since—since—you know?"

"Yes, yes; be still now. I think you might acquire a little more self-control if you tried, considering that excitement does you so much harm."

"It weakens me; it lays me prostrate for three or four days. I don't know what other harm it does me."

"Is not that enough? Where is Mrs. Freeman?"

"She is in my dining-room. I will tell you what happened. We were at luncheon—that is, I was, for she sat by the window, and would not take any: she has complained of illness latterly, as I told you. 'I think you might take a little of this fowl,' I said to her; 'it is very nice.' Well, she made no answer; so I spoke again. Still she said nothing, and I got up to look at her, wondering whether she could have dropped asleep in a minute. I went round the chair, and there she was with a face drawn in the most frightful manner you can conceive, and the next moment she had slipped from the chair to the carpet. And you and Lady Chandos blame me for not retaining my calmness."

"Will you take anything?" he inquired, pointing to the luncheon-tray; and it struck me that he wished to get the scene she had described out of her memory.

"No, thank you. The sight of Mrs. Freeman has taken my appetite away. Suppose you come and see her for yourself: I don't mind going with you."

Mrs. Chandos put her arm within his, and they departed. Hill ran upstairs; two or three of the maids followed her. Hickens looked after them in curiosity, and then came back to his luncheon-table. Not to be in the way of any one, I went up to my room.

For some hours I saw none of them. There was bustle in the house. Lady Chandos's voice I heard now and then, and once I caught a glimpse of Mr. Chandos in the grounds. Growing tired of my confinement, I looked out, and asked a maid-servant, who was passing in the corridor, what had been the matter.

"It was a sort of fit, miss, but she's better now," was Harriet's reply. "The doctor says she must be still, and have rest for some time to come, and she is going away this evening."

"Going away! Do you speak of Mrs. Freeman?"

"Yes, miss. She is going by her own choice. She has a sister who lives about thirteen miles from this, and she wishes to go at once to her house. My lady urged her to wait, at any rate until to-morrow, but Mrs. Freeman said she would rather go, especially as she can be of no further use at present to Mrs. Chandos. They have a suspicion that she fears another attack, and thinks she had better get to her sister's without delay. So it's all settled, and Hill is to accompany her."

Harriet departed, leaving my door on the latch. I sat, reading and listening by turns, and presently there sounded two more encountering voices outside. Those of Lady Chandos and Hill, her attendant.

"My lady," said the latter, in one of those loud whispers which penetrate to the ear more than open speaking, "is it right that I should go to-night? I could not allude to it before Mrs. Chandos."

"Why should it not be right, Hill?"

"It is the full of the moon, my lady."

Lady Chandos paused before replying, possibly in reflection. "There is no help for it, Hill," she said, at last. "Mrs. Freeman is too ill to be trusted to the care of any one but you."

The carriage was brought to the lower door in the wing, unbarred and unbolted for the occasion, and Mrs. Freeman was taken down the enclosed stairs to it, by Mr. Chandos and the doctor, so that I and my curiosity saw nothing of the exit, which I looked upon as an unmerited wrong. She was placed in the carriage, and Hill and the doctor went with her.

It was getting near dinner-time. I scarcely knew whether to go down or not, or whether there would be any dinner at all, in the state of confusion the house seemed to be in, when my doubt was solved by Lady Chandos herself. Looking out at my door, she passed me, coming along the gallery from her own room.

"I think dinner is ready, Miss Hereford?"

Following her downstairs, I saw Mr. Dexter, the agent, in the open portico, having at that moment, as it appeared, come to the house. Lady Chandos crossed the hall to speak to him. He put a sealed parcel, or thick letter into her hands.

"I beg your pardon, my lady. As I was passing here, I brought up these papers for Mr. Chandos. The new tenant opposite says there's something amiss with the roof of the coach-house, and I'm going to call and look at it."

Lady Chandos glanced casually at the letter she held; and then a thought seemed to strike her.

"What is the name of the new tenant, Mr. Dexter?"

"Barley, my lady. Mr. Edwin Barley."

There was a startled pause. Lady Chandos suddenly put her hand to her heart, as if some pang had taken it.

"Barley!" she repeated. "Edwin Barley! Do you know whether he comes from Hallam?"

"Hallam?—Hallam?" debated Mr. Dexter with himself, in consideration. "Yes, that *is* the place he comes from. I remember now. 'Edwin Barley, Esquire, of the Oaks, Hallam.' That's the address in the deed of agreement. Good-day, my lady."

She did not attempt to detain him. With the look of awful consternation on her livid face, she turned to come back. I slipped into the dining-room, and sat down in a shady nook by the piano, hoping not to have been seen. The cloth was laid, but no servants were in the room. Only Mr. Chandos, and he stood at a side-table looking into his desk, his back to the room.

"Harry! Harry!"

Turning at the tones of unmistakable terror, Mr. Chandos came swiftly to his mother, and took her hand.

"The new tenant," she gasped—and I think it was the only time I ever saw Lady Chandos excited; she, who imparted always the idea of calmness intensified; who had reproached Mrs. Chandos with allowing emotion to sway her! "The man by our entrance-gates!"

"Yes, yes! what of him?" cried Mr. Chandos, when she stopped from pain. "My dear mother, what has alarmed you?"

"It is Edwin Barley."

"Who?" almost shouted Mr. Chandos.

"Edwin Barley. Here at our very gates!"

Whatever calamity the words might imply, it seemed almost to overwhelm Mr. Chandos. He dropped his mother's hands, and stood looking at her.

"Is the agreement signed, Harry?

"Yes."

"Then we cannot get rid of him! What can have brought him here? Here, of all places in the world! Chance, think you?"

"No. Chance it cannot have been. I told you the new tenant had an ill-favoured face. He—"

Mr. Chandos stopped: Hickens and the footman were coming in. The soup was put on the table, and we sat down to dinner. As I moved forward from my corner, quietly and unobtrusively, looking as if I had neither seen nor heard, Lady Chandos turned to me with a start, a red flush darkening her cheeks. But I do not believe she knows, to this hour, whether I had been present during the scene, or had come in with the soup and the servants.

Dinner was eaten in almost total silence. Lady and Mr. Chandos were absorbed in their own thoughts; I in mine. The chance words of the agent, "Mr. Edwin Barley of the Oaks," had disclosed the fact that the simple-minded old man who had been so kind to me was dead, and his brother reigned in his stead, lord of all. A rich man, indeed, Edwin Barley must be. I think the servants in waiting must have seen that something was amiss; though, perhaps, the silence did not strike upon them so ominously as it did on my own self-consciousness.

You cannot have failed to note—and I think I have said it—that there was little ceremony observed in the everyday life at Chandos. Ten minutes after dinner, tea was rung for. Lady Chandos sat whilst it was brought in, and the dessert taken away.

"Will you oblige me by presiding at tea this evening, Miss Hereford?"

Had Lady Chandos not preferred the request at once, I should have withdrawn to my own room, with an excuse that I did not wish for any tea. How miserably uncomfortable I felt, sitting with them, an interloper, when I knew they must want to be talking together, and were wishing me, naturally, at the other end of the earth, none but myself can tell. I poured out the tea. Lady Chandos drank one cup, and rose.

"I must go to sit with Ethel, Harry. Will you come?"

"She does not want me," was his reply. And Lady Chandos left the room.

He let his tea stand until it was quite cold, evidently forgetting it: forgetting all but his own thoughts. I sat in patient silence. Awakening later out of his reverie, he drank it at a draught, and rang the bell for the things to be taken away. As the man left the room with them, I happened to look at Mr. Chandos, who was then standing near the mantelpiece, and caught his eyes fixed on me, something peculiar in their expression.

"Mr. Chandos," I took courage to say, "I am very sorry to be in this position—an intruder here."

"And but for one thing I should be very glad of it," was his ready answer. "It is a pleasant in-break on our monotonous life."

"And that one thing, sir?"

"Ah! I cannot tell you all my secrets," he said, with a light laugh. "Do you make yourself at home, young lady. But for your book, that I know you are longing to be reading again, I should have compunction at leaving you alone."

He quitted the room, laughing still. I reached the book he alluded to, and sat down again. But I could not read; the surprise was too new, and thought upon thought kept crowding upon me. *They* evidently had cause to fear Edwin Barley, far more than I; perhaps then, after all, he had not come here to look after me? What the matter or the mystery could be, I knew not: but unmistakably there was something wrong between him and Chandos.

It was turned half-past ten when Lady Chandos came back again to the oak-parlour. I had returned to my book then, and was buried in it. Mr. Chandos followed her almost immediately, and began to wish us good-night.

"You must be tired, Harry," she observed. "You have had a fatiguing day."

"I am tired," was his reply. "I shall sleep to-night without rocking. Good-night, mother; good-night, Miss Hereford."

He left the room. Lady Chandos said she was tired too, and she and I went out together. Mr. Chandos, who had stayed in the hall, speaking to Hickens, went up just before us, entered his room and closed the door. I turned into mine; and I heard Lady Chandos traverse the long gallery and shut herself into the west wing.

Instead of undressing, what should I do but put back the curtains and shutters, sit down and open my book again. Only for two minutes, of course, said I to my conscience. It was that most charming of all romances, whether of Scott's or of others', "The Bride of Lammermoor," which Mr. Chandos had given me out the previous day. The two minutes grew into—but that I have to do it, I should not confess how many, especially as I could only guess at the number. My watch—the pretty watch of Selina's, given me so long ago by Mr. Edwin Barley—had latterly acquired a trick of stopping. It had been so delightful! sitting there with that enchanting romance, the window open to the bright night and balmy air.

Perhaps, after all, it was not more than twelve o'clock. I wound up the defaulting watch, shook it until it went again; set it at twelve by guess, and undressed slowly, and in silence. Then, putting out the light, I threw on a warm shawl, and leaned out of the window for a last look, before closing it. Which, of course, was a very senseless proceeding, although romantic. If Mademoiselle Annette could have seen me!

I stayed there, lost in thought; various interests jumbling themselves together in my mind. Lucy Ashton and the Master of Ravenswood; my own uncertain future and present disagreeable position; the curious mysteries that seemed to envelop Chandos; and the ominous proximity of Mr. Edwin Barley. As I leaned against the corner of the window, still as a statue, I was startled by observing a movement in the garden.

And a very extraordinary movement, too, if it was that of a rational being. Something dark, the height of a tall man, appeared to emerge from the clusters of trees skirting the lawn opposite, approach a few steps, and then dart in again; and this was repeated over and over again, the man advancing always nearer to the other end of the house. It was like the motions of one who wished to come on, yet feared being seen; a full minute he stood within those dark trees, each time that he penetrated them.

I watched, still as a mouse, and gazed eagerly, feeling like one chilled with a sudden fear. It was certainly very singular. When opposite the west wing, he stood for a minute out on the open greensward, and took off his round broad-brimmed hat as he looked up at the windows. Then I recognized the features of Mr. Chandos. He wore a short cloak, which in a degree hid his figure; but there was no mistaking the face, for the moon shone full upon it. The next moment he crossed the grass, and disappeared within the narrow laurel path that led to the private entrance of the west wing.

How had he got out of his room? That he had not come out by its door, I felt sure; for I had been so silent that I must have heard it, had it opened; besides, that door of his would only open with a creaking noise. If there was another door to his apartment, it must lead into the wing inhabited by Mrs. Chandos. Why had he been dodging about in that strange way in the grounds? and put on a cloak and broad hat to do it in, just as if he wished to disguise himself? And what could he want in the apartments of Lady Chandos in the middle of the night? Truly there was mystery at Chandos. But I could not solve it, and went to bed.

"Good-morning, Miss Hereford."

The salutation came from Mr. Chandos, who was following me into the breakfast-room, having that instant quitted his own. I was going quickly; so was he; for we were late, and Lady Chandos liked punctuality. But she was not in the oak-parlour.

"That's right," he cried, when he saw the room empty. "I hope my mother has overslept herself too, and had as good a night as I have."

"Have you had a good night, sir?" came the involuntary question.

"Too good: a man does not want eight or nine hours' sleep. I dropped asleep the minute I got into bed last night; did not even hear my clock strike eleven, though it only wanted a few minutes to it; and I never woke until twenty minutes to eight this morning. I was very tired last night."

Was Mr. Chandos mystifying me? Somehow it caused me vexation. My eyes had a resentful expression as I fixed them on his; which, of course, they had no right in the world to have.

"You did not go to sleep at eleven o'clock, sir."

"Indeed I did, Miss Hereford."

"Then you must have got up again, sir."

"Nothing of the sort! Why do you say that? I never woke until this morning."

Standing there and deliberately saying this to my face, with every appearance of truth, could only be done to mislead—to deceive me. I had far rather he had struck me a blow; though *why*, I did not stay to ask myself.

"Mr. Chandos, I saw you in the grounds in the middle of the night!"

"Saw me in the grounds in the middle of the night!" he echoed. "You were dreaming, Miss Hereford."

"No, sir; I was wide awake. It must have been getting on for one o'clock. You had on a cloak and a low broad-brimmed hat, and were dodging in and out of the trees."

"What trees?"

"Those opposite."

"Wearing a cloak and broad hat, and dodging in and out of the opposite trees! Well, that is good, Miss Hereford!"

His face wore an amused expression: his dark eyes—and they

were looking dark as purple in the morning light—were dancing with mirth. I turned cross. Some foolish thought, that Mr. Chandos would make a confidant of me in the morning, had run into my mind in the night.

"I don't possess a cloak, young lady."

"At any rate, sir, I saw you in one. A short one; a sort of cape. I saw your face quite plainly when you were looking up at the windows. The moon was as bright as day, and shining full upon you."

"It must decidedly have been my ghost, Miss Hereford."

"No, sir; it was yourself. I don't believe in ghosts. When you had finished your dance in and out of the trees, you crossed the grass to the laurel walk that leads down by the west wing."

"What do you say?"

The tone was an abrupt one; the manner had entirely changed: something like a glance of fear shot across the face of Mr. Chandos. But at that moment Hill came in.

"So you are back again, Hill!" he exclaimed.

"I have been back an hour, sir. Mrs. Freeman's no worse, and I came by the Parliamentary train. And it is well I did come," added she, "for I found my lady ill!"

Mr. Chandos swung himself round on his heel. "My mother ill! what is the matter with her?"

"Well, sir, I hardly know. I came to ask you to go up and see her."

"She was very well last night," he observed, striding upstairs on his way to the west wing.

"You had better begin breakfast, miss," Hill said to me. "My lady won't be down; I'll go and order it in."

"Am I to send any up to Lady Chandos, Hill?"

"I have taken my lady's breakfast up," was her answer. The tea and coffee came in, and I waited; waited, and waited. When I had nearly given Mr. Chandos up, he came. His face was pale, troubled, and he appeared lost in inward thought. From the signs, I gathered that Lady Chandos's malady was serious.

"I fear you have found Lady Chandos worse than you anticipated, sir?"

"Yes—no—yes—not exactly," was the contradictory answer. "I hope it is nothing dangerous," he more collectedly added; "but she will not be able to leave her rooms to-day."

"Is she in bed, sir?"

"No; she is sitting up. My tea? thank you. You should not have waited for me, Miss Hereford."

He took his breakfast in silence, ringing once for Hickens, to ask after a paper that ought to have come. Afterwards he quitted the room, and I saw him go strolling across to the Pine Walk.

# CHAPTER 15

## IN THE IRONING-ROOM

"Will you allow me to repose a word of confidence in you, Miss Hereford, and at the same time to tender an apology?"

Playing a little bit of quiet harmony, reading a little, musing a little, half-an-hour had passed, and I was leaning my back against the frame of the open window. Mr. Chandos had come across the grass unheard by me, and took me by surprise.

I turned, and stammered forth "Yes." His tones were cautious and low, as though he feared eavesdroppers, though no one was within hearing; or could have been, without being seen.

"You accused me of wandering out there last night," he began, sitting on the stone ledge of the window outside, his face turned to me, "and I rashly denied it to you. As it is within the range of possibility that you may see me there again at the same ghostly hour, I have been deliberating whether it may not be the wiser plan to impart to you the truth. You have heard of sleep-walkers?"

"Yes," I replied, staring at him.

"What will you say if I acknowledge to being one?"

Of course I did not know what to say, and stood there like a statue, looking foolish. The thought that rushed over my heart was, what an unhappy misfortune to attend the sensible and otherwise attractive Mr. Chandos.

"You see," he continued, "when you spoke, I did not know I had been out, and denied it, really believing you were mistaken."

"And do you positively walk in your sleep, sir?—go out of your room, out of the locked doors of the house, and pace the grounds?" I breathlessly exclaimed.

"Ay. Not a pleasant endowment, is it? Stranger things are heard of some who possess it: they spirit themselves on to the roofs of houses, to the tops of chimneys, and contrive to spirit themselves down again, without coming to harm. So far as I am aware, I have never yet attempted those ambitious feats."

"Does Lady Chandos know of this?"

"Of course. My mother saw me last night, I find: she felt unable to sleep, she says, thinking of poor Mrs. Freeman, and rose from her bed. It was a light night, and she drew aside her curtains and looked from the window. But for her additional testimony, I might not have believed you yet, Miss Hereford."

"You seemed to be making for her apartments, sir—for the little door in the laurel walk."

"Did I?" he carelessly rejoined. "What freak guided my steps thither, I wonder? Did you see me come back again?"

"No, sir. I did not stay much longer at the window."

"I dare say I came back at once. A pity you missed the sight a second time," he continued, with a laugh that sounded very much like a forced one. "Having decorated myself with a cloak and broad hat, I must have been worth seeing. I really did not know that I had a cloak in my dressing-closet, but I find there is an old one."

He sat still, pulling to pieces a white rose and scattering its petals one by one. His eyes seemed to seek any object rather than mine; his dark hair, looking in some lights almost purple like his eyes, was impatiently pushed now and again from his brow. Altogether, there was something in Mr. Chandos that morning that jarred upon me—something that did not seem *true*.

"I cannot think, sir, how you could have gone down so quietly from your room. For the first time since I have been in your house—for the first time, I think, in my whole life—I sat up reading last night, and yet I did not hear you; unless, indeed, you descended by some exit through the east wing."

"Oh, you don't know how quiet and cunning sleep-walkers are; the stillness with which they carry on their migrations is incredible," was his rejoinder. "You must never be surprised at anything they do."

But I noticed one thing: that he did not deny the existence of a second door. In spite of his plausible reasoning, I could not divest myself of the conviction that he had not left his chamber by the entrance near mine.

"Is it a nightly occurrence, sir?"

"What—my walking about? Oh dear, no! Months and years sometimes elapse, and I have nothing of it. The last time I 'walked'—is not that an ominous word for the superstitious?—must be at least two years ago."

"And then only for one night, sir?"

"For more than one," he replied, a strangely grave expression settling on his countenance. "So, if you see me again, Miss Hereford, do not be alarmed, or think that I have taken sudden leave of my senses."

"Mr. Chandos, can nothing be done for you? To prevent it, I mean."

"Nothing at all."

"If—if Lady Chandos, or one of the men-servants were to lock you in the room at night?" I timidly suggested.

"And if I—finding exit stopped that way—were to precipitate myself from the window, in my unconsciousness, what then, Miss Hereford?"

"Oh, don't talk of it!" I said, hiding my eyes with a shudder. "I do not understand these things: I spoke in ignorance."

"Happily few do understand them," he replied. "I have given you this in strict confidence, Miss Hereford; you will, I am sure, so regard it. No one knows of it except my mother; but she would not like you to speak of it to her."

"Certainly not. Then the servants do not know it?"

"Not one of them: not even Hill. It would be most disagreeable to me were the unpleasant fact to reach them; neither might they be willing to remain in a house where there was a sleep-walker. The last time the roving fit was upon me, some of them unfortunately saw me from the upper window; they recognized me, and came to the conclusion, by some subtle force of reasoning, explainable only by themselves, that it was my 'fetch,' or ghost. It was the first time I had ever heard of ghosts of the living appearing," he added, with a slight laugh.

"Do you think they saw you last night?" was my next question.

"I hope not," he replied, in tones meant to be light, but that, to my ear, told of ill-concealed anxiety.

"But—Mr. Chandos!—there are no windows in the servants' part of the house that look this way!" I exclaimed, the recollection flashing on me.

"There is one. That small Gothic window in the turret. The fear that some of them may have been looking out is worrying my mother."

"It is that, perhaps, that has made Lady Chandos ill."

"Yes; they took me for my own ghost," he resumed, apparently not having heard the remark. "You now perceive, possibly, why I have told you this, Miss Hereford? You would not be likely to adopt the ghostly view of the affair, and might have spoken of what you saw in the hearing of the servants, or of strangers. You have now the secret: will you keep it?"

"With my whole heart, sir," was my impulsive rejoinder. "No allusion to it shall ever pass my lips." And Mr. Chandos took my hand, held it for a moment, and then departed, leaving me to digest the revelation.

It was a strange one; and I asked myself whether this physical infirmity, attaching to him, was the cause of what had appeared so mysterious at Chandos. That it might account for their not wishing to have strangers located at Chandos, sleeping in the house, was highly probable. Why! was not I myself an illustration of the case in point? I, a young girl, but a week or so in the house, and it had already become expedient to entrust me with the secret! Oh yes! no wonder, no wonder that they shunned visitors at Chandos! To me it seemed a most awful affliction.

As I quitted the oak-parlour and went upstairs, Hill stood in the gallery.

"Lady Chandos is up, I understand, Hill?"

"Well, I don't know where you could have understood that," was Hill's rejoinder, spoken in sullen and resentful tones. "My lady up, indeed! ill as she is! If she's out of her bed in a week hence it will be time enough. *I* don't think she will be."

I declare that the words so astonished me as to take my senses temporarily away, and Hill was gone before I could speak again. Which of the two told the truth, Mr. Chandos or Hill? He said his mother was up; Hill said she was not, and would not be for a week to come.

Meanwhile Hill had traversed the gallery, and disappeared within the west wing, closing the green-baize door sharply after her. I stood in deliberation. Ought I, or ought I not, to proffer a visit to Lady Chandos?—to inquire if I could do anything for her. It seemed to me that it would be respectful so to do, and I moved forward and knocked gently at the green-baize door.

There came no answer, and I knocked again—and again; softly always. Then I pushed it open and entered. I found myself in a narrow passage, richly carpeted, with a handsome oak door before me. I gave a stout knock at that, and the latch of the green-baize door closed with a sharp sound. Out rushed Hill. If ever terror was pictured on a woman's face, it was so in hers then.

"Heaven and earth, Miss Hereford! Do you want to send me into my grave with fright?" ejaculated she.

"I have not frightened you! What have I done?"

"Done? Do you know, miss, that no soul is permitted to enter these apartments when my lady is ill, except myself and Mr. Chandos? I knew it was not he; and I thought—I thought—I don't know what I did not think. Be so good, miss, as not to serve me so again."

Did she take me for a wild tiger, that she made all that fuss? "I wish to see Lady Chandos," I said, aloud.

"Then you can't see her, miss," was the peremptory retort.

"That is, if it be agreeable to her to receive me," I continued, resenting Hill's assumption of authority.

"But it is not agreeable, and never can be agreeable," returned Hill, working herself up to a great pitch of excitement. "Don't I tell you, Miss Hereford, my lady never receives in these rooms? Perhaps, miss, you'll be so good as to quit them."

"At least you can take my message to Lady Chandos, and inquire whether—"

"I can't deliver any message, and I decline to make any inquiries," interrupted Hill, evidently in a fever of anxiety for my absence. "Excuse me, Miss Hereford, but you will please return by the way you came."

Who should appear next on the scene but Lady Chandos! She

came from beyond the oak door, as Hill had done, apparently wondering at the noise. I was thunderstruck. She looked quite well, and wore her usual dress; but she went back again at once, and it was but a momentary glimpse I had of her. Hill made no ceremony. She took me by the shoulders as you would take a child, turned me towards the entrance, and bundled me out; shutting the green-baize door with a slam, and propping her back against it.

"Now Miss Hereford, you must pardon me; and remember your obstinacy has just brought this upon yourself. I couldn't help it; for to have suffered you to talk to my lady to-day would have been almost a matter of life or death."

"I think you are out of your mind, Hill," I gasped, recovering my breath, but not my temper, after the summary exit.

"Perhaps I am, miss; let it go so. All I have got to say, out of my mind or in my mind, is this: never you attempt to enter this west wing. The rooms in it are sacred to my lady, whose pleasure it is to keep them strictly private. And intrusion here, after this warning, is what would never be pardoned to you by any of the family, if you lived to be ninety years old!"

"Hill, you take too much upon yourself," was my indignant answer.

"If I do, my lady will correct me; so do not trouble your mind about that, Miss Hereford. I have not been her confidential attendant for sixteen years to be taught my duty now. And when I advise you to keep at a distance from these apartments, miss, I advise you for your own good. If you are wise, you will heed it: ask Mr. Chandos."

She returned within the wing, and I heard a strong bolt slipped, effectually barring my entrance, had I felt inclined to disobey her; but I never felt less inclined for anything in my life than to do that. Certainly her warning had been solemnly spoken.

Now, who was insane?—I? or Lady Chandos? or Hill? It seemed to me that it must be one of us, for assuredly all this savoured of insanity. What was it that ailed Lady Chandos? That she was perfectly well in health, I felt persuaded; and she was up and dressed and active; no symptom whatever of the invalid was about her. Could it be that her mind was affected? or was she so overcome with grief at the previous night's exploits of Mr. Chandos as to be obliged to remain in retirement? The latter supposition appeared the more feasible—and I weighed the case in all its bearings.

But not quite feasible, either. For Hill appeared to be full mistress of the subject of the mystery, whatever it might be, and Mr. Chandos had said she had no suspicion of his malady. And, besides, would it be enough to keep Lady Chandos in for a week? I dwelt upon it all until my head ached; and, to get rid of my perplexities, I went strolling into the open air.

It was a fine sunshiny day, and the blue tint of the bloom upon the pine trees looked lovely in the gleaming light. I turned down a shady path on the left of the broad gravel drive, midway between the house and the entrance-gates. It took me to a part of the grounds where I had never yet penetrated, remote and very solitary. The path was narrow, scarcely admitting of two persons passing each other, and the privet hedge on either side, with the overhanging trees, imparted to it an air of excessive gloom. The path wound in its course; in turning one of its angles, I came right in the face of some one advancing; some one who was so close as to touch me: and my heart leaped into my mouth. It was Mr. Edwin Barley.

"Good-morning, young lady."

"Good-morning, sir," I stammered, sick almost unto death, lest he should recognize me; though why that excessive dread of his recognition should be upon me, I could not possibly have explained. He was again trespassing on Chandos; but it was not for me, in my timidity, to tell him so; neither had I any business to set myself forward in upholding the rights of Chandos.

"All well at the house?" he continued.

"Yes, thank you. All, except Lady Chandos. She keeps her room this morning."

"You are a visitor at Chandos, I presume?"

"For a little time, sir."

"So I judged, when I saw you with Harry Chandos. That you were not Miss Chandos, who married the Frenchman, I knew, for you bear no resemblance to her: and she is the only daughter of the family. I fancied they did not welcome strangers at Chandos."

I made no answer; though he looked at me with his jet-black eyes as if waiting for it; the same stern, penetrating eyes as of old. How I wished to get away! but it was impossible to pass him without rudeness, and he stood blocking up the confined pathway.

"Are you a confidential friend of the family?" he resumed.

"No, sir; I am not to be called a friend at all; quite otherwise. Until a few days ago, I was a stranger to them. Accident brought me then to Chandos, but my stay here will be temporary."

"I should be glad to make your acquaintance by name," he went on, never taking those terrible eyes off me. Not that the eyes in themselves were so very terrible; but the fear of my childhood had returned to me in all its force—as a very bug-bear. I had made the first acquaintance of Mr. Edwin Barley in a moment of fear—that is, he had frightened me. Unintentionally on his own part, it is true, but with not less of effect upon me. The circumstances of horror (surely it is not too strong a word) that had followed, in all of which he was mixed up, had only tended to increase the feeling; and grown to womanhood though I was now, the meeting with him had brought it all back to me.

"Will you not favour me with your name?"

He spoke politely, quite as a gentleman, but I felt my face grow red, white, hot and cold. I had answered his questions, feeling that I dared not resist; that I feared to show him anything but civility; but—to give him my name; to rush, as it were, into the lion's jaws! No, I would not do that; and I plucked up what courage was left me.

"My name is of no consequence, sir. I am only a very humble individual, little more than a school-girl. I was brought here by a lady, who, immediately upon her arrival, was recalled home by illness in her family, and I am in daily expectation of a summons from her; after which I dare say I shall never see Chandos or any of its inmates again. Will you be kind enough to allow me to pass?"

"You must mean Miss Chandos—I don't recollect her married name," said he, without stirring. "I heard she had been here: and left almost as soon as she came."

I bowed my head and tried to pass him. I might as readily have tried to pass through the privet hedge.

"Some lady was taken away ill, yesterday," he resumed. "Who was it?"

"It was Mrs. Freeman."

"Oh! the companion. I thought as much. Is she very ill?"

"It was a sort of fit, I believe. It did not last long."

"Those fits are ticklish things," he remarked. "I should think she will not be in a state to return for some time, if at all."

He had turned his eyes away now, and was speaking in a dreamy sort of tone; as I once heard him speak to Selina.

"They will be wanting some one to fill Mrs. Freeman's place, will they not."

"I cannot say, I'm sure, sir. The family do not talk of their affairs before me."

"Who is staying at Chandos now?" he abruptly asked.

"Only the family."

"Ah! the family—of course. I mean what members of it."

"All; except Madame de Mellissie and Sir Thomas Chandos."

"That is, there are Lady Chandos, her son, and daughter-in-law. That comprises the whole, I suppose—except you."

"Yes, it does. But I must really beg you to allow me to pass, sir."

"You are welcome now, and I am going to turn, myself. It is pleasant to have met an intelligent lady; and I hope we often shall meet, that I may hear good tidings of my friends at Chandos. I was intimate with part of the family once, but a coolness arose between us, and I do not go there. Good-day."

He turned and walked rapidly back. I struck into the nearest side-walk I could find that would bring me to the open grounds, and nearly struck against Mr. Chandos.

"Are you alone, Miss Hereford? I surely heard voices."

"A gentleman met me, sir, and spoke."

"A gentleman—in this remote part of the grounds!" he repeated, looking keenly at me, as a severe expression passed momentarily across his face. "Was it any one you knew?"

"It was he who came into the broad walk, and whom you ordered out—the new tenant. He is gone now."

"He! I fancied so," returned Mr. Chandos, the angry flush deepening. And it seemed almost as though he were angry with me.

"I found out the walk by accident, sir, and I met him in it. He stopped and accosted me with several questions, which I thought very rude of him."

"What did he ask you?"

"He wished to know my name, who I was, and what I was doing at Chandos; but I did not satisfy him. He then inquired about the family, asking what members of it were at home."

"And you told him?"

"There was no need to tell him, sir, for he mentioned the names to me; yourself, Lady and Mrs. Chandos."

"Ethel! he mentioned her, did he! What did he call her?—Mrs. Chandos?"

"He did not mention her by name, sir; he said 'daughter-in-law'." I did not tell Mr. Chandos that the designation made an impression upon me, establishing the supposition that Mrs. Chandos *was* a daughter-in-law.

"And pray what did he call me?"

"Harry Chandos."

"Well, now mark me, Miss Hereford. That man accosted you to worm out what he could of our everyday life at home. His name is Barley—Edwin Barley. He is a bitter enemy of ours, and if he could pick up any scrap of news or trifle of fact that he could by possibility turn about and work so as to injure us, he would do it."

"But how could, he, sir?" I exclaimed, not understanding.

"His suspicions are no doubt aroused that—that—I beg your pardon, Miss Hereford," he abruptly broke off, with the air of one who has said more than he meant to say. "These matters cannot interest you. You—you did not tell Mr. Barley what I imparted to you this morning, touching myself?"

"Oh, Mr. Chandos, how can you ask the question? Did I not promise you to hold it sacred?"

"Forgive me," he gently said. "Nay, I am sorry to have pained you."

He had pained me in no slight degree, and the tears very nearly rose in my eyes. I would rather be beaten with rods than have my good faith slighted. I think Mr. Chandos saw something of this in my face.

"Believe me, I do not doubt you for a moment; but Edwin Barley, in all that regards our family, is cunning and crafty. Be upon your guard, should he stop you again, not to betray anything of our affairs at Chandos, the little daily occurrences of home life. A chance word, to all appearance innocent and trifling, might work incalculable mischief to us, even ruin. Will you remember this, Miss Hereford?"

I promised him I would, and went back to the house, he continuing his way. At the end of the privet walk a gate led to the open country, and I supposed Mr. Chandos had business there. As I reached the portico a gentleman was standing there with the butler, asking to see Lady Chandos. It was Mr. Jarvis, the curate.

"My lady is ill in bed, sir," was Hickens's reply, his long, grave face giving ample token that he held belief in his own words.

"I am sorry to hear that. Is her illness serious?"

"Rather so, sir, I believe. Mrs. Hill fears it will be days before her ladyship is downstairs. She used to be subject to dreadful bilious attacks; I suppose it's one of them come back again."

The curate gave in a card, left a message, and departed. So it appeared that Hill was regaling the servants with the same story that she had told me. I could have spoken up, had I dared, and said there was nothing the matter with the health of Lady Chandos.

At six o'clock I went down to dinner, wondering who would preside. I have said, that no ceremony was observed at Chandos, the everyday life was simple in the extreme. Since the departure of Emily de Mellissie we had sat in the oak-parlour, and all the meals were taken there. In fact, there was nobody to sit but myself. Lady Chandos had been mostly in the west wing; Mr. Chandos out, or in his study; Mrs. Chandos I never saw. The servants were placing the soup on the table. In another moment Mr. Chandos came in.

"A small company this evening, Miss Hereford; only you and I," he laughed, as we took our seats.

"Is Lady Chandos not sufficiently well to dine, sir?" I asked.

"She will take something, no doubt. Hill takes care of her mistress. I met her carrying up the tray as I came down."

"I hope I am not the cause of your dining downstairs," I rejoined, the unpleasant thought striking me that it might be so. "Perhaps, but for me, you would dine with Lady Chandos?"

"Nothing of the sort, I assure you. Were it not for you, I should sit here in solitary state, and eat my lonely dinner with what appetite I might. And a solitary dinner is not good for digestion, the doctors tell us. Did any one call while I was out, Hickens?"

"Only Mr. Jarvis, sir. I think he wanted to see my lady about the new schools. He was very particular in asking what was the matter with her, and I said I thought it might be one of those old bilious attacks come on again. My lady had a bad one or two at times, years ago, sir, you may remember."

"Ay," replied Mr. Chandos: but it was all the comment he made.

"Is Lady Chandos subject to bilious attacks?" I inquired of Mr. Chandos.

"Not particularly. She has been free from them latterly."

"Did you know, sir," continued Hickens, "that we have had news of Mrs. Freeman?"

"No. When did it come? I hope it's good."

"Not very good, sir. It came half-an-hour ago. She had another fit to-day in the forenoon, and it's certain now that she won't be able to come back here for a long while, if she is at all. The relation that she is with wrote to Mrs. Hill, who took up the note to my lady. Hill says, when she left her there were symptoms of a second attack coming on."

Mr. Chandos leaned back for a moment in his chair, forgetful that he was at dinner, and not alone. He was in a reverie; but, as his eye fell on me, he shook it off, and spoke.

"Her not returning will prove an inconvenience to Mrs. Chandos."

"I am afraid it will, sir," rejoined Hickens, who had fancied himself addressed; though, in point of fact, Mr. Chandos had but unconsciously spoken aloud his thoughts. Hickens had been a long time in the family, was a faithful and valued servant, consequently he thought himself at liberty to talk in season and out of season. "I warned Mrs. Chandos's maid, sir, not to tell her mistress about Mrs. Freeman's being worse," he went on; "It would do no good, and only worrit her."

Mr. Chandos slightly nodded, and the dinner then proceeded in silence. At its conclusion, Mr. Chandos, after taking one glass of wine, rose.

"I must apologize for leaving you alone, Miss Hereford, but I believe my mother will expect me to sit with her. Be sure you make yourself at home; and ring for tea when you wish for it."

"Shall you not be in to tea, sir?"

"I think not. At all events, don't wait."

Dreary enough was it for me, sitting in that great solitary room—not solitary in itself, but from want of tenants.

I went and stood at the window. The wax-lights were burning, but nothing but the muslin curtains was before the windows. There was no one to overlook the room; comers to the house did not pass it; the servants had no business whatever in the front; and very often the shutters were not closed until bedtime. It was scarcely yet to be called dark: the atmosphere was calm and clear, and a bright white light came from the west. Putting on a shawl, I went quietly out.

It was nearly, for me, as dreary out of doors as within. All seemed still; no soul was about; no voices were to be heard; no cheering lights gleamed from the windows. I was daring enough to walk to the end and look up at the west wing; a slight glimmering, as of fire, sparkled up now and again in what I had understood was Lady Chandos's sitting-room. Back to the east wing, and looked at the end of that. Plenty of cheerful blaze there, both of fire and candle; and, once, the slight form of Mrs. Chandos appeared for a minute at the window, looking out.

I passed on to the back of the house, by the servants' ordinary path, round the east wing. It was a good opportunity for seeing what the place was like. But I did not bargain for the great flood of light into which I was thrown on turning the angle. It proceeded from the corner room; the windows were thrown wide open, and some maid-servants were ironing at a long board underneath. Not caring that they should see me, I drew under the cover of a projecting shed, that I believe belonged to the brewhouse, and took a leisurely survey. Plenty of life here; plenty of buildings; it seemed quite a colony. Lights shone from several windows of the long edifice—as long as it was in front. The entrance was in the middle; a poultry-yard lay at the other end; and a pasture for cows opposite; the range of stables could be seen in the distance.

Harriet and Emma were the two maids ironing; Lizzy Dene, a very dark young woman of thirty, with a bunch of wild-looking black curls on either side of her face, sat by the ironing-stove, doing nothing. Why they added her surname, Dene, to her Christian name in speaking of her, I did not know, but it seemed to be the usual custom. These three, it may be remembered, have been mentioned as the housemaids. Another woman, whom I did not recognize, but knew her later for the laundry-maid, was at the back, folding clothes. They were talking fast, but very distinctly, in that half-covert tone which betrays the subject to be a forbidden one. The conversation and the stove's heat were alike wafted to me through the open window.

"You may preach from now until to-morrow morning," were the first words I heard, and they came from Harriet; "but you will never make me believe that people's ghosts can appear before they die. It is not in nature's order."

"*His* appears. I'll stand to that. And what's more, I'll stand to it that I saw it last night!" cried Lizzy Dene, looking up and speaking in strong, fierce jerks, as she was in the habit of doing. "I sat up in the bedroom sewing. It's that new black silk polka of mine that I wanted to finish, and if I got it about downstairs, Madam Hill would go on above a bit about finery. Emma got into bed and lay awake talking, her and me. Before I'd done, my piece of candle came to an end, and I thought I'd go into Harriet's room and borrow hers. It was a lovely night, the moon shone slantways in at the turret-window, and something took me that I'd have a look out. So I went up the turret-stairs and stood at the casement. I hadn't been there a minute before I saw it—the living image of Mr. Chandos!—and I thought I should have swooned away. Ask Emma."

"Well, I say it might have been Mr. Chandos himself, but it never was his ghost," argued Harriet.

"You might be a soft, but I dare say you'd stand to it you are not," retorted Lizzy. "Don't I tell you that in the old days we saw that apparition when Mr. Harry was safe in his bed? When we knew him to be in his bed with that attack of fever he had? I saw it twice then with my own eyes. And once, when Mr. Harry was miles and miles away—gone over to that French place where Miss Emily was at school—it came again. Half the household saw it; and a fine commotion there was! Don't tell me, girl! I've lived, in the family seven years. I came here before old Sir Thomas died."

There was a pause. Harriet, evidently not discomfited, whisked away her iron to the stove, changed it, and came back again before she spoke.

"I don't know anything about back times; the present ones is enough for me. Did you see this, Emma, last night?"

"Yes, I did," replied Emma, who was a silent and rather stupid-looking girl, with a very retreating chin. "Lizzy Dene came rushing back into the room, saying the ghost had come again, and I ran after her up to the turret window. Something was there, safe enough."

"Who was it like?"

"Mr. Chandos. There was no mistaking him: one does not see a tall, thin, upright man like him every day. There was his face, too, and his beautiful features quite plain; the moon gave a light like day."

"It was himself, as I said," coolly contended Harriet.

"It was not," said Lizzy. "Mr. Chandos would no more have been dancing in and out of the trees in that fashion, like a jack-in-the-box, than he'd try to fly in the air. It was the ghost at its tricks again."

"But the thing is incredible," persisted Harriet. "Let us suppose, for argument's sake, that it is Mr. Chandos's ghost that walks, what does it come for, Lizzy Dene?"

"I never heard that ghosts stooped to explain their motives. How should we know why it comes?"

"And I never heard yet that ghosts of live people came at all," continued Harriet, in recrimination. "And I don't think anybody else ever did."

"But you know that's only your ignorance, Harriet. Certain people are born into the world with their own fetches or wraiths, which appear sometimes with them, sometimes at a distance, and Mr. Chandos must be one. I knew a lady's-maid of that kind. While she was with her mistress in Scotland, her fetch used to walk about in England, startling acquaintances into fits. Some people call 'em doubles."

"But what's the use of them?" reiterated Harriet; "what do they do? That's what I want to know."

"Harriet, don't you be profane, and sot up your back against spirituous things," rebuked Lizzy Dene. "There was a man in our village, over beyond Marden, that never could be brought to reverence such; he mocked at 'em like any heathen, saying he'd fight single-handed the best ten ghosts that ever walked, for ten pound a-side, and wished he could get the chance. What was the awful consequences? Why, that man, going home one night from the beer-shop, marched right into the canal in mistake for his own house-door, and was drownded."

Emma replenished the stove, took a fresh iron, singed a rag in rubbing it, and continued her work. The woman, folding clothes at the back, turned round to speak.

"How was the notion first taken up—that it was Mr. Chandos's fetch?"

"This way," said Lizzy Done, who appeared from her longer period of service in the family to know more than the rest. "It was about the time of Sir Thomas's death, just before it, or after it, I forget which now. Mr. Harry—as he was mostly called when he was younger—was ill with that low fever; it was said something had worried him and brought the sickness on. My lady, by token, was poorly at the same time, and kept her rooms; and, now that I remember, Sir Thomas *was* dead, for she wore her widow's caps. At the very time Mr. Harry was in his bed, this figure, his very self, was seen at night in the grounds. That was the first of it."

"If there's one thing more deceptive than another, it's night-light," meekly observed the woman.

"The next time was about two years after that," resumed Lizzy, ignoring the suggestion. "Mr. Harry was in France, and one of the servants stopped out late one evening without leave: Phoeby it was, who's married now. She had missed the train and had to walk, and it was between twelve and one when she got in, and me and Ann sitting up for her in a desperate fright lest Mrs. Hill should find it out. In she came, all in a fluster, saying Mr. Harry was in the Pine Walk, which she had come across, as being the nearest way, and she was afraid he had seen her. Of course, we thought it was Mr. Harry come home, and that the house would be called up to serve refreshments for him. But nothing happened; no bells were rung, and to bed we went. The next morning we found he had not come home, and finely laughed at Phoeby, asking her what she had taken to obscure her eyesight—which made her very mad. Evening came, and one of them telegraph messages came over the sea to my lady from Mr. Harry, proving he was in the French town. But law! that night, there he was in the dark pine-path again, walking up and down it, and all us maids sat up and saw him. My lady was ill again then, I remember; she does have bad bouts now and then."

"Do you mean to say you all saw him?" questioned Harriet. "We all saw him, four or five of us," emphatically repeated Lizzy. "Hickens came to hear of it, and called us all the simpletons he could lay his tongue to. He told Hill—least-ways we never knew who did if he didn't—and didn't she make a commotion! If ever she heard a syllable of such rubbish from us again, she said, we should all go packing: and she locked up the turret-door, and kept the key in her pocket for weeks."

"You see, what staggers one is that Mr. Chandos should be alive," said Harriet, "One could understand if he were dead."

"Nothing that's connected with ghosts, and those things, ought to stagger one at all," dissented Lizzy.

"According to you, Lizzy Dene, the ghost only appears by fits and starts."

"No more it does. Every two years or so. Anyway it has been seen once since the time I tell you of when Mr. Chandos was abroad, which is four years ago, and now it's here again."

"One would think you watched for it, Lizzy!"

"And so I do. Often of a moonlight night, I get out of bed and go to that turret-window."

Some one came quickly down the paths at this junctures brushing by me as I stood in the shade. It was the still-room maid. She had a bundle in her hand, went on to the entrance, and then came into the ironing-room. Hill followed her in; but the latter remained at the back, looking at some ironed laces on a table, and not one of the girls noticed her presence. The still-room maid advanced to the ironing-board, let her bundle fall on it, and threw up her arms in some excitement.

"I say, you know Mrs. Peters, over at the brook! Well—she's dead."

"Dead!" echoed the girls, pausing in their work. "Why, it was not a week ago that she was here."

"She's dead. They were laying her out when I came by just now. Some fever, they say, which took her off in no time; a catching fever, too. A mortal fright it put me in, to hear that; I shouldn't like to die yet awhile."

"If fever has broken out in the place, who knows but it's fever that has taken my lady!" exclaimed Emma, her stupid face alive with consternation: and the rest let their irons drop on their stands. "All our lives may be in jeopardy."

"Your places will be in greater jeopardy if you don't pay a little more attention to work, and leave off talking nonsense," called out the sharp voice of Mrs. Hill from the background. The servants started round at its sound, and the irons were taken up again.

# CHAPTER 16

## DISTURBED BY MRS. CHANDOS

No candles yet in Lady Chandos's rooms, but a great flood of light in those of Mrs. Chandos. The commotion in the ironing-room, that followed the discovered presence of Hill, had given me the opportunity to come away, and so exchange (not willingly) the gossiping cheerfulness of the back, for the dreary front of the house. I had almost laughed aloud at those foolish servant-girls; nevertheless, in what they had said there was food for speculation. For when Harry Chandos was in bed, ill with fever; when he was over in France, with the broad sea and many miles of land between him and his home; how could they have seen him, or fancied they saw him, in these dark walks, night after night, at Chandos?

Pacing the dark gravel-walk from wing to wing, glancing, as I passed each time, through the window-panes and the muslin curtains into the oak-parlour, where the solitary tea waited, I thought over it all, and came to the conclusion that, taking one curious thing with another, something uncanny was in the place. How long should I have to stay here?—how long would it be before Emily de Mellissie came back to me?

The hall-door stood open, and the hall-lamp threw its light across the lawn in a straight line. It seemed like a ray of companionship amidst the general dreariness. I took a fancy to walk along the pleasant stream, forgetting or unheeding the dew that might lie on the grass. On reaching the other side, I stood a moment at the top of the Pine Walk, and then advanced a few steps down it.

Some one was there before me. A white figure—as it looked—was flitting about; and I gave a great start. What with the night-hour, the solitary loneliness of all around, the soft sighing sound from the branches of the trees, and the servant-girls' recent talk of the "ghost," I am not sure but I began to think of ghosts myself. Ghost, or no ghost, it came gliding up to me, with its slender form, its lovely face: Mrs. Chandos, in a white silk evening-dress, with a small white opera-cloak on her shoulders. It was her pleasure, as I learnt later, to dress each day for her own lonely society just as she would for a state dinner-table.

"How you startled me!" she exclaimed. "With that great brown shawl on your head, you look as much like a man as a woman. But I saw by the height it was not *he*. Did you know that he came—that he was here last night?" she added, dropping her voice to the faintest whisper.

It was the first time Mrs. Chandos had voluntarily addressed me.

Of course I guessed that she alluded to Mr. Harry Chandos: but I hesitated to answer, after the caution he had given me. Was there anything *wild* about her voice and manner as she spoke?—had her spirits run away with her to-night?—or did the fact of her flitting about in the white evening-dress in this wild way, like any school-girl, cause me to fancy it?

"Did you know it, I ask?" she impatiently rejoined. "Surely you may answer *me*."

"Yes!" There seemed no help for it. "I saw him, madam, but I shall not mention it. The secret is safe with me."

"You saw him! Oh, Heaven, what will be done?" she cried, in evident distress. "It was so once before: the servants saw him. You must not tell any one; you must not."

"Indeed I will not. I am quite trustworthy."

"What are you doing out here?" she sharply said. "Looking for him?"

"Indeed no. I was dull by myself, and came across unthinkingly. I am as true as you, Mrs. Chandos. I would not, for the world, say a word to harm him."

The assurance seemed to satisfy—to calm her; she grew quiet as a little child.

"To talk of it might cause grievous evil, you know; it might lead to—but I had better not say more to a stranger. How did you come to know of it?"

I made no answer. Some feeling, that I did not stay to sift, forbade me to say it was from himself.

"I know; it was from Madame de Mellissie. It was very foolish of her to tell you. It was wrong of her to bring you here at all."

As Mrs. Chandos spoke, there was something in her words, in her tone, in her manner altogether, that caused a worse idea to flash across me—that she was not quite herself. Not insane; it was not that thought; but a little wanting in intellect; as if the powers of the mind were impaired. It startled me beyond measure, and I began to think that I ought to try and get her indoors.

"Shall you not take cold out here, Mrs. Chandos?"

"I never take cold. You see, I am my own mistress now: when Mrs. Freeman's here, she will never let me come out after dusk. Lady Chandos sent my maid to sit with me this evening, but I lay down on the sofa, and told her I was perhaps going to sleep and she could not stay with me. And I came out; I thought I might see *him*."

Every word she spoke added to the impression.

"And so you saw him last night! I did not; I never do. The windows looking this way are closed. And perhaps if I were to see him like that, and be taken by surprise, it might make me ill: Mrs. Freeman says it would. It is so sad, you know!"

"Very sad," I murmured, assuming still that she alluded to the infirmity of Mr. Chandos.

"They never told me. They are not aware that I know it. I found it out to-day. I was going about the gallery early this morning, before Hill came home, and I found it out. When Mrs. Freeman's here, I can only get out when she pleases. You cannot think what a long time it is since—since—"

"Since what?" I asked, as she came to a stop.

"Since the last time. Harry has not said a word to me all day; it is a shame of him. He ought to have told *me*."

"Yes, yes," I murmured, wishing to soothe her.

"You see, Harry's not friends with me. He tells me he is, but he is not in reality. It is through my having treated him badly: he has been the same as a stranger ever since. But he ought to have told me this. You must not tell them that I know it."

"Certainly not."

"They might lock me in, you know; they did once before; but that was not the last time, it was when Harry was in France. If Mrs. Freeman had been here to-day, I should not have known it so soon. It is very cruel: I think I shall tell Lady Chandos so. If Harry—"

During the last few words, Mrs. Chandos's eyes had been strained on a particular spot near to us. What she saw, or fancied she saw, I know not, but she broke into a low smothered cry of fear, and sped away swiftly to the house. Rather startled, I bent my eyes on the place, as if by some fascination, half expecting—how foolish it was!—to see Mr. Chandos perambulating in his sleep. And I believe, had I done so, I should have run away more terrified than from any ghost.

Something did appear to be there that ought not to be. It was between the trunks of two trees, in a line with them, as if it were another tree of never-yet-witnessed form and shape. A great deal more like the figure of a man, thought I, as I gazed. Not a tall slender man like Mr. Chandos: more of the build of Mr. Edwin Barley.

Why the idea of the latter should have occurred to me, or whether the man (it certainly was one!) bore him any resemblance, I could not tell. The fancy was quite enough for me, and I sped away as quickly as Mrs. Chandos had done. She had flitted silently through the hall towards her rooms, and met her maid on the stairs; who had probably just discovered her absence.

"Are you ready to make tea, Miss Hereford? I have come to have some."

It was the greeting of Mr. Chandos, as I ran, scared and breathless, into the oak-parlour. He was sitting in the easy-chair near the table, a review in his hand, and looked up with surprise. No wonder—seeing me dart in as if pursued by a wild cat, an ugly shawl over my head. But, you see, I had not thought he would be there.

However, he said nothing. I sat down, as sedate as any old matron, and made the tea. Mr. Chandos read his paper, and spoke to me between whiles.

"Don't you think, sir, we ought to have heard to-day from Madame de Mellissie?"

"Why to-day?"

"It is getting time that I heard. Except the short note to Lady Chandos, written upon her arrival in Paris, she has not sent a syllable. It is very strange."

"Nothing is strange that Emily does. She may be intending to surprise us by arriving without notice. I fully expect it. On the other hand, we may not hear from her for weeks to come."

"But she has left me here, sir! She said she should be sure to come back the very first day she could."

Mr. Chandos slightly laughed. "You may have passed from her memory, Miss Hereford, as completely as though you never existed in it."

I paused in consternation, the suggestion bringing to me I know not what of perplexity. He looked excessively amused.

"What can I do, sir?"

"Not anything that I see, except make yourself contented here. At least until we hear from Emily."

With the tea-things, disappeared Mr. Chandos; and a sensation of loneliness fell upon me. At what? At his exit, or at my previous alarm in the Pine Walk? I might have asked myself, but did not. He came back again shortly, remarking that it was a fine night.

"Have you been out, sir?"

"No. I have been to my mother's rooms."

"Is she better this evening?"

"Much the same."

He stood with his elbow on the mantelpiece, his hand lifted to his head, evidently in deep thought, a strange look of anxiety, of pain, in the expression of his countenance. I went over to a side-table to get something out of my work-box; and, not to disturb him by going back again, I softly pulled aside the muslin window-curtain to look out for a minute on the dusky still night.

What was it made me spring back with a sudden movement of terror and a half-cry? Surely I could not be mistaken! That *was* a face close to the window, looking in; the dark face of a man; and, unless I was much mistaken, bearing a strong resemblance to that of Mr. Edwin Barley.

"What is it?" asked Mr. Chandos, coming forward. "Has anything alarmed you?"

"Oh, sir! I saw a face pressed close to the window-pane. A man's face."

Without the loss of a moment, Mr. Chandos threw up the window, and had his head out. All I felt good for was to sit down in a chair out of sight. He could see no one, as it appeared, and he shut the window again very quietly. Perhaps his thoughts only pointed to some one of the servants.

"Are you sure you saw any one, Miss Hereford?"

"I am very nearly sure, sir."

"Who was it?"

In truth I could not say, and I was not obliged to avow my suspicions. Mr. Chandos hastened outside, and I remained alone, as timid as could be.

A curious and most unpleasant suspicion was fixing itself upon my mind, dim glimpses of which had been haunting me during tea—that Mr. Edwin Barley's object was myself. That it was he who had been in the Pine Walk, and again now at the window, I felt a positive conviction, He must have recognized me; this stealthy intrusion at odd times, seasonable and unseasonable, must be to watch me, to take note of my movements, not of those of the owners of Chandos. But for his motive I searched in vain.

"I cannot see or hear any one about," said Mr. Chandos, when he returned; "all seems to be quite free and still. I fancy you must have been mistaken, Miss Hereford."

I shook my head, but did not care to say much, after the notion that had taken possession of me. Words might lead to deeper questions, and I could not for the world have said that I knew Edwin Barley.

"Possibly you may be a little nervous to-night," he continued, ringing the bell; "and at such times fancy considers itself at liberty to play us all sorts of tricks. My having told you what I did this morning relating to myself, may have taken hold of your imagination."

"Oh no; it has not."

"I shall be very sorry to have mentioned it, if it has. Believe me, there's nothing in that to disturb you. When you ran in at tea-time I thought you looked scared. Close the shutters," he added, to the servant, who had appeared in answer to his ring. "And if you will pardon my leaving you alone, Miss Hereford, I will wish you good-night. I am very tired; I have some writing to do yet."

He shook hands with me and departed. Joseph bolted and barred the shutters, and I was left alone. But I went up to my room before ten o'clock.

Would Mr. Chandos—or his ghost, as the servants had it—be out again that night in his somnambulant state? The subject had taken hold of my most vivid interest, and after undressing I undid the shutters and stood for a few minutes at the window in a warm wrapper, watching the grounds. Eyes and ears were alike strained, but to no purpose. No noise disturbed the house indoors, and all appeared still without; it might be too early yet for Mr. Chandos.

But the silence told upon me. There was not a voice to be heard, not a sound to break the intense stillness. I began to feel nervous, hurried into bed, and went to sleep.

Not to sleep for very long. I was awakened suddenly by a commotion in the gallery outside. A loud, angry cry; reproachful tones; all in the voice of Mrs. Chandos; they were followed by low, remonstrating words, as if some one wished to soothe her. Were you ever aroused thus in the middle of the night in a strange, or comparatively strange, place? If so, you may divine what was my terror. I sat up in bed with parted lips, unable to hear anything distinctly for the violent beating of my heart; and then darted to the door, putting on my slippers and my large warm wrapper, before drawing it cautiously an inch open.

It was not possible to make out anything at first in the dim gallery. Three dusky forms were there, having apparently come from the west wing, which I took to be those of Lady, Mr., and Mrs. Chandos. She, the latter, had her hair hanging down over a white wrapper; and Mr. Chandos, his arm about her waist, was drawing her to her own apartments. It was by that I knew him; who else would have presumed so to touch her?—his coat was off, his slippers were noiseless. The moonlight, coming in faintly on the gallery from above, made things tolerably clear, as my eyes got used to them.

"You never would have told me," she sobbed, pushing back her hair with a petulant hand; "you know you never meant to tell me for ever so long. It is cruel—cruel! What am I here but a caged bird?"

"Oh, Ethel! Ethel! you will betray us all!" cried Lady Chandos, in a voice of dire, reproachful tribulation. "To think that you should make this disturbance at night! Did you forget that a stranger was sleeping here?—that the servants may hear you in their rooms? You will bring desolation to the house."

Scarcely had they disappeared within the doors of the east wing, when Mr. Chandos came swiftly and suddenly out of his own chamber. Only a moment seemed to have elapsed, yet he had found it sufficient time to finish dressing, for he was now fully attired. His appearing from his chamber, after disappearing within the east wing, established the fact that his room did communicate with it. Almost simultaneously Hickens ran up the stairs from the hall, a light in his hand. Mr. Chandos advanced upon him, and peremptorily waved him back.

"Go back to bed, sir. You are not wanted."

But as the light fell on Mr. Chandos's face, I saw that he was deadly pale, and his imperative manner seemed to proceed from fear, not anger.

"I heard a scream, Mr. Harry," responded poor Hickens, evidently taken aback. "I'm sure I heard voices; and I—I—thought some thieves or villains of that sort had got in, sir."

"Nothing of the kind. There's nothing whatever the matter to call for your aid. Mrs. Chandos is nervous to-night, and cried out—it is not the first time it has happened, as you know. She is all right again now, and my mother is with her. Go back, and get your rest as usual."

"Shall I leave you the light, sir?" asked Hickens, perceiving that Mr. Chandos had none.

"Light? No. What do I want with a light? Mrs. Chandos's ailments have nothing to do with me."

He stood at the head of the stairs, watching Hickens down, and listening to his quiet closing of the doors dividing the hall from the kitchen-passages. Hickens slept downstairs, near his plate-pantry. He was late in going to rest, as it was explained afterwards, and had heard the noise overhead in the midst of undressing.

Mr. Chandos turned from the stairs, and I suppose the slender inch-stream of moonlight must have betrayed to him that my door was open. He came straight towards it with his stern, white face, and I had no time to draw back. He and ceremony were at variance with each other that night.

"Miss Hereford, I beg your pardon, but I must request that you retire within your room and allow your door to be closed," came the peremptory injunction. "Mrs. Chandos is ill, and the sight of strangers would make her worse. I will close it for you; I should so act by my sister, were she here."

He shut it with his own hand, and turned the key upon me. Turned the key upon me! Well, I could only submit, feeling very much ashamed to have had my curiosity detected, and returned to bed. Nothing more was heard; not the faintest movement to tell that anything unusual had happened.

But how strangely mysterious it all appeared! One curious commotion, one unaccountable mystery succeeding to another. I had heard of haunted castles in romances, of ghostly abbeys; surely the events enacted in them could not be more startling than these at Chandos.

Morning came. I was up betimes; dressed, read; found my room unlocked, and went out of doors while waiting for breakfast. Mr. Chandos passed on his way from the house, and stopped.

"Did I offend you last night, Miss Hereford?"

"No, sir."

"Walk with me a few steps, then," he rejoined. "I assumed the liberty of treating you as a sister—as though you were Emily. I thought you would have the good sense to understand so, and feel no offence. What caused you to be looking from your door?"

"The commotion in the gallery awoke me, sir, and I felt frightened. It was only natural I should look to see what caused it."

"What did you see?"

"I saw Lady and Mrs. Chandos; and I saw you, sir. You were supporting Mrs. Chandos."

"Did you see any one else?"

"No; not any one else."

For the space of a full minute Mr. Chandos never took his eyes from me. It looked as if he questioned my veracity.

"I forgot Hickens, sir; I saw him. At least, in point of fact, I did not see him; he did not come forward enough; I only heard him."

"Suppose I were to tell you it was not Mrs. Chandos you saw?"

"But it was Mrs. Chandos, sir; I am sure of it. I recognized her in spite of her hanging hair, and I also recognized her voice."

"You are equally sure, I presume, that it was myself?"

"Of course I am, sir. Why, did you not speak to me at my door afterwards?"

Could I have been mistaken in thinking that a great relief came over his face?

"Ah, yes," he continued after a pause, while his gaze went out into the far distance, "Mrs. Chandos is one of our troubles. She is not in good health, and has disturbed us before in the same manner. The fact is, she is what is called nervous; meaning that she is not so collected at times as she ought to be. I am very sorry you were disturbed."

"Pray don't think anything of that, sir. She feels strange, perhaps, now Mrs. Freeman is gone."

"Yes, that is it. But it has very much upset my mother."

"I fancied yesterday evening that Mrs. Chandos was not quite right; though, perhaps, I ought not to repeat it. Her manner was a little wild."

"Yesterday evening! When did you see her yesterday evening?"

"I saw her out in the grounds, sir, in the Pine Walk."

"Alone?"

"Quite alone, sir, in her white silk evening-dress. It was at dusk; just before I ran in to the oak-parlour, if you remember. Mrs. Chandos and I came in together."

"What took *you* there?" he asked, abruptly.

I told him what—that I had stepped out, being alone, and crossed the grass.

"Well," he said, gravely, "allow me to caution you not to go out of doors after dusk, Miss Hereford; there are reasons against it. I will take care that Mrs. Chandos does not. We might have you both run away with," he added, in a lighter tone.

"There is no fear of that, sir."

"You do not know what there is fear of," he sharply answered.

"Last night you looked as scared as could be. You will be fancying you see ghosts in the Pine Walk next, or me, perhaps, walking in my sleep."

"We thought we did, sir. At least, something was there that looked like a man."

"What sort of man?" he hastily asked.

"One short and thick-set. I suppose it was only the trunk of a tree."

"Stay indoors; don't go roaming about at dark," he emphatically said. "And now I have another request to make to you, Miss Hereford."

"What is it, sir?"

"That you will leave off calling me 'sir.' It does not sound well on your lips."

He smiled as he spoke. And I blushed until I was ashamed of myself.

"Have you any love for the appellation?"

"No, indeed! But Madame de Mellissie—"

"Just so," he interrupted. "I suspected as much. You would not have fallen into it yourself."

"I don't know that, sir."

"Sir?"

"It was a slip of the tongue. I used to say 'Sir' and 'Madam' to Mr. and Mrs. Paler. I was told to do so when I went there as governess."

"Well, you are not governess here, and we can dispense with it. Good-morning!" he added, as we neared the gates. "It is too bad to bring you so far, and send you back alone."

"Are you not coming to breakfast, sir?" Another slip.

"My breakfast was taken an hour ago. I am going to see how Mrs. Freeman is. You will be condemned to a solitary breakfast this morning. Good-bye!"

A very pleasant one, for all that. It *is* pleasant to live amidst the luxuries of life. The fare of a governess had been exchanged for the liberal table of Chandos. Not that I cared much what I ate and drank: I was young and healthy; but I did like the ease and refinement, the state and the innocent vanities belonging to the order of the Chandos world.

Half sitting, half lying in one of the garden-chairs in the balmy sunshine, I partly read and partly dreamed away the morning. The house was within view; servants and comers passed to it within hail; cheery voices could be heard; snatches of laughter now and again. On that side all was busy life; on the other lay the silent mass of trees that surrounded Chandos. The sun was twinkling through their foliage; the glorious tints of ruddy autumn lighted them up. A charming tableau!

Uncertain though my stay was, unusual and perhaps undesirable as the position was for a young girl, I was beginning to feel strangely happy in it. Madame de Mellissie did not come; another post in, that day, and no letter from her. And there I sat on unconcerned, in my pretty lilac muslin, with the ribbons in my chestnut hair, watching the little birds as they flew about singing; watching the gardener sweeping up his leaves at a distance; and feeling more joyous than the morning. I ought not to have felt so, I dare say, but I did, and broke out into snatches of song as gay as the birds.

Mr. Chandos passed to the house with a quick step, not seeing me. He was back, then; I followed, for it was the luncheon-hour, and I was not on a sufficient footing at Chandos to keep meals waiting. Hill was in the oak-parlour, inquiring after the state of Mrs. Freeman.

"Her state is this, Hill—that it admits no probability whatever of her returning here," said Mr. Chandos, throwing back his velveteen coat, for he was in sporting clothes. And well he looked in them! as a tall, handsome man generally does.

"There's a bother!" was Hill's retort. "Then some one else must be seen about, Mr. Harry, without loss of time."

"I suppose so. Things seem to be going tolerably cross just now."

"Cross and contrary," groaned Hill. "As they always do, I've noticed, when it's specially necessary they should go smooth. My lady was speaking about Miss White, you know, sir."

"Yes. I'll go up and speak with my mother. But I must have something to eat, Hill."

"The luncheon ought to be in," was Hill's reply. And she crossed to the bell and gave it a sharp pull.

"Have you been walking to Mrs. Freeman's?" I asked of Mr. Chandos, as he was quitting the room.

"That would be more than a twenty-mile walk, there and back," he answered, turning to speak. "I honoured the omnibus with my company as far as the station, and then went on by train; coming back in the same way."

The luncheon was on the table when he descended from his mother's rooms, and he hastily sat down to it. He was dressed differently then.

"I will not invite you to take it with me," he observed, "for I must not sit five minutes, and can barely snatch a mouthful."

"Are you going far?"

"Not very far; but I wish to be home to dinner. That will do, Joseph; you need not wait."

"Let me wait upon you, Mr. Chandos," I said, springing up.

"Very well. How will you begin?"

"I don't know what to begin with. I don't know what you want first."

"Nor I. For I do not want anything at all just now. What have you been doing with yourself all the morning?"

"Working a little, and reading. Not Shakespeare, but a play of Goldsmith's; 'She Stoops to Conquer.'"

"Why, where did you pick that up?" he interrupted. "I did not know the book was about."

"I saw it lying in the window-seat near the east wing, and dipped into it. After that, I could not put it down again—although it was not in the list of the books you gave me."

"You thought you would enjoy the mischief first, as the children do, whether the scolding came afterwards or not."

"Ought I not to have read it?"

"You may read it again if you like. It is an excellent comedy; more entertaining, I fancy, to read than to witness, though. Did you fall in love with Tony Lumpkin?"

"Not irrevocably. Here comes your horse round, Mr. Chandos."

"My signal for departure. And I believe I am speeding on a useless errand."

"Is it an important one?"

"It is to inquire after a lady to replace Mrs. Freeman as companion to Mrs. Chandos. Some one my mother knows; a Miss White. Miss White was seeking such a situation a few months ago; but the probabilities are that she has found one."

A strong impulse came over me to offer to supply the place—until I should be called away by Madame de Mellissie.

*Miss* White! she might be only a young person. If I could only make myself useful, it would take away the compunction I felt at having been thrust upon them at Chandos. I spoke on the impulse of the moment, blushing and timid as a schoolgirl. Mr. Chandos smiled, and shook his head.

"It is not a situation that would suit you; or you it."

"Is Miss White older than I?"

"A little. She is about fifty-six."

"Oh! But as a temporary arrangement, sir? Until we have news from Madame de Mellissie. I should like to repay a tithe of the obligation I am under to Lady Chandos."

"A great obligation, that! No, it could not be. We should have you and Mrs. Chandos running into the shrubberies after sleep-walkers and ghosts, as it seems you did last night. Besides," he added, taking up his gloves and riding-whip, "if you became Mrs. Chandos's companion, what should I do for mine?"

He nodded to me after he got on his horse; a spirited animal, Black Knave by name: and rode away at a brisk canter, followed by his groom.

# CHAPTER 17

## THE STRANGER APPLICANT

"Is Mr. Chandos gone, do you know, miss?"

The question came from Hill, who put her head in at the oak-parlour to make it.

"He rode away not three minutes ago."

"Dear me! My lady wanted him to call somewhere else. I suppose the note must be posted."

"Stay an instant, Mrs. Hill," I said, detaining her. "There's a new companion wanted, is there not, for Mrs. Chandos?"

"Of course there is," returned Hill. "What of it?"

"Can I see Lady Chandos?"

Hill turned hard directly, facing me resolutely.

"Now, miss, you listen; we have had that discussion once before, and we don't want it gone over again. So long as my lady keeps her rooms, neither you nor anybody else can be admitted to her; you wouldn't be if you paid for it in gold. And I'm much surprised that a young lady, calling herself a lady, should persist in pressing it."

"Hill, I am not pressing it. I only asked the question. As I cannot see Lady Chandos, will you deliver a message to her for me? If I can be of any use in taking the duties of companion to Mrs. Chandos in this temporary need, I shall be glad to be so, and will do my very best."

To see the countenance with which Hill received these words, was something comical: the open mouth, the stare of astonishment.

"*You* take the duties of companion to Mrs. Chandos!" uttered she, at length. "Bless the child! you little know what you ask for."

"But will you mention it to Lady Chandos?"

Hill vouchsafed no answer. She cast a glance of pity on my ignorance or presumption, whichever she may have deemed it, and quietly went out of the room.

That it was perfectly useless persisting, or even thinking of the affair further, I saw, and got out my writing-desk. Not a word had come to me from Mrs. Paler, not a hint at payment; and I wrote a civil request that she would kindly forward me the money due.

This over, I sat, pen in hand, deliberating whether to write or not to Emily de Mellissie, when a loud ring came to the house-door. One of the footmen crossed the hall to answer it.

"Is Lady Chandos at home?" I heard demanded, in a ladylike and firm voice.

"Her ladyship is at home, ma'am," answered Joseph, "but she does not receive visitors."

"I wish to see her."

"She is ill, madam; not able to see any one."

"Lady Chandos would admit me. My business is of importance. In short, I must see her."

Joseph seemed to hesitate.

"I'll call Mrs. Hill, and you can see her, ma'am," he said, after a little pause. "But I feel certain you cannot be admitted to my lady."

She was ushered by Joseph into the oak-parlour. A good-looking woman, as might be seen through her black Chandlly veil, dressed in a soft black silk gown and handsome shawl. She was of middle height, portly, and had a mass of fiery red hair, *crêpé* on the temples, and taken to the back of her head. I rose to receive her. She bowed, but did not lift her veil; and it struck me that I had seen her somewhere before.

"I presume that I have the honour of speaking to a Miss Chandos?"

"I am not Miss Chandos. Will you take a seat?"

"I grieve to hear that Lady Chandos is ill. Is she so ill that she cannot see me?"

What I should have answered I scarcely know, and was relieved by the entrance of Hill. The visitor rose.

"I have come here, some distance, to request an interview with Lady Chandos. I hear she is indisposed; but not, I trust, too much so to grant it to me."

"I'm sorry you should have taken the trouble," bluntly returned Hill, who was in one of her ungracious moods. "My lady cannot see any one."

"My business with her is of importance."

"I can't help that. If all England came, Lady Chandos could not receive them."

"To whom am I speaking?—if I may inquire," resumed the lady.

"I am Mrs. Hill. The many-years' confidential attendant of Lady Chandos."

"You share her entire confidence?"

"Her entire confidence, and that of the family."

"I have heard of you. It is not every family who possesses so faithful a friend."

"Anything you may have to say to her ladyship, whatever its nature, you can, if you please, charge me with," resumed Hill, completely ignoring the compliment. "I do not urge it, or covet it," she hastily added, in an uncompromising tone. "I only mention it because it is impossible that you can see Lady Chandos."

"Mrs. Chandos requires a companion, at the present moment, to replace one who has gone away ill"

"What of that?" returned Hill.

"I have come to offer myself for the appointment," said the visitor, handing her card, which Hill dropped on the table without looking at. "I flatter myself I shall be found eligible."

Hill looked surprised, and I felt so. Only a candidate for the vacant place?—after all that circumlocution!

"Why could you not have said at first what you wanted?" was Hill's next question, put with scant politeness. Indeed, she seemed to resent both the visit and the application as a personal affront. "I don't think you'll suit, madam."

"Why do you think I shall not?"

"And we are about somebody already. Mr. Chandos is gone to inquire for her now."

A flush, and a shade of disappointment, immediately hid under a smile, appeared on the lady's face. I felt sorry for her. I thought perhaps she might be wandng a home.

"Mr. Chandos may not engage her," observed the visitor.

"That's true enough," acknowledged Hill. "Yet she would have suited well; for she is not a stranger to the Chandos family."

"Neither am I," quietly replied the applicant. "My name is Penn—if you will have the goodness to look at the card—Mrs. Penn."

"Penn? Penn?" repeated Hill, revolving the information, but paying no attention to the suggestion. "I don't recognize the name. I remember nobody bearing it who is known to us."

"Neither would Lady Chandos recognize it, for personally I am unknown to her. When I said I was no stranger to the Chandos family, I meant that I was not strange to certain unpleasant events connected with it. That dreadful misfortune—"

"It's not a thing to be talked of in the light of day," shrieked Hill, putting up her hands to arrest the words. "Have you not more discretion than that? Very fit, you'd be, as companion to young Mrs. Chandos!"

"Do not alarm yourself for nothing," rejoined Mrs. Penn, with soothing coolness. "I was not going to talk of it, beyond the barest allusion: and the whole world knows that the Chandos family are not as others. I would only observe that I am acquainted with everything that occurred; all the details; and therefore I should be more eligible than some to reside at Chandos."

"How did you learn them?" asked Hill.

"Lady Chandos had once an intimate friend—Mrs. Sackville; who is now dead. I was at Mrs. Sackville's when the affair happened, and became cognizant of all through her. Perhaps Lady Chandos may deem it worth while to see me, if you tell her this."

"How can she see you, when she's confined to her bed?" irritably responded Hill, who appeared fully bent upon admitting none to the presence of Lady Chandos. The very mention of it excited her anger in a most unreasonable manner, for which I could see no occasion whatever.

More talking. At its conclusion, Hill took the card up to Lady Chandos; also the messages of the stranger; one of which was, that she would prove a faithful friend in the event of being engaged. Hill returned presently, to inquire how Mrs. Penn heard that a companion to Mrs. Chandos was required; that lady replied that she had heard it accidentally at Marden. She had lived only in three situations, she said: with Mrs. Sackville and Mrs. James, both of whom were dead, and at present she was with Mrs. Howard, of Marden, who would personally answer all inquiries.

Hill appeared to regard this as satisfactory. She noted the address given, and accompanied Mrs. Penn to the portico, who declined the offer of refreshments. They spoke together for some minutes in an undertone, and then Mrs. Penn walked away at a brisk pace, wishing, she said, to catch the omnibus that would presently pass Chandos gates on its way to the station. I put my head out at the window, and gazed after her, trying to recall, looking at her back, what I had not been able to do looking at her face. Hill's voice interrupted me.

"Is not there something rather queer about that person's looks, Miss Hereford?"

"In what way, Hill? She is good-looking."

"Well, her face struck me as being a curious one. What bright red hair she has!—quite scarlet!—and I have heard say that red hair is sometimes deceitful. It is her own, though: for I looked at it in the sunlight outside."

"She puts me in mind of some one I have seen, and I cannot recollect who. It is not often you see red hair with those very light blue eyes."

"I never saw hair so red in all my life," returned Hill; "it looks just as if it had been burnished. She seems straightforward and independent. We shall see what the references say, if it comes to an inquiry."

"If you and Lady Chandos would only let me try the situation, Hill! I'm sure I should suit Mrs. Chandos as well as this lady would. I am only twenty; but I have had experience one way or another."

As if the words were a signal to drive her away, Hill walked off. I wrote to Madame de Mellissie, finished a drawing, and got through the afternoon; going up to dress at half-past five.

Now that Lady Chandos was secluded, and Mr. Chandos my sole dinner companion, instinct told me that full dress was best avoided. So I put on my pretty pink barége, with its little tucker of Honiton lace at the throat, and its falling cuffs of Honiton lace at the wrists. Nothing in my hair but a bit of pink ribbon. I had not worn anything but ribbon since I came to Chandos.

The dinner waited and I waited, but Mr. Chandos did not come. I had seen a covered tray carried upstairs by Hickens; at the door of the west wing Hill would relieve him of it, the invariable custom. At the special request of Lady Chandos, Hickens alone went up there; the other men-servants never. Joseph carried up the meals for Mrs. Chandos and stayed to wait on her.

"Would you like to sit down without Mr. Chandos, miss?" Hickens came to inquire of me when half-past six o'clock had struck.

No, I did not care to do that. And the time went on again; I wondering what was detaining him. By-and-by I went out of doors in the twilight, and strolled a little way down the open carriage drive. Surely Mr. Chandos's prohibition could not extend to the broad public walk. It was not so pleasant an evening as the previous one; clouds chased each other across the sky, a dim star or two struggled out, the air was troubled, and the wind was sighing and moaning in the trees.

There broke upon my ear the sound of a horse's gallop. I did not care that its master should see me walking there, and turned to gain the house. But—what sort of speed was it coming at? Why should Mr. Chandos be riding in that breakneck fashion? Little chance, in truth, that I could outstrip that! So I stepped close to the side trees, and in another moment Black Knave tore furiously by without its rider, the bridle trailing on the ground.

Mr. Chandos must have met with an accident; he might be lying in desperate need. Where could it have happened? and where was the groom who had gone out in attendance on him? I ran along at my swiftest speed, and soon saw a dark object in the distance, nearly as far as the entrance-gates. It was Mr. Chandos trying to raise himself.

"Are you hurt?" I asked, kneeling down beside him.

"Some trifling damage, I suppose. How came you here, Miss Hereford?"

"I saw the horse gallop in, and ran to see what the accident might be, sir. How did it happen?"

"Get up, child. Get up, and I will tell you."

"Yes, sir," I said, obeying him.

"I was riding fast, being late, and in passing this spot some creature—I should say 'devil' to any one but a young lady—darted out of those trees there, and threw up its hands with a noise right in front of my horse, to startle it, or to startle me. Black Knave reared, bounded forward, and I lost my seat. I had deemed myself a first-rate horseman before to-night; but I was sitting carelessly."

"Was it a man?"

"To the best of my belief, it was a woman. The night is dusk; and I saw things less accurately than I might have done in a more collected moment. It was a something in a grey cloak, with a shrill voice. I wonder if you could help me up?"

"I will do my best."

I stooped, and he placed his hands upon me, and raised himself. But it appeared that he could not walk: but for holding on to me, he would have fallen.

"I believe you must let me lie on the ground again, and go and send assistance, Miss Hereford. Stay: who's this?"

It was one of the servants, Lizzy Dene, who had been, as was subsequently explained, on an errand to the village. She exclaimed in dismayed astonishment when she comprehended the helpless position of Mr. Chandos.

"Now don't lose your wits, Lizzy Dene, but see what you can do to help me," he cried. "With you on one side, and Miss Hereford on the other, perhaps I may make a hobble of it."

The woman put her basket down, concealing it between the trees, and Mr. Chandos laid his hand upon her shoulder, I helping him on the other side. She was full of questions, calling the horse all sorts of treacherous names. Mr. Chandos said the horse was not to blame, and gave her the explanation that he had given me.

"Sir, I'd lay a hundred guineas that it was one of those gipsy jades!" she exclaimed. "There's a lot of them camped on the common."

"I'll gipsy them, should it prove so," he answered. "Miss Hereford, I am sorry to lean upon you so heavily. The order of things is being reversed. Instead of the knight supporting the lady, the lady is bearing the weight of the knight."

"Where was your groom, sir?" I inquired. "He went abroad with you."

"Yes, but I depatched him on an errand, and rode back alone."

"Should you know the woman again, sir?" asked Lizzy.

"I think I should know her scream. It was as shrill as a sea-gull's. Her head was enveloped in some covering that concealed her face; probably the hood of the grey cloak."

"Who's to know that it was not a man? " resumed Lizzy Dene. "If so, he wore petticoats," said Mr. Chandos. "A seat at last!" he added, as we approached one. "I will remain here whilst you go and send two of the men."

"Can't we get you on further, sir?" said Lizzy.

"No. I have taxed your strength too much in this short distance. And my own also, through endeavouring to ease my weight to you."

In point of fact, the weight had been felt, for the one foot seemed quite powerless. He sat down on the bench, his brow white and moist with pain, and motioned to us to go on. "I think they had better bring my mother's garden-chair," he said.

"I'll run and send it," cried Lizzy. "Miss had better stop with you, sir."

"What for?" asked Mr. Chandos.

"Look you here, sir. That woman, whoever she might have been, was trying to do you an injury; to cause you to lose your life, I should say; and the chances are that she's concealed somewhere about here still. Look at the opportunities for hiding there are here! Why, a whole regiment of gipsies and murderers and thieves might be skulking amid the trees, and us none the wiser till they showed themselves out with guns and knives. That woman—which I'll be bound was a man—may be watching to come out upon you, sir, if you can be caught by yourself."

Mr. Chandos laughed, but Lizzy Dene seemed in anything but a laughing mood. "I will stay with you, sir," I said, and sat down resolutely on the bench. Lizzy went off with a nod.

"Now, Miss Hereford, you and I have an account to settle," he began, as her footsteps died away in the distance. "Why am I 'sir' again?"

"Lizzy Dene was present," I answered, giving him the truth. I had not liked that she should see me familiar with him—putting myself, as it were, on a level with Mr. Chandos; and in truth the word still slipped out at odd times in my shyness. Lizzy Dene might have commented upon the omission in the household: but this I did not say. Mr. Chandos turned to look at me.

"Never mind who is present, I am not 'sir' to you. I beg you to recollect that, Miss Hereford. And now," he continued, taking my hand, "how am I to thank you?"

"For what?"

"For coming and looking for me. I might have lain until morning, inhaling the benefit of the night dews; or until that grey witch had 'come out again with a gun' and finished me."

The last words, a repetition of Lizzy Dene's, were spoken in jest. I laughed.

"You would soon have been found, without me, Mr. Chandos. Lizzy Dene was not many moments after me, and scores of others will be coming in before the night is over."

"I don't know about the 'scores.' But see how you destroy the romance of the thing, Miss Hereford! I wish there *was* a probability that the woman had gone into hiding in the groves of Chandos; I would soon have her hunted out of them."

"Do you suppose it was one of the gipsies?"

"I am at a loss for any supposition on the point," he replied. "I am unconscious of having given offence to any person or persons."

"Do you think you are much injured?"

"There are worse misfortunes in hospitals than the injury to my foot. I believe it to be nothing but a common sprain, although it has disabled me. The pain—"

"That's great, I am sure."

"Pretty well. I should not like you to experience it."

That it was more than pretty well, I saw, for the drops were coursing down his face. The men soon came up with the garden-chair, and Mr. Chandos sent me on.

He was laid on the sofa in the oak-parlour. Hill examined the foot and bound it up, one of the grooms having been despatched for a medical man. He arrived after dinner—which was taken in a scrambling sort of manner—a Mr. Dickenson, from the village, who was left with Mr. Chandos.

At tea-time, when I went in again, things looked comfortable. The surgeon had pronounced it to be only a sprain, and Mr. Chandos was on the sofa, quietly reading, a shaded lamp at his elbow. From his conversation with Hill, I gathered that the lady he had been inquiring after, Miss White, had taken a situation at a distance, and could not come to Chandos.

"We have had another applicant after the place, Mr. Harry," observed Hill, who was settling the cushion under his foot. And she proceeded to tell him the particulars of Mrs. Penn's visit.

"Is she likely to suit?"

"My lady thinks so. Mr. Harry"—dropping her voice to a whisper, which she, no doubt, thought would be inaudible to me, busy with the tea-cups at the table ever so far off—"she knows all about that past trouble."

Mr. Chandos laid down his book and looked at her.

"Every unhappy syllable of it, sir; more than my lady knows herself," whispered Hill. "She mentioned one or two particulars to me which I'm sure we had never known; and she said she could tell my lady more than that."

"That is extraordinary," observed Mr. Chandos, in the same subdued tone. "Who is this Mrs. Penn? Whence could she have heard anything?"

"From Mrs. Sackville. You must remember her, sir. She stayed a week with us about that time."

"This comes of my mother's having made a confidant of Mrs. Sackville!" he muttered. "I always thought Mrs. Sackville a chattering woman. But it does not account for Mrs. Penn's knowing particulars that my mother does not know," he added, after a pause. "I shall be curious to see Mrs. Penn."

"That's just the question I put to her, sir: where Mrs. Sackville could have learnt these details. Mrs. Penn answered that she had them from Sir Thomas himself. Therefore, I conclude, Sir Thomas must have revealed to her what he spared my lady."

Mr. Chandos shook his head with a proud, repellant air.

"I don't believe it, Hill. However Mrs. Sackville might have learnt them, rely upon it it was not from Sir Thomas. She was no favourite of his."

"Misfortunes never come singly," resumed Hill, quitting the subject with a sort of grunt. "Mrs. Freeman could not have fallen ill at a worse time."

"And now I am disabled! Temporarily, at least."

"Oh, well, sir, let's hope for the best," cried she, getting up from her knees. "When troubles come, the only plan is to look them steadily in the face, and meet them bravely."

"It is rather curious, though," cried Mr. Chandos, looking at Hill. "What is, sir?"

"That I should be laid aside now. It has been so each time. There's something more than chance in it."

Hill appeared to understand. I did not. As she was quitting the room, Hickens came in.

"Mr. Dexter has called, sir," he said. "Would you like to see him?"

"Does he want anything particular?" asked Mr. Chandos. "No business, sir. He heard of this accident to you, and hurried here, he says."

"Let him come in. You need not leave us, Miss Hereford," he added to me, for I was rising. "Dexter will thank you for a cup of tea."

"Well, now, Mr. Chandos, how was this?" cried the agent, as he bustled in, wiping his red face. Mr. Dexter gave me the idea of being always in a hurry.

"I can hardly tell you," replied Mr. Chandos. "I don't quite know myself."

"News was brought into my office that Mr. Chandos's horse had thrown him, and he was supposed to be dying. So I caught up my hat and came rushing off. Hickens says it is only an injury to the ankle."

"And that's enough, Dexter, for it is keeping me a prisoner. However, it might have been as you heard, so I must not grumble. The question is, what ill-working jade caused it?"

"Ill-working jade?" repeated Mr. Dexter. "Was it not an accident? I don't understand."

"An accident maliciously perpetrated. Some venomous spirit in the guise of a woman sprang before my horse with a scream and threw up her arms in his face. Black Knave won't stand such jokes. I was riding carelessly, and lost my seat."

"Bless my heart!" exclaimed Mr. Dexter, after a pause, given to digest the words. "Who was it? Is she taken?"

"A tramp, probably. Though why she should set on me I am unable to conjecture. Where she vanished to, or what became of her, I know not. I raised myself on my elbow directly I could collect my wits, which I assure you were somewhat scattered, but the coast was already clear: and I had not been down a minute then."

"What was the woman like?" pursued the agent, as I handed him some tea.

"I can tell you nothing about that. She wore a grey cloak, or something that looked like one, which enveloped her person and shaded her face. I should not know her if she stood before me this minute."

"Was the cloak assumed for the purpose of disguise, sir, think you?" eagerly questioned the agent, who seemed to take the matter up with much warmth, as if he had a suspicion.

"It looked uncommonly like it."

"Then I tell you what, Mr. Chandos; it was no ordinary tramp, or gaol-bird of that description. Depend upon it, you must look nearer home."

"Nearer home!" repeated Mr. Chandos. "Do you allude to our household servants?"

"I don't allude to any party or parties in particular, sir. But when a disguise is assumed for the purpose of molesting a gentleman, riding to his home in the dusk of night, be assured that the offender is no stranger. This ought to be investigated, Mr. Chandos."

"I sent two of the men to seek round about, and they scoured the plantations near the spot, but without result. So far as they could ascertain, no living body, worse than a hare, was concealed there."

"I could understand if you were obnoxious to the tenants, or to any others, in the neighbourhood, but the exact contrary is the case," pursued Mr. Dexter, stirring his tea violently round and round. "The tenants often say they wish Mr. Chandos was their real landlord. Not that they have any cause of complaint against Sir Thomas; but Sir Thomas is a stranger to them, and you, sir, are in their midst; one, as it were, of themselves."

"Talking about tenants—and to leave an unprofitable subject, for we shall make nothing of it in the present stage of the affair," resumed Mr. Chandos—"I don't like the new tenant by the gates here, Dexter."

"No? Why not, sir?"

"And I should like to get rid of him."

Our visitor put his bread-and-butter down on the plate, and stared at Mr. Chandos, as if questioning whether he might be in jest or earnest.

"What is your objection to him, sir?" he asked, after a pause.

"I cannot state any objection in detail. I have seen the man, and I don't like him. How can he be got rid of, Dexter?"

"He cannot be got rid of at all, sir, until the lease is out—three years—unless he chooses to quit of his own accord. There's a clause in the lease that he can leave at the end of any twelvemonth, by giving proper notice."

"That's his side—as regards the agreement. What is mine?"

"You have no power to dismiss him until the three years are up."

"How came you to draw up a one-sided deed, such as that?"

"Haines said his client wished to have the option of quitting at the end of any year, though he would probably continue for the three. In point of fact, Mr. Edwin Barley is a yearly tenant; but he wished to have the power in his own hands of remaining the three years. I did speak to you, Mr. Chandos, and you made no objection."

Mr. Chandos sat, twirling the watch-key and beautiful transparent seal that drooped from his gold chain. It was self-evident to him that what might appear to be just terms for any other man on the face of the earth who had offered himself as tenant, looked anything but just now that the tenant proved to be Mr. Edwin Barley.

"And the agreement is signed, of course?"

"Signed, sealed, and delivered," was the answer of Mr. Dexter, who had taken the remark as a question.

"Just so. And there are no legal means of getting rid of the man?"

"None at all, sir, for three years, if he pleases to stop. But, Mr. Chandos, he appears to me to be an exceedingly eligible tenant—a very wealthy and respectable gentleman!"

"Wealthy and respectable though he may be, I would give a thousand pounds to be quit of him, Dexter."

"But why, sir?" repeated the agent, in surprise.

"He is not likely to prove an agreeable neighbour. I don't like the look of him."

"Pardon the suggestion, Mr. Chandos, but you are not obliged to have anything to do with him," returned the agent, who looked as though the views propounded were quite different from any he had ever met with. "So long as Mr. Edwin Barley keeps his house respectable and pays his rent, that's all you need know of him sir, unless you like."

"What brought him settling himself here?" abruptly asked Mr. Chandos.

"Well, I inquired once, but got no satisfactory answer. They say his own place by Nettleby is quite magnificent compared with this house that he has taken. I remarked upon it to Haines. 'Gentlemen like to go about the country and please their fancy for change,' Haines answered me. Which is true enough, sir."

Mr. Chandos gave a sort of incredulous nod, and the agent rose.

"Now that I have seen you, sir, and had the pleasure of ascertaining that the injury is less than report said, I'll be going back again. But I shall keep my eyes open for a woman in a grey cloak. If I meet one, I'll pounce upon her, as sure my name's Bob Dexter. Pray don't trouble yourself, young lady! I know my way out."

I had risen to ring the bell. Mr. Dexter was gone beforehand, and we heard the hall-door close after him with a sharp click.

Just as the tea-things were taken away, Lizzy Dene came in. The woman looked wild to-night; her eyes were shining as with fire; her dark cheeks had a glow in them as of fever; the bunches of black curls on either side were tangled; and she had not removed her bonnet and shawl before appearing in the presence of Mr. Chandos.

"I beg your pardon, sir!" she said, "but I thought I'd tell you where I've been to."

"Well?" returned Mr. Chandos, turning his head to her from the sofa.

"I couldn't get it out of my head, sir, that the woman who served you that trick must be one of the gipsies, so I just put my best foot foremost, and walked over to the common. They are encamped at the far end of it, down in the hollow amid the trees. Such a sight! A big tent lighted with a torch stuck in the ground, and four or five women and children in it, and straw beds in the corner, with brown rugs, and a pot a-boiling on the fire outside. But I had my walk for nothing; for the women seemed quiet and peaceable enough; one of them was sewing, and, so far as I saw, they had never a grey cloak between 'em. There was an old creature bent double, she could scarce hobble, and two young women with babies in their arms, and there was a growing girl or two. I'm bound to confess that none of them looked wicked enough to have been the one that set on you, sir."

"Well?" repeated Mr. Chandos, regarding Lizzy with some wonder. "What else?"

"Why, sir, this. If it was one of the gipsies that attacked you, she's not back at the camp yet; she must be in hiding somewhere; and most likely it's in these very grounds, where they're thickest. If all the men went out to beat the place, they might drop upon her."

There was something curiously eager about the woman as she spoke, with her cheeks and eyes glowing, and her tone full of passion. I think it struck Mr. Chandos. It certainly struck me, and to a degree that set me wondering. But Mr. Chandos betrayed no curiosity, and answered with quiet decision.

"We will forget this, Lizzy Dene; at any rate for the present. I am tired of this subject; and I do not suppose it to have been any of the gipsies. Some poor mad woman, more probably, escaped from the county asylum. Don't trouble yourself about it further."

Lizzy looked hard at him, as if she would have said more, but finally withdrew in silence.

"Tired of everything, I think, to-night!" he added, with a weary sigh, as she closed the door. "Tired even of reading!"

"Can I do anything to amuse you, Mr. Chandos?" I asked, for he threw his book on the stand.

"Ay. Sit you down on that low chair, and tell me the stories of your past life, after the manner of fairy-tales."

The chair was on the opposite side to the sofa, and I sat down upon it. He made me come quite close to him, lest he should not hear. Which must have been said in jest, for his ears were quick. But I drew it nearer.

"Now for fairy-tale the first. How shall you begin?"

"I don't know how to begin, sir. My life has had no fairy-tales in it. I have not had a home, as other girls have."

"Not had a home!"

"I had one when I was a little girl. Mamma lived in a cottage in Devonshire, and I was with her."

"So you are a little Devonshire woman?"

"No; I was born in India. Mamma brought me over when I was three years old."

"And your father?"

"He had to stay behind in India. He was in the army. After that he sold out to come home, and died very soon. Mamma died when I was eleven, and since that I have been at school."

"Had you no relatives to offer you a home?"

"No!" And I felt my face flush as I thought of Mr. Edwin Barley. He must have noticed it: he was looking at me.

"No home all those years! How you must long for one!"

"I keep my longings down. It may never be my happiness to know a home; certainly there is no present prospect of it. I resign myself to my position, doing my duty, as it is placed before me, and not looking beyond it."

"What do you call your 'position'?"

"That of a governess."

"I should say you are of gentle blood?"

"Oh yes."

He paused. I paused. I saw that he expected I should tell him something more about myself and my family; and I would willingly have told all, but for having to bring in the names of Mr. and Mrs. Edwin Barley. The fear of doing that; of alluding to the dreadful events of the past, clung to me still as a nightmare. Mr. Chandos, who did not fail to detect the reluctance, concluded there must be some reason for it, not expedient to relate; he quitted the subject at once, with the innate delicacy of a refined man, and did not again, then or later, make allusion to my family.

"Well, now for the fairy-tales. Begin. If you don't tell me something worth hearing, I shall fall asleep."

I laughed; and related to him one or two short anecdotes of my school life, and then remembered the supper-scene at Miss Fenton's, and the setting on fire of Georgina Digges. He had grown interested in that, and we were both talking very fast, when the clock struck ten. I got up and put away the low chair.

"Good-night, sir."

"Good-night—miss!"

It made me laugh. He took my hand, kept it for a minute in his, and said he wished me pleasant dreams.

"I shall dream of a woman in a grey cloak. But, Mr. Chandos! in one sense, the accident is a good thing for you."

"You must explain how. I don't see it."

"With that disabled foot you may make sure of uninterrupted rest. There is no fear that you will leave your bed to-night to walk in the moonlight."

"You go to bed, and to sleep, and never mind looking for me in the moonlight; to-night, or any other night."

His mood had changed: his brow had grown angry, his voice stern. The thought of having alluded to his infirmity brought back all my humiliation.

"I beg your pardon, sir," I meekly said. And he released my hand without another word.

I thought of it all the time I was undressing; I thought of it after I was in bed. Not of that only, but of other things. If Mr. Edwin Barley was the enemy of the family, as hinted at by Mr. Chandos, and could do them at will irreparable injury; and if he, Edwin Barley, had thus brought himself into proximity, because he had learnt in some unaccountable manner that I was staying there, how they would have cause to detest me! Of course it might not be. Mr. Edwin Barley might have come for his own purposes to Chandos, irrespective of me. I could only hope it was so; but the doubt caused me most jealously to guard his name, as a connection of mine, from Mr. Chandos.

I dropped into peaceful sleep. My last thought, as it stole over me, was to wonder whether Lizzy Dene and the other maids were watching from the turret-window for the ghost in the Pine Walk.

# CHAPTER 18

## THE NEW COMPANION

A solitary breakfast for me. Mr. Chandos remained in his room, nursing his foot; Lady Chandos was in hers. As I was eating it, Hill came in.

"Will you transact a commission for my lady, this morning, Miss Hereford?"

"With great pleasure," I answered, starting up with alacrity, glad that they were going to give me something to do at last. "What is it?"

"Well, it's nothing that you need be in such a hurry for as to lose your breakfast," grimly responded Hill. "My lady is ill, Mr. Chandos is disabled, I can't be spared; so we want you to go to Marden, and make some inquiries."

"Oh yes; I will go anywhere. It is very dull here, by myself all day. Is it about Mrs. Penn?"

"It is about Mrs. Penn," returned Hill, in her stiffest manner. "You will have to see Mrs. Howard, the lady she referred to, and ask certain questions of her, which will be written down for you."

"Am I to go by train, Hill?"

"My lady would not send you alone by train. Her own carriage will be round by ten o'clock to convey you to Marden."

At ten the carriage drew up. I was quite ready for it. Vain girl! I had put on one of my prettiest dresses, and a white bonnet; my chestnut hair rippled back from my brow, and the pink flowers mingled with it. I had grown fairer in complexion than I was as a child, and my cheeks wore generally a soft bright colour.

Stepping in, I was bowled away, in the same state that my lady would have gone. The fine barouche had its handsome hammercloth, its badge on the panels, its attendant servants. I was born to this social state, if I had not been brought up in it, and it was very delightful. The old lodge-keeper touched his hat to me as we passed through the gates to the smooth road. The sun was shining, the birds were singing, the leafy trees were dancing.

"Now mind!" Hill had said to me. "All you have to do is to put by word of mouth these questions written down for you, and to take strict note of the answers, so as to report them accurately when you come back. They are but ordinary questions: or else you would not be sent. Be discreet, young lady, and don't talk on your own score."

I opened the paper and read over the questions as we went along. Simple queries, as Hill had said; just such as are put when a dependent, whether lady or servant, is being engaged. The address given was "Mrs. Charles Howard, number nine, King Street,

Marden." And there the carriage drew up. Carrying the paper, I was shown upstairs to the drawing-rooms, sending in my name—Miss Hereford.

Handsome rooms, two communicating with each other. A lady, very much dressed in elaborate morning costume, rose to receive me. I found it was Mrs. Howard, and entered upon my queries.

They were most satisfactorily answered. A higher character than she gave to Mrs. Penn could not be tendered. Mrs. Penn was faithful, good, discreet, and trustworthy; very capable in all ways, and invaluable in a sick room, Her regret at parting with her was great, but she, Mrs. Howard, was going to Brussels on a long visit to her married daughter, and it would be inconvenient to take Mrs. Penn. She should be so glad to see her settled elsewhere comfortably, before leaving England.

So voluble was Mrs. Howard, saying ten times more than she need have said, that I could not get in a word. I should have liked her better had she been less flourishing in speech, and not worn quite so many ornaments. As soon as I could speak, I asked if I might see Mrs. Penn, such having been Hill's instructions to me, in case the references proved satisfactory.

Mrs. Howard rang for her, and she came in. She wore a bright violet gown of some soft material; her red hair was disposed in waving bands low on her forehead and taken back underneath her cap. *Had* I seen her anywhere in my past life? The expression of her full face when her eyes were turned on me seemed so familiar: striking upon the mind like something we may have seen in a dream; but when I examined her features I could not trace in them any remembrance. Perhaps I was mistaken. We do see faces that resemble others as we go through the world.

I told her she was to proceed with as little delay as possible to Chandos, to hold an interview with its mistress when she would probably be engaged.

My mission over, I entered the carriage to be driven home again. We had nearly reached Chandos when I missed my pocket-handkerchief. It was one that had been embroidered for me by a favourite schoolfellow at Miss Barlieu's, Marguerite Van Blumm, and I valued it for her sake. Besides, I only possessed two handsome handkerchiefs in the world: that, and one I had bought in Paris. I hoped I had left it at Mrs. Howard's, and that Mrs. Penn would bring it to me.

To my great amazement, when I arrived home, I found Mrs. Penn was already there. Not engaged: Hill was waiting to hear my report of what Mrs. Howard said. Mr. Chandos laughed at the expression of my face.

"The triumph of steam over carriage wheels, Miss Hereford. She took a train immediately, and a fly on at Hetton Station."

The fly was outside the windows as he spoke; it had drawn away from the door to allow the carriage to set me down. I did not see Mrs. Penn; she was waiting in the large drawing-room; and I did not like to make the fuss of going to her to ask about my handkerchief.

But a quarter-of-an-hour, and it was driving her back to Hetton. She was engaged; and had agreed to enter that same evening. She came, quite punctually. But for a day or two afterwards it so fell out that I did not see her.

The first time we met was one morning, when I was finishing breakfast. Mrs. Penn came into the oak-parlour with her bonnet and shawl on. She had been out of doors.

"I don't know what your grim old butler will say to me, but I have forestalled him with the postman," she began, without any other greeting. "Unless I take a turn for ten minutes in the open air of a morning, I feel stifled for the day: the postman came up while I was in the broad walk, and I took the letters from him. Only two," she continued, regarding the addresses in a free and easy sort of manner scarcely becoming her position. "Both foreign letters," she went on in a running comment. "One is for Harry Chandos, Esquire; the other for Miss Hereford. That is yourself, I think."

"I am Miss Hereford."

"It is a pretty name," she observed, looking at me: "almost as pretty as you are. Do you remember in the school history of England we are told of the banishment of Lord Hereford by his sovereign, and how it broke his heart? Is your Christian name as pretty?"

"It is Anne."

"Anne Hereford! A nice name altogether. Where do your friends live?"

Instead of answering, I rose and rang the bell for the butler; who came in.

"The letters are here, Hickens," I said, putting the one for Mr. Chandos in his hand, whilst I kept mine. Hickens, with a dubious air, looked alternately at me, and the letters, as if wondering how they came there. I explained.

"Mrs. Penn brought them in. She tells me she met the postman in the broad walk, and took them from him."

"Please to let the man bring the letters to the house, ma'am, should you meet him again," Hickens respectfully observed, turning to Mrs. Penn. "My lady never allows any one to take them from the postman: he brings them into the hall, and delivers them into my hand. Once when Miss Emily was at home, she took them from the man in the grounds, and my lady was very much displeased with her. Her ladyship is exceedingly strict in the matter."

"How particular they seem about their letters!" exclaimed Mrs. Penn in an undertone, as Hickens departed with his master's.

"Many families are so. Mr. Paler was worse than this, for he always liked to take the letters from the facteur himself."

"Who is Mr. Paler?" she questioned.

"I have been living as governess in his family in Paris. Mrs. Penn, may I ask you whether I left a handkerchief at Mrs. Howard's the day I went there?"

"Not that I know of. I did not hear of it. Have you lost one?"

"Yes; one that I valued: it was a keepsake. I know I had it in the carriage in going to Marden, but I remember nothing of it subsequently. When I arrived home I missed it."

"You most likely dropped it in stepping out of the carriage."

"Yes, I fear so."

She quitted the room with a remark that her time was up. I opened my letter, which was in Emily de Mellissie's handwriting; and read as follows:—

"The idea of your making all this fuss! Though I suppose it is mamma's fault, not yours. She is neither poison nor a tiger, and therefore will not do the house irretrievable damage. It's not my fault if Alfred has taken this gastric fever, and I am detained here. I would rather be in the wilds of Africa, I assure you, scampering over the sandy desert on a mad pony, than condemned to be pent up in sick-chambers. Fancy what it is! Alfred reduced to a skeleton, in his bed on alternate days, taking nothing but *tisane,* and that sort of slops, and lamenting that he won't get over it: Madame de Mellissie in *her* bed, groaning under an agonizing attack of sciatica; and I doing duty between the two. It's dreadful. I should come off to Chandos to-morrow and leave them till they were better, but that the world would call me hard-hearted, and any other polite name it could lay its hand upon. Every second day he seems nearly as well as I am, and says I shall be sure to start for Chandos on the next. When the next comes, there he is, down again with fever. And that is my present fate!—which is quite miserable enough without your reproaching me for being thoughtless, and all the rest of it. How I should get through the dreary days but for some novels and a few callers, I don't know; but the novels are not exciting, and the visitors are stupid. Paris is empty just now, and as dull as a dungeon. Don't go worrying me with any more letters reflecting on my 'prudence,' or I shall send them back to you. If mamma orders you to write, tell her plainly that you won't. Pray who is Anne Hereford, that she should be allowed to disturb the peace of Chandos? Indeed, Harry, she is *nobody*! and you need not stand on ceremony with her. I am sorry that her staying there just now should be so very inconvenient—as you hint that it is. Mamma has a great dislike to have people in the house, I know; but leaving her was really not my fault, as you ought to see. I will come over as soon as I can, for my own sake, and relieve you of her:—you cannot form an idea what it is here, no soirées going on, no fêtes, no anything. But if you really cannot allow her to remain until then, the shortest way will be to let her go to Nulle.

    "Love to mamma, and believe me, your affectionate sister,
       "EMILY DE MELLISSIE."

I read nearly to the end before suspecting that the letter was not meant for me. I had supposed it to be the answer to the one I despatched to Emily in the previous week. Some one else—as it would appear—had despatched one also, remonstrating at the inconvenience my presence caused at Chandos.

With a face that was burning in its every lineament—with hands that trembled as they closed—with a heart that felt half-sick with shame—I started up. That very moment I would write word to Madame de Mellissie that I was quitting Chandos, and to Miss Barlieu, to say I was coming. In the midst of which paroxysm there entered Mr. Chandos, between Hickens and a stick.

He sat down in an arm-chair, wishing me good-morning. When the man had gone I advanced to him with the open letter.

"This letter must be intended for you, I think, Mr. Chandos, although it was addressed to me. It is from Madame Alfred de Mellissie."

"Just so," he said, taking it, and handing me the one he himself held. "This, I presume, is for you, as it begins 'My dear Anne Hereford.' Emily has betrayed her characteristic heedlessness, in sending my letter to you, and yours to me."

He ran his eyes over the note, and then called to me. I stood looking from the window.

"Have you read this?"

"Every word. Until I came to my own name I never suspected that it was not written for me. I am very sorry, Mr. Chandos; but I hope you will not blame me; indeed it was done inadvertently."

"So am I sorry," he answered, in a joking sort of tone, as if he would pass the matter over lightly. "Emily's letters ought to be preserved in the British Museum."

Before he could say more, Hill came in, and began talking with him in an undertone, looking crossly at me. Of course it drove me away. I went to the portico, and read my letter.

    "MY DEAR ANNE HEREFORD,
      "You need not trouble yourself at all about being what you call 'an encumbrance' at Chandos, but just make yourself contented until I can come over. Mamma and my brother ought to be

glad to have you there, for they are immured alone from year's end to year's end. Keep out of their way as much as possible, so as not to annoy them.

"Yours sincerely,

"EMILY DE MELLISSIE.

"P.S.—Of course you might go to Miss Barlieu's, if Lady Chandos deems it expedient that you should do so."

A fine specimen of contradiction the note presented. I folded it and went upstairs, one determination strong upon me—to depart for Nulle.

Mrs. Penn was standing at the gallery-window between my room and the library. She was dressed handsomely, this new companion: a grey silk robe, a gold chain, a pretty blonde-lace cap mingling with her almost scarlet hair, valuable rings on her fingers. Just as I took likes and dislikes when a child, so I took them still. And I did not like Mrs. Penn.

"I cannot divest myself of the notion that I have met you before, Mrs. Penn," I said. "But I am unable to recollect where."

"I can tell you," she answered. "You were at school at Nulle, and attended the English Protestant Church. It was there you and I used to see each other."

"There?" I repeated, incredulously, thinking she must be wrong.

"Yes, there," said Mrs. Penn. "I was staying in the town for some weeks two or three years ago; I remembered your face again here directly, though you have grown much. You were wont to study my face nearly as much as you studied your Prayer-book. I used to wonder what you found in me to admire."

Throw my recollection back as I would, I could not connect the face before me with my associations of Nulle. It certainly might have been there that we met—and indeed why should she say so, were it not?—but it did not seem to be. As to the looking off the Prayer-book part, I was sure that there could not have been much of that, the English governess who succeeded Miss Johnstone always watched us so sharply.

"Did you know the Miss Barlieus, Mrs. Penn?"

"Only by sight; I had no acquaintance with them. Quite old maids they are."

"They are kind, good women," I broke out, indignantly, and Mrs. Penn laughed.

"Somewhat careless withal, are they not? I think that was exemplified in the matter relating to Miss Chandos."

I could not answer. The whole blame had lain with Emily, but I did not choose to say that to Mrs. Penn. She was turning her gold chain round and round her finger, her very light blue eyes seemingly fixed on the opposite pine-trees, and when she spoke again her voice had dropped to a low tone.

"Do you believe in ghosts, Miss Hereford?"

"Ghosts?" I echoed, astonished at the question.

"Ghosts," she repeated. "Do you believe that the dead come again?"

"When I see any ghosts I will tell you whether I believe in them or not," I said, jokingly. "Up to the present time it has not been my good fortune to fall in with any."

"It is said," she proceeded, looking round with caution, "that a ghost haunts Chandos. Have you not seen any strange sights?"

"No, indeed. It would very much astonish me to see such—if by 'strange sights' you mean ghosts."

"I saw one once," she said.

"Mrs. Penn!"

"A lady died in a house where I was staying; died almost suddenly. If ever I saw anything in my life, I saw her after she was in her grave. You look at me with incredulity."

"I cannot fancy that a real genuine ghost was ever seen. I am aware that strange tales are told—and believed: but I think they are only tales of the imagination."

"In speaking of strange tales, do you allude to Chandos?"

"Certainly not. I spoke of the world in general."

"You take me up sharply. Nevertheless, strange tales are whispered of Chandos. On a moonlight night, as report runs, the spirit of Sir Thomas may be seen in the walks."

"Does it swim over from India to take its promenade?" I mockingly asked.

"You are thinking of the present baronet: he is not dead. I spoke of the late one. Look out some of these light nights, will you, and tell me whether you see anything. I cannot; for the available windows of the east wing do not face this way. They say he takes exercise there," pointing to the Pine Walk.

"Did you say Sir Thomas's ghost, Mrs. Penn?" I asked, laughing.

"The world says so. I hear that some of the maids here, seeing the sight, have arrived at the notion that it is only Mr. Harry Chandos given to come out of his room at night and take moonlight promenades."

There was a ball in the window-seat, and I tossed it with indifference. She had got hold of the wrong story, and it was not my place to set her right. Hill came up, saying Mr. Chandos wished to speak to me; but I did not hurry down.

I had made my mind up to borrow sufficient money of him to take me to Nulle, and was trying to call up courage to ask for it. His leg was upon a rest when I went in, and he leaned back in his chair reading a newspaper.

"I want to speak to you, Miss Hereford."

"And I—wanted—to speak to you, sir, if you please," I said, resolutely, in spite of my natural hesitation.

"Very well. Place aux dames. You shall have the first word."

It appeared, however, that Lizzy Dene was to have that. She came in at the moment, asked leave to speak, and began a recital of a second visit she had paid the gipsies the previous night, in which she had accused them of having attacked Mr. Chandos. The recital was a long one, and delivered curiously, very fast and in one tone, just as if she were repeating from a book, and imparting the idea that it had been learnt by heart. She wound up with saying the gipsies quitted the common in the night; and therefore no doubt could remain that one of the women had been the assailant. Mr. Chandos regarded her keenly.

"Lizzy Dene, what is your motive for pursuing those gipsies in the way you do? No one accuses them but you."

"Motive, sir?" returned the woman.

"Ay; motive," he pointedly said. "I shall begin to suspect that you know more about the matter than you would like made public. I think it is you to whom we must look for an explanation, not the gipsies."

Did you ever see a pale face turn to a glowing, fiery red?—the scarlet of confusion, if not of guilt? So turned Lizzy Dene's to my utter amazement, and I think to that of her master.

Could *she* have had anything to do with the attack upon him? She stammered forth a few deprecatory words, that, in suspecting the gipsies, she had only been actuated by the wish to serve Mr. Chandos, and backed out of the parlour.

Backed out to find herself confronted by a tall swarthy man, who had made his way into the hall without the ceremony of knocking for admittance. One of the gipsies unquestionably. Lizzie Dene gave a half-shriek and flew away, and the man came inside the room, fixing his piercing eyes upon those of Mr. Chandos.

"It has been told to me this morning that you and your people accuse us of having assaulted you," he began, without prelude. "Master, I have walked back ten miles to set it right."

"I have not accused you," said Mr. Chandos. "The assault upon me—if it can be called such—proceeded from a woman; but I have no more reason to suspect that it was one of your women, than I have to suspect any other woman in the wide world."

"'Twas none of ours, master. We was camped upon your common, and you let us stop there unmolested; some lords of the soil drive us off ere we can pitch our tent, hunt us away as they'd hunt a hare. You didn't; you spoke kind to us, more than once in passing; you spoke kind to our little children; and we'd have protected you with our own lives, any of us, had need been. Do you believe me, master?"

The man's voice was earnest, and he raised his honest eyes, fierce though they were, to Mr. Chandos, waiting for the question to be answered.

"I do believe you."

"That's well, then, and what I came back hoping to hear. But now, master, I'll tell ye what I saw myself that same night. I was coming up toward this way, and you overtook me, riding fast. Maybe you noticed me, for I touched my hat."

"I remember it," said Mr. Chandos.

"You rode in at the gates at a hand gallop; I could hear the horse's hoofs in the silence of the evening. I met one of our fellows, and stopped to speak to him, which hindered me three—or four minutes; and—you know them trees to the left of the gate, master, with posts afore em?"

"Well?" said Mr. Chandos.

"There stood a woman when I got up. She was taking off a grey cloak, and she folded it small and put it on her arm and walked away. Folks put on clothes at night, instead of taking 'em off, was in my thoughts, and I looked after her."

"Did you know her?"

"I never saw her afore. She was one in your condition of life, master, for her clothes were brave, and the rings glittered on her fingers. Next morning when we heard what had happened, we said she was the one. I have not seen her since. She seemed to be making for the railroad."

"Why did you not come and tell me this at the time?"

"Nay, master, was it any business of mine? How did I know I should be welcome? or that our people was suspected? That's all, sir,"

"Will you take some refreshment?" said Mr. Chandos. "You are welcome to it."

"Master, I don't need any."

The man, with a rude salute to me, turned and departed, and we saw him treading the gravel walk with a fearless step. Mr. Chandos turned to me with a smile.

"What do you think of all this?"

"I am sure that the gipsies are innocent."

"I have been tolerably sure of that from the first, for I knew that their interest did not lie in making an enemy of me; rather the contrary; what puzzles me, is Lizzy Dene's manner. But let us return to the matter we were interrupted in, Miss Hereford. Go on with what you were about to say."

Very shrinkingly I began, standing close to him, giving him a sketch of the circumstances (Mrs. Paler's tardy payment) that caused me to be without money; and asking him to lend me a trifle: just enough to take me back to Nulle. About a guinea, I thought, or a guinea and a half: I had a few shillings left still. Mr. Chandos seemed highly amused, smiling in the most provoking way.

"Does Mrs. Paler really owe you thirty guineas?"

"Yes, sir. It is half a year's salary."

"Then I think she ought to pay you."

"Will you lend me the trifle, sir?"

"No. Not for the purpose you name. I will lend you as much as you like to put in your pocket; but not to take you to Nulle."

"I must go, sir. At least I must go somewhere. And I only know the Miss Barlieus in all the world."

"You wish to go because, in consequence of Emily's letter, you are deeming yourself an encumbrance at Chandos?"

I made no answer in words: the colour that flushed into my cheeks was all-sufficient.

"Let me speak to you confidentially," he said, taking my hand in his; "for a few minutes we will understand each other as friends. I am grieved that Emily's carelessness should have been the cause of annoyance to you; my mother will be sadly vexed when I tell her; but you must now listen to the explanation. There are certain family reasons which render it inexpedient for a stranger to be located at Chandos; even Emily herself would not at all times be welcome. Emily left you here. As the days went on, and we heard nothing from her, my mother desired me to write and inquire when she would be over, and to reprove her thoughtlessness in leaving you at Chandos, when she knew why it was more expedient that we should be alone; I simply wrote what my mother desired me; no more; and this letter of Emily's to-day is the answer to it. Now you have the whole gist of the affair. But I must ask you fully to understand that it is not to you personally my mother has an objection; on the contrary, she likes you; the objection applies to *any* one, except its regular inmates, who may be at Chandos. If a royal princess offered a visit here, she would be equally unwelcome. Do you understand this?"

"Quite so. But, understanding it, I can only see the more necessity for my leaving."

"And where would you go?"

"To Nulle. To the Miss Barlieus."

"No; that would not do," he said. "Emily has left you here under our charge, and we cannot part with you, except to her. You said you must be guided by me in your reading; you must be guided by me also in this."

"I should only be too willing under happier circumstances. But you cannot imagine how uncomfortable is the feeling of knowing that I am intruding here in opposition to the wish of Lady Chandos."

"Lady Chandos does not blame you for it; be assured of that. And I can tell you my mother has other things to think of just now than of you—or Emily either. Will you try and make yourself contented?"

"You must please not say any more, Mr. Chandos. If I had nowhere else to go to, it would be a different thing; but I have Miss Barlieu's house."

"And suppose you had not that? Would you make yourself contented and stay?"

"Yes," I said, rashly.

"Then be happy from this moment. Miss Barlieu's house is a barred one to you at present."

Something like a leap of joy seemed to take my heart. His tone of truth was not to be mistaken.

"Lady Chandos had a note from Miss Annette on Saturday," he said, his beautiful truthful eyes fixed on my face with the same steady earnestness that they had been all along. "Amidst other news it contained the unpleasant tidings that fever had broken out at Nulle; one of their young ladies had been seized with it, and was lying very ill; and another was sickening for it."

"Oh, Mr. Chandos!"

"So you see we should not allow you to go there just now. Neither would the Miss Barlieus receive you. As my mother observed, that news settled the question."

I remained silent: in my shock and perplexity.

"Fever seems to be busy this autumn," he remarked, carelessly. "It is in this neighbourhood; it is in Paris; it is in Nulle: and probably in a great many more places."

"But, Mr. Chandos! what am I to do?"

"There is only one thing that you can do—or that Lady Chandos would allow you to do: and that is, stay here. Not another word, Miss Hereford. You can't help yourself, you know," he added, laughing; "and we are happy to have you."

"But the objection that Lady Chandos feels to having any one?"

"Ah well—you will not be a dangerous visitor. If the worst came to the worst, we shall have to enlist you on our side, and make you take a vow of fidelity to Chandos and its interests."

He was speaking in a laughing, joking way, so that one could not tell whether his words were jest or earnest. Still they were curious ones.

"That is the situation, young lady. You can't help yourself, you see, if you would. How much money will you have?"

"Oh, sir, none. I do not require it, if I am not to go. I wish—as I am to stay here—I could make myself useful to some one."

"So you can; you can be useful to me. I will constitute you my head-nurse and walking companion. I shall use your shoulder at will until my foot has its free use again. Take care I don't tire you out."

He had kept my hand in his all that time, and now those deep blue speaking eyes of his, gazing still into mine, danced with merriment or pleasure. A thrill of rapture ran through me, and I never asked myself wherefore. Could it be that I was learning to love Mr. Chandos?

I sat in the oak-parlour through the live-long day; I had nowhere else to sit but in my bedroom. Dangerous companionship!—that of an attractive man like Mr. Chandos.

Calling Hickens to his aid in the afternoon, he went slowly up to the apartments of Lady Chandos, and I saw no more of him until dinner-time. Meanwhile I wrote a long letter to Miss Annette, expressing my great sympathy with the illness amidst the school-girls, and begging her to write and tell me which of them were ill, and also to let me know the very instant that the house should be safe again, for that I wanted to come to it.

In the evening Mr. Chandos, his lamp at his elbow, read aloud from a volume of Tennyson. I worked. Never had poetry sounded so sweet before; never will it sound sweeter; and when I went upstairs to bed, the musical measure, and that still more melodious voice, yet rang in my ears.

To bed, but not to rest. What was the matter with me? I know not, but I could not sleep. Tossing and turning from side to side, now a line of the poems would recur to me: now would rise up the face of Mr. Chandos; now the remembrance of Lady Chandos's vexation at my being there. As the clock struck one, I rose from my uneasy bed, determined to try what walking about the chamber would do. Pulling the blind aside, quietly opening the shutters, I paused to look out on the lovely night, its clear atmosphere and its shining stars almost as bright as day.

Why!—was I awake? or was I dreaming? There, under the shade of the thick trees, keeping close to them, as if not wishing to be seen, but all too plain to me, nevertheless, paced Mr. Chandos, wrapped in a large overcoat. What had become of his lame foot? That he walked slowly, as one does who is weak, there was no denying, but still he did not walk *lame*. Did, or would, a state of somnambulancy cause a disabled limb to recover temporary service and strength? Every sense I possessed, every reason, answered no. As I gazed at the sight with bewildered brain and beating heart, Mrs. Penn's words flashed over me—that it was the ghost of the dead Sir Thomas which was said to haunt the groves of Chandos.

Could it be? Was I looking at a real ghost? We all know how susceptible the brain is to superstition in the lonely midnight hours, and I succumbed in that moment to an awful terror. Don't laugh at me. With a smothered cry, I flew to the bed, leaped in, and covered my face with the bedclothes.

One idea was uppermost amid the many that crowded on me. If that was indeed the spirit of Sir Thomas, he must have died a younger man than I supposed, and have borne a great likeness to his son, Harry Chandos.

The morning's bright sun dispelled all ghostly illusions. I went out of doors as soon as I got down, just for a run along the broad walk and back again. At the corner where the angle hid the house, I came upon Mrs. Penn and the postman, only a few yards off. She had stopped to look at the addresses of the letters he was bringing. The sight sent me back again; but not before she turned and saw me. Not only did the action appear to me dishonourable—one I could not have countenanced—but some instinct seemed to say that Mrs. Penn was unjustifiably prying into the affairs of the Chandos family.

As Hickens took the letters from the man in the hall, Mrs. Penn came into the oak-parlour. I was pouring out my coffee then.

"I am quite in despair," she exclaimed, flinging herself into a chair, with short ceremony. "These three days have I been expecting news of an invalid friend; and it does not come. I hope and trust she is not dead!"

"Perhaps she is unable to write?"

"She is. I said news of her; not from her. When I saw the postman come in at the gates just now, hope rose up within me, and I ran to meet him. But hope was false. The man brought me no letter, nothing but disappointment."

I am not sure but I must have had a wicked heart about that time. Instead of feeling sympathy with Mrs. Penn and her sick friend, a sort of doubt came over me, that she was only saying this to excuse her having stopped the postman. She untied the strings of her black lace bonnet, and rose, saying she supposed breakfast would be ready by the time she got upstairs.

"Mrs. Penn," I interposed, taking a sudden resolution to speak, "was that a joke of yours yesterday, about Sir Thomas Chandos?"

"About his ghost, do you mean? It was certainly not my joke. Why?"

"Nothing. I have been thinking about it."

"I don't tell you the ghost comes; but I should watch if I had the opportunity. The shutters in the front of the east wing are unfortunately fastened down with iron staples. I conclude—I *conclude*," repeated Mrs. Penn, slowly and thoughtfully—"as a precaution against the looking out of Mrs. Chandos."

"I dare say it is the greatest nonsense in the world. A ghost! People have grown wise now."

"I dare say it may be nonsense," she rejoined. "But for one thing I should heartily say it is nothing else."

"And that one thing, Mrs. Penn?"

"I will not disclose it to you, Anne Hereford. The report is common enough in the neighbourhood. Inquire of any of the petty shopkeepers in the hamlet, and you will find it to be so. They will tell you that rumours have been afloat for a long while that Sir Thomas may be seen at night in the Pine Walk."

She quitted the room as she spoke, leaving on my mind a stronger impression than ever that I had met her somewhere in my lifetime, had talked with her and she with me. There was in her manner an unconscious familiarity rarely indulged in save from old acquaintanceship. It was strange that she and Mr. Chandos should both strike on chords of my memory. Chords that would not be traced.

They were fortunate in this new companion. Gathering a word from one and another, I heard she was thoroughly efficient. And they made much of her, treating her essentially as a lady. She went out in the carriage with Mrs. Chandos; she talked to Mr. Chandos as an equal; she patronized me. But a whisper floated through the house that the only one who did not take kindly to her was Mrs. Chandos.

# CHAPTER 19

## TELEGRAPHING FOR A PHYSICIAN

Some uncomfortable days passed on. Uncomfortable in one sense. Heaven knows I was happy enough, for the society of Mr. Chandos had become all too dear, and in it I was basking away the golden hours. Looking back now I cannot sufficiently blame myself. Not for staying at Chandos; I could not help that; but for allowing my heart to yield unresistingly to the love. How could I suppose it would end? Alas! that was what I never so much as thought of: the present was becoming too much of an Elysium for me to look questioningly beyond it; it was as a very haven of sweet and happy rest.

With some of the other inmates, things seemed to be anything but easy. Lady Chandos was still invisible; and, by what I could gather, growing daily worse. Mr. Chandos, his lameness better, looked bowed down with a weight of apprehension. Hill was in a state of fume and fret; and the women-servants, meeting in odd corners, spoke whisperingly of the figure that nightly haunted Chandos.

What astonished me more than anything was, that no medical man was called in to Lady Chandos. Quite unintentionally, without being able to help myself, I overheard a few words spoken between Hill and Mr. Chandos. That Lady Chandos was dangerously ill, and medical aid an absolute necessity, appeared indisputable; and yet it seemed they did not dare to summon it. It was an unfathomable riddle. The surgeon from Hetton, Mr. Dickenson, came still to Mr. Chandos every day. What would have been easier than for him to go up to Lady Chandos? He never did, however; he was not asked to do so. Day after day he would say, "How is Lady Chandos?" and Mr. Chandos's reply would be, "Much the same."

The omission also struck on Mrs. Penn. One day, when she had come into my chamber uninvited, she spoke of it abruptly, looking full in my face, in her keen way.

"How is it they don't have a doctor to her?"

"What is the use of asking me, Mrs. Penn? I cannot tell why they don't."

"Do you never hear Mr. Chandos say why?"

"Never. At the beginning of her illness, he said his mother knew how to treat herself, and that she had a dislike to doctors."

"There's more in it than that, I think," returned Mrs. Penn, in a tone of significance. "That surly Hill won't answer a single question. All I get out of her is, 'My lady's no better.' Mrs. Chandos goes into the west wing most days, but she is as close as Hill. The fact is—it is very unfortunate, but Mrs. Chandos appears to have taken a dislike to me."

"Taken a dislike to you!"

Mrs. Penn nodded. "And not a word upon any subject, save the merest conversational trifles, will she speak. But I have my own opinion of Lady Chandos's illness: if I am right, their reticence is accounted for."

Again the tone was so significant that I could but note it, and looked to her for an explanation. She dropped her voice as she gave it.

"I think that the malady which has attacked Lady Chandos is not bodily, but mental; and that they, in consequence, keep her in seclusion. Poor woman! She has had enough trouble to drive her mad."

"Oh, Mrs. Penn! Mad!"

"I mean what I say."

"But did you not have an interview with her when you came?"

"Yes, a short one. Harry Chandos was sitting with her, and went out, after a few words to me, staying in the next room. It seemed to me that she was impatient to have him back again: anyway, she cut the meeting very short. I am bound to say that she appeared collected then."

Mrs. Penn lifted her hand, glittering with rings, to her brow as she spoke, and pushed slightly back her glowing hair. Her face looked troubled—that sort of trouble that arises from perplexity.

"Allowing it to be as you fancy, Mrs. Penn, they would surely have a doctor to her. Any medical man, if requested, would keep the secret."

"Ah! it's not altogether that, I expect," returned Mrs. Penn, with a curious look. "You would keep it, and I would keep it, as inmates of the family; and yet you see how jealously we are excluded. I suspect the true motive is, that they dare not risk the revelations she might make."

"What revelations?"

"You do not, perhaps, know it, Miss Hereford, but there is a sword hanging over the Chandos family," she continued, dropping her voice to a whisper. "An awful sword. It is suspended by a hair; and a chance word of betrayal might cause it to fall. Of that chance word the Chandoses live in dread that Lady Chandos, if she be really insane, might inadvertently speak it."

"Over which of them?" I exclaimed, in dismay.

"I had rather not tell you which. It lies over them all, so to say. It is that, beyond question, which keeps Sir Thomas in India: when the blow comes, he can battle with it better there than at home. They lie under sufficient disgrace as it is: they will lie under far greater then."

"They appear to be just those quiet, unpretending, honourable people who could not invoke disgrace. They—surely you cannot be alluding to Miss Chandos's runaway marriage!" I broke off, as the thought occurred to me.

"Tush! Runaway marriages are as good as others for all I see," avowed Mrs. Penn, with careless creed. "I question if Miss Chandos even knows of the blow that fell on them. I tell you, child, it was a fearful one. It killed old Sir Thomas; it must be slowly killing Lady Chandos. Do you not observe how they seclude themselves from the world?"

"They might have plenty of visitors if they chose."

"They *don't* have them. Any one in the secret would wonder if they did. Looking back, there's the disgrace that has fallen; looking forward, there's the terrible blow that has yet to fall."

"What is the nature of the disgrace?—what is the blow?"

Mrs. Penn shook her head resolutely. "I am unable to tell you, for two reasons. It is not my place to reveal private troubles of the family sheltering me; and its details would not be meet for a young lady's ears. Ill doings generally leave their consequences behind them—as they have here. Harry Chandos—"

"There is no ill-doing attaching to *him*," I interrupted, a great deal too eagerly.

A smile of derision parted the lips of Mrs. Penn. I saw that it must be one of two things—Harry Chandos was not a good man, or else Mrs. Penn disliked him.

"You don't know," she said. "And if you did, Harry Chandos can be nothing to you."

Her light eyes were turned on me with a searching look, and my cheeks went into a red heat. Mrs. Penn gathered her conclusions.

"Child," she impressively said, "if you are acquiring any liking for Harry Chandos, dis-acquire it. Put the thought of him far from you. That he may be a pleasant man in intercourse, I grant; but he must not become too pleasant to you, or to any other woman. Never waste your heart on a man who cannot marry."

"Cannot *he* marry?"

"No. But I am saying more than I ought," she suddenly added. "We get led on unconsciously in talking, and one word brings out another."

I could have boxed her ears in my vexation. Never, never had the idea of marrying Mr. Chandos crossed my mind; no, not in the wildest dream of dreams. I was a poor dependent governess; he was heir-presumptive to Sir Thomas Chandos.

"To return to what I was saying of Lady Chandos," resumed Mrs. Penn. "Rely upon it, I am right: that she has been suddenly afflicted with insanity. There is no other way of accounting for the mystery attaching to that west wing."

I sat down to think when she left me. To think. Could her theory possibly be true? were there sufficient apparent grounds for it? My poor brain—bewildered with the strange events passing around on the surface or beneath the surface, this new supposition one of the strangest—was unable to decide.

Had some one come in to say I had had a fortune left me, I could not have been more surprised than when Hill appeared with a gracious face. Lady Chandos's carriage was going into Marden on an errand—would I like the drive there and back? It might be a change for me.

"You dear good Hill!" I cried, in my delight. "I'll never call you cross again."

"Then just please to put your things on at once, and leave off talking nonsense, Miss Hereford," was Hill's reproval.

Again, as before, it was a lovely day, and altogether the greatest treat they could have given me. I liked the drive, and I liked the state it was taken in. A magnificent carriage and horses, powdered servants, and one pretty girl seated inside. Which was ME!

It was a good opportunity to inquire after my lost handkerchief, and I told James to stop at Mrs. Howard's. Accordingly the carriage drew up there the first thing. But the answer was not satisfactory. Mrs. Howard was gone. "On the Continent," they believed.

"When will she be back again?" I asked, leaning from the carriage to speak.

The servant girl, rather a dirty one and slipshod, did not know. Not at all, she thought. Mrs. Howard had left for good.

"But does Mrs. Howard not live here? Is not this her house?"

"No, ma'am. She lodged here for a little while; that was all."

I don't know why the information struck on my mind as curious, but it did so. Why should she have been there one day, as it were, and be gone the next? It might be all right, however, and I fanciful. Mrs. Penn had said—Mrs. Howard herself had said—she was going to visit her daughter in Brussels. Only I had thought she lived in that house at Marden.

That evening I found I had to dine alone. Mr. Chandos was rather poorly, not able to eat any dinner, Hickens said. How solitary it was to me, no one knows.

Afterwards, when I was sitting at the window in the dusk, he came downstairs. He had been in the west wing nearly all day. Opening his desk, he took out a bundle of letters: which appeared to be what he had come for.

"You must feel lonely, Miss Hereford?"

"A little, sir."

"That 'sir!'" he said, with a smile. "I am sorry not to be able to be down here with you. When I get better, we will have our pleasant times again."

I was standing up by the table. He held out his hand to shake mine. Thin and shadowy he always looked, but his face wore a grey hue in the dusk of the room.

"I fear you are very ill, sir. Suppose it should be the fever?"

"It is not the fever."

"But how can you tell it is not?"

"Do not be alarmed. It is nothing but—but what I have had before. Good-night, and take care of yourself."

His tone was strangely sad, his spirits were evidently depressed, and a foreboding of ill fell upon me. It was not lessened when I heard that a bed was made up for him in the west wing, that Lady Chandos and Hill might be within call in the night in case of need.

Therefore, when consternation broke over the house next morning, I was half prepared for it. Mr. Chandos was alarmingly ill, and a telegraphic express had gone up at dawn for a London physician.

It was so sudden, so unexpected, that none of the household seemed able to comprehend it. As to Hill, she bustled about like one demented. A large table was placed at the west wing door, and things likely to be wanted in the sick-room were carried up and put there, ready to her hand.

The physician, a Dr. Amos, arrived in the afternoon, the carriage having been sent to await him at the Hetton terminus. A slight-made man, dressed in black, with a Roman nose, and glasses resting on it. Hickens marshalled him to the door of the west wing, where Hill received him.

He stayed a long time; but they said he was taking refreshments as well as seeing his patient. The servants all liked Mr. Chandos, and they stood peeping in doorways, anxious for the doctor to come out. Hill came down and caught them, a jug in hand.

"Hill, do wait a moment and tell me!" I cried, as they flew away. "Does he find Mr. Chandos dangerously ill?"

"There's a change for the better," she answered. "Mr. Chandos will be about again to-morrow or next day. For goodness sake don't keep me with questions now, Miss Hereford!"

Not I. I did not care to keep her after that good news; and I ran away as light as a bird.

The carriage drew up to the portico, and Dr. Amos came down to it attended by Hickens and Hill. After he passed the parlour-door, I looked out of it, and saw Mr. Dexter come up. He had heard the news of Mr. Chandos's illness, and had come to inquire after him. Seeing the gentleman, who carried physician in his every look, about to step into the carriage, Mr. Dexter had no difficulty in divining who he was. Raising his hat, he accosted him.

"I hope, sir, you have not found Mr. Harry Chandos seriously ill?"

"Mr. Harry Chandos is very ill indeed!—very ill!" replied Dr. Amos, who appeared to be a pleasant man. "I fear there are but faint hopes of him."

"Good Heavens!" cried the thunderstruck agent when he was able to speak. "But faint hopes? How awfully sudden it must have come on!"

"Sudden? Not at all. It has been coming on for some time. He may have grown rapidly worse, if you mean that. In saying but faint hopes, I mean, of course, of his eventual recovery. He will not be quite laid by yet."

Dr. Amos entered the carriage with the last words, and it drove away, leaving his hearers to digest them; leaving me with a mist before my eyes and pulses that had ceased to beat Hill's sharp tones broke the silence, bearing harshly upon Mr. Dexter.

"What on earth need *you* have interfered for? Can't a doctor come and go from a place but he must be smothered with questions? If you have anything to ask, you can ask me."

"Why, Mrs. Hill, what do you mean?" remonstrated the agent. "I intended no harm, and I have done no harm. But what a pitiable thing about Mr. Chandos!"

"Doctors are not always oracles," snapped Hill. "My opinion's as good as his, and I know Mr. Chandos *will* get better: there's every chance that he'll be about to-morrow. The bad symptoms seem to be going off as suddenly as they came on."

"Hill," I whispered, laying hold of her gown as she was flouncing past me, "you say he may be about to-morrow; but will he get well eventually?"

"That's another affair," answered Hill.

"Dr. Amos said it had been coming on a long time," I pursued, detaining her still. "What complaint is it?"

"It's just a complaint that you had better not ask about, for your curiosity can't be satisfied, Miss Hereford," was Hill's response, as she broke away.

Broke away, leaving me. In my dreadful uncertainty, I went up to Hickens, who was standing still, looking so sad, and asked him to tell me what was the matter with Mr. Chandos.

"I don't know any more than you, miss. Mr. Chandos has had a vast deal of grief and trouble, and it may be telling upon him. He has looked ill of late."

No comfort anywhere—no rest. How I got through the day I don't know, it seemed as if I had received my death-knell, instead of he his.

Hill's opinion, in one respect, proved to be a correct one, for the next day Mr. Chandos appeared to the household. He came down about twelve o'clock, looking pale and subdued—but so he often looked—and I must say I could not detect much change in him. Starting from my seat in the oak-parlour, as he entered it, I went up to him in the impulse of the moment. He took both my hands.

"Glad to see me again?"

"Yes, I am glad," I whispered, calming down my excitement, and swallowing the intrusive tears that had risen. "Mr. Chandos, are you so very ill?"

"Who has been telling you that I am?" he inquired, walking to an arm-chair by help of my shoulder, for his ankle was weak yet, but not releasing me when he had sat down in it.

"I heard Dr. Amos say so. He said—"

"What did he say? Why do you stop?"

I could not answer. I could not disclose the opinion I had heard.

"I suppose you were within hearing when the doctor said he had but faint hopes of me?"

"Yes, I was. But, Mr. Chandos, who could have told you that Dr. Amos said it?"

"I was told," he smiled. "All are not so cautious as you, my little maid."

"But I hope it is not true, I hope you will get well."

"Would it give you any concern if I did not?"

My face flushed as I stood before him. Instead of answering, I bent it like a culprit—like a simpleton.

"I may cheat the doctors yet," he said, cheerfully.

"Have you been ill long?"

"I have not been quite well. Anxiety of mind sometimes takes its revenge upon the body."

He moved away to his desk as he spoke, which stood on a side-table. It was quite evident he did not wish to pursue the topic. What could I do but let it drop? Taking up my work, I carried it to the window, whilst he stood rummaging the desk, evidently searching for something. Every individual thing was at length turned out of it and put back again.

"Well, it's very strange!"

"What is it, sir?" That sir! as he would say. But I felt too shy, in my new and all-conscious feeling for him, to discard it entirely.

He had missed his note-book. One he was in the habit of using for any purpose; as a sort of diary, and also to enter business matters. That he had locked it up in his desk when he last wrote in it, two days ago, he felt absolutely certain.

"Have you left your keys about, sir?"

"I don't know. I generally put them in my pocket. But if I did leave them about, no one would use them. Our servants are honest."

The book, however, could not be found. Mr. Chandos looked for it, I looked, the servants looked. He said, in a joking sort of manner, that some sleight-of-hand must have been at work; and sat down to write a letter. I saw its address: London, Henry Amos, M.D.

Whilst making tea for Mr. Chandos in the evening, a discussion arose about the date of Emily's last letter, and I ran to my room to get it. Just within the door I encountered Lizzy Dene, darting out with a haste that nearly knocked me down.

"What did you want in my room, Lizzy?"

She murmured some incoherent answer about taking the housemaid's place that evening. A lame excuse. All work connected with the chambers had to be done by daylight; it was a rule of the house. I had had doubts, vague and indefinable, of Lizzy Dene for some days—that the girl was not altogether what she seemed. She looked red and confused now.

Emily's letter was not to be found. And yet I knew that I had tied it up with two or three others and left the packet in a certain compartment of my smaller trunk. Both boxes looked as though they had been searched over, for the things were not as I placed them. But I missed nothing, except the letters. Lizzy was in the gallery now, peering out at the window close by; I called to her to come in, and bade her shut the door.

"Boxes opened! Letters gone!" she retorted, in a passionate tone—though I had only mentioned the fact. "I have never laid a finger on anything belonging to you, miss. It's come to a pretty pass if I am to be suspected of that."

"Will you tell me what you were doing in my room, Lizzy?"

"No I won't!" Doggedly.

"I insist upon knowing: or I shall call Mrs. Hill."

"Well then, I *will* tell; I can't be hung for it," she returned, with sudden resolution. "I came into your room, miss, to look for something in the grounds that I thought might come there."

"The ghost?" I said, incautiously.

"So *you* know of it, miss!" was her answer. "Yes; it is walking again: and I'm veering round to their way of thought. Mrs. Hill has locked up the turret, so that look-out is barred to us."

She pulled open the door with a jerk, and departed. The draught of air blew out my frail wax taper, and I went to the window: Lizzy had left the curtains and shutters open. I had no fear; it never occurred to me that there could be anything to see. But superstition is catching, and—what did my eyes rest upon?

In the old spot, hovering about the entrance to the Pine Walk, was a man's shadowy figure; the one I had been told to believe was looked upon as the ghost of Sir Thomas Chandos.

These things can be laughed at in the open day, in the broad sunshine. We are ready then to brave ghosts, to acknowledge them to be myths of the fancy, as indisputably as we know the bogies of children to be puppets dressed up to frighten them; but all alone in the darkness the case is different. I was by myself on that vast floor; Lizzy Dene had gone down, the wing doors were shut, silence reigned. Once more terror got the better of me, the pacing figure was all too shadowy, and downstairs I flew, crossed the lighted hall, and burst into the oak-parlour to Mr. Chandos.

"Have you been waiting to re-write the letter?" he asked, "oblivious that your tea stood here, getting cold!"

I could make no answer just yet, but sank into my seat with a white face.

"You look as though you had seen a ghost," he jestingly said.

And then I burst into tears, just for a moment; the effect no doubt of nervous excitement. Mr. Chandos rose at once, his manner changing to one of tender kindness.

"Has anything alarmed you?"

"I cannot find Madame de Mellissie's letter," was all I answered, feeling vexed with myself.

"But that is not the cause of *this*. Something has frightened you. Come, Miss Hereford; I must know what it is," he concluded, with that quiet command of manner so few resist.

I did not: perhaps did not care to: and told him briefly what had occurred. Not mentioning suspicions of Lizzy Dene or what she said; but simply that the woman had opened the door too hastily, thereby putting my candle out—and then on to what I had seen.

"It must have been one of the gardeners," he quietly observed. "Why should that have alarmed you?"

That the gardeners never remained in the gardens after twilight, obeying the strict orders of the house, I knew. "Not a gardener" I answered, "but a ghost." And, taking courage, I told him all I had heard—that a ghost was said to walk nightly in the grounds.

"Whose ghost?" he asked, with angry sharpness.

"Your late father's, sir; Sir Thomas Chandos."

He turned quickly to the mantelpiece, put his elbow on it, and stood there with his back to me. But that his face had looked so troubled, I might have thought he did it to indulge in a quiet laugh.

"Miss Hereford, you cannot seriously believe in such nonsense!"

"No, indeed; not in collected moments; but I was left alone in the dark, and the surprise at seeing some one changed to fright."

"May I inquire from whom you heard this fine tale?"

"From Mrs. Penn first. But the women-servants talk of it. Lizzy Dene confessed she had gone up now to watch for it."

He turned round quickly. "*What* do you say? Lizzy Dene went up to watch for it?"

"I was not pleased at finding Lizzy in my room; she has no business to take her there, and I insisted upon knowing what took her to it, At first she would not say, but presently confessed: she had gone to watch for the ghost."

If ever a man's countenance betrayed a sickly dread, Mr. Chandos's did then. He went to the door, hesitated, and came back again, as if scarcely knowing what to be about.

"And she saw it?—saw some one walking there? She, and you?"

"I don't think she did; I saw it after she had gone. Oh, Mr. Chandos; I can see you are angry with me! I am very sorry; I—"

"Angry? no," he interrupted, in a gentle tone. "I only think how foolish you must be to listen to anything of the sort. I wish I could have shielded you from this alarm! I wish you had not come just now to Chandos!"

He rang the bell; a loud peal; and desired that Hill should be sent to him. I had never seen his face so stern as when he turned it upon her.

"Can you not contrive to keep the women-servants to their proper occupations, Hill? I hear they are going about the house looking after ghosts."

"Sir!"

"Miss Hereford went to her room just now, and found Lizzy Dene at its window. The woman said she was watching for the ghost."

Hill's face presented a picture. She stood more like a petrifaction than a living woman. Mr. Chandos recalled her to herself.

"Hill!" was all he said.

"I'll see about it, sir. I'll give that Lizzy Dene a word of a sort."

"I think you had better give her no 'word' at all, in the sense you indicate," returned Mr. Chandos. "Keep the women to their duties below at night, and say nothing. *Let the ghost die out, Hill.*"

"Very well, sir."

"As I dare say it will do, quietly enough. Sit with them yourself, if necessary. And—Hill—there's no necessity to mention anything of this to Lady Chandos."

"But—Mr. Harry—"

"Yes, yes; I know what you would say," he interrupted; "leave that to me."

He went limping out at the hall-door as he spoke. Hill disappeared in the direction of the kitchens, muttering angrily.

"That wretch of a Lizzy! If she should get spreading this among the outdoor men! I always said that girl brought no good to Chandos."

# CHAPTER 20

## LIZZY DENE

*"For my heart was hot and restless:*
*And my life was full of care;*
*And the burden laid upon me*
*Seemed greater than I could bear."*

Seated back in the shade, where the sunlight of the afternoon did not fall upon him, I saw him lift his hands at the last line, with a gesture half of despair, half of prayer, and then lay them on his pale face. Whatever his burden might be, it was a heavy one. It was he who had asked me to sing—Mr. Chandos; for the first time since I was in the house. Not much of a singer at the best, I never ventured on any but the most simple songs: and, of modern ones, "The Bridge," set to music by Miss Lindsay, is the sweetest.

"But now it has fallen from me;
It is buried in the sea;
And only the sorrow of others
Throws its shadow over me."

Rather boisterously the door was opened, and Mrs. Penn came in. Her hair was decidedly of a more glowing red than usual; but her light green gown of damask silk, her point-lace lappets thrown behind, her gold ornaments, ay, and herself, were altogether handsome. Mr. Chandos rose.

"Oh, I beg your pardon," she said, "for entering so unceremoniously. Hearing the piano, I though Miss Hereford was alone."

I turned round on the music-stool and sat facing the room. Mr. Chandos handed her a chair.

"Thank you," she said, hesitating to take it. "Mrs. Chandos is in the west wing: but perhaps I shall be intruding if I remain?"

"Not at all," replied Mr. Chandos. "Miss Hereford may be glad of your company. I am going to the west wing myself."

"Have you found your manuscript, Mr. Chandos?"

"What manuscript?"

She paused a moment. "I heard yesterday you had lost one. When Emma came in about her housemaid's duties last evening, she mentioned it."

It may as well be said, en passant, that Emma was housemaid to the east wing; Harriet to the chambers on the first floor generally, mine included; Lizzy Dene to the west wing: but it would frequently be the pleasure of Lady Chandos that Lizzy did not enter her apartments for days together, only Hill.

"It was a memorandum-book; not a manuscript," said Mr. Chandos.

"Oh; I understood her to say a manuscript."

"I have not found it," he continued. "Fortunately the contents are of little consequence. They consist chiefly of notes relative to the everyday business of the estate, and a few private items concerning myself. Some things are entered in hieroglyphics of my own," he continued, with a half-laugh, "and I'll defy the thief to make them out, however clever he may be. The singular thing is, how it could have disappeared from my desk."

"You must have left your keys about," she quickly said.

"That is more than likely. Having honest people about me at Chandos, I have not been very particular."

"It is a bad practice to leave keys where they may be picked up and used; it gives opportunities that otherwise might never have been seized upon," observed Mrs. Penn, in a dreamy tone.

"Not a bit of it, madam. Unless dishonest people are at hand to take advantage of the opportunities."

"Then how do you think your book can have gone, Mr. Chandos?"

"Well, I cannot think. I am content to leave the elucidation to time."

Mrs. Penn looked at him: she seemed to be hesitating over something. It was so palpable that Mr. Chandos noticed it.

"What is it?" he asked.

"I think I will speak," she said, with sudden decision. "Though indeed I do not like to do so, Mr. Chandos: and I certainly should not, but for hearing of this loss of yours. I have had a small loss too."

Mr. Chandos sat down; he had been standing since she came in; and waited for her to continue.

"It is not of much value; but—as you say by your book—it is the fact of its having gone that troubles me. Only a bit of what we call Honiton lace, about three yards of it, two inches in width. That it was safe in my work-box yesterday morning I know. This morning it was no longer there."

"Was the work-box locked?"

"It was. I had left it in the library, locked. My keys were in a drawer of my bedroom, where I keep them, for they are heavy, and weigh down my dress-pockets. Curious to say, upon looking for my keys this morning, I found them not in the usual drawer, but in the fellow-drawer beside it. Whoever had taken them out forgot which was the right drawer and put them back in the wrong one."

"And you missed the lace?"

"Yes. It happened that I was going to use it to trim some sleeves:

but for that I might not have missed it for weeks. It was in the bottom of the work-box, lying on the top of some other things: as soon as I lifted the upper tray, I saw it was gone. Of course I searched the box over, but without result."

"Have you spoken to the servants?"

"I have not said much, lest they should think I accused them. What I said was that I had lost or mislaid some lace; and described it. They all appear to be quite innocent. Still, the lace could not go without hands."

"I don't like this," observed Mr. Chandos, after a pause.

"It is not the loss in itself—as I say: it is the feeling of insecurity that it leaves," returned Mrs. Penn. "One cannot be sure that other things will not follow. But I must not detain you longer," she added, rising. "I hope, Mr. Chandos, you will not think I have been wrong or unkind in mentioning this."

"I think you have done quite right, Mrs. Penn," he warmly replied, as he opened the door for her. "If we really have a thief in the house, the sooner we are upon our guard the better. Take greater care of your keys for the present. As to the lace, Mrs. Chandos will make it good to you—"

"Sir!" she interrupted, rather fiercely. "Oh, pray don't talk in that way; I shall be vexed to have mentioned it. The loss is nothing."

She left the room. Not a word had I spoken all the time; not a syllable as to my own boxes having been visited. I did not care to throw any accusation upon Lizzy Dene. Besides, the matter seemed to present contradiction to my mind: as I found by the next words it was doing to that of Mr. Chandos.

"I cannot fathom this at all: unless we have two light-fingered people in the house. Mrs. Penn's lace must have been cribbed by one of the maids, I fear; but it is hardly likely that she would take a memorandum-book. Where would be the use of it to any one of them? There were things of value in my desk, not touched: a gold paper-knife; a large gold seal; and some loose silver. Well, we must wait; and meanwhile take care of our keys," he concluded, as he left the parlour.

I finished my interrupted song in a low voice, sang another one or two, and then went up to my room. Mrs. Penn was standing at the library-door.

"Has Mr. Chandos gone into the west wing, do you know, Miss Hereford?"

"I think so. He left the parlour almost as soon as you did."

"I am sorry to have missed him. I don't know what he'll think of me. Did you notice my omission?"

"What omission?"

"Never to have asked after his health. I feel ashamed of myself. I have not seen him since the day's illness he had, when the physician came down to him. I hate to be unfeeling," added Mrs. Penn. "But what with seeing him in the oak-parlour when I expected only you were there, and what with the thought of my lace, I completely forgot it."

"He says he is better. I think he must be very much better from the alarming state they said he was in that day. But he looks ill."

"That's caused by worry," said Mrs. Penn. "I should wonder if he could look well. Look at his figure: it's no better than a skeleton's."

We had been walking together to the end of the library. I don't know whether I have mentioned it before, but every evening, a good hour before dusk, the door of this library was locked for the night by Hill, and the key carried away in her pocket. Mrs. Penn turned to me as we stood together at the window, dropping her voice to a whisper.

"Was there not something mysterious about his illness?"

Frankly speaking, I thought there was. But in mind I had connected it in some undefined way with his sleep-walking. I could not say this.

"But that he is so remarkably unlikely a subject for it, I should think it had been a fit," she continued. "Did you hear whether the London doctor also saw Lady Chandos?"

"No, I did not. There's no one to inquire of, except Hill. And you know how much information we should be likely to get from her."

"Except him," corrected Mrs. Penn, with emphasis. "With all his sins, Harry Chandos is a gentleman, and would give you an answer."

I shook my head. It was not my place, a young visitor there on sufferance, to inquire of things they seemed to wish to keep secret: and I said as much to Mrs. Penn.

"You are too fastidious, Miss Hereford; you are no better than a school-girl. Look here," she added, turning briskly, "this is the work-box. I will show you where the lace was."

It was a large, handsome box of tortoise-shell inlaid with silver, its fittings of silver and sky-blue velvet; its scissors, thimble, bodkin, and stiletto of gold.

"I wonder they did not take these as well as the lace."

"They might be afraid to do that," said Mrs. Penn. "See!" she cried, lifting the tray, "it lay there. It was a very handsome piece of lace, and I am sorry to lose it."

The sweeping of a silk dress along the corridor gave token of the approach of Mrs. Chandos. She passed into the east wing, and Mrs. Penn hastened after her. Standing at the door of the west wing, as if he had attended Mrs. Chandos from it, was Mr. Chandos. He saw us both come out of the library.

Where he had his dinner that day I don't know. Mine was over and the things were taken away before I saw him again. I had been upstairs for a book and met him in the hall. He followed me to the oak-parlour and threw himself into a chair, like one utterly weary.

"You have not been walking much, have you, Mr. Chandos?"

"Not much; my foot's too weak yet. I have been taking a turn or two in the Pine Walk. And you? Have you been spirit-gazing again?"

I did not answer, except by a shake of the head, and he sat for a long while in silence, breaking it at last abruptly.

"Does Mrs. Penn get looking from the front windows, after that—that sight—that you professed to see the night before last?"

"I think she would like to do so: but there's no opportunity. The rooms in the east wing do not look to the front, you know."

"Ah, I see you and she get talking of this together."

"The talking has been very little, and of her seeking, not mine. I would rather she never spoke to me at all about it: it embarrasses me."

"Why does it embarrass you?"

"I—"

"Well?" he said, looking straight at me.

"I don't like to say, Mr. Chandos."

He left his chair and came to the window, where I stood playing with the jessamine. How soft the air was! how sweet the perfume of the flowers in the approaching night!

"Now then. I have come to hear what you mean."

The tones were persuasive: the face, as it drooped a little, wore a smile that invited confidence. I bent my head and told him—that I thought what people had seen at midnight and taken for a ghost might be himself walking in his sleep; but that I could not say this to Mrs. Penn. He made no rejoinder whatever. He lifted his head and gazed straight out towards the entrance to the Pine Walk.

"Shall I tell Mrs. Penn that it is not a ghost at all, sir, and set her mind, so far, at rest? I need not give any particulars."

"But suppose it is a ghost, Miss Hereford?"

The tones were very sad and serious. My heart beat a little quicker.

"Did you not assure me you saw it the other night—when I was safe in this very parlour?"

"Yes; but I thought afterwards it might be what you said—one of the gardeners. Night-light is so deceptive."

"Come back for his tools," added Mr. Chandos. "Mrs. Penn, however, says it is something else that walks there—my late father's spirit. Do you think she believes it?"

"Yes. She spoke as if she did believe it: and dreaded it. Shall I tell her she need not do so?"

"No," he sadly said. "I cannot unfortunately ask you to do that."

What did the speech mean? Did it really bear the intimation that he could not in truth deny it? Something like a tremor, with that dark and weird Pine Walk within sight, crept over me. Mr. Chandos leaned from the window, plucked a white rose, and put it into my hand.

"There," he said, "that's better than talking of ghosts. And, Miss Hereford—keep your curtains above closed after dark: I don't like to be watched when I go out there."

He rang the bell for lights and tea. Ah, that rose, that rose! Does any one, reading this, remember receiving one from a beloved hand? Had it been a flower from Paradise it could not have borne for me a greater charm. The skies were brighter, the coming night was sweeter, the whole atmosphere seemed impregnated with a bliss, not of this world. My heart was wild with happiness; the rose was worth more than Golconda's costliest diamonds. I have it still. I shall keep it for ever.

"And now for a cup of tea, if you'll give me one, Miss Hereford."

I turned from the window, the rose held carelessly in my fingers, and put it down, as of no moment, beside the tray. Afterwards he remained talking to me a little time, and then rose to leave for the evening.

"I wish I could stay longer; it is very lonely for you," he said, as he shook hands. "But my mother feels lonely too; and so—I must divide myself as I best may."

"Is not Lady Chandos better?" I asked, interrupting his light laugh.

"Some days she is. Not much so on the whole."

"And you, sir?"

I suppose I looked at him wistfully, for he put his hand for a moment on my head, and bent his kind face.

"Don't be anxious for me. I am sorry you heard what Amos said. I am very much better than I was the day he was here. Good-night."

It was all dreary again; sunshine had gone out; and I went up to bed at half-past nine. The first thing I did was to kiss the rose before putting it away: my cheeks burn at confessing it as they burnt then. And in the very midst of the sweet folly my chamber-door was knocked at, and Mrs. Penn came in. "How early you have come up! Dull? Ay, I dare say you do find it so. But I can't stay a moment. I want you to do me a favour, Anne Hereford. When Mrs. Chandos shall be in bed and asleep to-night, let me come to your room."

"What for?" I exclaimed, in great surprise.

"I want to watch from your windows. I want to see whether it is a ghost that is said to haunt the walks at nights: or—whether it is anything else. I knew the late Sir Thomas, and should recognize—"

"Hush, Mrs. Penn," I interrupted. Every impulse my mind possessed prompted me to deny the request. "It is what I cannot do. I might grow very frightened myself; but it is not that; it is that I am a visitor in the family, and would not pry into an affair that must no doubt be one of pain and annoyance to them. Don't you perceive that it would be dishonourable? I keep my curtains closed at night, you see; and no persuasion would induce me to allow them to be opened."

"You are a foolish girl," she said, with good humour. "Hill locks up the other rooms at dusk: and if she did not, I should be too great a coward to watch alone in them. A love of the marvellous was born with me; I may say a terror of it; and my early training served to increase this. As a child I was allowed to read ghost-stories; my nurse used to tell them in my hearing to her companions; of course it could but bear fruit. I think it perfectly wicked to allow such tales to penetrate to the impressionable imaginations of young children; they never wholly recover it."

"But you cannot seriously believe in ghosts, Mrs. Penn!"

"I should be ashamed to avow that I do believe in them. And yet the subject bears for me both a terror and a charm: nay, a strange fascination."

That she spoke the truth now was evident; though I could not think she always did. I stood waiting for her to go.

"And so you will not let me come, Miss Hereford! Well, perhaps you are right: it never occurred to me that the family might feel annoyed at it. Good-night."

But I did not trust her: she might steal in while I slept: and I turned the key of my door inside for the first time since I was at Chandos.

The next day was a gloomy one. Not as to weather; that was bright enough; but for me. Mr. Chandos was away. Gone out somewhere by rail, very far; and would not be back until night.

"Is he well enough to bear the fatigue, Hickens?" I could not help asking the butler as he stood by me at breakfast.

"Well, miss, I should say he is not well enough. Hill says it is some pressing business for my lady that he has gone upon; and Mr. Harry is one to go through with any duty, let him be well or ill; ay, though he died for it."

Idling away the morning desultorily, I got through an hour or two. Was this new feeling making me worthless? Half ashamed of myself as the question flashed over me, I took out a German book of study, and settled down to it on a bench amidst the trees, not far from the entrance-gates, and near the Privet Walk where I had once met Edwin Barley. Whilst I was reading steadily, a voice began speaking at a little distance, and I recognized it as *his*.

Edwin Barley's. Did he habitually come to the shady walk? The intervening shrubs hid me from him, and him from me; for some minutes I could do nothing but give way to my fear; and did not dare to stir hand or foot.

Some one was speaking with him; whether man or woman I

could not tell, the voice was so faint. And it seemed that while Mr. Barley must have had his face turned to me, and the wind, setting this way, bore his accents with it, the other person must have faced the opposite way, and the voice was lost.

"You are stupid, woman!" were the first distinct words I heard from him, seemingly spoken in sudden petulance. "Where's the use of your telling me this much, if you can't tell more?"

It was a woman, then. Sure and swiftly came the conviction of her identity to me with a force I could not account for. Lizzy Dene.

"It must have been a very serious attack, for a physician to be telegraphed for in such haste," resumed Mr. Edwin Barley. "And to be well again now to go out for a whole day by rail!"

A pause. It was taken up by the answer, but of that I could not hear so much as a tone. Mr. Edwin Barley resumed.

"There's a mystery about it all that I can't fathom. A mystery altogether about Harry Chandos. That attack upon him in the avenue was a curious thing. And his mother? Is she visible yet?"

Another inaudible reply.

"Well, you must work better, if you work at all. This is your affair, mind; not mine; I did not ask you to bring me news, or to look into letters—what do you say? Not able to look into letters? You can read, I suppose?"

It is Lizzy Dene, my conscience whispered me; for a half doubt had been crossing me of Mrs. Penn.

"Oh, I understand; don't get the chance of looking into them?" he went on. "Well—it is your own affair, I repeat; but as you chose to make the offer of looking out for discoveries, I shall expect you to make some. Do you hear?" he continued, in his voice of determination. "What? Speak low, for fear of hearers? Nonsense; there's no one to hear. If you want money for bribery, of course I can furnish you with it, if you undertake to use it legitimately."

Again a pause. The higher Mr. Edwin Barley raised his voice, the lower the other seemed to speak.

"No, you are wrong; the greatest enemy to your plans would be Harry Chandos; the rest are women. That there's something to be discovered connected with *him*, and at this present time, I am absolutely certain of. Discovered it shall be," emphatically pronounced Mr. Edwin Barley. "About his wife?" he suddenly asked.

"All that's wanted is the clue," he recommenced, after listening to the answer. "*It is to be had*, I know. They would not live in this dark, retired manner for nothing; and I have my theory about it. What do you say?—oh, well, yes, if you like; I did not ask you to repeat things about the family to me, you know; you are doing it of your own free will. How long have you lived in this neighbourhood?"

Strain my ears as I would, I could not catch more than a faint whisper in reply:

"Eh? What?" briskly resumed Mr. Edwin Barley. "The ghost walks again! Sir Thomas Chandos! Give my compliments to it, and ask if it remembers me! You foolish woman!" he went on, scornfully. "A troubled conscience may cause people to 'walk' in life; but it never yet brought them back after death. Now don't—oh, I thought you were going to insist on the ghost. Upon thorns lest you should be missed and called for? Hill looks you all up so sharply? I'll go then. Advice? I have none to give."

I heard his steps walking leisurely away. Stealing swiftly along the bye-paths, I went round to the servants' entrance, determined to see whether Lizzy Dene was out of doors or not. A miserable gnat had bitten me, affording an excuse; but I should have made one in case of need. The cook stood by her kitchen fire.

"Oh, cook, would you please give me a little warm water? A gnat has just stung my wrist. Perhaps if I bathe it at once, it will not inflame."

She gave it me immediately, putting the basin on the table underneath the window, Harriet ran and brought a little sponge. At that moment Mrs. Hill came in.

"Where's Lizzy Dene? Is she not here?"

"No, she's not here," was the quick retort of the cook, spoken with irritation. "She's off again—as she always is. I sent her to get the eggs, for the boy never brought them in this morning, and she has been gone pretty near an hour! It's a shame."

"It is not Lizzy's work, that you should send her," remarked Mrs. Hill; "but she has no business to stop out. Have you hurt your hand, Miss Hereford?"

I told her what it was, and she left the kitchen again, leaving orders for Lizzy Dene to come to her in the linen-room as soon as she entered.

"You need not have told," remonstrated Harriet to the cook, in an undertone, on account of my presence. "Mother Hill finds enough fault with us without being helped to more."

"I'm not going to put up with Lizzy, if you are!" cried out the cook, not caring whether I was present or not. "Send her but for the least thing, and there she stops. My custard ought to have been made, and set to cool by this time. She gets talking to the outdoor men; I know she does. What else can she do?"

"That woman was here again last night," rejoined Harriet, as they stood over the fire.

"Who is that woman?—coming after Lizzy Dene, as she does! Why shouldn't Lizzy be open about it?"

"I asked her who it was, the other day, but she'd give me no answer," replied Harriet. "You know that weeping ash, yonder to the right. Well, there they stood with their heads together, last night, Lizzy Dene and the woman. Lizzy's very much altered of late. I can't make her out. At the time of the accident to Mr. Chandos, she was like one out of her mind. I asked her if she had frightened the horse. There was always something odd about her."

"There'll be something odder about her yet, if she don't speedily bring them eggs," retorted the cook. "I won't put up with this."

I took my hand out of the water, wrapped a handkerchief loosely round it, and went out at the back-door, taking my way leisurely round. Truth to say, I was watching for Lizzy Dene.

And I saw her. She came darting down one of the paths, and caught up a basket of eggs that stood behind a tree; her face was red and flushed, as if she had been walking or talking herself into a heat.

"Lizzy," I said, confronting her, "they are waiting for the eggs. Where have you been?"

"Don't stop me, miss, please; cook's in a rage as it is, I know," was all the answer I received; and the woman bore on to the kitchen.

# CHAPTER 21

## IN THE PINE WALK

Really mine was just now a strange life. A young girl—young in experience as well as in years—living in that house without any companion except Mr. Chandos. More unrestrained companionship could scarcely have existed between us had we been brother and sister. Our meals were taken together; he presiding at luncheon and dinner, I at breakfast and tea. The oak-parlour was our common sitting-room; the groves and glades of Chandos, glowing with the tints of autumn, our frequent walks. It was very pleasant; too pleasant; I say nothing about its prudence.

Later, when I grew more conversant with the ways of the world and its exactions, I wondered that Lady Chandos had not seen its inexpediency. But that love should supervene on either side never crossed her thoughts. Had it been suggested to her, she would have rejected the idea as altogether improbable. I was a school-girl, her son (as she had reason to think) was love-proof. In regard to other considerations, Mr. Chandos was one of those men with whom a young girl would be perfectly safe; and she knew it.

Three or four days passed on. Mr. Chandos had recovered from his lameness, and went to church with us on Sunday. Our order of going was, as usual, this: he walked by the side of Mrs. Chandos, almost in silence: I and Mrs. Penn walked behind. In a pew at right angles with ours sat Mr. Edwin Barley alone; and his dark stern eyes seemed to be fixed on me from the beginning of the service to the end.

Well from his lameness; but anything but well as to his health, if looks might be relied upon. He seemed to grow more shadowy day by day. What his illness was I could not think and might not ask: it certainly seemed of the mind more than of the body. A conviction grew gradually upon me that some curious mystery, apart from the sleep-walking, did attach to Mr. Chandos; and the words I overheard spoken by Edwin Barley strengthened the impression: "That there is something to be discovered connected with him, and at this present time, I am absolutely certain of." What did he allude to?

Surely it was nothing in the form of disgrace! As he sat there before me, with his calm pale face and its sweet expression, it was against the dictates of common sense to suppose that evil or wicked antecedents attached to him. No; I would not believe it, let Madam Penn say what she chose.

It was a lovely autumn morning to begin the week with. The fire burnt briskly in the grate, but the window, near which we sat, was open. Mr. Chandos seemed low and depressed. His moods were changeable. Sometimes he would be lively, laughing, quite gay; as if he put away the inward trouble for a time. During breakfast, which he ate this morning almost in silence, he took a letter from his pocket and glanced at its contents, heaving an involuntary sigh. I recognized it as one that had been delivered the previous morning. The name "Henry Amos" on the corner of the envelope proved the writer; I wondered then—I wonder still—why people put their names outside the letters they send, as some do.

"Does he write instructions to you still, Mr. Chandos?"

"Who? Dr. Amos? Well, yes; in a measure."

"I hope he thinks you are getting better?"

"I tell him that I am. You have forgotten the sugar. A small lump, please. Thank you."

It was ever so. If I did summon up courage to ask about his health he only turned it off. His tea did not want further sweetening more than mine did.

We went out that day for a drive in the large open carriage; Mrs. Chandos, Mrs. Penn, and I. It was the first time we had gone together. Mr. Chandos was away; attending some county meeting. It was nearly five when we returned home. Later, when I had my hair down and was dressing for dinner, Mrs. Penn came in.

"Oh, this dreary life at Chandos!" she exclaimed, sinking into a chair, without ceremony or apology for entering. "I am not sure that I can continue to put up with it."

"Dreary, do you find it?"

"It *is* dreary. It is not pleasant or satisfactory. Mrs. Chandos grows colder and more capricious; and you are not half the companion you might be. It was on the tip of my tongue just now to give her warning. If I *do* give it, I shall be off the next day. I never found a place dull in all my life before."

"Something has vexed you, perhaps, Mrs. Penn?"

"If it has, it's only a slight vexation. I hastened to write this as soon as we came in"—turning her left hand, in which lay a sealed letter—"and I find the letters are gone. I thought the man called for them at half-past five."

"No; at five."

"So Hickens has just informed me. What few letters I have had to write since I came have been done in the morning. It can't be helped; it must wait until to-morrow."

She put the letter into her bag, shutting it up with a sharp click that spoke of vexation; a small morocco bag with a steel clasp and chain; took her keys from her pocket and locked it.

"What a pretty thing that is!"

"This reticule? Yes, it is pretty: and very convenient. Have you one?"

"Not like that. Mine is an ugly one, made out of a piece of carpet; I bought it ever so long ago at the fair at Nulle."

"Shall you ever go back to Nulle?"

"I should be there at this present time, but for a fever that has broken out at Miss Barlieu's. It is passing away, though; I heard from Miss Annette on Saturday."

"Fever, or no fever, I should say it would be a happy change for you from this dull place."

Dull! It was my Elysium. I felt guilty in my self-consciousness, and the bright colour stole over my face and neck.

"Allow me to fasten your dress for you."

I thanked her, but laughingly said that I was accustomed to dress myself. She laughed too; observed that school-girls generally could help themselves, having no choice upon the point, and turned to look from the window.

She stood there with her back to me until I was ready to go down, sometimes turning her head to speak. We left the room together, and she seemed to have recovered her good temper. I had reached the foot of the stairs when I happened to look up the well of the staircase. There was the face of Mrs. Penn, regarding me with a strange intensity. What did she see in me?

Is this to be a full confession? When my solitary dinner was brought in, and Hickens said his master dined at Warsall, I felt half sick with disappointment. What was I coming to? Something not good, I feared, if I could feel like that; and I sat down after dinner to take myself to task.

Why did I love him? *That* I could not help now; but I could help encouraging it. And yet—*could* I help it, so long as I stayed at Chandos? I foresaw how it would be: a short period of time—it could not be a long one—and Madame de Mellissie would be there and carry me away with her, and and it. I should find another situation, and never see or hear of Chandos again, or of him. Better go away at once than wait until my heart broke! better go to the fever, as Mrs. Penn had said!

"Why! What's the matter?"

He had come up to the open window, riding-whip in hand, having alighted at the gates, and left his horse to the groom. There was no possibility of concealment, and my eyes were red with crying.

"I felt a little dull, sir."

"Dull! Ah, yes; of course you do," he continued, as he came into the room, and stood with me at the window. "I wish I could be more with you, but duties of various kinds call me elsewhere."

The very thing I had been thinking ought not to be! My tears were dried, but I felt ashamed of my burning face.

"Would you please to let me have that money, Mr. Chandos?"

"What money?"

"Some that I asked you for. Enough to take me to Nulle."

"You shall have as much money as you please, and welcome. But not to take you to Nulle."

"Oh, sir! I must go."

He paused, looking at me. "Will you tell me *why* you want to go there, knowing that it might be dangerous?"

"I have not anywhere else to go to. I don't suppose the fever would attack me. In all French schools there is, you know, an infirmary."

"Then your motive is to quit Chandos. Why?"

I did not speak.

"Is it because you find it dull? Are you so unhappy in it?"

"It is not dull to me; only at moments. But I ought to leave it, because—because the longer I stay, the worse the going away will be."

But that I was confused and miserable, I should not have said anything so near the truth. The words slipped from me. There was no reply, and I looked up to find his eyes fixed earnestly upon mine.

"Only think, sir, for yourself," I stammered. "I am only a governess, accustomed to be at work from morning until night. After this life of ease and idleness, how shall I be able to reconcile myself to labour again?"

"It seems to me that you ought to welcome this interval as a rest. You know best about that, of course. But, whether or not, there is no help for it. Do you think my mother would suffer you to go to the fever?"

"I don't know," I answered.

"Yes, I think you do know. *I* should not."

"You are too kind to me, Mr. Chandos."

"Am I? Will you repay it by giving me some tea? I am going up to my mother, and shall expect it ready when I come down. Put out, and cool, mind, ready to drink. I am as thirsty as a fish."

I ran to the bell; he meant to forestall me, and his hand fell on mine as it touched the handle; he kept his there while he spoke.

"Can you not be happy at Chandos a little longer?"

"Oh, sir, yes. But it will only make the leaving worse when it comes."

"Well, that lies in the future."

Yes, it did lie in it. And in the throbbing bliss his presence brought, I was content to let it lie. Parting could not be worse in the future than it would be now.

The tea had time to grow cold, instead of cool, for he stayed a long time in the west wing. He seemed very tired; did not talk much, and said good-night early.

It must have been getting on for eleven o'clock the next morning.

Mr. Chandos had been asking me to sew a button on his glove. "They are always coming off," he cried, as he watched my fingers. "My belief is, they are just pitched on to the gloves, and left there. I have heard Harriet say the same; she sews them on generally."

"Why did you not give her this one?" I had been laughing, and was in high spirits; and until the words were out, it did not strike me that it was not quite the right thing for me to say, even in joke.

"Because I like you to do it."

"There it is, sir. Are there any more?"

If there were, he had no time to give them to me. A sharp decisive knock at the room door, and Mrs. Penn came in, looking pale and angry.

She has been coming to a rupture with Mrs. Chandos, thought I. But I was wrong.

It appeared, by what she began to say, that she had left, unintentionally, the small bag, or reticule as she called it, in my room the previous evening, and had not thought of it until just now. Upon sending one of the maids for it, she found it had been opened.

"Mrs. Penn!" I exclaimed.

"It's quite true," she rejoined, almost vehemently, as she held out the bag. "Do you remember seeing me put the letter in the bag, Miss Hereford? The letter I was too late to post?"

"Yes; I saw you put it in and lock the bag."

"Just so. Well, while I talked with you afterwards, I presume I must have let the bag slip on the window-seat; and forgot it. This morning, not long ago, I missed it, looked everywhere, and it was only by tracing back to when I last remembered to have had it, that I thought of your room, and that I might inadvertently have left it there. I sent Emma to look; and when she brought me the bag, I found it had been opened."

"Opened!" I repeated.

"Opened," she angrily affirmed. And then, perhaps our very calmness recalling her to herself, she went on in quieter tones. "I am sure you will make allowance for me if I appear a little excited. I do not wish to throw suspicion upon any one: but I cannot deny that I am both annoyed and angry. You would be so yourself, Mr. Chandos, if such a thing happened to you," she added, suddenly turning to him.

"Take a seat, and explain to me what it is that has happened," replied Mr. Chandos, handing her a chair. "I scarcely understand."

"Thank you, no," she said, declining the seat. "I cannot stay to sit down, I must return to Mrs. Chandos: it was she who recommended me to come and speak to Miss Hereford. Upon Emma's bringing me the reticule I unlocked it, suspecting nothing, and—"

"I thought you said it had been opened, Mrs. Penn?"

"It had been opened. You shall hear. The first thing I saw was my letter, and the seal looked cracked across. I thought perhaps the bag had fallen to the ground; but upon my looking at it more attentively I saw it had been opened. See."

She put the envelope into Mr. Chandos's hand for examination. It had been opened with a penknife, cut underneath, and afterwards fastened down with gum. Of this there was no doubt; part of the letter had also been cut.

"This is very extraordinary," said Mr. Chandos, as he turned the envelope about. It was addressed to London, to a medical man.

"Yes, it *is* extraordinary, sir," said Mrs. Penn, with some slight temper, which I am sure he considered excusable. I did so. "The note was a private note to the gentleman who has attended me for some years; I didn't write it for the perusal of the world. But that is not the chief question. There must be false keys in the house."

"Did you leave your key in the bag, Mrs. Penn?"

"No, sir. I had my keys in my pocket. The lock has not been injured, therefore it can only have been opened with a false key."

Remembering my own boxes and Mr. Chandos's desk, I felt no doubt that false keys must be at hand. Mrs. Penn said she had not yet spoken to the servants, and Mr. Chandos nodded approval: he would wish to deal with it himself. For my part I had not seen the bag in my room, except in her possession, and did not notice whether she had carried it away or left it.

She quitted the parlour, taking the bag and note with her. Mr. Chandos called Hickens and desired that Emma should be sent to him. The girl arrived in some wonder. But she could tell nothing; except that she found the bag lying on the floor by the window-seat, and carried it at once to Mrs. Penn. Harriet was next questioned. She had seen the bag lying in the window-seat the previous evening, she said, when she put the room to rights after Miss Hereford went down to dinner, and left it there, drawing the curtains before it.

"Did you touch it?" asked Mr. Chandos.

"Yes, sir. I took it up in my hand, and thought what a pretty thing it was: I had never seen it before."

"Did you open it?"

"Open it? No, sir, that I did not. I think it was locked, for I saw there was a key-hole: at any rate, it was closely shut. I did not keep it in my hands a moment, but put it down where I found it, and drew the curtains."

"Who else went into Miss Hereford's room last evening?"

"Why, sir, how can I tell?" returned Harriet, after a pause of surprise. "What I have to do in the room does not take five minutes, and I am not near it afterwards. Twenty folk might go in and out without my knowing it."

That both the girls were innocent there could be no question.

Then who was guilty? In undrawing the curtains that morning I must have pulled the bag off the window-seat, which caused me not to see it. Hill went into a temper when she heard of the affair.

"I don't believe there's one of the maids would do such a thing, Mr. Harry. What should they want with other folk's letters? And where would they get gum from to stick them down?"

"There's some gum on my mantelpiece, Hill: I use it with my drawings," I said to her.

"Ah, well, gum or no gum, they wouldn't cut open letters," was Hill's reply, given obstinately.

"There must be false keys in the house, Mr. Chandos," I began, as Hill went out.

"There's something worse than that—a spy," was his answer, "Though the one implies the other."

And I thought I could have put my hand upon her—Lizzy Dene. But it was only a doubt. I was not certain. And, being only a doubt, I did not consider that I ought to speak.

Some days elapsed with nothing special to record, and then some money was missed. Mr. Chandos and I were together as usual in the oak-parlour. Opening his desk, he exclaimed rather sharply, and I looked up from my work.

"So! they have walked into the trap, have they!" he cried, searching it here and there. "I thought so."

"What is it, Mr. Chandos?" I asked, and he presently turned to me, quitting the table.

"These matters have been puzzling me, Miss Hereford. Is it a petty thief that we have in the house, one to crib lace and such trifles; or is it a spy? I have thought it may be both: such a thing is not beyond the bounds of possibility. A person who took Mrs. Penn's lace would not be likely to take my memorandum-book: for *that* must have been done to pry into my private affairs, or those of the Chandos family: and a spy, aiming at higher game, would keep clear of petty thefts. The taking Mrs. Penn's letter, I mean breaking its seal, I do not understand: but, before that was done, I marked some money and put it into my desk; two sovereigns and two half-crowns. They are gone."

"You locked the desk afterwards?"

"Yes. Now I shall act decisively. Mrs. Penn has thought me very quiet over her loss, I dare say, but I have not seen my way at all clear. I do not, truth to say, see it now."

"In what way, sir?"

"I cannot reconcile the one loss with the other. Unless we have two false inmates amongst us. I begin to think it is so. Say nothing at all to any one, Miss Hereford."

He wrote a hasty note, directed it, and sealed it with the Chandos coat-of-arms; then ordered his own groom, James, into his presence.

"Saddle one of the horses for yourself, James. When you are ready, come round with him, and I will give you directions."

The man was soon equipped. He appeared leading the horse. Mr. Chandos went out, and I stood at the open window.

"Are you quite ready?"

"Quite, sir."

"Mount then."

The servant did as he was bid, and Mr. Chandos continued, putting the note he had written into his hands.

"Go straight to Warsall, to the police-station, and deliver this. Do not loiter."

James touched his hat and cantered off.

Ever since I had seen the police at Mr. Edwin Barley's, at the time of the death of Philip King, I had felt an invincible dread of them; they were always associated in my mind with darkness and terror. The French gendarmes had not tended to reassure me; with their uniform, their cocked hats, their conspicuous swords, and their fiery horses; but the police there were quite another sort of people, far more harmless than ours. The worst I saw of them was the never-ending warfare they kept up with the servant-maids for being late in washing before the doors in a morning. The cook at Miss Barlieu's, Marie, called them old women, invariably setting them at defiance: but one day they cited her before the tribunal, and she had to pay a fine of five francs.

The police arrived in the afternoon; two, in plain clothes; and Mr. Chandos was closeted with them alone. Then we heard—at least, I heard—that the servants' pockets were to be examined, and their boxes searched. I was standing in the hall, looking wistful enough, no doubt, when Mr. Chandos and his two visitors came forth from the drawing-room.

"You appear alarmed," he paused to say, smiling. "Have no fear."

They were disappearing down the passage that led to the kitchens and thence to the servants' rooms above, when Mrs. Penn came in with her bonnet on. She gazed after the strangers.

"Those look just like police!" she whispered. "What have they come for?"

"About these losses, I believe. Mr. Chandos has again lost something from his desk."

"What! besides the first loss the other day?"

"Yes. He feels very much annoyed: and it is enough to make him feel so."

"I would forgive a little pilfering—that is, I would not be too harsh upon the thief," she remarked. "Pretty lace and such vanities do bear their attractions. But when it comes to violating letters and private papers, that is essentially another affair. What are the police going to do in it? Do you know?"

"I believe the servants' boxes and pockets are about to be examined."

"I should think, then, my lace, at any rate, will come to light," she laughed, as she tripped up the stairs.

The process of searching seemed to be a pretty long one. Mr. Chandos was in the oak-parlour, when one of the officers, who seemed to be superior to the other, came in.

"Well, sir," said he, as he took the seat to which Mr. Chandos invited him, "there's no trace of any stolen property about the maids or their boxes. One or two of them had some love-letters: and seemed much more afraid of my reading them than of finding lace or money," he added, with a broad smile. "I just glanced over the epistles, enough to convince myself that there was nothing wrong in them: but there is no game more formidable to be found."

Mr. Chandos made no reply. I thought he looked puzzled.

"We have hitherto placed great trust in our servants," he observed, presently. "But the disappearance of these things is unaccountable."

"There does seem some mystery about it," returned the policeman. "You say, sir, that you are sure of the housekeeper."

"As sure as I am of myself."

"Shall we search the rooms in the front, above here, sir? Thieves have a trick of hiding things, you know."

"No," decisively replied Mr. Chandos. "My mother might hear you; I could not risk annoying her in her invalid state. Besides, the rooms have been fully searched by the housekeeper."

"Would you like a watch placed in the house, sir, unknown to the servants?"

"No, no," said Mr. Chandos. "It—"

The appearance of Mrs. Penn caused the pause. She came in, after knocking quietly at the door. Mr. Chandos rose; the officer rose.

"I beg your pardon for my interruption, Mr. Chandos. Will it not be better that the police"—slightly bowing to the one present—"should come up now? Mrs. Chandos has gone into my lady's rooms: if they can come up at once, she will be spared the sight."

"Come up for what?" asked Mr. Chandos.

"I understood that our boxes were to be examined."

She evidently meant her own and mine. Mr. Chandos laughed pleasantly.

"Your boxes? Certainly not, Mrs. Penn. Why, you are the chief sufferer! It would be a new thing to search the very places from which the articles have been taken."

But Mrs. Penn pressed it. It was not pleasant, although she had lost a bit of lace: and she thought the boxes should all be treated alike, excepting those belonging to the Chandos family: it would be more satisfactory to our minds. Mr. Chandos repeated his No, courteously, but somewhat imperatively, and left the room with the officer.

"Did you offer your boxes for their inspection?" she asked of me.

"Of course not. They know quite well I should not be likely to take the things."

"I may say the same of myself. But I cannot help remembering that you and I are the only strangers in the place; and it makes me, for my part, feel uncomfortable. Such a thing never before happened in any house where I have been."

"At any rate, Mrs. Penn, *you* must be exempt from suspicion."

"It is not altogether that. I look at it in this light. These servants are searched: they are proved innocent; at least nothing is found upon them to imply guilt. They may turn round and say—why don't you search these two strangers?—and suggest injustice. However—of course Mr. Chandos must do as he pleases: he seems sole master here."

"Do not fear that he will suspect either you or me, Mrs. Penn. And Lady Chandos, as I gather, knows nothing of the matter."

The search and commotion had the effect of delaying dinner. It was late when the men departed, and I grew tired of being alone in the oak-parlour. Mr. Chandos had gone out somewhere. Throwing a shawl over my shoulders, for the evenings were not so warm as they had been, I went out and walked down the avenue.

Suddenly, as I paced it, it occurred to me that Mr. Chandos might be coming home. Would it look as though I had gone to meet him! Love was making me jealously reticent, and I plunged thoughtlessly into the shady walks opposite, trusting to good luck to take me back to the house. Good luck proved a traitor. It lost my way for me: and when I found it again I was at the far end of the Pine Walk.

To my dismay. The superstitions attaching to this gloomy walk flashed into my mind. Outside, it had been a grey twilight; here it was nearly as dark as night: in fact, night had set in. There was nothing for it but to run straight through: to turn back would be unwise now: I should inevitably lose myself again. I was about half-way up the walk, flying like the wind, when in turning a corner I almost ran against Mr. Chandos, who was coming quickly down it.

But, in the first moment I did not recognize him; it was too dark. Fear came over me, my heart beat wildly; and I almost screamed.

"I beg your pardon, sir," I said. "I did not know you quite at first."

"*You* here!" he exclaimed in astonishment, and (as it sounded to me) alarm. "Why did you come into this dreary portion of the grounds, and at this hour? I have already warned you not to do it."

I told him quite humbly how it was: that I had inadvertently got into it, after losing my way. Humbly, because he seemed to be angry at my disobedience.

"I had better take you out of it," he said, drawing my arm within his, without the ceremony of asking leave. "When dusk approaches, you must confine your rambles to the open walk, Miss Hereford,"

"Indeed, yes. This has been a lesson to me. But it seemed quite light outside."

He went on without another word, walking as though he were walking for a wager, so swift was his pace. The dark boughs meeting overhead, the late hour, the still atmosphere, imparted altogether a sensation of strange dreariness.

All at once a curious thing occurred. What, I scarcely know to this day. I saw nothing; I heard nothing; but Mr. Chandos apparently did, for he stopped suddenly, and his face became livid with terror. At this portion of the walk there was no outlet on either side; the trees and the low shrubs around them were too thickly planted. His eyes and ears alike strained—not that he could see far, for the walk wound in and out—Mr. Chandos stood; then he suddenly drew me against those said trees, placed himself before me, and bent my face down upon his breast, so that I could see nothing.

"You will be safe thus; I will take care of you," he whispered, the words trembling as they left his lips. "Be still, for the love of Heaven."

So entirely was I taken by surprise, so great was my alarm, that "still" I kept, unresistingly; there as he placed and held me. I heard measured footsteps advance, pass us—they must have touched him—and go on their way. Mr. Chandos's heart was beating more violently than is common to man, and as the steps went by, he clasped me with an almost painful pressure so that to look up, had I been so inclined, was impossible. When the sound of the footsteps had died away, he raised his head, went on a few yards up the walk, and drew me into one of the narrow intersecting paths. Then he released me.

"Anne, I could not help it. You must forgive me."

The name, Anne—the first time he had called me by it—sent a whole rush of joy through my veins. What with that, what with emotion, what with the fright, I burst into tears.

"You are angry with me!"

"Oh no, not angry. Thank you for sheltering me: I am sure you must have had good cause. I am only frightened."

"Indeed I had cause," he replied, in passionate tones. "But you are safe now. I wish—I wish I could shelter and protect you through life."

He must have felt my heart beating at the words; swifter, far, than his had done just now.

"But what was the danger?" I took courage to ask.

"A danger that you may not inquire into. You have escaped it; let that suffice. But you must never encounter the risk again; do you hear, Anne?"

"Only tell me how I am to avoid it."

"By keeping away from these gloomy walks at nightfall. I feel as if I could never be thankful enough for having come up when I did."

He had turned into the Pine Walk again, my arm within his now, and was striding up it. At the end he released me.

"Shall you be afraid to run across the lawn alone?"

"Oh no; the hall-lamp is lighted."

"To be sure. One moment yet. I want a promise from you." He held me before him, looking straight into my eyes, and took my hand between both of his, not in affection, I saw that well enough, but in painful anxiety.

"A promise not to mention what has occurred to any one."

"Trust me. I will not. *Trust* me, Mr. Chandos."

"Yes, I do trust you. Thank you, my dear little friend." But all the time his face had remained cold and white. He turned back into the walk again, and I ran swiftly across in the stream of light thrown on the grass by the hall-lamp, and went indoors; one bewildering query haunting me—did ghosts emit sounds as of footsteps when they walked?

My dinner was getting cold on the table. Hickens stared as I went in, wondering, doubtless, where I had been. Mr. Chandos's place remained unoccupied; and the things were taken away. I did marvel at his remaining out of doors so long. By-and-by, Hill came in to get something from the sideboard; she ran in and out of the rooms at will, without ceremony. To speak to her was a sort of relief.

"Hill, don't you think it is very imprudent of Mr. Chandos to be out in the night-air so long, considering that he was ill recently?"

"I should if he was in it," responded Hill, in the abrupt tone she always gave me. "Mr. Chandos is in the west wing with my lady."

It had occurred to my mind many times—and I think I was right—that Hill resented the fact of my unfortunate detention at Chandos.

On the following day a new feature was to be added to the mysterious illness of Lady Chandos—a doctor at length came to see her. He had travelled from a distance, as was understood; but whether by train or other conveyance did not appear. They called him Dr. Laken. He was a short, thin man, getting on in years, with dark eyes, and a benevolent, truthful countenance. His appearance was unexpected—but it seemed more welcome than gold. Mr. Chandos came to him in the oak-parlour, shaking hands warmly.

"Doctor! how glad I am to see you! So you have at last returned!"

"Ay, safe and sound; and considerably refreshed by my two months' change. Where do you think I have been, Mr. Harry? All the way to the other end of Scotland."

"And you were such a stay-at-home!"

"When I was obliged to be so. I'm growing old now, and my son has taken to the patients. Well, and who is it that is in urgent need of me? Your flourishing self?"

"My flourishing self is in no need of medical aid just now," replied Mr. Chandos, something constrained in his voice. "Will you take anything at once, doctor?"

"I'll see my patient first. It is my lady, I suppose?"

Mr. Chandos nodded.

"Ah," said the doctor, following him from the parlour. "I said, you may remember, that the time might come when you would be glad of me at Chandos. No skill in these remote parts; a set of muffs, all of them; known to be."

Mr. Chandos echoed his laugh; and leading the way to his study, shut himself in with the doctor. Afterwards he took him up to the west wing.

Why should Mr. Chandos have denied that he was ill?—as by implication he certainly did—was the question that I kept asking myself. Later, when he came to the oak-parlour, I asked him.

"One patient is enough in a house," was all his answer. He had come down from the west wing, grave even to sadness.

"But—to imply that you were well—when you know what the other doctor said!"

"Hush! Don't allude to that. It was a painful episode, one that I like to be silent upon. The—the danger, as I thought it, passed with the day, you know."

"But are you really better?"

"I am well enough, now," he answered, the gloom on his face breaking. "At least, I should be if—I mean that I am as well as I can expect to be."

"Oh, Mr. Chandos! I think you are only saying this to satisfy me."

"Anne—I must call you 'Anne;' I did so last night, you know, and I cannot go back to the formality of 'Miss Hereford'—"

"Yes, yes, please call me Anne," I interrupted all too earnestly. And he looked down with a sad sweet smile into my eyes and my blushing face.

"Anne, whether I am ill or well, you must not make it of moment to you. I wish it might be otherwise."

I felt ready to strike myself. Had I so betrayed my own feelings? The soft blush of love turned to the glow of shame, and I could only look down, in hope of hiding it.

"My dear little friend!" he softly whispered, as if to atone for the former words: "in saying I wish it might be otherwise—and perhaps I owe it to you to say as much—the subject must close. You and I may be the best friends living, Anne; and that is all I can be to you, or to any one."

Quitting the parlour rather hastily, in the hall he encountered Dr. Laken, who had just come down from the west wing. Mr. Chandos said something in low tones; I presume, by the answer, it was an inquiry as to what he thought of his patient.

"Emaciated, and as obstinate as—"

Mr. Chandos checked the raised voice; and the doctor, turning into the parlour, caught sight of me.

"I never was famous for civility, you know, Mr. Harry, but I confess I ought not to abuse Lady Chandos before this young lady. I was going to say 'obstinate as a mule.' Your mother *is* obstinate."

"I know it," replied Mr. Chandos, lifting his eyes to the doctor's. "That is one of the worst features of the case. They are all bad enough."

"And it can't be remedied. Unless—but there might be danger attending that. Besides—well, well, we must do the best we can; it would not answer to try experiments on Lady Chandos."

Up to the word "besides," Dr. Laken seemed to forget that I was in the room; with the recollection he made the break. Mr. Chandos rang for refreshments to be served, and I gathered up my work to leave them alone.

"I wish you could remain for the night, Dr. Laken."

"So do I. But it's of no use wishing it, Mr. Harry. I'll see what I can do towards spending a couple of days here next week."

They were the last words I heard. In half-an-hour the pony carriage was ordered round, and the doctor went away, Mr. Chandos driving.

# CHAPTER 22

## A NIGHT ALARM

It was the loveliest autumn I had ever remembered. Clear, soft, balmy; the foliage glowing with its ruddy tints, the sky blue and beautiful.

There would be a fire in the grate of the oak-parlour, and the window thrown open to the lawn and the scent of the sweet flowers. One afternoon I sat there, a bit of work in my hand, the sprays of jessamine almost touching me, and the far-off Pine Walk looking almost as bright as though no ghost had the reputation of haunting it. Mr. Chandos sat at the table writing. Out of doors or in, we were very much together, and my heart was at rest. I fear I had taken to think that the heaven of hereafter could not be more blissful than this that I seemed to be living in now.

His foot was weak again. Not sufficient to disable him from getting about; only to deter him from walking more than was absolutely necessary. It was all his own fault; as Mr. Dickenson, the surgeon, told him; he had persisted in using the ankle too much before it was quite strong again.

Lady Chandos kept her rooms still; report said her bed; and the impression in the house was that she was in danger. The discovery of the petty pilferer, or pilferers, appeared to be as far off as ever: but one or two strange things connected with the subject were about to occur.

"Will you put these on the hall-table for me, Anne?"

I turned to take the letters from him. When he did not allow me to save his foot in these little things, it made me cross, and I told him so. One of the letters was addressed to his sister.

"You have been writing to Madame de Mellissie, Mr. Chandos!"

"Yes. We heard from her this morning. She expects to be here in a day or two. Stay! I think I will show my mother what I have said. You shall place only the other one on the table."

The news fell on my heart like an ice-shaft. Chandos had become all too dear to me.

The other letter was to Mr. Haines; I remembered the name as that of an agent who had taken the house near the lodge-gates for Mr. Edwin Barley. It was sealed with the Chandos coat-of-arms in black wax. I had never seen Mr. Chandos use red. Lizzy Dene was passing through the hall as I laid the letter down. I observed that she looked at me; seemed to look at what I was doing; and Mrs. Penn and Hill were speaking on the stairs, almost beyond view; whether they saw me or not, I could not say.

"Thank you," said Mr. Chandos, when I went in again. "What

should I do without you to fetch and carry? I want that book now."

It lay on the side-table; a dreadfully dry scientific work. He locked his desk and took the book from me.

"You must put down your slavery to my stupid foot. When you become disabled, Anne, I'll do as much for you."

"You know the fault is yours, Mr. Chandos. Had you only been a little patient when the foot was recovering, it would have been strong before now. As to the slavery—"

"Well? What as to the slavery? Are you going to strike?"

I had been about to say that I *liked* the slavery, but stopped in time. The colour of embarrassment was coming into my cheek, and I turned it off with a light laugh and light words.

"I won't strike just yet. Not until Madame de Mellissie comes."

"Then suppose you lend me your shoulder?"

He could have walked quite well without it, as he knew and I knew; I dare say if put to it he might have walked to the railway-station. But ah! the bliss of feeling his hand on me! if it were only half as great to him he had kept his ankle weak for ever!

"As to Emily, with her proverbial uncertainty, she is just as likely to be here in two months as in two days, Anne."

I took up my work again; a pretty bag I was embroidering in grey and black silk for Lady Chandos. He sat on the other side the window, reading his book and talking to me between whiles. All things seemed full of rest and peace and love; a very paradise.

Soon—I dare say it was an hour, but time passed so swiftly—we heard footsteps come along the broad walk to the portico. I looked out to see whose they were.

"It is Mr. Dexter," I said to Mr. Chandos.

"Dexter! The very man I wanted to see. You need not go away," he added, as I began to gather up my work; "we are not about to talk treason. Don't you know, Anne, that I like to have you with me whilst I may."

He must have been thinking of the approaching separation that the advent of Emily would bring about. But I wanted some more silk, and went to fetch it, remaining in my room some minutes. When I got back they were both seated at the table, some papers before them. I turned to the window, and went on with my work.

The conversation appeared to be of little moment; of none to me. It was of leases, rents, repairs, and other matters connected with the estate. Presently Mr. Dexter mentioned that he had received a letter from Haines.

"Have you?" said Mr. Chandos. "I wrote to him this afternoon. What does he say?"

Mr. Dexter took a letter from his pocket-book, and put it into his master's hand, who ran his eyes over it.

"My letter will be useless, then, and I must write another," he observed when he had finished. "I'll get it, and show you what I said. It will save explanation."

"Let me get it for you, Mr. Chandos," I interposed, anxious to save him. And without waiting for permission I left the room. But the letter was not on the table.

"It is not there, Mr. Chandos; it is gone."

"It cannot be gone," he said, taking out his watch. "It is only four o'clock. Emily's letter is not there yet."

Hickens was called. Hickens, in a marvel of consternation—at being asked what he had done with the letter—protested he had not seen it; he had not been in the hall that afternoon.

We all went out; it seemed so strange a thing; and I showed Mr. Chandos where I had placed the letter. It had not slipped down; it could not be seen anywhere. Mr. Chandos looked at me: he was evidently thinking that the spy was again at work.

"Was any one in the hall when you put the letter here, Miss Hereford?"

"Lizzy Dene was passing through it. And Mrs. Penn and Hill were standing on the stairs."

"They would not touch it," said Mr. Chandos, just as Lizzy Dene, hearing the commotion, looked from the door of the large dining-room. It was her place to keep the room in order, and she seemed to choose odd times to do it in. Mr. Chandos questioned her, but she said she had not touched the letter; had not in fact noticed it.

At this juncture Mrs. Chandos came down the stairs, dressed for going out, attended by Mrs. Penn. She inquired of Mr. Chandos what the matter was.

"A letter has mysteriously disappeared from the hall, Ethel," he replied.

"A letter disappeared! how strange!" she returned, in the rather vacant manner that at times characterized her. "Was it of consequence?"

"In itself, no. But these curious losses are always of consequence in another sense of the word. I beg your pardon, Mrs. Penn: did you speak?"

For Mrs. Penn, who first stood back in her surprise, had advanced behind him, and was saying something in low tones.

"Mr. Chandos! rely upon it, the same hand that opened my letter has taken this one. You ought not to leave a stone unturned to discover the culprit. I speak in the interest of all."

Mr. Chandos gravely nodded assent. He seemed to be in a hopeless puzzle. I fully suspected Lizzy Dene; and I think she saw something of this in my face.

"What should I do with a letter that was not mine?" she cried, resentfully, addressing no one in particular. "If Mr. Chandos offered me a dozen of his letters to read, I'd rather be spared the trouble; I am no great scholar. And what good would they do me?"

The argument seemed conclusive; at least to Mr. Chandos. I suspected the girl more and more.

"Well, Harry, I must leave you to your investigation, if I am to have a walk this afternoon," concluded Mrs. Chandos.

She went out and turned down the broad walk. Lizzy resumed her work in the dining-room, I and Mr. Dexter went back to the oak-parlour and stood at the window: and then I became aware that Mrs. Penn had lingered in the portico, talking with Mr. Chandos.

"Until recently I believed we had the most trustworthy set of servants that it is possible for any family to possess," he was saying. "What can there be in my letters that should interest them?"

"Nay," said Mrs. Penn, "I think it is the greater wonder what there should be in mine. I am a stranger to your servants: my affairs cannot be supposed to concern any one of them."

"It is my habit to leave letters on the table every day. They have never been touched or tampered with, so far as I know, until this afternoon."

"You cannot be sure of that. But what shall you do in the matter now?"

"I don't know what to do; it is the sort of thing that causes me to feel at a nonplus. Were I to have an officer in the house to watch, as you suggest, it might prove useless."

"Have you a suspicion of any one in particular?" she asked abruptly. And by this time Mr. Dexter had grown interested in the conversation, and was listening as attentively as I.

"Not the slightest. Neither can you have, I suppose."

Mrs. Penn was silent.

"Have you?" repeated he, thinking her manner peculiar.

"I would rather not answer the question, Mr. Chandos; because it would inevitably be followed by another."

"Which is equivalent to admitting that your suspicions are directed to some one in particular," he returned, with awakened interest. "Why should you object to avow it?"

"Well, it is so," she replied. "I do think that all the circumstances—taking one loss, one disagreeable event with another—tend to point to a certain quarter. But I may be wrong."

"To whom?" he asked.

"That is just the question that I knew would follow," returned Mrs. Penn, "and I must decline to answer it. No, Mr. Chandos; you possess the same facilities for observing and judging that I do: in fact, greater ones: and if you cannot draw your own deductions, I certainly will not help you to them. I might be wrong, you know."

"You must allude to an inmate of Chandos?"

"I should deem it impossible that any but an inmate of Chandos could play these tricks. Where would be their opportunity?"

"Mrs. Penn, if you possess any clue; nay, if you think you have any well-founded cause for suspicion, you ought to impart it to me," he gravely said.

"Were I *sure* that my suspicions were correct, I would do so; but, as I say, they may be mistaken. Forgive me, if I hint that perhaps your own eyes are shut closer than they need be."

She hastened away, leaving the impression of her mysterious words behind. I wondered very much if she alluded to Lizzy Dene.

That same evening I had an opportunity of asking her. Mr. Chandos went to the west wing after dinner, I sat near the lights, working at my bag, when Mrs. Penn came into the oakparlour, not having troubled herself to knock for admittance.

"It's good to be you, Anne Hereford," she said, putting herself into Mr. Chandos's chair by the fire. "I wish I had this room to sit in."

"Are the rooms upstairs not comfortable?"

"I don't know about comfort: they are wretchedly dull. I'd as soon be cooped up in a prison. Not a soul to speak to from morning to night, but Mrs. Chandos. Here you have Mr. Chandos; are full of state and ceremony; and have the chance of seeing all the visitors."

"All the visitors consist of a doctor now and then, and Mr. Dexter once a week, or so," I said, laughing.

"A doctor and an agent are better than no one. I suppose," she added, after a pause, "they are all assembled in conclave in the west wing; Mr. Chandos, Mrs. Chandos, and my lady."

"I wish Lady Chandos was better," I remarked.

Mrs. Penn turned eagerly, her eye lighting with excitement.

"I *wish* I knew what is the matter with her! I wish I knew! Do you never gather a hint of it from Mr. Chandos?"

"Never. But why should you be so desirous of learning? What is it to you, Mrs. Penn?"

"I have my reasons," she replied, nodding her head. "I won't tell them to you this evening, but I have not made a vow that I never will. If she is insane, as I suspect, why then—but I'll say no more now. What a strange thing it is about that letter!"

"Very. You are suspecting some one in particular?"

"Well?" she answered, sharply, turning her face to me.

"Is it Lizzy Dene?"

"Who it is, or who it is not, is nothing to you," she rejoined, in the crossest tone I ever heard. "I know this: I would give the worth of a dozen letters ten times over to bring the mystery to light. They may be suspecting you and me next."

"Mrs. Penn!"

"Yes, Mrs. Penn!" she retorted, in a mocking, tone. "We are the only strangers in the house, Anne Hereford."

As if my words had angered her beyond redemption, she quitted the room abruptly. Very soon Mr. Chandos returned to it, and the tea came in. He began talking of the lost letter—of the unpleasantness altogether. Should I tell him my doubt? The old proverb runs, that if a woman deliberates she is lost: it proved so in my case, and I mentioned Lizzy Dene.

"Lizzy Dene!" repeated Mr. Chandos, in great surprise. "*Lizzy Dene!*"

"But indeed it is a doubt more than a suspicion; and it arises chiefly from my having found her in my room that night," I eagerly added, feeling half-afraid of what I had done, and determined not to hint at her supposed alliance with Mr. Edwin Barley.

"Rely upon it, you are wrong, Anne," Mr. Chandos decided.

"Lizzy Dene would be the very last woman to act treacherously towards our family. She may be foolishly superstitious, but she is honest as the day. I'll answer for *her.*"

How could I say more?—unless my grounds against Lizzy Dene had been surer. Joseph took away the tea-things, and Mr. Chandos went to his own sitting-room. I stood at the little table in the corner of the room nearest the window, putting my work-box to rights. Some of its reels were on the window-ledge, and I moved to get them.

I don't know why I should have done it; unthinkingly, I believe; but I drew aside the muslin curtain to look out on the lovely night, and found my face in contact (except for the glass between us) with that of another face, peering in. Terribly startled, I drew away with a scream. Mr. Chandos came back at the moment, and I gave a frightened word of explanation. Quick as lightning, he laid forcible hold of me, put me in a chair, ordered me to stay in it in the most peremptory manner—and turned to the window to fling it up. One moment and he had leaped out: but in his haste he broke a pane of glass.

I sat there, trembling; the window open, the curtain waving gently in the night breeze—and the thought of that terrible face without. Mr. Chandos looked stern and white when he returned—not through the window—and blood was dripping from his hand.

"I can see no one: but I could not stay long, my hand bled so," he said, taking up his white handkerchief which lay on the table, and winding it round the palm. "But now—Anne, do you think these can be fancies of yours? This is the second time."

"I wish I could think so. I am *certain* a man stood there, looking in. He had not time to draw away. I just moved to the window from that corner, so that he did not see me approaching."

"Whose face was it? That man's by the lodge-gates—Edwin

Barley?"

My very fear. But I did not dare say so. What I did say was the strict truth—that it had all passed so momentarily, and I was so startled, as to allow no chance of recognition.

"Can you find a piece of linen rag, Anne? I don't care to make a commotion over this. I dare say I can do up my hand myself: I'm a bit of a surgeon."

I ran upstairs to get some, and began turning over the contents of my large trunk in search of it. In doing this, a small parcel, very small, came into my hands, and I looked at it with some curiosity, not remembering what it contained.

As I undid the paper two sovereigns fell into my hand. They were not mine; I possessed none. As I looked and wondered, a strange thought flashed through my mind: were they the two lost sovereigns marked by Mr. Chandos?

There was no time for speculation; Mr. Chandos was waiting for the rag. Finding it, I went down.

"You ought to put your hand in warm water, Mr. Chandos. There may be fragments of glass in it."

"I was thinking so," he said; when at that moment Hickens came in with a letter. The man noticed the white handkerchief and its stains.

"You have met with an accident, sir."

"Ah," said Mr. Chandos, in a tone of raillery, making light of the affair; "this comes, Hickens, of doing things in a hurry. You must bring me a basin of warm water. I attempted to open the window, not observing it was fastened, and my hand slipped through the glass. Close the shutters. At once."

Hickens went to the window: I stood by Mr. Chandos with the linen rag. "Presently," he nodded; "I must wait for the water. Open this for me, will you, Anne?"

I unsealed the letter, and opened it. In handing it to him, my eyes accidentally fell upon my own name.

"It is about me!" I exclaimed, impulsively.

Mr. Chandos ran his eyes over the lines—there were very few—and a scowl contracted his brow. He read them over again, and then folded the letter with his one hand.

"Hickens, who brought this? When did it come?"

"It came but now, sir. A lad brought it to the back-door. I happened to be standing there, and took it from him. 'For Mr. Chandos,' he said, and turned away. I thought how quickly he made off."

"Should you know him again?"

"No, sir, I think not. I'm not sure, though."

"Well, bring the warm water."

"Is the letter from Madame de Mellissie?" I asked.

"I don't know who it is from," said Mr. Chandos. "It is anonymous."

"Anonymous! And about me!"

I stood looking at him. I connected this letter with the two sovereigns I had just found: was any one at work to ruin me in the estimation of Chandos House?

"Mr. Chandos, that is not a pleasant letter, is it?"

"Anonymous letters never are pleasant," he rejoined. "If I had my way, the writers of such should all be shaken in a bag together and sunk in the bottom of the sea. Do not let it trouble you; it defeats its own ends."

"Will you allow me to read it?"

"It would give you no pleasure."

"But it might afford me some light; and light is what I want just now; I do indeed. Let me see it, Mr. Chandos! I request it as a favour."

"Very well. My showing it to you will prove the sort of estimation I have for it."

Taking the letter from his unresisting hand, I opened it and laid it before me. It ran as follows:

"MR. CHANDOS,

"It is rumoured that you have some trouble in your house, and are suspecting your servants. The probability is that they are honest; they have been with you long enough to be proved. There are two strangers under your roof: the companion to Mrs. Chandos, and the younger lady, Miss Hereford. Just reflect that all the misfortunes have occurred since these ladies entered Chandos. In doing this, perhaps you will find a way out of the wood. The suggestion is offered by
"A FRIEND."

"This would implicate Mrs. Penn as well as myself!" I exclaimed.

"Yes," he said. "Forgetting that Mrs. Penn is a sufferer. Or perhaps not knowing it."

The tears rose to my eyes: I could not help it. "Then—do you doubt *me*, Mr. Chandos?"

He touched my arm; and those grave eyes of his, half laughing then, looked into mine.

"Doubt you? So greatly that I am deliberating whether I shall not call in the police again and give you in charge."

It was said in jest I knew, but at that moment it told upon me, and the tears were palpably near the surface. Hickens was heard approaching with the basin of water.

"Oh, Anne, Anne! you are a very simple child."

"Will you see to your hand, sir?"

"Ay, it wants seeing to."

It was the palm that was cut; badly, I thought. Mr. Chandos seemed to understand what to do, and dressed it himself with the butler's help, I watching the process. When we were alone again, I took the little parcel from my pocket, and gave it to Mr. Chandos.

"Will you please to open that, sir?"

"Two sovereigns," he cried, as he did so. "What of them?" I told him all about it, where I had found them. He held them to the light, and smiled.

"They are the sovereigns I lost out of my desk, Anne."

"Are you sure?"

"Sure? here are the marks. See."

Standing close, I looked where he pointed. The marks were quite plain. I went to my seat and sat down.

"And you found them in your trunk! Anne, who is your enemy in the house?"

"I did not know I had one, sir. So far as I am aware, I have not given offence to any one within it. I must quit it now."

"Oh, indeed! What else would you like to do?"

I could no longer keep my tears back. "It seems to me, Mr. Chandos, that I am no longer safe in it."

"You are perfectly safe, Anne, for you possess in it a strong protector. One who will not suffer harm to reach you; who will guard annoyance from you so far as shall be practicable."

I knew that he alluded to himself, and thanked him in my heart. But—so far as was practicable! There it lay. If I really had a hidden enemy, who might shield me? Mr. Edwin Barley it could not be; and I fell back upon Lizzy Dene.

Mr. Chandos began telling off the inmates on his fingers.

"There's my mother, Mrs. Chandos, myself, Hill, Hickens; for all these I can answer. Then come the servants. For some of them I can equally answer, Lizzy Dene being one of them; but I regard them all as honest and trustworthy."

"Therefore the uncertain ones are only Mrs. Penn and myself."

"And Mrs. Penn is certainly exempted," he rejoined. "For she has been interfered with in an equal degree with any of us."

"That leaves only me!"

"Just so; only you. But, Anne," bending those earnest eyes upon me, "I would answer for you with my *life*."

"If it is not Lizzy Dene that is my enemy, who else can it be?" I exclaimed, foolishly speaking what was in my thoughts.

"Why should you think it Lizzy Dene more than any one else?" he hastily cried, in resentful tones. "She can have no cause of enmity against you."

There flashed across me that interview with Mr. Edwin Barley. If it was Lizzy Dene who had held it, who was in league with him, no need to search for a motive.

"That I have an enemy is indisputable. The letter you have just received and these sovereigns prove it."

"Anne, Lizzy Dene could not have written such a letter as this."

That he was prejudiced in favour of Lizzy Dene, determined to admit nothing against her, seemed evident; and I let the subject drop.

But now the strangest incident was to occur; an alarming incident; nay, it might rather be called a scene. In the short silence that supervened, Mrs. Penn glided into the room without notice. The word "glided" is not inapplicable; she came softly in, scarcely seeming to move, her face scared, her voice sunk to a whisper.

"Mr. Chandos! Do you know that there are mounted police outside the house?"

He rose from his seat, looking at her as if he thought she must be dreaming.

"Mounted police!" he repeated.

"They are riding quietly up, three of them; I saw their swords flash in the starlight. I had gone to the library to get a book for Mrs. Chandos; she had sent to Hill for the key; when I thought I heard a noise as of horsemen, and opened the shutters to look out. Oh, Mr. Chandos! what can they have come for? They once rode up to a house where I was staying, in the same silent manner; it was to make investigations in a charge of murder."

I had seen Mr. Chandos turn pale before; you have heard me say so; but I never saw a tinge so livid in man or woman as that which overspread his countenance now. He retained nevertheless his self-possession; ay, and that quiet tone of command which somehow is rarely disobeyed.

"You will be so kind as to return immediately to Mrs. Chandos," he calmly said to Mrs. Penn. "*Close the doors of the east wing as soon as you have entered, and keep her attention amused. She is excitable—as you by this time probably know—and this visit must be kept from her cognizance.*"

Allowing no time for answer or dissent, he took Mrs. Penn by the hand somewhat peremptorily, and watched her upstairs. Then he stole to the hall-door and silently put up its bar. As for me, I do not know that I had ever in my whole life felt so sick and frightened. All the past scene at Mr. Edwin Barley's, when the mounted police had come there, recurred to me: and Mr. Chandos's manner completed the dread. I put my hands on his arm; reticence was forgotten in the moment's terror; as he stood listening in the middle of the oak-parlour.

"Tell me what it is! Tell me!"

"Oh, Anne, this is an awful blow," he said, in the deepest agitation, as if he had never heard my words. "I joked about the police coming to take you in charge, but—"

"Not for me! They cannot have come for me!" I reiterated foolishly, in my confused alarm.

"Would to Heaven they had come for you! I mean, would they had come for one who could as readily be exonerated as you! Mercy! mercy! so the blow has fallen at last!"

The words brought to my memory what Mrs. Penn had said, about a sword hanging by a single hair over Mr. Chandos and his family. I don't think he knew what he was about. He walked across the hall towards the stairs, hesitated, and came back, listening evidently for the summons of the police; all in the deepest agitation and alarm.

"It may be well not to go!" he muttered. "Better that I should be here to face them when they enter! Anne, run and find Hill: bring her hither quickly: but make no alarm."

I knew it was the supper hour in the housekeeper's room, and ran to it. Hill was seated at the head of the table, the upper-servants round her.

"Mrs. Hill," I said, appearing among them without ceremony, "Mr. Chandos wants you for a moment. Instantly, if you please."

"There! His hand has begun bleeding again!" surmised Hickens, who occupied the chair opposite Hill. Mrs. Hill said nothing, but rose and followed me. As we passed through the hall, there came a loud ring at the front-door.

"Hill," Mr. Chandos whispered, drawing her into the oak-parlour, and there was a world of dread and terror in his tone, "mounted police are outside the house."

She shrieked aloud, making the room ring. The woman actually trembled all over.

"Hush!" interrupted Mr. Chandos. "Don't lose *your* senses, Hill."

"Oh, Mr. Harry! the police at last! It's what I have dreamt of ever since that awful night!"

"Well, you and I must be calm. You know the plan decided upon; if it ever came to this. I may not go; I must stay and face it. Make haste! And—Hill! *lock* the outer door of the east wing on the outside; Mrs. Chandos must not see these men."

Hill did not stay to listen. She appeared to take in all, and was flying up the stairs, breathless and panting. There came another ring: and Robin, one of the under men, who was coming across the hall, increased his speed. Mr. Chandos arrested him.

"Robin, desire Hickens to attend himself. I wish it."

The man turned back, and Mr. Chandos stood for a moment against the wall, his hands up to his pale face.

"Mr. Chandos!" I said, in emotion great as his, "what are you afraid of? what dreadful thing is this? Confide in me! tell me!"

"That you may run from me, as the rest will do! You have said the word, Anne—dreadful. That is it."

Hickens was advancing to the hall. Mr. Chandos went out to him; I looked from the parlour-door.

"Hickens," said Mr. Chandos, speaking with apparent carelessness, "these may be the police at the door. If so, they may enter."

"The police again, sir!" returned Hickens, in consternation. "Weren't they satisfied with their last visit? What can they want at this hour?"

"That's my business," replied Mr. Chandos. And Hickens turned to the entrance.

"What a cowardly donkey that Joseph is, barring up the house before bed-time!" quoth Hickens to himself as he threw wide the door.

Threw it wide, and admitted two of the officers. The third remained in charge of the horses.

# CHAPTER 23

## IN THE GALLERY

**M**r. Chandos advanced with suavity; the officers saluted him and took off their hats. He held his handkerchief to his face, as if fearing the draught; *I* knew that it was to shade his livid countenance.

"A late visit, gentlemen! To what am I indebted for it?"

He had been gradually withdrawing to the oak-parlour as he spoke, and they came with him. I drew back in confused indecision, and stood in the remotest and darkest corner. I had not courage to quit the room, for I must have brushed by them: I hoped that Mr. Chandos would see and dismiss me. But no; he never looked my way. He closed the door, in the face of Hickens, whose state of mind seemed an even balance between wonder and dismay.

"We could not get here sooner, sir," observed one of the officers, who spoke quite like a gentleman, "but we hope the delay has not been inconvenient to you. The inspector, to whom your note was addressed, was out when it arrived, so that it was not opened immediately."

Had the sentence been spoken in an unknown tongue, it could not more completely have puzzled Mr. Chandos, to judge by his looks.

"What note do you speak of?"

"The note you sent in to-day."

This appeared to be no elucidation to Mr. Chandos.

"Will you tell me what its contents were?"

"We received but one, sir. It requested two or three of us to be here to-night, mounted. It intimated that the thief, who has been playing tricks in your house, was discovered, and would be given up to us. Our inspector wondered why we were wanted to come mounted."

The change that fell over the face of Mr. Chandos! the light of hope, the rush of renewed colour! It was as one awakening from death to life.

"Gentlemen," he said, with a smile, as he pointed to seats, "I fear a trick has been played upon you. I have not written to your inspector, and most certainly possess, as yet, no clue to the parties who have been so disagreeably busy at Chandos."

They seemed scarcely to believe him. For my own part I could hardly tell what was real, what not.

"But you must not return without refreshment, although you have had a useless ride," concluded Mr. Chandos, when some further explanation had passed. "It shall be brought in at once," he added, ringing for Hickens. "And this young lady," looking at me for the first time, "will obligingly see the housekeeper and bid her hasten it."

I obeyed the look and followed him into the hall. Hickens was there.

"Supper, Hickens. These gentlemen will take some before their departure. Bring the best of what you have, and be quick over it."

Hickens moved away with alacrity: the word "departure" had reassured him, and also seemed to afford hope that his curiosity would be satisfied. Mr. Chandos caught my hand and drew me through the door to the foot of the stairs. His own hand was trembling, and cold as ice: unconsciously, I think, to himself, he laid it on my shoulder, and spoke in the gentlest whisper.

"Go to the west wing, Anne. Knock at the outer door, but do not attempt to enter. Hill will answer you. Tell her to inform Lady Chandos that it is a false alarm; that the officers have only come respecting what was recently lost from my desk, and I have ordered supper for them. Say that I will be with my mother as soon as possible, but I remain at present to entertain them."

He returned swiftly to the parlour, closing the door, leaving me to proceed on my errand. Hill answered my knock, her face and her cap of an equal whiteness, and I delivered the message, speaking in whispers. Strangely relieved seemed she, at least in an equal degree with Mr. Chandos, and she made me repeat the little I had heard said by the officers, as if scarcely daring to believe the good tidings, without confirmation.

"Heaven be praised!" she exclaimed; "it would just have killed my lady. Bless you, child, for the good news."

That Hill's mental relief must have been something extraordinary for her to bless *me*, one could only acknowledge; and. I excused her shutting the baize door in my face.

In less than half-an-hour, I heard the police ride away, as I sat in my chamber, and Mr. Chandos passed to the west wing. It was very dull for me in that lonely bedroom, and only half-past nine o'clock; so I thought I might go down again. Hickens was putting the things together on the supper tray.

"Miss, do you know what those men came for?" he asked.

"Well, Hickens, not exactly. Nothing at all to be afraid of, so far as I could gather. I heard Mr. Chandos laughing with them when they went away."

"Oh, I heard that; I was rung for to show 'em out," returned Hickens. "My opinion is this, miss, that it's just a scandal for policemen to ride up at will on a dark night to a gentleman's seat, and if I were Mr. Chandos I'd let them know it. Swords, indeed! What next?"

He went away with his tray. Five minutes afterwards Mr.

Chandos came down. He was gay; his step was light, his face smiling. It was the reaction that sometimes sets in after deliverance from great fear. I had not thought to see him again that night: and stupidly said so.

"No! I came to look after you; lest you should have melted away with terror. Were you very much alarmed, Anne?"

"Yes; just at first."

"Take it for all in all, this has been a sensational evening," he resumed, laughing. "My accident at the window; your discovery of the marked money in your box; and the visitation of the police. Private families cannot often boast of so much entertainment all at once."

I looked at him wistfully. After the intense agitation and dread he had betrayed, this light tone sounded unnatural; almost like a pretence.

"Mr. Chandos, I fear you live in some great peril," was my timid rejoinder. "I suppose I may not be told what it is; but I wish I could help you; I wish I could avert it from you, whatever it may be."

As if by magic, his mood changed, and the shadow came back to his countenance. "So you won't let me cheat myself, Anne! I was trying to do so."

"If you would only tell me what it is! If I could avert it from you!"

"No living being can do that, child. I wish I could forget it, if only for a moment."

"And you cannot?"

"Never; by night or by day. I appear as the rest of the world does; I laugh and talk; but within lies ever that one terrible care, weighing inc down like an incubus."

How terrible it was, I could see even then, as he covered his eyes for a moment with his wasted hand.

"But to-night has brought me a great relief—though it may be only temporary," he resumed, looking up. "How thankful I felt when the police explained their errand, God alone can ever know."

"But what errand did you fear they had come upon?"

"That I cannot tell you. Not upon quite so harmless a one as it turned out to be."

"Better, perhaps, that they had come for me."

Mr. Chandos smiled—as well he might at the words; and passed to a gayer strain.

"Which of the three would you have preferred to ride before, had I given you into custody for finding that money of mine in your possession? We must have searched for a pillion!"

But I did not answer in the same spirit; I could not so readily forget my alarm, or their hidden trouble, Very gravely, for it was nearly bed-time, I put my hand out to wish him good-night. He took it within his, and there was a moment's silence.

"Anne," he said, his low voice sounding very solemn in the stillness of the room, "you have to-night been forced into what may be called a species of confidence as to our unhappy secrets; at least, to have become cognizant that Chandos has things to be concealed. Will you be true to us—in so far as not to speak of this?"

"I will, sir."

"In the house and out of it?"

"I will be true as Heaven," I answered in my earnestness. "I will seem to forget that I know anything of it myself."

"Thank you, my best friend. Good-night."

I had come up earlier than usual; it was not ten o'clock; and. I thought I might read for half-an-hour without transgressing any good rule. But where had I left my book? Looking about, I could not see it.

Then it occurred to me that I had been sitting reading in the gallery window for some minutes before dinner, and must have left the book there. It was only a few steps, and I went to fetch it.

There it was. I found it by feel, not by sight. The moon was bright again, but the shutters were closed and barred. It was that beautiful story, the "Heir of Redclyffe." Madame de Mellissie had bought the Tauchnitz edition of it in Paris, and had left it behind her at Chandos. Soon after she departed, I had found it and read it; and was now dipping into it again.

But as I took it in my hand, a strange thing occurred, frightening me almost to death. Turning from the window, the whole length of gallery was before me up to the door of the west wing, the moonlight streaming into it here and there from the high windows above. Midway in the passage, revealed by the moonlight, was a shadowy form; looking like nothing on earth but an apparition.

I was in the dark; remember that. Gliding slowly along, one of its arms stretched out, looking just as if it were stretched out in warning to me to escape—and I had not the sense then to remember that I must be invisible—on it came. A tall, thin form, with a white and shadowy face. There was no escape for me: to fly to my own room would be to meet it; and no other door of refuge was open.

It has never been your fate, as I feel sure, my gentle reader, to be at one end of a gallery in a haunted house at night and see a ghost gliding towards you from the other; so please do not laugh at me. What my sensations were I can neither describe nor you conceive: I cannot bear to think of them even now. That I beheld the ghost, said to haunt Chandos, my fainting heart as fully believed, in that moment, as it believed in Heaven. Presence of mind forsook me; all that the wildest imagination can picture of superstitious terror assailed me: and I almost think—yes, I do think—that I might have lost my senses or died, but for the arrival of succour.

Oh, believe me! In these awful moments, which have on occasion come to people in real life far more certainly and terribly than anything ever represented in fiction, believe me, God is ever at hand to send relief. The overstrung mind is not abandoned to itself: very, very rarely indeed are our guardian angels absent, or unready to work by an earthly instrument.

It came to *me* in the person of Mr. Chandos. Ascending the stairs, a candle in his hand, softly whistling in unconcern, he came. It was no moment for deliberation: had it been a king or an emperor, it had been all the same to me. With a great cry of anguish that escaped from me in the tension of nerves and brain, I clasped his arm, as if I dare not let him go again; dropping the book on the carpet of the gallery.

I suppose he put the wax-light down; I suppose he got over his astonishment in some way: all I knew was that in a moment he was holding me in his arms, trying to soothe my fears. Reaction had come, and with it tears; never before had I cried so violently; and I clung to him still in an agony of terror, as one, drowning, clings to the living. But nothing remained in the gallery. Whatever had been in it had vanished.

"What is all this? What has alarmed you?"

"It was there; coming towards me!" I whispered hysterically in answer. "Oh forgive me! I feel as though I should die."

"What was coming?" he inquired.

"The same—I think—that is seen in the grounds. The ghost. I saw it distinctly."

"How can you be so foolish? How can you take up these absurd fancies?" he remonstrated, in sharp tones, moving some steps away from me.

"I saw it, Mr. Chandos; I did indeed. It came onwards with its arm raised, as if to warn me away: a tall skeleton of a form, with features the hue of the dead. Features that bore, in their outlines, a great resemblance to yours."

Was it fancy? or was it fact?—that his own features, as I spoke, assumed a livid hue, just as they had done when the police-officers came?

"What were you doing out here?" he asked, in the same sharp accent.

"I only came to the window-seat to get a book. I saw it as I turned to go back."

"You saw nothing," he persisted with some warmth. "I am astonished at you, Miss Hereford: the fancy was the creation of your own brain, and nothing more. Pray, if the ghost was here then, where is it now?"

"I don't know. It disappeared: I think it seemed to go back

towards the west wing. It was certainly there."

"You are certainly silly," was his response, "A great deal more so than I had given you credit for."

"Ah, Mr. Chandos, you cannot reason me out of my senses. Thank you, thank you ever for coming up the stairs just then: I do believe I should have died, or lost my reason."

Taking up the "Heir of Redclyffe," I walked to my room, went in, and shut the door. Mr. Chandos pulled it open again sharply.

"Forgive me if I have been harsh. Good-night."

"Oh yes, sir; I know how foolish it must seem to you. Good-night."

"Go to rest in peace and safety, Anne. And be assured that no ill, ghostly or human, shall work you harm whilst I am at hand to prevent it."

I closed the door and bolted it, a vague idea in my mind that a bolted door was some sort of safeguard against a ghost. Mr. Chandos's footsteps died away in the direction of the west wing.

With the morning, a little of the night's impression had vanished, for the sun was shining brilliantly. Ghosts and sunlight don't accord with each other. Ghosts that are ghosts at midnight, in the warm and cheery morning sun have vanished into unknown regions. I dressed as usual, in better spirits than might be supposed, and went down. Mr. Chandos was earlier than I, and stood at the window in the oak-parlour. He took my hand and retained it for some moments in silence. I stood looking from the window as he did.

"And how is the ghost this morning, Anne?"

"I wish you would regard me as a rational being, Mr. Chandos! Do anything but treat me as a child."

"Nay, I think you proved yourself both irrational and a child last night," he laughingly said.

"Indeed I did not. I wish you had seen what I saw."

"I wish I had," was the mocking answer. "Anne, trust me: there is no ghost inside Chandos, whatever they may say as to there being one out of it."

"I don't know how I shall be able to go upstairs alone at night again."

"Nor I. You will want Hill and half-a-dozen lighted torches to escort you. Do you remember my remarking, that last evening, taking one event with another, was a sensational one? But I did not suppose it was to wind up with anything so grand as a ghost."

The ridicule vexed me. It was as if he ridiculed me. In spite of my good sense, the vexation appeared in my eyes.

"There! We will declare a truce, Anne, and let the ghost drop. I don't want to make you angry with me."

"I am not angry, sir. I can never repay all your kindness to me;

and especially that last one of coming to my relief last night."

"Which was accidental. Shall I tell you how you can repay it all, Anne?" His voice dropped to seriousness; his eyes, a strange sadness seated in their depths, looked into mine.

"I wish you could, sir."

"Let this matter of your ghost be a perfect secret between you and me. One to be disclosed to no one."

"Certainly. I promise."

That some great reason prompted the request was unmistakable: that there were certain interests attaching to this "ghost," whether it might walk without doors or within, could only be apparent. How I wished he would take me into his confidence!—if it were only that I might show him that I would be true and faithful. But for the strange reticence imposed by love when once it takes possession of the soul, I might have boldly suggested this.

He leaned out of the window inhaling the crisp air of the bright October morning. Courage at length came to me to say a word.

"Of course, sir, I do not fail to see that there are interests here that involve caution and care, though I cannot think how, or what they are. If you would entrust me with them—and I could help in any way—I should be glad. I would be so true."

"Ay, I am sure you would be. Latterly a vision has crossed me of a time—a possible future when it might be disclosed to you. But it is neither probable nor near. Indeed, it seems like a dream even to glance at it."

The urn was brought in, and I went to the table to make the tea. Newspapers and letters arrived; he was buried in them during breakfast, and carried them afterwards to his own sitting-room.

I saw his horse brought to the door in the course of the morning. In crossing the hall, he looked in at the oak-parlour. I was mending gloves.

"Hard at work! Do you wear mended gloves?"

"Every one is not Mr. Chandos of Chandos. Poor governesses have to wear many things that the gay world does not. And Mrs. Paler has not paid me."

"Shall I bring you some gloves home to-day?"

"Oh no, indeed; no, thank you," I answered, speaking and colouring much more vehemently than the occasion called for. "Are you going for a ride?"

"I am going to the police-station at Warsall, to endeavour to obtain a sight of that note."

"Who could have written it? It seems so useless a hoax to have played."

"Useless? As it turned out, yes. But it strikes me the intention was neither harmless nor useless," he added, in a thoughtful tone.

"Shall you not institute an inquiry into it, Mr. Chandos?"

"No. I shall pick up what there may be gathered in a quiet way; but I shall make no stir in it, I have my reasons for this. Good-bye, Anne. Mind you mend those gloves neatly."

"Good-bye, sir. Take care that Black Knave does not throw you again."

He went away laughing at his own remark about the gloves, or mine about Black Knave, went up to the west wing, and was down again in a minute. The horse was a favourite, and he patted him and spoke to him before mounting. The groom rode a bright bay horse; a fine animal also.

Surely there was no harm in my looking from the window to watch them away! But Mrs. Penn, who came into the oak-parlour at the moment, appeared to think so. Her lips were drawn in and her brow had a frown on it as I turned to her. With that want of ceremony that distinguished her ordinary behaviour to me, she threw herself back in an easy-chair. Her gown was a bright muslin; her glowing hair was adorned with purple ribbons and black lace lappets.

"What a place this Chandos seems to be!" she exclaimed. "Did you ever see such a house, Miss Hereford? That visit of the police—riding up with their drawn swords!"

"The swords were sheathed."

"I can tell you it gave me a turn. And after all, after terrifying us nearly to death, Mr. Chandos, I hear, entertained them amicably at supper."

"It was as well to be civil; it was not their fault that they came here. A trick had been played on them."

"A trick? I don't understand."

"A note was written in Mr. Chandos's name to the inspector of police at Warsall, asking for mounted officers to be sent over. They supposed they were coming to take into custody the person who had been playing tricks at Chandos. Tricks was the word used."

Mrs. Penn stared. "Who wrote the note?"

"Mr. Chandos does not know. He received a note himself also last night, an anonymous one: insinuating that as you and I were the only strangers at Chandos, one of us must be the guilty person."

"What next?" demanded Mrs. Penn, angrily. "Does Mr. Chandos suppose I stole my own lace and rifled my own letter? But it is only what I have anticipated."

"Mr. Chandos knows better. I say it was the anonymous letter that suggested the idea to him. I thought it seemed to point more to me than to you."

"Mr. Chandos would not admit the idea—would he?"

"Oh no. I am quite easy on that point. Mr. Chandos knows he may trust me."

Whether Mrs. Penn thought this remark seemed to reflect on herself; to shift the imputation on her, failing me, I could not tell; certainly no such thought had been in my mind. Her eyes grew angry: she rose from the chair, and shook her finger in my face.

"Anne Hereford, I have warned you once not to allow yourself to grow attached to Mr. Chandos; I now warn you again. There are reasons—I may not speak them—why it could bring you nothing but misery. Misery is only a faint word for it: disgrace, shame; more than you in your inexperience can imagine of evil. Better that you fell in love with the lowest man-servant attached to the place, than with Harry Chandos."

The tell-tale crimson rose to my cheeks, and I bent to pick one of the late rose-buds, entwining themselves about the trellis-work outside.

"Child! should harm ever come of this, recollect that I did my best to warn you. I am older than you by many years; had I ever possessed a daughter, she might have been of your age."

"Thank you, Mrs. Penn," I gently said; "there is no cause to fear for me."

"Where has Mr. Chandos gone to?"

"To Warsall. He would like to discover the writer of the note to the police."

"You seem to be quite in his confidence," remarked Mrs. Penn.

"He told me so much—that he intended to ride there. It was no very great confidence."

"There are many things I don't like in this house," she continued, after an interval of silence. "What do you suppose they did last night? Actually locked us up in the east wing! Turned the key upon us! I was coming forth to see if I could find out what those police were doing, and I found myself a prisoner! Madam Hill's act and deed, no doubt."

"Indeed!" was my reply, not choosing to tell her that I had heard the order given by Mr. Chandos.

"Hill takes a great deal too much upon herself." I thought it could be no one else, and taxed her with it, asking how she could presume to lock me up. She coolly replied that she had never thought of me at all in the affair, but of Mrs. Chandos, who was of a timid nature, and would not like to see policemen inside the house. "Poor thing! she has cause," added Mrs. Penn, in a sort of soliloquy.

"Mrs. Chandos has!"

"No unhappy prisoner escaped from Portland has more cause to dread the officers of justice than she. Your friend, Harry Chandos, has the same. I would not lead the life of apprehension he does, for untold gold. Look at the skeleton it makes of him! he is consuming away with inward fever. You were surprised when that London physician was brought down to him; the household were surprised: I was not."

"How came you to be so deep in their secrets?"

"Had I not been in their secrets, and shown them that I was, I should not have been admitted an inmate of that east wing," she answered. "Do you know, when the police came last night—But I had better hold my tongue, or I might say too much."

To avoid doing so, possibly, she left the room. But there were few women—as I believed—less likely than Mrs. Penn to be betrayed into speaking on impulse what it might be inexpedient to disclose.

The adventures of the day were not over for me. I wish they had been! I finished my gloves; I practised; I did a little German; and in the afternoon, when it was getting late, I strolled out with my book, and sat down between the house and the lodge-gates in a sheltered seat; where I could see who passed to and from the house, without being seen.

The morning had been very lovely; the evening was becoming less so; the wind sighed amidst the trees, clouds passed rapidly over the face of the sky, and the autumn leaves whirled about the paths. Did it ever strike you that there is something melancholy in these lying leaves? Many people like autumn best of the four seasons; but I think there is in it a great deal of sadness. It brings our own autumn of life too forcibly to the mind: as the leaves of the trees decay, and fall, and die; so must we when our time shall come.

I was listening to the rustle of the leaves, and watching—this is to be a true confession—for Mr. Chandos, when he rode by to the house. Inclination would have led me to follow him; common sense and propriety kept me where I was. Presently, I saw Lizzy Dene advancing quietly along one of the dark and private paths. She wore her cloak and bonnet, and had a basket on her arm, as if she had been on an errand to the village. In a moment some gentleman had met her and they were talking together. It was Edwin Barley. There were so many outlets from the broad walk that almost any of these private paths could be gained at will. Lizzy Dene came on almost directly; she seemed to be in a hurry, and turned off towards the kitchens. The next to appear in the same walk was Mrs. Penn, who immediately went up to Mr. Edwin Barley.

I was so sheltered by trees that they could not see me; but as they came nearer, walking side by side, Mrs. Penn's eye caught mine. She quickened her pace, and Mr. Edwin Barley turned back, raising his hat to her.

"Here you are with your book," she began. "Is it not too dark to see to read?"

"Almost. Have you been for a walk, Mrs. Penn?" I asked, hoping she would not mention the name of Edwin Barley.

"I have been to the village post-office. I don't care to entrust my letters now to the hall-table. Did you notice a gentleman with me down there, Miss Hereford?"

"I think I did see some one walking with you. It is dark amidst all those trees."

"I want to know his name," she continued, looking at me. "He has accosted me once or twice lately. A very civil, gentlemanly man."

"*Is* he! He has spoken to me, and I—I did not think him so. At least, I did not much like him. He lives in that house by the lodge-gates."

"Oh, then, it must be Mr. Edwin Barley, I suppose. Did you know his name?"

"Yes."

"He is a friend of the people here, I imagine. He stopped me just now and began asking after the health of Lady Chandos, as if he had an interest in it."

"I should not answer any of his questions at all, if I were you, Mrs. Penn."

"Why not?"

"You don't know anything about him, or what his motives may be for inquiry. I once heard Mr. Chandos warn him off these grounds; after that, he has no right to enter them. I think his doing so looks suspicious."

"I think you must be a suspicious young lady to fancy it," returned Mrs. Penn with a laugh. "You were certainly born to be an old maid, Anne Hereford. They are always ultra-cautious."

"I dare say I was."

"When a gentleman—and a neighbour, as you now say he is—makes inquiries in passing after the invalids of the family you may be staying with, *I* do not see any harm in answering them. One can't turn away like a bear, and say, I will not tell you."

"As you please. I do not think Mr. Chandos would approve of your speaking to him."

"Talking of Mr. Chandos, has he returned from that police errand yet?"

"I saw him ride past half-an-hour ago."

"I must hasten home," she returned, beginning to move away. "Mrs. Chandos cannot be left for long. I have run all the way back from the post, and I ran to it."

What a strangely persevering man that Edwin Barley seemed to be! If Mrs. Penn knew—as she evidently did know—the dark secrets of the Chandos family, what might he not get out of her? I almost made up my mind to inform Mr. Chandos.

Alas for my poor courage! Turning a sharp corner to go home, I came upon him standing there; Edwin Barley. Was he waiting for me, or for Mrs. Penn? But she had gone on by the other path. It was too late to retreat. I essayed to do it, but he placed himself in my way.

"Not so fast, young lady. I have been expecting you to come up: I saw you in the distance, and waited to exchange a word with you. Why! you won't be so discourteous as to refuse me!"

"I cannot stay now, thank you."

"Oh yes, you can—when I wish it. I want to inquire after the health of the family. There's no getting anything out of any one: they 'can't tell me how my lady is, except from hearsay;' they 'never see her,' they 'see nearly as little of Mr. Chandos.' You and I can be more confidential with each other."

"No, we cannot, sir. I never see Lady Chandos, any more than others do,"

"You cannot say that of Mr. Harry; you see a good deal of him," retorted Mr. Edwin Barley, with a parting of the lips that showed the subject vexed him. "You and he are always together—as news is brought to me."

"Did Mrs. Penn tell you that?" I asked, my colour and my anger rising together.

"Mrs. Penn!"

"The lady you have just parted with," I answered, supposing he did not know her by name.

"Mrs. Chandos's companion? *She's* none too civil to me. You had a visit from the mounted police last evening; an unexpected one, rumour runs. Did their sudden appearance confound Mr. Harry Chandos?"

How he seemed to know things! Did he get them from mere rumour, or from Lizzy Dene? I remained silent.

"Did they bring, I ask, confusion to Mr. Chandos? Did he exhibit the aspect, the terror, of one who—who has been guilty of some great crime, and dreads to expiate it?"

"I cannot tell you, sir."

"You were with him, I know that much," he returned, in the same commanding, angry, imperative tones I had once heard him use to my aunt Selina.

"But what if I was? I cannot say how Mr. Chandos felt or thought."

"You *can*—if you choose to do so. I asked you how he looked; what his manner betrayed: not what he felt or thought."

Loving him as I did, bound to his interests, could I be otherwise than on my guard? Nevertheless there must have been something in my tone and look that carried doubt to Mr. Edwin Barley.

"Mr. Chandos spoke to the officers quite calmly, sir. They were admitted at once, and he invited them into the sitting-room."

He looked at me keenly: I say, there must have been some doubt on his mind. "Are you aware that I know you, Anne? I think you must know me. As your uncle, your only living relative, I have a right to question you of these and other things."

My heart beat violently. Almost too sick to speak felt I: and the words shook as they issued from my lips.

"You are not my uncle, sir. Selina was my aunt, but—"

"And as Selina's husband, I became your uncle, Anne, by law. She is dead, but I am living: your uncle still. So you did know me?"

"I have known you, sir, ever since the day I first saw you here."

"It is more than I did you, young lady; or I should not have allowed you to remain so quietly at Chandos. For the sake of my dead wife, I take an interest in your welfare: and *that* will not be enhanced by your companionship with Harry Chandos."

The hint conveyed by the words frightened me. *He* allow me! *He* assume a right to control me! I spoke out in my terror.

"You cannot have any power over me or my actions, Mr. Edwin Barley."

"Indeed I have, Anne. The law would say so. Do you know who Mrs. Penn is?" he abruptly asked.

"I don't know who Mrs. Penn is or where she comes from," was my quick reply, glad he had put a question at last that I could answer honestly. "Will you please to let me go, sir. It is getting dark."

"Not just yet. You must first reply to a question or two I wish to ask touching Harry Chandos. To begin with: Does he go often from home?"

"I cannot tell you anything whatever about Mr. Chandos—or what he does—or what any one else does. As long as I am in the family, protected by them, trusted by them, it is dishonourable even to listen to such questions. But indeed I know nothing. If the Chandos family have secrets, they do not tell them to me."

"I should not imagine they would. I am not asking you for secrets. There are reasons why I wish to learn a little of their ordinary everyday doings. This, at any rate, is a simple question: Does Mr. Harry Chandos—"

"It is of no use, sir; I will not answer that question or any other. Pray do not stop me again! I hope you will pardon me for reminding you that I heard Mr. Chandos desire you not to intrude on these grounds: I think you ought to obey him, sir."

His face, always stern, grew fierce in its anger. Perhaps it was only natural that it should do so. He raised his hand.

"I hold the Chandoses under my finger and thumb. A little movement" (here he closed them), "and they may go trooping out of the kingdom to hide their disgrace; your friend, Mr. Harry, with all his high and mighty pride, leading the van. It will not be long first. By the obedience you owed your aunt Selina, my dead wife, by the tenderness for her cherished memory, I order you to speak. You must do so,

Anne."

One single moment of hesitation—I am ashamed to confess to it; but his voice and manner were so solemn—and my resolve returned, fixed and firm.

"I have said that I will not, now or ever."

He seized my two arms as if he were going to shake me; his angry face, with its beautiful white teeth—he always showed them when in anger—close to mine. The old fear I used to have of him as a child clung to me still, and I cried aloud in my terror. I had always been wanting in presence of mind.

It all passed in a moment. *What* I hardly knew. There was a crash as if the slender hedge gave way; and Mr. Chandos was holding me behind him, having flung Mr. Edwin Barley against the opposite tree.

# CHAPTER 24

## MRS. PENN'S REVELATION

Against the tree to which the push had flung him, he stood quietly. There had been no blow. Mr. Chandos had but come between us, calmly put me behind him, laid his hand on Mr. Edwin Barley's chest, and sent him backwards. These slender, delicate-looking men sometimes possess unusual strength—as he did. Edwin Barley, in an encounter, would have been as a reed in his hand.

Neither of them seemed in a passion: at least their manner did not betray it. Mr. Chandos's face was a little paler than common; it was stern and haughty; but otherwise he looked cool and collected. And Mr. Edwin Barley stood gazing at him, a strange look of power in his eye and lip.

"How dare you presume to molest this young lady?" were the first words of Mr. Chandos. "What do you mean by it?"

"As to 'molesting,' I do not understand the term, as applied to Miss Hereford," returned Mr. Edwin Barley, with cool equanimity. "I possess the right to talk to her, and touch her; you don't. Neither possess you the right to protect her! I do. What relative may she be of yours?"

"None. But she is my mother's guest."

"None; just so. She is my niece."

Mr. Chandos, with a gesture of astonishment, looked at me for confirmation or refutation. He received neither. I only clung to him for protection, the tears running down my cheeks.

"She has no relative save myself; she has no other relative, so far as I know, or she knows, in the world, except a lad younger than herself," pursued Mr. Edwin Barley, no anger in his tone, only the firmness of conscious power. "My niece, I tell you, sir."

"Whatever she may be, she is residing under my mother's roof, and as such, is in my charge. If you ever dare to touch her against her will again, sir, I will horsewhip you."

Mr. Chandos held his riding-whip in his hand as he spoke (he had brought it out by chance), and it trembled ominously. Mr. Edwin Barley drew back his lips: not in laughter; in all he did he was in earnest; and his teeth were momentarily seen.

"Harry Chandos, you know that you will one day have to pay for your incivility."

"I know nothing of the sort; and if I did, the Chandoses are not given to calculation. I can tell you what you shall be made to pay for, Mr. Edwin Barley—trespassing upon my domains. I warned you off them once; I will not warn you again—the law shall do it for me."

"*Your* domains!" retorted Mr. Edwin Barley.

"Yes, sir, mine," was the haughty answer. "They are mine so long as I am the representative of Sir Thomas Chandos. Have the goodness to quit them now, or I will call my servants to escort you."

Whatever Mr. Edwin Barley might do privately, he knew he had no legal right to remain within the domains of Chandos, when ordered off them, and he was not one openly to defy usages. He moved away in the direction of the gates; turning his head to speak, and halting as he did so.

"The law, so far, lies with you at present, Mr. Harry Chandos. A short time, and perhaps it will lie with me, in a matter far more weighty. As to you, Anne, I shall officially claim you."

Nothing else was said. Mr. Chandos watched him to the turning of the dark wall, then walked by my side to the house, flicking the shrubs with his whip.

"I happened to have it with me," he said, whether addressing the whip, or me, or the air, was not clear. "I was fastening the handle, which had got loose. *Is* that man your uncle?"

He turned to me, a look of stern pain on his pale, proud face. The tears gushed forth again at the question; I was wishing my heart could break.

"Oh no, no; indeed I am no blood-relation of his."

Mr. Chandos went on without another word. I thought he was despising me: would think that I h*ad* been in league with his enemy, Edwin Barley. I who had pretended not to know him!

The cloth was laid in the oak-parlour, but there were no lights yet. Mr. Chandos flung his whip into a corner, and stood in the shade of the curtain. I went up to him, feeling very hysterical.

"Do not misjudge me, Mr. Chandos. I will tell you all, if you please, after dinner. I should have told you before but that I have felt so frightened of Mr. Edwin Barley."

"Since when have you felt frightened?"

"Since I was a little girl. I had not seen him for many years until I saw him here at Chandos, and I was afraid to speak of him—afraid also that he would recognize me."

"He says he can claim you. Is that an idle boast?"

"I don't now; I don't understand English laws. Perhaps he might, but I would a great deal rather die."

Mr. Chandos bent towards me, a strange look of tenderness in his earnest eyes. I think he was going to lay his hand on my shoulder to assure me of his care, when at that moment some one passed the window, whom I took to be Edwin Barley. It was only the gardener—as I learned later—he had put on his coat to go home; a short, dark man walking past, and the dusk was deceptive. I thought Edwin Barley had come to take me there and then.

For the minute I was certainly not in my senses: terror alone reigned. I laid hold of Mr. Chandos in hysterical excitement, clinging to him as one clings for dear life.

"Oh, keep me, keep me! Do not let him take me! Mr. Chandos! I know you are angry with me and despise me; but do not give me up to him!"

Before I had ceased speaking he had me in his arms, holding me to his breast. We stood there in the shade of the dark room, heart beating wildly against heart.

"I wish I could give myself the right to keep you from him, and from every other ill," he breathed. "Do you know, Anne, that I love you above all else in the world?"

I made no answer; but I should have liked to remain where I was for ever.

"But, my darling, it can only end here as it has begun; for I cannot marry. My brother, Sir Thomas, does not marry."

I looked at him. He saw that I would have asked why.

"Because we ought not to do so: it would not be right. There are dark clouds hanging over Chandos: should they open, it would be to hurl down desolation and disgrace upon us. How can either of us, he or I, think of exposing a wife to encounter this? Could I in honour do it?"

"It might be happier for you, if this sorrow should arrive, to have one with you to soothe your cares and share them."

"And there is one who would not shrink from it," be said, tenderly. "Had I not seen that, Anne, I should have been as much knave as fool to confess to my own state of feeling. For some days past I have been thinking it might be better to speak; that I owed as much to you; to speak and have done with it. Before I knew my danger, love had stolen over me, and it was too late to guard against it. It has not been our fault that we were thrown together."

He took some impassioned kisses from my face. I let him take them. I fear I did not think whether it was right or wrong. I'm not sure that I cared which it was: I only know that I felt as one in a blissful dream.

"I have been betrayed into this, Anne," he said, releasing me. "I ought to beg your pardon in all humility. It is not what I intended. Though I might just tell you of my love, I never thought to give you tokens of it. Will you forgive me?"

He held out his hand. I put mine into it, the silent tears running down my blushing face. "Do not fear a similar transgression for the future. The fleeting moment over, it is over for good. I would give half my remaining existence, Anne, to be able to marry, to make you my wife; but it cannot be. Believe me, my darling, it *cannot* be. No, though you are my darling, and will be for ever."

"Oh, look! look! It is from your hand! What has happened?"

On my dress of white muslin there were two red stains. The straps on his hand had loosened, perhaps in the encounter with Mr. Edwin Barley, and it had begun to bleed again. I ran upstairs to put on another dress, leaving Mr. Chandos to attend to his hand.

I was in a glow of happiness! He had said he could not *marry*. What was marriage to me? Had there been no impediment on his side, there might have been one on mine: a poor friendless young governess was no match for Mr. Chandos of Chandos. He loved me: that was quite sufficient for present bliss; and, as it seemed to me, for future.

Mr. Chandos presided at dinner as usual, himself once more calm, collected, courteous, and gentlemanly. The servants in waiting could never have suspected he had been making me a declaration of love, and pressing kisses on my lips not many minutes before.

"Did you succeed in seeing the letter at Warsall?" I asked, when the servants had left again, and silence was growing too self-conscious for me.

"Yes, but I don't know the handwriting. It looks like a lady's. They let me bring the note home; I will show it you presently. Talking of that—"

Without concluding, he rose, went to a side-table, and brought me a box, done up in paper.

"There! Don't say I forget you."

It contained gloves; many pairs. Beautiful French gloves of all colours; some dark and useful, others delicate and rare. But I thought it would not be right to accept them, and the tell-tale pink flushed my cheeks.

"Don't scruple; they are not from me. Look at the little note."

I took it out of the box. It contained a few words pencilled by Lady Chandos, asking me to wear the gloves.

"It happened that I was going to buy some for my mother to-day. When I went up to her after Black Knave was brought round, I told her Miss Hereford had no gloves left, and she asked me to bring you some. There, Miss Hereford."

I supposed I might wear them now, and began putting on a glove to cover my confusion. Mr. Chandos ate his grapes with his usual equanimity.

"Six-and-a-half. How did you guess my size?"

"By your hand."

As if jealous of the interview—it seemed so to me at the moment—Hill came in to break it. Lady Chandos wanted him in the west wing.

He went up at once. I sat thinking of all that had occurred. Would Mr. Edwin Barley indeed claim me? *Could* he do so? Would the law allow him? I shivered at the thought.

The tea waited on the table when he came down again. It seems very monotonous, I feel sure, to be alluding so continually to the meals, but you see they were the chief times when I was alone with Mr. Chandos; so I can only crave pardon for doing so.

Mr. Chandos's countenance wore a sad and gloomy look: but that was nothing unusual after his visits to the west wing. I wondered very much that he did not have the shutters closed after what had taken place the previous night; but there they were open, and nothing between the room and the window but the thin lace curtains. The silk curtains, at the extreme corners of the windows, were not made to draw. Long afterwards I found that he had the shutters left open because I was there. As the habit had been to leave them open in the past, he did not choose to alter it now: people inclined to be censorious, might have remarked upon it. That aspect of the affair never occurred to me.

"What led to the scene with that man to-day?" he abruptly asked, after taking a cup of tea in silence. "How came you to meet him?"

I briefly explained. Mentioning also that I had seen Mrs. Penn with him, and what she said to me of his inquiries. And I told him of Mr. Edwin Barley's questions about the visit of the police-officers.

"If Mrs. Penn is to make an acquaintance of Mr. Edwin Barley, she cannot remain at Chandos," he coldly remarked. "Have you finished tea? Then it shall go away."

He rose to ring the bell, did not resume his seat again, but stood with his back to the fire, and watched the servants remove the things. I got my work about as usual.

"Now then, Anne, I claim your promise. What are you to Edwin Barley? and what is he to you?"

A moment's pause. But I had made my mind up to tell him all, and would not flinch now the moment had come. Putting down the work, I sat with my hands clasped on my lap.

"Did you know that there was once a Mrs. Edwin Barley?"

"Unfortunately, I had too good cause to know it." I thought the answer a strange one, but went on. "She was a Carew. Miss Selina Carew of Keppe-Carew."

"I know she was."

"And my aunt."

"Your aunt!" he repeated, looking at me strangely. "Why, whose daughter are you?"

"My father was Colonel Hereford. A brave officer and gentleman."

"Thomas Hereford? Of the —th?"

"Yes."

"And your mother?"

"My mother was Miss Carew of Keppe-Carew. She was a good deal older than Selina. They were sisters."

The information appeared to surprise him beyond expression. He sat down in front of me, his eyes fixed earnestly on my face.

"The daughter of Colonel Hereford and of Miss Carew of Keppe-Carew! And we have been thinking of you as only a governess! Je vous en fais mes compliments empressés, Miss Hereford! You are of better family than ours."

"That does me no good. I have still to be a governess."

"Does it not, young lady? Well—about Mrs. Edwin Barley. Did you see much of her?"

"Not much until the last. I was there when she died."

"There! At Edwin Barley's! She died at his place near Hallam."

"Yes." And I gave him the outline of what had taken me there: to spend the short interval between mamma's death and my being placed at school.

"You must have heard of a—a tragedy"—he spoke the words in a hesitating, unwilling manner—"that occurred there about the same time. A young man, a ward of Edwin Barley's died."

"Philip King. Yes; he was killed. I saw it done, Mr. Chandos."

"Saw what done?"

"Saw Philip King murdered. That is not a nice word to repeat, but it is what they all called it at the time. I was in the wood. I saw the shot strike him, and watched him fall."

"Why, what a strange girl you are!" Mr. Chandos exclaimed, after a pause of astonishment. "What else have you seen?"

"Nothing like that. Nothing half so dreadful. I trust I never shall."

"I trust not, either. Anne," he continued, dropping his voice to a low, solemn tone, "you say you saw that shot strike him. *Who fired it?*"

"It was said to be—but perhaps I ought not to mention the name even to you, Mr. Chandos," I broke off. "Mrs. Hemson cautioned me never to repeat it under any circumstances."

"Who is Mrs. Hemson?"

"She was also once a Miss Carew of Keppe-Carew. Her father was John Carew; and my grandfather, Hubert Carew, succeeded him. She married Mr. Hemson; he was in trade, and the Carews did not like it: but oh, he is one of the noblest gentlemen in mind and manners."

"As I have heard my mother say. Go on, Anne."

"After Mrs. Edwin Barley died, I was sent to Mrs. Hemson's at Dashleigh; she had undertaken the charge of fixing on a school for me. It was she who told me not to mention the name."

"You may mention it to me. Was it George Heneage?"

"You know it, then, Mr. Chandos!"

"I know so much—as the public in general knew. They said it was

George Heneage; a gentleman staying there at the time. Did you see who it was fired the shot? Pray answer me."

"I did not see it fired: but I think it was George Heneage. Quite at first I doubted, because—but never mind that. I did not doubt afterwards, and I think it was certainly George Heneage."

"'Never mind' will not do for me, Anne. I mind it all; have too much cause to do so; and from me you must conceal nothing. Why did you at first doubt that it was George Heneage?"

"I saw Mr. Edwin Barley coming from the direction where the shot was fired, with his gun in his hand, and I wondered at the moment whether he had done it. I used to feel afraid of him; I did not like him; and he disliked George Heneage."

"Did you hear or know the cause of his dislike to George Heneage?"

"I gathered it," I answered, feeling my face flush.

"Mrs. Edwin Barley was beautiful, was she not?" he asked, after a pause.

"Very beautiful."

"Are you anything like her?"

I could not help laughing. I like Selina!

"Not one bit. She had a very fair, piquante face, light and careless, with blue eyes and a great deal of light curling hair."

"Do you remember George Heneage?" he continued, stooping for something as he asked the question.

"No; not his face. When I try to recall it, it always seems to slip from me. I remember thinking him good-looking. He was very tall. Charlotte Delves called him a scarecrow; but I thought she disliked him because Mr. Edwin Barley did so."

"Who was Charlotte Delves?"

"She lived there. She was distantly related to Mr. Edwin Barley. Jemima—one of the maids—once said that Charlotte Delves liked Mr. Edwin Barley too well to be just."

"I remember hearing of her—of some relation, at least, who was in the house at the time," he observed, in a dreamy sort of tone. "Delves? perhaps that was the name. A pleasant-mannered, lady-like woman—as described to me."

"I don't recollect much about her, or what she was like, except that she was very kind to me after my aunt Selina's death. It is a good while ago, and I was only a little girl."

"Ay. But now, Anne, I want you to relate to me all the particulars of that bygone miserable tragedy: anything and everything that you may remember as connected with it. Understand me: it is not curiosity that prompts me to ask it. Were I to consult my own wishes, I would bury the whole in a stream of Lethe; every word spoken of it is to me so much agony. Nevertheless, you may do me a service if you will relate what you know of it."

"I would tell you willingly, Mr. Chandos. But—I fear—I—should have to seem to throw blame on Selina."

"You cannot throw so much blame on her as has already been thrown on her to me. Perhaps your account may tend to remove the impression it left on my mind."

I began at the beginning, and told him all, as far as I could recollect, giving my childish impressions of things. I told him also my own early history. When I came to the details of Philip King's death, Mr. Chandos sat with his elbow on the arm of the chair, his face turned from me and buried in his hand.

"You saw George Heneage just afterwards?" he remarked.

"Yes. He was hiding in the wood, trembling all over, and his face was very white."

"Had he the look of a guilty man?"

"I think he had. Had he not been guilty, why should he not have come openly forward to help Philip King?"

"True. Did Mrs. Edwin Barley think him guilty?"

"Not at first. I don't know what she might have done later. Mr. Edwin Barley did."

"As he took care to let the world know. Go on with your narrative, Anne. I ought not to have interrupted it."

I went on to the end. Mr. Chandos heard me without comment; and remained so long silent that I thought he was never going to speak again.

"Has George Heneage ever been heard of, do you happen to know, Mr. Chandos?"

"It is said not."

"Then I think he must be dead. Or perhaps he has kept out of the country. Mr. Edwin Barley said at the time that he would bring him to justice, were it years and years to come."

"Mr. Edwin Barley was excessively bitter against him. He, Barley, succeeded to Philip King's fine property. Were I on the jury when George Heneage was brought to trial, I should require strong proof—stronger than Mr. Edwin Barley's word—ere I convicted him."

"Mr. Edwin Barley did not shoot him," I said, gravely.

"I do not accuse him; I feel sure he did not. But there were one or two private doubts entertained upon the matter; I can tell you that, Anne. He was suspiciously eager in his accusations of George Heneage!"

"Think of his provocation! Selina and George Heneage had both lived only to provoke him; and people said he was really attached to Philip King."

"Good arguments, Anne. I believe I am unjust in all that relates to

Edwin Barley."

"But why should you be so, Mr. Chandos? Don't you think it must have been George Heneage who committed the murder?"

"I beg you will not use that ugly word, Anne. My full and firm belief is that it was an accident—nothing more."

"Then why should George Heneage stay away?"

"A natural question. Of course we cannot answer for what George Heneage does or does not do. Were he to appear in England, Mr. Edwin Barley would instantly cause him to be apprehended; there's no doubt of that; innocent or guilty, he must stand his trial; and to some men that ordeal would be just as bad as conviction. Besides, he might not be able to prove that it was only an accident; I think he would not be; and, failing that proof, he would be condemned. In saying this, I am not seeking to defend George Heneage."

"Did you ever see George Heneage, Mr. Chandos?"

"Yes."

"Perhaps you knew him?"

He made no reply; but rose from his seat and began to pace the room.

"About that will of Mrs. Edwin Barley's, Anne?" he presently asked. "Did her husband destroy it?"

If I had thought so as a child, and thought so still, it was not possible for me to say it; but Mr. Chandos had acquired a habit of reading what I hesitated to speak.

"I see; you think it better not to avow dangerous doctrines."

"Indeed, I should be grieved to know that he really took it. Its disappearance was very strange."

"You don't think he took it; you only had an instinct that way. But, Anne, your instincts are generally true ones. Mr. Barley has the character of being a grasping man, loving money better than anything else in the world, except bringing George Heneage to punishment. He could not bear that the little trifle should go from him; compared with his large property, it was only as a drop of water to the ocean. He did not want it, you did; you have but little."

"I have nothing, nothing but what I earn. Mamma sank for my education the trifle of money she had saved."

"But—the daughter of Colonel Hereford ought to enjoy a pension," he debated, stopping in his walk.

"Papa sold out before his death."

"Oh, I see," and he resumed his walk.

"Mr. Chandos, may I ask you a question?"

"You know you may. I will answer it if I can."

"What has Mr. Edwin Barley to do with you? Why should he be your enemy?"

"That is what I cannot answer," he quickly rejoined. "He is an implacable enemy to me and my family; and likely ever to remain so. I cannot divest myself of the idea that he was the author of that visit we were favoured with last night by the police. Between the two—him and his wife—we have suffered enough. I should be puzzled to say which of them did us most harm, Miss Hereford."

Miss Hereford! And I was the Barley's relative! My heart felt sick and faint within me.

"Well, what now?" asked Mr. Chandos, who happened to be looking, and he came up and stood close before me.

"Nothing, sir, nothing; only I cannot help Selina's having been my aunt. Perhaps you will never care to be kind to me again."

His eyes, so grave before, quite danced with their pleasant light.

"Anne, the only kind thought I have had of your aunt Selina is since I knew she was of your kindred. If—"

I rose with a vivid blush. Inside the door, having come in so quietly as to be unheard, stood Mrs. Penn. Mr. Chandos turned, a haughty frown on his brow.

"I beg your pardon, madam; did you want anything?"

"I beg yours, sir, for my intrusion," she answered, civilly. "I only had a little errand with Miss Hereford. Will you"—turning to me—"kindly let me have my embroidery scissors, if you have done with them?"

I took them from my basket and gave them to her. "Thank you, Mrs. Penn, for the loan of them. They cut my strip of work beautifully."

"It is a chilly evening," she remarked, moving to depart. "I fancy we are going to have rain."

Mr. Chandos opened the door for her, and when she left slipped the bolt. Ere he was half-way across the room on his return, however, he went back and undid it, some reflection appearing to strike him. His brow was stern and displeased.

"That Mrs. Penn is a curious woman!"

"Curious! In what way, sir? Do you mean her hair?"

He slightly laughed. "I spoke the word literally, Anne. She came in, I fancy, just to see what was going on, the scissors being the excuse."

"She complains of it being dull in the east wing. I think she is glad to escape from it for a moment when she can do so."

"Ay, no doubt; we must not judge her harshly. She is a contrast to Mrs. Freeman, who never put herself into any one's way. I wish I could discover the author of these losses in the house," he continued, passing to another subject. "Had it been alone the looking into letters or stealing them, I might have suspected Edwin Barley. That is, that some, one was at work for him here. That he would like to get my private memoranda into his fingers, and peep at my letters, I know; but he could have no possible motive for causing lace and money to be stolen."

My head was full of Lizzy Dene, and I thought the time had come for me to speak. Ah, what would I not tell him in this bond of confidence that seemed to be established between us.

"But, Mr. Chandos—suppose, for argument's sake—that he has an agent in the house; suppose that it is a woman, that agent may be transacting a little business on her own account whilst she does his."

Mr. Chandos came and stood before me. "Have you a motive in saying this?"

"Yes. I think, I do think, if there is one, that it is Lizzy Dene."

Of course, having said so much, I told all. Of the interview that some one (I suspected Lizzy Dene) had held with Edwin Barley in the grounds; the chance meeting they had held that afternoon. Mr. Chandos was terribly displeased, but still he could not—I saw it—be brought to believe that it was Dene.

"You have great faith in her, Mr. Chandos?"

"I have, because I believe Lizzy Dene to be true and honest. I do not think her capable of acting as a spy, or in any other false part. She is an inveterate gossip; she is superstitious, and looks after ghosts; but I believe her to be faithful to the backbone."

It was useless to contend: he had his opinion, I had mine. To look at Lizzy's face, to listen to her voice, I should have thought her honest too; but I could not close my eyes to facts and circumstances. Mr. Chandos rang for Hill.

"I want to say a word to Lizzy Dene, Hill; incidentally, you understand. Can you contrive to send her here on some ostensible errand?"

Hill nodded her head and withdrew. Presently Lizzy Dene came in with a knock and a curtsy; she went to the sideboard and began looking in it for something that appeared difficult to find. Mr. Chandos, standing with his back to the fire, suddenly accosted her; her head was nearly inside one of the sideboard cupboards.

"How long have you known Mr. Edwin Barley, Lizzy?"

"Known who, sir?" she returned, standing up and looking round at him.

"Mr. Edwin Barley."

"I don't know him at all, sir," she replied, after a minute's pause, given apparently to surprise and consideration. "Not but what I seem to have heard that name—lately, too."

"He is the new tenant at the house outside the gates."

"Dear! yes, to be sure! Two of the men were talking of him one day; that was the name, for I remember I said it put me in mind of the fields. I have seen him once or twice, sir; a short, dark man."

"Where did you first see him?"

"It was coming home from church one Sunday, sir. We were crossing the road to the gates, me and Robin and Harriet, when I noticed a swarthy gentleman standing stock-still and staring at us. 'I hope he'll know us again,' said I; 'he's ugly enough.' 'Hush!' says Robin, 'that's master's new tenant at the house there!'"

"Have you spoken to him?" inquired Mr. Chandos.

"Well, sir, if you can call it speaking, I have. This evening, as I was coming home, I met him in one of the walks. He wished me good-evening, and asked how my lady was. I stood to answer him, saying my lady was still very ill. That's all, sir."

"Has he spoken to you at any other time?"

"No, sir, never. I had forgotten his name, sir, till you mentioned it now."

She did seem to speak truthfully, and Mr. Chandos looked at me. Lizzy, finding nothing more was asked, turned to the sideboard again, and presently left the room.

"The traitor is not Lizzy Dene, Anne!"

Certainly it did not appear to be so. I felt puzzled. Mr. Chandos continued his walk, and the clock struck ten. Putting up my work, I held out my hand to wish him good-night, and took courage to speak the question lying so heavily on my heart.

"Do you think, sir, Mr. Edwin Barley can really claim me?"

"I cannot tell, Anne. At any rate, he would have, I imagine, to make you first of all a ward in Chancery, and get himself appointed guardian; and that would take time."

"He could not come into your house and take me forcibly out of it?"

"Certainly not; and I—acting for Lady Chandos—will take very good care he does not do it."

"Good-night, sir!"

"It is to be 'sir' to the end—is it? Good-night, Anne," he went on, shaking me by the hand. "I wish I dare offer you a different good-night from this formal one! I wish I could feel justified in doing it."

I don't know what I stammered; something foolish and incoherent; and in tone, at any rate, full of my depth of love.

"No, it may not be," he answered, very decisively. "If a wavering crossed my mind before, when I thought you—forgive me, Anne—an unpretending governess, as to whether I should lay the good and the ill before you, and let you decide, it has passed now. The daughter of Colonel Hereford and of Miss Carew of Keppe-Carew must not be trifled with. Good-night, child!"

The tears were very near my eyes when I entered my bedroom. Had Mr. Chandos cast me off for ever? Since that unlucky remark of his, that my family was better than his own, I know not what sweet visions had been floating in my mind. I *was* of good descent, with a lady's breeding and education; surely, if he could forgive my want of money and my having lived as a dependent at Mrs. Paler's, there had been no very great barrier between me and a younger brother of Chandos!

Dwelling upon this, it startled me to see Mrs. Penn quietly seated in my room. She pointed to the door.

"Shut it and bolt it, Miss Hereford. I have been waiting to talk to you!"

I shut it, but did not slip the bolt. Where was the necessity? No one ever came into my room at night—Mrs. Penn excepted.

"Come and sit down, and tell me why you are crying!"

"I am not crying. I have no reason to cry," I resentfully answered, vexed beyond everything. "I thought of something as I came upstairs, which brought the tears into my eyes: we often laugh until we cry, you know."

"Oh, indeed," said Mrs. Penn, "perhaps yours are tears of joy?"

"I should be so very much obliged if you could put off what you wish to say until the morning. You don't know how sleepy I am."

"I know that you can tell a parcel of fibs, you wicked child," she returned, in fond accents. "Anne—I shall call you so to-night—I have come to talk to you; and talk I shall. I want to save you."

"Save me from what?"

"From the—what shall I call it?—the machinations of Harry Chandos."

"Mr. Chandos is working no machinations against me."

"I know that he *is*. He has been making you a declaration of love."

The tell-tale crimson lighted up my face. Mrs. Penn continued, taking my hand.

"I felt uneasy, and made my scissors an excuse for coming to the oak-parlour. You should not have heard it from him. I warned you that any attachment between you and Mr. Chandos could not end happily; you cannot marry him!"

My nerves were completely unstrung, and I burst into tears; I could play a false part no longer. It was bitter enough to hear her confirm his own words. Mrs. Penn gently stroked my hair.

"Child, do you know why I thus interfere between you and Mr. Chandos? I will tell you. A few years ago I became attached to a young girl of eighteen—a connection of mine. She was under my charge and under my eye; her name, Lottie Penn. A stranger came, fascinating as Mr. Chandos; and I, believing him to be upright and honourable, exercised little caution. He gained her love, just as Mr. Chandos is gaining yours—"

"Mrs. Penn!"

"Hush! do you think I am blind? He gained Lottie's love; and, when marriage came to be spoken of as a natural sequence, we found out that we had been entertaining a Jesuit in disguise. He could not marry."

"A Jesuit?"

"I am speaking metaphorically. The man called himself a Protestant, if he called himself anything. I heard him say he was a Christian. Very Christian work it was to gain Lottie's heart, and then confess that he had gained it for no end. Lottie died. The blow was too sharp for her. She was a timid, gentle flower, and could not stand the rough blast. Anne, believe me, there is no fate so cruel in the whole catalogue of the world's troubles as that of misplaced love."

"Why could he not marry?" I asked, growing interested in the tale.

"Ah! why, indeed!" she answered, curling her lips with mockery. "Why cannot Harry Chandos? The cases are somewhat parallel. It is the remembrance of Lottie which causes me to feel this interest in you, for you put me very much in mind of her, and I must try to save you."

"There is nothing to save me from!" I answered, touched with her kindness, and feeling ashamed of myself not to be more touched with it than I was. "I am not likely to marry Mr. Chandos, or to be asked to marry him!"

"My dear, I don't think I can be deceived. There *is* love between you!"

"You did not finish about Lottie," I said, evading the question. "Why could he not marry her?"

"Because he had a wife living, from whom he was separated."

"At least, Mr. Chandos has not that."

She remained silent, only looking at me. I am not sure but an idea struck me that the silence was strange. I could never tell afterwards whether or not it so struck me *then*.

"I said the cases were somewhat parallel," she slowly observed.

"Scarcely, Mrs. Penn. Mr. Chandos at least does not deceive me. He says he cannot marry. His life is given up to sorrow."

"Given up to sorrow? He says that, does he? Anne, I have half a mind to tell you the truth. What is his sorrow compared with that of poor Mrs. Chandos. I pity *her*."

"Who *is* Mrs. Chandos?" I interrupted, seizing the opportunity to inquire on the subject that remained a puzzle, and thinking this kind woman might satisfy me. "They call her Lady Chandos's daughter-in-law, but I cannot see how she can be so."

"Mrs. Chandos was once Miss Ethel Wynne."

"But who is her husband?"

"Ah, *you* may well ask. It is curious though that you should do so."

Was it the stress on the pronoun?—or that her face was so suggestive as it gazed into mine?—or that the previous vague idea was growing into life? I knew not; I never have known. I only felt that I turned sick with an undefined doubt and dread as I waited for Mrs. Penn's answer. She was a full minute, looking into my whitening face, before she gave it.

"My poor stricken lamb! Has it never struck you who it might be?"

I put up my trembling hand as if to beat off her words. That unholy idea—yes, it seemed to me unholy in those first confused moments—was growing into a monster of fear. Mrs. Penn looked as if she could not sufficiently note the signs.

"What if her husband were Harry Chandos?

With the strange surging in my ears—with my pulses standing cold and still, and then coursing on to fever-heat—with my temples beating to pain—no wonder I could not weigh my words.

"Oh, Mrs. Penn! Do not tell it me!"

"Think you that you need telling, Anne? I can add something more. Never will Harry Chandos love again in this world, you or any one else, as he once loved Ethel Wynne."

My senses were growing confused; I no longer seemed to understand things. She went on.

"Husband and wife live apart sometimes, although they may live under the same roof. She and Harry Chandos parted; it is years ago now; she used him very ill; and I don't suppose he has ever so much as touched her hand since, except in the very commonest courtesies of everyday life: and that only when he could not help himself. Passion has long been over between them; they are civil when they meet; nothing more. My poor child, you look ready to fall."

I did fall. But not until she had left the room. I fell on the ground, and let my head lie there in its misery. Much that had been obscure before seemed to shine out clearly now; things to which I had wanted a clue, appeared to be solved. I wished I could die, there as I lay, rather than have found him out in deceit so despicable.

# CHAPTER 25

## MISERY

The sun shone brightly into my room in the morning, but there would be no more sunshine for me. What a night I had passed! If you have ever been deceived in the manner I had, you will understand it; if not, all the writing in the world would fail to convey to you a tithe of the misery that was mine—and that would be mine for years to come. *Her* husband! whilst he pretended to love *me!*

All my study would now be to avoid Mr. Chandos. Entirely I could not do so; for we must meet at the daily repasts when he chose to sit down to them. In that I could not help myself. I was very silent that morning, and he was busy with his newspapers.

He rode out after breakfast; to attend some county meeting, it was said; and returned at four o'clock. I remained in my own room until dinner-time; but I had to go down then.

He appeared inclined to be thoroughly sociable; talked and laughed; and told me of a ludicrous scene which had occurred at the meeting; but I was cold and reserved, scarcely answering him. He looked at me keenly, as if debating with himself what could have so changed my manner. When the servants had withdrawn, I left my place at table, and sat down in a low chair near the fire.

"Why do you go there?" said Mr. Chandos. "You will take some dessert?"

"Not this evening."

"But why?"

"My head aches."

He left the table, came up, and stood before me. "Anne, what is the matter with you?"

My breath was coming quickly, my heart seemed as if it must burst. All the past rose up forcibly before me; he, a married man, had mocked me with his love; had—oh, worse than all!—gained mine. It was a crying insult; and it was wringing bitterly every sense of feeling I possessed. Anything else I could have borne. Mrs. Penn had hinted at some great crime; words of his own had confirmed it. Had he committed every crime known to man, I could better have forgiven it. But for this deliberate deceit upon me, there could be no forgiveness: and there could be no cure, no comfort for my lacerated heart.

"Are you angry with me for any cause? Have I offended you?"

The question unnerved me more than I was already unnerved. It did more, it raised all the ire of my spirit. A choice between two evils only seemed to be left to me; either to burst into hysterical tears, or to reproach Mr. Chandos openly. The latter course came first.

"Why did you deceive me, Mr. Chandos?"

"Deceive you!"

"Yes, deceive me, and wretchedly deceive me," I answered in my desperation; neither caring nor quite knowing what I said. "How came you to speak to me at all of love, knowing *why* it is that you cannot marry?"

He bit his lip as he looked at me. "Do *you* know why it is?"

"I do now. I did not yesterday, as you may be very sure!"

"It is impossible you can know it," he rejoined, in some agitation.

"Mr. Chandos, I *do* know. Spare me from saying more. It is not a subject on which either you or I should enlarge."

"And pray, Anne, who enlightened you?"

"*That* is of no consequence," I passionately answered, aroused more and more by his cool manner of taking the reproach. "I know now what the barrier is you have more than once hinted at, and that is quite enough."

"You consider that barrier an insuperable one—that I ought not to have avowed my love?"

I burst into hysterical tears. It was the last insult: and the last feather, you know, breaks the camel's back. Alas! we were at cross-purposes.

"Forgive me, Anne," he sadly cried, "Before I remembered that there might be danger in your companionship; before I was aware that love could ever dawn for me, it had come, and was filling every crevice of my heart. It is stirring within me now as I speak to you. My pulses are thrilling with the bliss of your presence; my whole being tells of the gladness of heaven."

In spite of the cruel wrong; in spite of my own bitter misery; in spite of the ties to which he was bound, to hear the avowal of this deep tenderness, stirred with a rapture akin to his every fibre of my rebellious love. I know how terribly wrong it must seem; I know how worse than wrong is the confession; but *so it was.* I was but human.

"I am aware that I have acted unwisely," he pursued, his tones very subdued and repentant. "Still—you must not blame me too greatly. Circumstances are at least as much in fault. We were thrown together, unavoidably; I could not, for reasons, absent myself from home; you were located in it. Of course I ought to have remembered that I was not free to love: but then, you see, the danger did not occur to my mind. If it had, I should have been cold as an icicle."

To hear him defending himself seemed worse than all. I had thought if there lived one man on the face of the earth who was the soul of nobility, uprightness, honour, it was Harry Chandos.

"It was the cruelest insult possible to be offered to me, Mr. Chandos."

"What was?"

"What was! Telling me of your love."

"Anne, I told it you because—forgive my boldness!—I saw that you loved me."

Heaven help me! Yes, it was so; I did love him. My face grew hot; I beat my foot upon the carpet.

"I did the best that could be done: at least I strove to do it. It was my intention to lay before you the unhappy case without disguise, its facts and deterrent circumstances, and then to say—'Now marry me or reject me!'"

"How can you so speak to me, sir? Marry me! with—with—that barrier?"

"But that barrier may be removed."

Oh! I saw now, or fancied I saw, the far-off thought he was driving at. Staying seemed to make matters worse; and I got up from my seat to leave him.

"Your turning out to be who you are of course made the difficulty greater. I said so last night—"

"No, it does not," I interrupted, with an impassioned sob, partly of love, partly of anger. "Whether I am regarded as a poor governess, or the daughter of Colonel Hereford, there could never, never be any excuse for you."

"Is that your final opinion?" he asked, standing before me to ask the question.

"It is, Mr. Chandos. It will never change. You ought to despise me if it could."

"Forgive, forgive me, Miss Hereford! Nothing remains for me now but to ask it."

I could not forgive him; but I was spared saying so, for Hill opened the parlour-door in haste.

"Mr. Harry, will you please go up to the west wing? At once, sir."

"Any change, Hill?"

"No, sir; it's not that. A little trouble."

"Oh; Mrs. Chandos is there, I suppose?"

"Yes, sir."

*Need* he have asked that question, have mentioned her name in my presence? It struck me that it was a gratuitous insult. Mr. Chandos followed Hill from the room, and as soon as I thought he was safe within the west wing, I flew up to my own chamber.

Flew up with a breaking heart: a heart that felt its need of solitude, of being where it could indulge its own grief unseen, unmolested. I was not, however, to gain my chamber; for, at the entrance to the east wing stood Mrs. Penn, and she arrested me.

"Come into my sitting-room," she said. "Mrs. Chandos will not be back for an hour. She is paying a visit to the west wing."

"Mr. Chandos also," I replied, as indifferently as I could speak.

"Mr. Chandos also," she assented. "They meet there more frequently than the house suspects."

"But why may they not meet? Why is it that they live estranged—or appear to do so?"

"Sit down," she said, drawing me along the passage and into a small sitting-room. "Here is a warm seat by the fire. There is estrangement between Mr. and Mrs. Chandos, but how far it precisely extends I cannot tell you."

"I did not ask you how far the estrangement extended; I asked you its cause."

"Be content with knowing what you do know, Miss Hereford, without inquiring into causes. The advice is offered you in kindness. I can tell you one thing, that never was more impassioned love given to woman than he at one time felt for Mrs. Chandos."

Ashamed I am to confess that the words caused my heart to chill and my face to burn. Mrs. Penn continued.

"He says he loves you, but, compared with the passion he once bore for Mrs. Chandos, his love for you is as *nothing*. Contrast the pale cold beams of the moon with the burning rays of a tropical sun, and you have a type of that passion, and of this one."

"Why do you say this to me? Is it well?"

"I deem it well. I say it because I think it right that you should know it: were you my own child I should say more. You have one course only before you, my dear, a plain and simple one."

"What is it?"

"To quit Chandos."

"I shall not do that."

"Not do it?"

"No."

"Miss Hereford, you *must*. Your own good sense ought to show you the necessity for leaving. By this time to-morrow evening you must have put miles between yourself and Chandos," she eagerly continued, as though she had a personal interest in my going. Hot, angry, flushed, I resented both the words and the advice.

"Mrs. Penn, you are making too much of this. I think you have taken a wrong view of things. My heart is all right, thank you."

"Is it!" she retorted. "You cannot stay on here, his companion. You *cannot*, Anne Hereford."

"I will! Whether with him as a companion or without him is not of any moment—he will not eat me. But I do not quit Chandos until my legitimate plans call me away."

In point of fact I had nowhere to go; but I did not say that. All this, and her assumption of reading my love, drove me into a perfect fit of anger.

Mrs. Penn paused, seemingly in deliberation, and when she next spoke it was in a whisper.

"Has he given you any hint of what the dark cloud is that hangs over Chandos? Of the—the crime that was committed?"

"No."

"It was a very fearful crime: the greatest social crime forbidden in the Decalogue. When the police rode up here the other night, I thought they had come for him. I know Mr. Chandos thought so."

"For whom?"

"For Mrs. Chandos's husband," she answered, in a sharp, irascible tone. "Why do you make me repeat it?"

At least I thought she need not repeat the word "husband" in my ears.

"It was murder," she continued, "if you wish to hear the plain English of it."

"Was there a trial?"

"No. That has to come. Certain"—she seemed to hesitate—"proofs are being waited for. Poor Mrs. Chandos has not been quite right since: when the moon is at the change and full they think her worse; but at all times it is well that she should be under surveillance. That is why I am here."

I did not speak; I was thinking. No doubt it was all true.

"Poor thing! the blow was enough to turn her brain," observed Mrs. Penn, musingly. "But I fancy she could never have been of strong intellect. A light, frivolous, butterfly girl, her only recommendation her beauty and soft manner."

"What you told me before was, that she had used Mr. Chandos ill."

"And so she did; very ill. But that was altogether a different matter, quite unconnected with what followed."

"How did you become acquainted with these things, Mrs. Penn?"

"In a perfectly legitimate manner. Believe me, Anne, this house is no proper home for you; Harry Chandos is an unfit companion. Quit both to-morrow."

The pertinacity vexed me almost beyond bearing. "I will think of it," I said, sharply; and getting up quickly made my escape from the room and the east wing.

Not any too soon. To go to the east wing was against the law, and as I turned into my own room, Mrs. Chandos was coming down the gallery, Mr. Chandos by her side.

"When will you get it for me, Harry?" she was saying as they passed my door.

"Shortly, I hope. The booksellers here may have to send to London for it, but I'll see that you have it as soon as possible."

He held open the door of the east wing for her to enter, and then took his way downstairs. I followed presently. Tea would be waiting and I was expected to preside at it. How could I absent myself from the routine of the house and the oak-parlour—I, who was only there on sufferance, an interloper? Were the circumstances that had passed such as I—a lady born, and reared to goodness and modesty and all rightful instincts—ought to make a commotion over? No. And I felt as if I could bite my tongue for having said what I did to Mr. Chandos just now. Henceforth, I would hold on my course in calm self-respect; meeting him civilly, forgetting, and believing that he forgot anything undesirable that had passed. As to the "crime" spoken of by Mrs. Penn—well, I thought it *could not be*: crime of any sort seemed so entirely incompatible with Mr. Chandos.

And my love? I could only resolve to beat it down, down, when-ever it rose in my heart. Others had suffered it, so must I.

He did not appear at tea. I drank mine, and Joseph came for the things. Ah, what passion is like unto! None can control it. I had resolved to put it away from me, and that whole evening it was upper-most in my thoughts! Fifty times I caught myself yearning for his presence, and saying to myself that life was a blank without him. Very shortly after taking away the tea-tray, Joseph came in again.

"I am going to close the shutters, miss."

"Very well. Who ordered it to be done?"

"The master."

"The master" meant Mr. Chandos. As Joseph put aside the cur-tains to get to the shutters, I looked out. Pacing the lawn in the moon-light, his arms folded and his head bent, was Mr. Chandos; pacing it as one in pain. And yet he had thought of me in the midst of it—of my possible timidity, and desired that the shutters should be closed.

It was nearly ten o'clock when he came into the parlour for some papers. I concluded he was going to his own sitting-room.

"Good-night!" he said, holding out his hand as usual.

Should I take it? A momentary debate with myself, and then I shook hands coldly with him. Had I not decided to let the past be as though it had never been? And all the display of resentment possible would not turn bad into good.

Days went on: days of an unsatisfactory life. Dr. Laken came over, and stayed two of them. Of Mr. Chandos I saw little: he was out and about, and more than usual in the west wing. I seemed estranged from every one. Mrs. Penn I shunned; Mr. Chandos was courteous to me, but nothing more; and I had never been intimate with any one else in the house.

And now I resolved to leave. It would not look *now* as though I hurried away in anger, or because I feared my own love. Heaven knows I wished to do right, whatever it cost me; and reason pointed out that to remain longer was not only inexpedient but might be so looked upon. The life for me was beginning to be intolerable. He was with me at times, the very fact of his presence feeding the love that held possession of me; and the image of Mrs. Chandos upstairs began to haunt me as a spectre. It was not possible any longer to deceive myself with fine resolutions; my eyes were opened to the fact that I could not begin to forget him or to love him less as long as I stayed at Chandos.

I wrote to Madame de Mellissie, telling her that I felt obliged to cancel my engagement with her, and should leave Chandos. Then I wrote to the Misses Barlieu, asking them to receive me whilst I looked out for another situation, and begging them not to refuse me on the score of the fever: I was not afraid of it; and I need not go near the infirmary. But I truly hoped and expected it had by that time passed away.

It was a fine afternoon, and a fancy came over me to take the letters to the village post-office instead of leaving them on the hall-table, so I put on my things. In going out at the portico I met Mrs. Penn.

"Do you know that you are looking ill—that this struggle is telling upon you?" she abruptly exclaimed, but in tones full of kindness. "Why don't you make an effort, and quit it?"

"The effort is made," I answered, half in anger, half in despair, as I held up the letters in my hand. "Here is the announcement to those who will, I hope, receive me. I must await the answer, and then I bid adieu to Chandos."

"My dear, you have done well," she answered, as she passed into the house, and I out of the portico.

Leaning against the wall, on the far side, was Mr. Chandos, who must have heard what had been said. That she was unconscious of his vicinity, I was certain, and, for myself, I started when I saw him. He said something, but I made as if I did not hear, and went quickly on.

The post-office was farther than I thought. I picked a few ferns, and lingered on my road in miserable musing. By the time I turned homeward again, it had grown dusk. There was a lane near to Chandos, which led to a small entrance-gate at an obscure part of the grounds: it was called the laurel-gate, because many laurels grew near it. By taking this way I should cut off a good deal of the road, and down the lane I turned. Very much to my surprise, I came by-and-by to a cottage. A cottage I had never seen before; and was very sorry to see it now, for it proved to me that I had turned down the wrong lane.

It was the waste of time that vexed me; but all I could do was to retrace my steps back to the right lane. It was almost dark night when I at length reached the laurel-gate; some of the stars were beginning to shine.

The gate was unlatched, as if the last person who passed through had omitted to close it. A narrow path led to other narrow paths, which branched off through the trees; I hesitated which to take, not being certain which would lead me soonest to the house; and as I stood thinking, a dark form came following me down the lane. It was Mr. Edwin Barley's.

The darkness of the night, the superstition attaching to the place, the proximity of the man I so dreaded, brought sufficient terror with them. He might be coming to seize me and claim me! Fear lent me wings. Flying up a path at hazard, I never ceased until I was in the broad walk, and close—it was rather curious that it should be so—to Mr. Chandos. He was coming in from an errand to the lodge.

With a sense of protection, I rested my hand on his arm. All considerations were merged in the moment's terror. I forgot his great offence; I forgot my own self-esteem: standing there, he appeared to me only as a protector, one in whom I might find safety and shelter.

"Oh, Mr. Chandos! In mercy take care of me!"

"What has alarmed you?" he asked, in tones a great deal too full of tenderness.

My only answer was to draw back amidst the side trees, that I might be hidden from Edwin Barley. Mr. Chandos came and stood there also.

"What is it, Anne? The ghost? Or Edwin Barley again?"

My senses were in a degree returning to me, and I told him what had occurred; turning my head to listen still.

"He will not follow you here. As to the lane, usage has made it public property, and he has a right to walk in it if he chooses."

I turned to the house. He quietly put my arm within his. "Suffer it to be so for an instant, Anne; you are trembling still."

And so we went on thus.

"What was it I heard you say to Mrs. Penn about leaving Chandos?"

"I think the time has come for me to leave it. If the Miss Barlieus can receive me, I shall go to them. I have written to ask."

"That's the letter you have been so far to post! Were you afraid I should intercept it?—as mine was intercepted?"

"Not that. I thought the walk would be pleasant."

"Rather too late a one, nevertheless!"

I did not tell him that I had wasted my time in it, picking ferns, thinking, and finally losing my way. "What's this?" said Mr. Chandos.

He alluded to the handful of ferns I carried, and without ceremony took one of the best sprays and put it in his coat "as a keepsake."

"If you are to leave, Anne, I must have something to remind me of you!"

There was a light sound in his voice, which seemed to say he treated the idea of my leaving as a jest; as if he knew I should not go.

"I *shall* leave, Mr. Chandos!"

"Not just yet, at any rate. Madame de Mellissie left you with us, and to her only can we resign you!"

"I have written to Madame de Mellissie also, telling her I now take my plans upon myself."

"Oh, been posting that letter also, I suppose! Go you must not, Anne; I cannot part with you."

Every right feeling within me rose in rebellion against the avowal, and I strove to withdraw my arm, but my strength was as nothing in his firm grasp.

"I cannot part with you, I say; it would be like parting with life. These last few days—when we have been living in estrangement—have sufficed to show me what it would be were you to be away entirely. And so—"

"But you know you ought not to say this to me, Mr. Chandos!" I interrupted, speaking passionately through my blinding tears. "It is unworthy of you. What have I done that you should so insult me?"

"Listen to me for a minute, Anne. I have been weighing things calmly and dispassionately; it has been my employment since the night of the explanation, when you told me you had become cognizant of deterring circumstances. I have endeavoured to judge unselfishly, as though the interest lay with another—not with myself; and I confess I cannot see any good reason why you should not become my wife. I mean, of course, later; when difficulties that exist now shall be removed from my path."

It was strangely puzzling to hear him speak in this manner. I had always deemed him to be of a most honourable nature, one to whom the bare allusion of anything not good and perfect and upright, would be distasteful. Before I knew of existing circumstances, it had been bad enough to speak to me of love; but now—Whether he had taken my silence for acquiescence I know not; I suppose there can be no doubt of it; but he suddenly bent his head and left some kisses on my face. Was he insane, or only a bad man?

"I could not help it," he hastily murmured in agitation. "I know it is wrong and foolish, but a man has not always his actions under cold control, Forgive me, Anne! Stay here to gladden me: and hope, with me, that things will work round for us. I should not bid you do so without good reason,"

A variety of emotions nearly choked me. His words told upon me more than his kisses. How could things work round so that he might be free, except by one event, the death of his wife?—and she was young and healthy! How dared he during this, her lifetime, urge me to remain there to gladden him? But for the strongest control, I should have burst into hysterical tears, born of indignation and excitement; and little reeked I what I said in my anger, as I wrenched my arm away from him.

"Things work round, Mr. Chandos! Are your thoughts glancing to a second murder?"

I borrowed the word from Mrs. Penn's mysterious communication—which I had never believed. It was very bad of me to say it; I know it only too well; but in such moments one does not wait to choose words.

"Anne, you might have spared me that reproach," he rejoined, in a subdued tone of pain.

"How have you spared me?"

"It may end brightly yet; it may indeed. What's that?"

A rustling amidst the dense shrubs on the right caused the question. Possibly with an idea that it might be Edwin Barley, Mr. Chandos quitted me to look. I darted across the road, and plunged into the trees, intending to go on by a by-path, and so escape him. Suddenly I came upon Lizzy Dene, talking to a man. She started back, with a faint cry.

"I am going right for the house, am I not, Lizzy?"

"Quite so, miss. Take the path on the right when you come to the weeping elm."

I had nearly gained the tree, when Lizzy Dene came up with me. The woman seemed to be in agitation as great as mine.

"Miss," she began, "will you do me a favour, and not mention who you saw me talking to?"

"I should be clever to mention it, Lizzy. I don't know him."

"But, please miss, not to say you saw me talking to any one. The young man is not a sweetheart, I assure you; he is a relation; but those servants are dreadful scandal-mongers."

"You need not fear; it is no affair of mine. And I am not in the habit of carrying tales to servants."

She continued to walk a little behind me. It seemed I was to have nothing but encounters. There, on a garden-chair, as we turned on to the lawn, sat Mrs. Penn.

"I am sitting here to recover breath," she said, in answer to my exclamation. "It has been taken away by surprise. I don't quite know whether I am awake or dreaming."

"Have you seen the ghost, ma'am?" asked Lizzy, breathlessly, putting her own comment on the words.

"Well, I don't know; I should just as soon have expected to see one as Lady Chandos. She was in the Pine Walk."

"Impossible, Mrs. Penn," I exclaimed.

"Impossible or possible, Miss Hereford, Lady Chandos it was," she answered, resolutely. "I can tell you I rubbed my eyes when I caught sight of her, believing they must see things that were not. She wore a black silk cloak, and had a black hood over her head. It was certainly Lady Chandos; and she seemed to be walking to take the air."

To hear that any lady, confined to her bed, was suddenly walking abroad in a damp, dark night to take the air, was inconceivable. It was altogether so to Lizzy Dene. Her eyes grew round with wonder as they were turned on Mrs. Penn.

"Then I say with miss here that it's just impossible. My lady's no more capable of walking out, ma'am, than—"

"I tell you I saw her," conclusively interrupted Mrs. Penn. "It was twenty minutes ago, just before it grew quite dark. I came and sat down here, waiting for her to pass me: which she has not done. But I suppose there are other paths by which she could gain the house. Lizzy, how obstinate you look over it!"

"And enough to make me, ma'am; when I know that my lady it *could not* be."

"Do you see much of her?" asked Mrs. Penn.

"Me! Neither me nor nobody else, ma'am. If ever Hill calls me to help with a room in the west wing, my lady has first been moved out of it. Since her illness, Hill does the work there herself. No, no; it never was my lady. Unless—unless—oh, goodness grant it may not be—unless she's dead!"

"Why, what does the girl mean?" cried Mrs. Penn, tartly.

Lizzy Dene had suddenly flown into one of her rather frequent phases of superstition, and began to explain with a shiver.

"It is just this," she whispered, glancing timidly over her shoulder. "Hill was in some distress at mid-day; we servants asked her what was the matter, and she said my lady was worse; as ill as she could be. Now, it is well known, in the moment of death people have appeared to others at a distance. I think my lady must have died, and it was her spirit that Mrs. Penn has just seen in the Pine Walk. Oh! ah! oh!"

Lizzy Dene wound up with three shrieks. In some curiosity—to say the least of it—we crossed the lawn. It *was* curious that Lady Chandos, if worse, should be abroad. Hickens was at the hall-door, looking out probably for me. It was past dinner-time.

"How is Lady Chandos?" I impulsively asked.

"I have not thought to inquire this evening, miss. I suppose much as usual."

"Isn't she dead?" put in Lizzy.

"Dead!" he echoed, staring at the girl. "Anyway, there's a basin of arrowroot just gone up for her, and I never heard that dead people wanted anything to eat. What crotchet have you in your head now, Lizzy Dene?"

I think we all looked a little foolish. Mrs. Penn laughed as she ran in; Lizzy Dene went round to the servants' entrance.

"Hickens," I said, in a low tone, passing him to go upstairs, "I have a headache, and shall not take any dinner. Perhaps Harriet will kindly light a fire in my room, and bring me up some tea."

For I had caught a glimpse of Mr. Chandos and dinner both waiting for me in the oak-parlour.

# CHAPTER 26

## GETTING INTO THE WEST WING

Sitting by the fire in the pretty bedroom with the candles on the table, and the chintz curtains drawn before the window, shutting out the Pine Walk and any unearthly sight that might be in it, I thought and resolved. To remain at Chandos with its ostensible master in his present mood was almost an impossibility; and I began to think I might leave it without waiting for an answer from Miss Barlieu. The chief difficulty would be getting away; the actual departure; for Mr. Chandos was certain to oppose it. Another difficulty was money.

It struck me that the only feasible plan would be to see Lady Chandos. I would tell her that I must go, not mentioning the reason; ask her to sanction it, and to lend me sufficient money to take me to Nulle. I did not see that I could leave without seeing her; certainly not without making her acquainted with the fact, and thanking her for her hospitality and kindness. Heroines of romance might take flight from dwellings by night; but I was nothing of the sort; only a rational girl of sober, everyday life, and I must act accordingly.

"Do you happen to know how Lady Chandos is to-night, Harriet?" I asked, when the maid came in to inquire whether I wanted anything more.

"Her ladyship's a trifle better, miss, I have just heard Hill say so."

Harriet left the room; and I sat thinking as before. That seeing Lady Chandos could only be accomplished by stratagem I knew, for Hill was a very dragon in guarding that west wing. If it was really Lady Chandos who had been pacing the grounds—and Mrs. Penn was positive in her assertion and belief—she must undoubtedly be well enough to speak to me. It was only a few words I had to say to her; a few minutes that I should detain her. "Circumstances have called me away, but I could not leave without personally acquainting you, madam, and thanking you for your hospitality and kindness." Something to that effect: and then I would borrow the money—about forty or fifty francs; which Miss Barlieu would give me to remit, as soon as I reached Nulle. If Lady Chandos sanctioned my departure, Mr. Chandos could not put forth any plea to detain me.

Never were plans better laid than mine—as I thought. Rehearsing them over and over again in my mind after I lay in bed, the usual sleeplessness followed. I tossed and turned from side to side; I counted, I repeated verses; all in vain. Sleep had gone from me, and I heard the clock strike two.

I heard something else: a stir in the gallery. It seemed as if some one rushed from the doors of the west wing, and came swiftly to the chamber of Mr. Chandos. In the stillness of night, sounds are plainly heard that would be inaudible by day. The footsteps were like Hill's. There was a brief whispering in Mr. Chandos's chamber, and the same footsteps ran back to the west wing.

What could be the matter? Was Lady Chandos worse? Almost as I asked myself the question, I heard Mr. Chandos come out of his room, go downstairs, and out at the hall-door. Curiosity led me to look from the windows The stars were shining brilliantly; I suppose it was a frosty night; and the dark pine-trees rose clear and defined against the sky. All was quiet.

A very few minutes and other sounds broke the silence: the foot-steps of a horse. Mr. Chandos—as I supposed it to be—came riding forth at a canter from the direction of the stables: the pace increasing to a gallop as he turned into the broad walk.

There seemed less sleep for me than ever. In about an hour's time I heard Mr. Chandos ride in again. I heard him ride round to the sta-bles, and return on foot. He let himself in at the hall-door, came softly upstairs, and went into the west wing. It was in that wing that some-thing must be happening.

I was almost dressed in the morning when Mrs. Penn knocked at my door and entered. I did wish she would not thus interrupt me! Once she had come when I was reading my chapter; once during my prayers.

"Did you hear any disturbance in the night?" she began. "Mr. Chandos went out at two o'clock. Do you know what for?"

"Mrs. Penn! How should I be likely to know?"

"I happened to be up, looking from the end window—"

"At that time of night?" I interrupted.

"Yes, at that time of night," she repeated. "I was watching for—for—the ghost if you will" (but I thought somehow she said this to mystify me), "and so I may as well confess it. I often do watch from my window at night. Suddenly a figure appeared making its way swiftly towards the stables; my heart stood still for a moment; I thought the ghost had come at last. But soon I recognized Mr. Chandos, and presently saw him return on horseback. Where did he go to? For what purpose?"

"You put the questions as though you thought I could answer them," I said to her; and so she did, speaking in a demanding sort of way. "I cannot tell where Mr. Chandos has gone."

"He is back again now: he was home again in about an hour. I would give the world to know!"

"But why? What business is it of yours or mine? Mr. Chandos's movements are nothing to us."

"They are so much to us—to me—that I would forfeit this to be able to follow him about and see where he goes and what he does," she said, holding up her right hand.

I looked at her in wonder.

"I would. Is it not a singular sort of thing that a gentleman should rise from his bed at two o'clock in the morning, saddle his horse by stealth, and ride forth on a mysterious journey?"

"It is singular. But he may not have saddled his horse by stealth."

"How now?" she tartly answered. "He did saddle it; saddled it himself."

"Yes: but that may have been only from a wish not to disturb the grooms from their rest. To do a thing one's self with a view of sparing others, and to do it stealthily are two things."

"So your spirit must rise up to defend him still! Take care of yourself, Anne Hereford!"

"Nay, there was no defence. What does it signify whether Mr. Chandos saddles a horse for himself or gets a man to saddle it?"

"Not much, perhaps; looking at it in the light you do."

"Mrs. Penn, I wish you would please to go, and allow me to finish dressing. I am afraid of being late."

Rather to my surprise, she moved to the door without another word, and shut it behind her.

I went down to breakfast: I could not help myself. It would not do to plead illness, and ask to have my meals sent upstairs. But we had a third at table, I found; and that was Dr. Laken. I am not sure how I and Mr. Chandos should have got on without him; with him all went smoothly.

But not merrily. For both he and Mr. Chandos spoke and looked as if under the influence of some great care. Listening to their conversation, I discovered a rather singular circumstance. Mr. Chandos's errand in the night had been to the telegraph-office at Warsall, to send an imperative message for Dr. Laken. That gentleman (almost as though a prevision had been upon him that he would be wanted) had started for Chandos the previous evening by a night train, and was at Chandos at seven in the morning. So that he and the message crossed each other. His visit was of course—though I was not told so—to Lady Chandos; and I feared there must be some dangerous change in her. They talked together, without reference to me.

"I wish you could have remained," Mr. Chandos suddenly said to the doctor.

"I wish I could. I have told you why I am obliged to go, and where. I will be back to-night, if possible; if not, early to-morrow. Remember one thing, Mr. Harry—that my staying here could be of no real use. It is a satisfaction to you, of course, that I should be at hand, but I can do nothing."

"Mr. Dexter is here, sir, and wishes to see you," said Hickens, entering the parlour at this juncture. "He says he is sorry to disturb you so early, sir, but he is off to that sale of stock, and must speak to you first. I have shown him into your private room, sir."

Mr. Chandos rose from his seat and went out. And now came my turn. I was alone with Dr. Laken, and seized the opportunity to inquire about Lady Chandos. See her I must, and would.

"Is Lady Chandos alarmingly ill, Dr. Laken?

He was occupied with an egg at the time, and he did not speak immediately: his attention seemed almost equally divided between looking at me and finishing the egg.

"What you young ladies might call alarmingly ill, we old doctors might not," were his words, when he at length spoke.

"Can she speak?"

"Oh yes."

"And is sufficiently well to understand, if any one speaks to her?"

"Quite so. Don't trouble yourself, my dear, about Lady Chandos. I trust she will be all right with time."

Not another word did I get from him. He began talking of the weather; and then took up a newspaper until Mr. Chandos returned. As I was leaving them alone after breakfast, Mr. Chandos spoke to me in a half-grave, half-jesting tone.

"You are one of the family, you know, Miss Hereford, and may be asked to keep its affairs close, just as Emily would be were she here. Don't mention that I went to Warsall in the night—as you have now heard that I did go. It is of no use to make the household uneasy."

And, as if to enforce the words, Dr. Laken nodded emphatically. I bowed and withdrew.

To see Lady Chandos? How was it to be done? And, in spite of Dr. Laken's reassuring answer, I scarcely knew what to believe. Hill went about with a solemn face, silent as the grave; and an impression ran through the household that something was very much amiss in the west wing. My impression was, that there was a great deal of unaccountable mystery somewhere.

"Harriet," I said, as the girl came to my room in the course of her duties, "how is Lady Chandos?"

"Well, miss, we can't quite make out," was the answer. "Hill is in dreadful trouble, and the doctor is here again; but Lizzy Dene saw my lady for a minute this morning, and she looked much as usual."

So far well. To Lady Chandos I determined to penetrate ere the day should close. And I am sure, had any one seen me that morning, dodging into the gallery from my room and back again, they would have deemed me haunted by a restless spirit. I was watching my opportunity. It did not come for nearly all day. In the morning Dr. Laken and Mr. Chandos were there; in the afternoon Hill was shut up in it. It was growing dusk when I, still on the watch, saw Hill come forth. She left the door ajar, as if she intended to return instantly, and went into a large linen-closet close by. Now was my time. I glided past the closet, quiet as a mouse, and within the green-baize door of the west wing.

But which was the room of Lady Chandos? No time was to be lost, for if Hill returned, she was sure to eject me summarily, as she had done once before. I softly opened two doors, taking no notice of what the rooms might contain, looking only whether Lady Chandos was inside. Next I came to one, and opened it, as I had the others; and saw—what? Who—who was it sitting there? Not Lady Chandos.

In a large arm-chair near the fire, propped up with pillows, sat an emaciated object, white, thin, cadaverous. A tall man evidently, bearing in features a great resemblance to Mr. Chandos, a strange likeness to that ghostly vision—if it had been one—I had seen in the gallery. Was he the ghost?—sitting there and staring at me with his large eyes, but never speaking? If not a ghost, it must be a living skeleton.

My pulses stood still; my heart leaped into my mouth. The figure raised his arm, and pointed peremptorily to the door with his long, lank, white fingers. A sign that I must quit his presence.

I was glad to do so. Startled, terrified, bewildered, I thought no more of Lady Chandos, but went back through the passage, and out at the green-baize door. There, face to face, I encountered Mr. Chandos.

I shall not readily forget his face when he looked at me. Never had greater haughtiness, rarely greater anger, appeared in the countenance of living man.

"Have you been in there?" he demanded.

"Yes. I—" More I could not say. The words died on my lips.

"Listen, Miss Hereford," he said, his face working with emotion. "I am grieved to be compelled to say anything discourteous to a lady, more especially to you, but I must forbid you to approach these rooms, however powerfully your curiosity may urge you to visit them. I act as the master of Chandos, and demand it as a right. Your business lies at the other end of the gallery; this end is sacred, and must be kept so from intrusion."

I stole away with my crimson face, with a crimsoned brain, I think, wishing the gallery floor would open and admit me. Hill came out of the closet with wondering eyes; Mr. Chandos went on, and closed the door of the west wing after him. I felt ashamed to faintness. My "curiosity!"

But who could it be, he whom I had just seen, thus closeted in the apartments of Lady Chandos? Could it be Sir Thomas, arrived from abroad? But when did he arrive? and why this concealment in his mother's rooms? for concealment it appeared to be. Whoever it was, he was fearfully ill and wasted: of that there could be no doubt; ill, as it seemed to me, almost unto death; and a conviction came over me that Dr. Laken's visits were paid to him, not to Lady Chandos.

"My dear child, how flushed and strange you look!"

The speaker was Mrs. Penn, interrupting my chain of thought. She was standing at the door of the east wing, came forward, and turned with me into my room.

"Anne," she continued, her tones full of gentle compassion, "was Mr. Chandos speaking in that manner to you?"

"I deserved it," I sighed, "for I really had no right to enter the west wing clandestinely. I went there in search of Lady Chandos. I want to leave, but I cannot go without first seeking her, and I thought I would try to do so, in spite of Hill."

"And did you see her?" questioned Mrs. Penn.

"No; I could not see her anywhere; I suppose I did not go into all the rooms. But I saw some one else."

"Who was it?"

"The strangest being," I answered, too absorbed in the subject, too surprised and bewildered, to observe my usual custom of telling nothing to Mrs. Penn. "He was sitting in an easy-chair, supported by pillows; a tall, emaciated man, looking—oh, so ill! His face was the thinnest and whitest I ever saw; but it bore a likeness to Mr. Chandos."

Had I been more collected, I might have seen how the revelation affected Mrs. Penn. Just then my eyes and senses were, so to say, blinded. She put her hand on my arm, listening for more.

"He startled me terribly; I declare that, at first sight, I thought it was a ghost. Why should he be hidden there?—if he is hidden. Unless it is Sir Thomas Chandos come home from India—Mrs. Penn! what's the matter?"

The expression of her countenance at length arrested me. Her face had turned white, her lips were working with excitement.

"For the love of Heaven, wait!" she uttered. "A tall man, bearing a family likeness to Mr. Chandos—was that what you said?"

"A striking likeness: allowing for the fact that Mr. Chandos is in health, and that the other looks as though he were dying. The eyes are not alike: his are large and dark, Mr. Chandos's blue. Why? Perhaps it is only Sir Thomas Chandos."

"It is not Sir Thomas; he is a short, plain man, resembling his mother. No, no; I know too well who it is; and it explains the mystery of that west wing. All that has been so unaccountable to me since I have dwelt at Chandos is quite plain now. Dolt that I was, never to have suspected it! Oh! but they were clever dissemblers, with their illnesses of my Lady Chandos!"

She went out, and darted into the east wing. So astonished was I, that I stood looking after her, and saw her come quietly forth again after a minute or two, attired to go out. She was gliding down the stairs, when Mrs. Chandos also came from the east wing and called to her.

"Mrs. Penn, where are you going? I want you."

Mrs. Penn, thus arrested, turned round, a vexed expression on her face.

"I wish to do a very slight errand for myself, madam. I shall not be long."

"I cannot spare you now; I cannot, indeed. You must defer it until to-morrow. I will not remain by myself now that it is getting dark. I am as nervous as I can be this evening. You are not half so attentive as Mrs. Freeman was: you are always away, or wanting to be away."

Mrs. Penn came slowly up the stairs again, untying her bonnet-strings. But I saw she had a great mind to rebel, and depart on her errand in defiance of her mistress.

What could it be that she was so anxious for? what was she going to do? As she had passed to the stairs before being called back, the words, "Down now with the Chandoses!" had reached my ears from her lips, softly spoken. I felt sick and frightened. What mischief might I not have caused by my incautious revelation? It seemed as though I had been treacherous to Chandos.

Restless and uncomfortable, I was going into the oak-parlour a little later, when Lizzy Dene, in a smart new bonnet and plaid shawl, a small basket on her arm, came into the hall to say something to Hickens, who was there.

"I suppose I may go out at this door, now I'm here?" said she, afterwards; and Hickens grunted out "Yes" as he withdrew. At that self-same moment Mrs. Penn came softly and swiftly down the stairs, and called to her. Neither of them saw me, just inside the parlour.

"You are going out, I see, Lizzy. Will you do a little errand for me?"

"If it won't take long," was the girl's free answer. "But I have got leave to go out to tea, and am an hour later than I thought to be."

"It will not take you a minute out of your way. You know where Mr. Edwin Barley lives—the new tenant. Go to his house with this note, and desire that it may be given to him: should he not be at home, say that it must be handed to him the instant he comes in. If you do this promptly, and keep it to yourself, mind! I will give you a crown piece!"

"I'll do it, and say 'thank ye,' too, ma'am," laughed Lizzy, in glee.

She opened the lid of her basket, popped in the note, and went out at the hall-door. Mrs. Penn disappeared upstairs.

But Lizzy Dene had halted in the portico, and had her face turned towards the skies.

"Now, is it going to rain?—or is it only the dark of the evening?" she deliberated aloud. "Better take an umbrella. I should not like my new shawl spoilt; and they didn't warrant the blue in it, if it got a soaking."

She put down the basket, and ran back to the kitchen. Now was my opportunity. I stole to the basket, lifted the lid, and took out the letter, trusting to good luck, and to Lizzy's not looking into the basket on her return.

She did not. She came back with the umbrella, snatched up the basket, and went down the broad walk, at a run.

With the letter grasped in my hand, I was hastening to my own room to read it in peace-

"Read it!" interposes the reader, aghast at the action. "Read it?"

Yes; read it. I believed that that letter was full of treachery to Chandos, and that I had unwittingly contributed to raise it, through my incautious revelation. Surely it was my duty now to do what I could to avert it, even though it involved opening Mrs. Penn's letter. A sudden light seemed to have opened upon her—whispering a doubt that she was treacherous.

But in the hall I met dinner coming in, and Mr. Chandos with it. Putting the note inside my dress, I sat down to table.

It was a silent dinner, except for the most ordinary courtesies. Mr. Chandos was grave, preoccupied, and sorrowful; I was as grave and preoccupied as he. When the servants had left, he drew a dish of walnuts towards him, peeled some, and passed them to me; then he began to peel for himself. I felt inclined to refuse them, but somehow words failed me.

"Anne, I have not understood you the last few days."

The address took me by surprise, for there had been a long silence. He did not raise his eyes to me as he spoke, but kept them on the walnuts.

"Have you not, sir?"

"What could have induced you to intrude into the west wing, to-day? Pardon the word, if it grates upon your ear; that part of Chandos House is strictly private; private and sacred; known to be so by all inmates; and, for any one to enter unsolicited, is an intrusion."

"I am sorry that I went in—very sorry; no one can repent of it now more than I do; but I had an urgent motive for wishing to see Lady Chandos. I wish to see her still, if possible; I do not like to leave Chandos without it."

"You are not going to leave Chandos?"

"I leave to-morrow, if it be practicable. If not, the next day."

"No," he said; "it must not be. I act for my mother, and refuse her sanction."

Too vexed to answer, too vexed to remain at table, I rose and went to the fire, standing with my back to him.

"What has changed you?" he abruptly asked.

"Changed me?"

"For some days now you have been unlike yourself. Why visit upon me the sins of another? I suffer sufficiently as it is; I suffer always."

I could not understand the speech any more than if it had been Greek, and glanced to him for explanation.

"I look back on my past conduct, and cannot see that I am to blame. We were thrown together by circumstances; and if love stole unconsciously over us, it was neither my fault nor yours. I was wrong, you will say, to avow this love; I believe I was; it might have been better that I had held my tongue. But—"

"It would be better that you should hold it now, sir. I do not wish to enter upon any explanation. Quit your house, I will. Lady Chandos, were she made acquainted with what has passed, would be the first to send me from it."

Mr. Chandos rose and stood up by me. "Am I to understand that you wish to quit it because I have spoken of this love?"

"Yes; and because—because it is no longer a fit residence for me."

"Do you wish to imply that under no circumstances—that is, with any barrier that may exist now against my marrying removed—would you accept my love?"

"I wish to imply—to say—that not under any alteration of circumstances that the world can bring about, would I accept your love, Mr. Chandos. The very fact of your naming it to me is an insult."

And yet how passionately was I loving him in my heart all the time, even as I spoke it!

"Very well. In that case it may be better that you quit Chandos. Should Miss Barlieu's answer prove favourable—I mean, if she assures you that danger from the fever is past—you shall be conveyed there under proper escort."

"Thank you," I interrupted, feeling, I do believe, not half as grateful as I ought.

"A moment yet. In case the danger is not past, you must remain here a little longer. There is no help for it. I will promise not to speak another unwelcome word to you, and to give you as little of my company as possible. We will both ignore the past as a pleasant dream, just as though it had not existed. Will this content you?"

"Yes, sir."

"Then I give you my honour that after this evening it shall be so. But we must have a few words together first. I have already intimated that I should not have spoken so soon but for perceiving that love had arisen on your side as well as mine. Now don't fly off at a tangent: I intend to have an explanation from you this night: an explanation that shall set things straight between us, or sever us for ever. We are not boy and girl that we should shrink from it. At least, if you are only a girl in years, you have sense and prudence and right feeling that belong rather to double your age."

Standing there before me, calm and resolute, I knew there could be no avoidance of the explanation he sought. His was the master-spirit. But it was cruel to wish me to give it in words. And so utterly needless!

"If I allude to your love for me, it is not needlessly to pain, or, as you may think, insult you: believe me, when I say it; but only to call to your notice the inconsistency of your conduct. It is of this that I require an explanation. Anne, you know you loved me. Whence, then, the sudden change?"

"I did not know your position then," I answered, meeting the words as I supposed he wished to force me to meet them, and taking a step backwards on the hearthrug.

"I can only think you must in some way be mistaking my position. Circumstances, very sad and grievous circumstances, are rendering it of brighter prospect. I am aware of the misfortune that attaches to my family, the disgrace that is reflected upon me: but you should not treat me as though the disgrace or the fault were mine. Surely there is no justice in resenting it on me! You might have rejected me with civility."

"I do not know what you are saying," I interrupted, passionately. "What is it to me, the disgrace attaching to your family? That could not sway me. It is unknown to me."

"Unknown to you?" he repeated in accents of surprise.

"Quite unknown, except for vague rumours that I have not cared to attend to. The disgrace lies with you, sir, not with your family."

"With me? What have I done? Do you mean in having spoken to you of love?" he added, finding I did not answer. "At least, I do not see that disgrace could be charged on me for that. I intended to lay the case openly before you, and it would have been at your option to accept or reject me."

"Do you call deceit and dishonour no disgrace, Mr. Chandos?"

"Great disgrace. But I have not been guilty of either."

"You have been guilty of both."

"When? and how?"

"To me. You know it. You know it, sir. Had my father been alive; had I any friend in the world to protect me, I do not think you would have dared to speak to me of love."

"Were your father, Colonel Hereford, alive, Anne, I should lay the whole case before him, and say—'Judge for yourself; shall, or shall not your daughter be mine?' I fancy he would find the objection less insuperable than you appear to do."

I believe I simply stared in answer to this. Calm, good, and noble he looked, standing there with his truthful eyes, speaking his apparently truthful words. It seemed that we must be at cross-purposes.

"When you spoke of the bar that existed to your marrying, you put it upon the misfortunes, the disgrace attaching to your family, Mr. Chandos. But you never alluded to the real bar."

"There is no other bar. But for that, I should like to make you my wife to-morrow. What have you got in your head?"

I knew what I was beginning to have in my temper. "If you continue to detain me here, sir, and to say these things, I will go straight with my complaint to Mrs. Chandos."

"To Mrs. Chandos! What good would that do?" he coolly questioned.

"Oh, sir, spare me! I did not think you would behave so. Don't you see, putting me and my feelings out of the question, how all this wrongs her?"

He looked at me strangely, his countenance puzzled. "What has Mrs. Chandos to do with it? She is nothing to you or to me."

"She is your wife, sir."

His elbow displaced some ornament on the mantelpiece; he had to turn and save it from falling. Then he faced me again.

"My wife, did you say?"

And very much ashamed I had felt to say it: with my hot face and my eyes bent on the carpet.

"Mrs. Chandos is no wife of mine. I never was married yet. Did you fall asleep and dream it?"

Ah, how that poor foolish heart of mine stood still! Was it possible that Mrs. Penn had been mistaken?—that my misery had been without foundation; my insults only fancied ones. No condemned criminal, called from his cell to hear the reprieve read that will restore to him the life he has forfeited, could experience a more intense revulsion of joy than I did then.

I put my hands up before him: it was no moment for affectation or reticence.

"Tell me the truth," I gasped; "the truth as before Heaven. Is, or is not, Mrs. Chandos your wife?"

He bent his head a little forward, speaking clearly and distinctly, with an emphasis on every word.

"Mrs. Chandos is my sister-in-law. She is my brother's wife. It is the truth, in the presence of Heaven."

I covered my face with my hands to hide the blinding tears, my cheeks of shame. To have made so dreadful a mistake! and to have spoken of it!

Mr. Chandos took the hands away, holding them and me before him.

"Having said so much, Anne, you must say more. Has this been the cause of your changed conduct? Whence could the strange notion have arisen?"

I spoke a few words as well as I could; just the heads of what I had heard, and from whom.

"Mrs. Penn! Why, she of all people must know better. She knows who Mrs. Chandos's husband is. Surely she cannot be mistaking me for my brother!"

"I thought, sir, you had no brother, except Sir Thomas."

"Yes, I have another brother," he answered in a whisper. "You saw him to-day, Anne."

"That poor sick gentleman, who looks so near the grave?"

"Even so. It is he who is the husband of Mrs. Chandos. The fact of his being at Chandos is unknown, not to be spoken of," he said, sinking his voice still lower, and glancing round the walls of the room, as though he feared they might contain eavesdroppers. "Take care that it does not escape your lips."

Alas! it had escaped them. I bent my head and my troubled face, wondering whether I ought to confess it to him. But he spoke again.

"And so—this is the silly dream you have been losing yourself in! Anne! could you not have trusted me better?"

"You must forgive me," I said, looking piteously at him through my tears.

"Will you recall your vow, child; never—under any circumstances that the world can bring forth—to accept any love?" he whispered. "Oh, Anne, my darling! it would be cruel of you to part us."

Never more would I doubt him, never more. True, kind, good, his face was bent, waiting for the answer. My whole heart, my trust went out to him, then and for ever. I lifted my eyes and stole my hand into his. Down came his kisses upon my lips by way of sealing the compact.

"And so you are willing to trust me without the explanation?"

"Quite willing," I whispered. "I am certain you have not been guilty of any crime."

"Never; so help me Heaven," he fervently answered. "But disgrace reflects upon me, for all that, and you must give your final decision when you have heard it."

I sat down: he put his elbow on the mantelpiece as before.

"Anne, you will not run away from Chandos now?"

"Not to-morrow, sir."

"Am I to be 'sir' always, you shy child? But about this fable of yours connecting me with Mrs. Chandos? It could scarcely have been Mrs. Penn who imparted it to you?"

"Indeed it was. She said a great deal more than that."

"It is not possible she can be mistaking me for my brother," he repeated, deliberating with himself. "That cannot be, for she believes him to be a fugitive. This is very strange, Anne."

Perhaps Mrs. Penn is false, I thought in my inmost heart. Perhaps she has a motive in wishing me to leave Chandos? She had certainly done her best to forward it—and to prejudice me against him.

"Do you know Mrs. Penn to be true to your interests, Mr. Chandos? I mean to those of the family?"

"I know nothing about her. Of course but for being supposed to be true and honourable, she would not have been admitted here. My mother—Hark! What's that?"

A sound of wheels was heard, as of a carriage being driven to the door. Mr. Chandos turned to listen. It struck me that a sort of dread rose to his countenance.

"What troubles you?" I whispered, approaching him. "You look as if there were cause for fear."

"There is every cause for fear in this unhappy house. Do you remember the night that the police rode up, Anne? I thought surely the blow had come. I know not whom this carriage may have brought: I am not expecting any one."

We heard the door opened by one of the servants.

"It may be Dr. Laken, sir."

"No; he could not be back yet."

In bustled Hickens, faster than was usual with that solemn personage.

"It's Miss Emily, sir," said he, addressing Mr. Chandos. "That is, Madame de Mellissie. Her foreign French name never comes free to me."

Miss Emily was in the room ere Hickens had done speaking—bright, handsome, gay as ever.

"There's plenty of luggage, Hickens, mind; you must see to it with Pauline," were her first words. "And how are you, Harry?" she continued, putting up her mouth to be kissed.

"This is an unexpected visit, Emily," he said, as he took the kiss. "You should have written us word, and I would have met you at the station with the carriage. How did you come from it?"

"Oh, I found a conveyance of some sort; a fly, or a chaise, I hardly know what it was, except that I believe it had no springs, for it shook me to pieces. How is mamma?"

"Won't you speak to me, Madame de Mellissie?" I asked, holding out my hand. I had stood there waiting for her to notice me, which she did not appear to have the least intention of doing.

"I hope you are well," was her reply, but she pointedly and rudely neglected my offered hand.

"How did you leave your husband?" Mr. Chandos hastily asked, as a sort of covering to her ill manners.

"Well neither in health nor in temper. I ran away."

"Ran away!"

"Of course I did. I received a letter, some days past—"

"Yes, I wrote to you," I interrupted.

"You!" she rudely said, in condemning tones. "I am not alluding to your letter. When this other letter arrived, I told Alfred I must go at once to Chandos. 'Very well,' said he, 'I shall be able to take you in a day or so.' But the days went on, and still he was too ill; or said he was. 'I must go,' I said to him yesterday morning. 'I must and I will,' and that put him up. 'Listen, ma chère,' cried he, in his cool way, 'I am too ill to travel, and there's no one else to take you, so you can't go; therefore let us hear no more about it.' Merci, monsieur! I thought to myself; and I forthwith told Pauline to pack up, and get the boxes out of the house en cachette. She did so, and I followed them, Alfred and Madame la Mère believing I had gone for a drive in the Bois de Boulogne. A pretty long drive they must think it by this time."

"Emily, how can you act so?" exclaimed her brother, in stern reproval.

"Now, Harry, I don't want any of your morality. Look at home, before you preach to me. What have you been doing the last few weeks? I have heard."

"Shall I pay for the chaise, ma'am?" inquired Hickens, putting in his head.

"Pay for anything and everything, Hickens," was her answer. "I have brought no money with me, to speak of. I ran away."

"Emily, how can you?" exclaimed Mr. Chandos, as the man withdrew.

"Nonsense! Who's Hickens? Pauline's sure to tell him all about it. I repeat to you, Harry, that you need not preach: you have more need to reform your own acts and doings. The letter I received was about you; and, from what it said, I began to think it high time that I should be at Chandos."

"Indeed!" he quietly answered. "Pray who may have taken the trouble to write it?"

"That is what I cannot tell you. It was anonymous."

Mr. Chandos curled his lip. "There is only one thing to do with an anonymous letter, Emily—put it in the fire, with a thought of pity for its miserable writer, and then forget it for ever. We have been dealing in anonymous letters here, lately. I received one; and the inspector of police at Warsall received one, falsely purporting to be from me. The result was that a descent of mounted police came swooping upon us one night, frightening sober Chandos out of its propriety."

"I never heard of such a thing!" exclaimed. Madame de Mellissie, her interest momentarily diverted from her own grievances. "What did they want?"

"The inspector was led to believe I required them to take some one into custody for theft. I assure you anonymous letters have been the fashion here lately. But they are not the less despicable."

"Shall I tell you what was in mine?"

"I do not wish to hear it."

"Ah, you are afraid," she answered, with a laugh. "Conscience makes cowards of us all."

Mr. Chandos looked anything but afraid: he stood very calm, his head raised. Emily began taking off her things, throwing a bonnet on one chair, gloves on another, a shawl on the floor. I went forward to assist her.

"Don't touch anything of mine," she haughtily interrupted. "Harry, how long has mamma kept her room?"

"Ever since you left," replied Mr. Chandos.

"Oh. And you and Anne Hereford have had the sole benefit of each other's company!"

"And a very pleasant benefit, too," boldly retorted Mr. Chandos. But my cheeks were crimson, and they both saw it.

"You wrote me word that you wished to leave," she said, turning to me. "You are no longer in my service, and are at liberty to do so. When can you be ready?"

"My preparations will not take me long," was my reply.

Little cause was there to ask what had been the purport of her anonymous letter. Who could have written it? Who could be concerning themselves about me and Mr. Chandos? Was it Mrs. Penn?

"I should like some tea," she said, as she poured herself out a glass of wine. "Ring the bell and order it in, Miss Hereford. Whilst they bring it I will run up to mamma's rooms, Harry. Won't she pull a long face when she hears that I decamped without the cognizance of le mari et la vieille mère!"

"Emily," said Mr. Chandos, gravely, "you cannot go into your mamma's rooms at present."

"But I will go."

"My dear, you must not; at least until I have spoken to you. There are urgent reasons against it."

"What are the reasons?"

"I will tell you later. You had better have some tea first. Shall I ring for Hill to show you to a chamber?"

"I will be shown to a chamber when I have been in to mamma," she defiantly responded. "Take yourself out of the way, Harry."

Poor Mr. Chandos was standing between her and the door. "Emily, did I ever advise you but for your good—your comfort? Pray attend to me."

"For my good, no doubt," she said, with a gay laugh. "I don't know about my comfort. Harry, we shall come to a battle royal, if you don't move from that door. I am quite determined to go into the west wing, and I will not be stopped. Why! you are trying to control me as though I were a child."

Mr. Chandos opened the door and followed her out. In the hall they stood for a moment talking together in a whisper, and I heard a cry of pain and dismay escape her lips.

# CHAPTER 27

## GEORGE HENEAGE

I sat down with my weight of happiness. Oh, the change that had passed over me! He was not married; he was true and honourable, and he loved me! Everything else went out of my head, even the letter I held, still unopened; and when I should have thought of it I cannot say, but that some time later I heard the voice of Mrs. Penn in the hall, speaking in covert tones.

I remembered it then. Was she going to steal out, as she had previously essayed to do? I went to the door and opened it about an inch. Lizzy Dene stood there.

"How early you are home!" Mrs. Penn was saying.

"Thanks to Madam Hill!" grumbled Lizzy. "She wouldn't give me leave to go unless I could be in by seven, or a bit later: with illness in the house, she said, there was no knowing what might be wanted."

"Did you deliver the letter?" resumed Mrs. Penn, in a whisper.

"Yes, ma'am," was the ready answer. "A young man came to the door, and I asked if Mr. Barley was at home, and he said, 'Yes, all alone,' so I gave him the note, and he took it in."

"Thank you, Lizzy," answered Mrs. Penn, complacently. "There's the five shillings I promised you."

"Many thanks all the same to you, ma'am, but I'd rather not take it," replied Lizzy, to my great astonishment, and no doubt to Mrs. Penn's. "I'm well paid here, and I don't care to be rewarded for any little extra service. It's all in the way of the day's work."

They parted, Mrs. Penn going up the stairs again. But a startling doubt had come over me at Lizzy Dene's words: could I have taken the wrong letter from the basket? I hastened back to the light and drew it forth. No, it was all right: it was directed to Mr. Edwin Barley. What could Lizzy Dene mean by saying she had delivered it, I wondered, as I tore it open.

"I am overwhelmed with astonishment. I was coming round to your house, in spite of your prohibition, to tell you what I have discovered, but was prevented by Mrs. Chandos. *He is here!* I am as certain of it as that I am writing these words: and it clears the mystery of that closely-guarded west wing, which has been as a closed book to me. Anne Hereford went surreptitiously in just now, and saw what she describes as a tall, emaciated object, reclining in an invalid-chair, whose face bore a striking resemblance to that of Harry Chandos. There can be no doubt that it is he, not the slightest in the world; you can therefore take immediate steps, if you choose, to have him apprehended. My part is now over.

"C. D. P."

The contents of the letter frightened me. What mischief had I not caused by that incautious revelation to Mrs. Penn! Mrs. Penn the treacherous—as she undoubtedly was. "Take immediate steps to have him apprehended." Who was he? what had he done? and how did it concern Mr. Edwin Barley? Surely I ought to acquaint Mr. Chandos, and show him the note without loss of time.

Tea waited on the table, when Hickens came in with a message from the west wing to the effect that Mr. Chandos and Madame de Mellissie were taking tea there. I poured out a cup, and sent the things away again, debating whether I might venture on the unheard-of proceeding of sending to the west wing for Mr. Chandos.

Yes. It was a matter of necessity, and I ought to do it. I sought Hill. Hill was in the west wing, waiting on the tea party. Should I send Hickens to the west wing door, or go myself? Better go myself, instinct told me.

I ran lightly up the stairs. Peeping out at the east wing door, listening and prying, was the head of Mrs. Penn.

"They have quite a soirée in the west wing to-night," she said to me, as I passed; "a family gathering: all of them at it, except Sir Thomas. Whither are you off to so fast?"

"I have a message for the west wing," I answered, as I brushed on, and knocked at the door. Hill came to the door. She turned desperately angry when she saw me.

"I have not come to intrude, Hill. Mr. Chandos is here, is he not?"

"What's that to any one?" retorted Hill.

"He is wanted, that is all. Be so good as ask him to step down to the oak-parlour. At once, please; it is very pressing."

Hill banged the door in my face, and bolted it. Mrs. Penn, whose soft steps had come stealing near, seized me by the gathers of my dress as I would have passed her.

"Anne, who wants Mr. Chandos? Have the police come?"

"I want him; I have a message for him," I boldly answered, the remembrance of her treachery giving me courage to say it. "Why should the police come? What do you mean?"

"As they made a night invasion of the house once before, I did not know but they might have done it again. How tart you are this evening!"

I broke from her and went down to the parlour. Mr. Chandos was in it almost as soon.

"Hill said I was wanted. Who is it, Anne? Do you know?"

"You must forgive me for having ventured to call you, Mr.

Chandos. I have been the cause of some unhappy mischief, and how I shall make the confession to you I hardly know. But, made it must be, and there is no time to be lost."

"Sit down and don't excite yourself," he returned. "I dare say it is nothing very formidable."

"When we were speaking of the gentleman I saw before dinner in the west wing, you warned me that his being there was a secret which I must take care not to betray."

"Well?"

"I ought to have told you then—but I had not the courage—that I had already betrayed it. In the surprise of the moment, as I left the west wing after seeing him, I mentioned it to Mrs. Penn. It was done thoughtlessly; not intentionally; and I am very sorry for it."

"I am sorry also," he said, after a pause. "Mrs. Penn?" he slowly continued, as if deliberating whether she were a safe person or not. "Well, it might possibly have been imparted to a worse."

"Oh, but you have not heard all," I feverishly returned. "I do not think it could have been imparted to a worse than Mrs. Penn; but I did not know it then. I believe she has been writing to Mr. Edwin Barley."

My fingers were trembling, my face was flushed. Mr. Chandos spoke.

"Anne, be calm. I shall understand you better."

I strove to do as he said, and tell my story in as few words as possible. That I had said it must be Sir Thomas Chandos: that Mrs. Penn, wildly excited, said it was not Sir Thomas; and so on to the note she gave Lizzy Dene. Mr. Chandos grew a little excited himself as he read the note.

"Nothing could have been more unfortunate than this. Nothing."

"The most curious thing is, that when Lizzy Dene came back she affirmed to Mrs. Penn that she had delivered the note," I resumed. "I cannot make that out."

Mr. Chandos sat thinking, his pale face full of trouble and perplexity.

"Could Mrs. Penn have written two notes, think you, Anne?"

"I fear to think so: but it is not impossible. I only saw one in the basket; but I scarcely noticed in my hurry."

"If she did not write two, the mischief as yet is confined to the house, and I must take care that for this night at least that it is not carried beyond it. After that—"

He did not conclude his sentence, but rang for Hickens. The man came immediately.

"Hickens, will you lock the entrance-doors of the house, back and front, and put the keys into your pocket. No one must pass out of it again to-night."

Hickens stared. It was the most extraordinary order ever given to him at Chandos. "Why, sir?" he cried. "What for?"

"It is my pleasure," replied Mr. Chandos, in his quiet tone of command. "Lock the doors and keep the keys; and suffer no one to go out on any pretence whatsoever. No one that the house contains, you understand, myself excepted. Neither Mrs. Chandos nor Mrs. Penn; Miss Hereford"—turning to me with a half smile—"or the servants. Should any one of them present themselves at the door, and, finding it fast, ask to be let out, say you have my orders not to do it."

"Very well, sir," replied the amazed Hickens. "There's two of the maids out on an errand now, sir; are they to be let in?"

"Certainly. But take care that you fasten the door afterwards. Go at once and do this; and then send Lizzy Dene to me."

Away went Hickens. Mr. Chandos paced the room until Lizzy Dene appeared.

"Did you want me, sir?"

"I do. Come in and shut the door. What I want from you, Lizzy, is a little bit of information. If, as I believe, you are faithful to the house you serve, and its interests, you will give it me truthfully."

Lizzy burst into tears, without any reason, that I could see, and hung her head. Evidently there was something or other on which she feared to be questioned.

"It's what I always have been, sir, and what I hope I shall be. What have I done?"

"Did Mrs. Penn give you a letter, some two or three hours ago, to deliver at Mr. Edwin Barley's?"

"Yes, sir," was the reply, spoken without hesitation or embarrassment. Apparently that was not Lizzy Dene's sore point.

"Did you deliver it?"

Lizzy hesitated, and Mr. Chandos repeated his question.

"Now only to think that one can't meet with an accident without its being known all round as soon as done!" she exclaimed. "If I had thought you had anything to do with the matter, sir, I'd have told the truth when I came back; but I was afraid Mrs. Penn would be angry with me."

"I shall be glad to hear that the letter was not delivered," said Mr. Chandos, "So tell the truth now."

"Where I could have lost it, sir, I know no more than the dead," she resumed. "I know I put it safe in my basket; and though I did run, it could not have shaken out, because the lid was shut down; but when I got to Mr. Barley's, and went to take it out, it was gone. Sleighted off right away; just like that letter you lost from the hall-table, sir. What to do I didn't know, for I had given a good pull at their bell before I found out the loss. But I had another letter in my basket—"

"Another letter?" interrupted Mr. Chandos, thinking his fears verified.

"Leastways, as good as a letter, sir. As luck would have it, when I was running down the avenue, I met the young man from the fancy-draper's in the village, and he thrust a folded letter in my hands. 'For Lady Chandos, and mind you give it her,' says he, 'for it's a list of our new fashions.' So, what should I do, sir, when I found the other was gone, but give in the fashions to Mr. Barley's young man. 'And mind you take it in to your master without any delay,' says I, 'for it's partic-ular,' He'll wonder what they want, sending him the fashions," con-cluded Lizzy.

"You said nothing to Mrs. Penn of this?"

"Well—no, sir, I didn't. I meant, when she found it out, to let her think I had given in the wrong letter by mistake. I don't suppose hers was of much consequence, for it was only writ in pencil. I didn't take the money she offered me, though; I thought that wouldn't be fair, as I had not done the service."

"And my desire is, that you say nothing to her," said Mr. Chandos. "Let the matter rest as it is."

Mr. Chandos looked very grave after Lizzy Dene withdrew, as though he were debating something in his mind. Suddenly he spoke.

"Anne, cast your thoughts back a few years. Was any one in Mr. Edwin Barley's house, at the time Philip King was killed, at all answering to the description of Mrs. Penn?"

I looked at him in simple astonishment.

"It has struck me once or twice that Mrs. Penn must have been in the house, or very near it, by the knowledge she has of the details, great and small. And it would almost seem now, as though she were in league with Edwin Barley, acting as his spy."

"No one whatever was there except the servants and Charlotte Delves?"

"Stop a bit. Charlotte Delves—C. B. P.; C. D. would stand for that name. Is Mrs. Penn Charlotte Delves?"

The question almost took my breath away.

"But, Mr. Chandos, look at Mrs. Penn's hair! Charlotte Delves had pretty hair—and very light; quite different from this."

He smiled sadly.

"You must be inexperienced in the world's ways, my dear, if you have believed the present colour of Mrs. Penn's hair to be natural. She must have dyed her hair, intending, no doubt, to change it to golden: instead of which it has come out of the ordeal a blazing ver-milion. I think Mrs. Penn *is* Charlotte Delves."

Little by little, as I compared the past Charlotte Delves with the present Mrs. Penn, truth dawned upon me. All that had puzzled me in the likeness I could not trace, became clear. She had grown older;

she had grown much stouter; form both of figure and face had changed. Mrs. Penn, with a plump face and glowing red hair drawn back, was quite another person from Miss Delves with a thin face and long fair ringlets shading it.

"You are right," I said, in low, earnest tones. "It is Charlotte Delves."

"And she has been here trying to find out what she can of George Heneage. I see it all."

"But, Mr. Chandos, what is George Heneage to you?"

"He is my brother, Anne. *He* is George Heneage," he added, pointing in the direction of the west wing.

He George Heneage! I sat in greater and greater amazement. But, as I had traced the likeness in Charlotte Delves, so, now that the clue was given me, did I see that the resemblance which had so haunted me in Mr. Chandos, was to the George Heneage of that unhappy time.

"You were but a child, you know, then. And a child's remembrance does not retain faces very long."

"But, Mr. Chandos, how can George Heneage be your brother?"

"Is it perplexing you? Soon after the sad time of which we know too much, my father, Sir Thomas Heneage, had a large estate—this one—bequeathed to him by Mr. Chandos, my mother's brother, on condition that he assumed the name. You may be sure we lost no time in doing so—too thankful to drop our own, which George had disgraced."

"Then—his name is no longer George Heneage, but George Chandos?" I said.

"Strictly speaking, our name is Heneage-Chandos; and Heneage-Chandos we should have been always styled. But we preferred to drop the name of Heneage completely. It may be—I don't know—that we shall take it up again hereafter,"

"And where has he been all this time?"

"Ah, where! You may well ask. Leading the life of a miserable exile, conscious that Edwin Barley was ever on the watch for him, seeking to bring him to trial for the murder of Philip King."

"Did your brother really do it?" I asked, in a low tone.

"In one sense, yes. He killed Philip King, but not intentionally. So much as this he said to me for the first time only two days ago. Were he brought to trial, there could be no doubt of his condemnation—and only think of the awful fear that has been ours! You can now understand why I and my brother, Sir Thomas, have felt ourselves bound in honour not to marry whilst that possible disgrace was hanging over us. Ill-fated George!"

"Has he been concealed here always?"

"That would have been almost impossible," replied Mr.

Chandos, with a half smile at my simplicity. "He has been here only a short time: and no end of stratagems have we had to resort to, to conceal the fact. My mother has been compelled to feign illness, and remain in the west wing, that an excuse might be afforded for provisions and things being carried up. I have assumed to you the unenviable character of a sleepwalker; we have suffered the report that my dead father, Sir Thomas, haunted the Pine Walk, without contradicting it—"

"And are you not a sleep-walker? and is there no ghost?" I breathlessly interrupted.

"The only ghost, the only sleep-walker, has been poor George," he sadly answered. "*You* saw him arrive, Anne."

"I!"

"Have you forgotten the night when you saw me—as you thought—dodging in and out of the trees, as if I wished to escape observation, and finally disappear within the west wing? It was George. The next morning you accused me of having been there; I knew I had not, and positively denied it. Later I found that George had arrived: and then I amused you with a fable of my being addicted to sleep-walking. I knew not what else to invent; anything to take suspicion from the right quarter; and I feared you would be seeing him there again."

"But is it not very dangerous for him to have ventured here?"

"Ay. After the misfortune happened he lay a short time concealed at Heneage Grange, where we then lived, and eventually escaped to the Prussian dominions. We heard nothing of him for some time, though we were in the habit of remitting him funds periodically for his support. But one night he made his appearance here; it was not long after we had settled at Chandos; startling my mother and Hill almost out of their senses. They concealed him in the west wing, and Lady Chandos feigned illness and remained in it with him, as she has done this time. He did not stay long; but henceforth we could be at no certainty, and took to leaving the lower entrance-door of the west wing unfastened at night, so that he might enter at once, should he arrive a second time. Three or four times in all has he come, including this time."

"But it must surely be hazardous?"

"Nothing can be more so; not to speak of the constant state of suspense and anxiety it keeps us all in. He declares he is obliged to come, or die; that he is attacked with the *mal du pays*, the yearning for home, to such an extent that when the fit comes on him, he is forced to risk it. More dangerous, too, than his actually being here, is his walking out at night in the grounds; and he will do it in spite of remonstrance. George was always given to self-will,"

"Does he walk out?"

"Does he? Why, Anne, need you ask the question? Sometimes at dusk, sometimes not until midnight, at any hour just as the whim takes him, out he will go. He has led so restless a life that without walking once or twice in the twenty-four hours he could not exist. Have you not seen the 'ghost' yourself more than once? Were you not terrified by him in the corridor? Do you forget the evening when I gathered your face to me in the dark walk, whilst some one passed? I feared that you should see him—should detect that it was a living man, real flesh and blood, not a harmless ghost. Very glad were we when the servants, at his first visit, took up the theory of a ghost, in place of any more dangerous notion. From them it spread outside, so that the Chandos ghost has become public rumour and public property."

"Do the servants know that you have this brother?"

"Hickens and some of the elder ones of course know it: know all he was accused of, and why he went into exile; but so many years have elapsed since, that I feel sure the remembrance of him has nearly died out. This visit has been worse for us than any, owing to the proximity of Edwin Barley."

"You think Edwin Barley has been looking out for him?"

"Think! I know it. Something must have arisen to give him the idea that George had returned to England, and was in hiding: though he could not have suspected Chandos, or he would have had it searched. Many things, that we were obliged to say and do, appear to have been very foolish, looking back, and they will seem still more so in after years; but they were done in fear. The singular thing is that Mrs. Penn—being here to find out what she could—should not have hit upon the truth before."

"Would Mr. Edwin Barley cause him to be apprehended, do you think?"

"He will apprehend him the very moment that the news reaches his ears," spoke Mr. Chandos, lifting his hands in agitation. "Living, or—dead, I had all but said—at any rate, living or dying, Edwin Barley will seize upon George Heneage. I do not say but he would be justified in doing so."

"Oh, Mr. Chandos! Can you not take him somewhere for escape?"

He sadly shook his head. "No. George is past being taken anywhere. He has grown rapidly worse. Yesterday I should have said his hours were numbered: to-day he is so much better that I can only think he has entered on a renewed lease of life. At least of some days."

"What is the matter with him?"

"In my opinion it is a broken heart. He has fretted himself away. Think what existence has been for him. In exile under a false name; no home, no comfort, an innocent man's death upon his conscience;

and living, whether at home or abroad, in the ever-constant dread of being called upon to answer publicly for what has been called murder. The doctors call his illness a decline. He is a living shadow."

"And Mrs. Chandos is his wife! Oh, poor thing, what a life of sadness hers must be!"

"Mrs. Chandos was his wife; in one sense of the word is his wife still, for she bears his name," he gravely answered. "But I have a word to say to you, Anne, respecting Mrs. Chandos. Mrs. Penn—I shall begin to doubt whether every word and action of that woman be not false, put forth with some covert motive—informed you that Mrs. Chandos was my wife, knowing perfectly well to the contrary. Mrs. Chandos was never my wife, Anne, but she was once my love."

A chill stole over my heart.

"I met with her when she was Ethel Wynne, a lovely, soft-mannered girl, and I learned to love her with impassioned fervour. We became engaged, and were to be married later: I was only two-and-twenty then, she seventeen. She came to Heneage Grange on a visit, she and her elder sister, since dead. Little thought I that my sweet, soft-mannered girl was eaten up with ambition. One morning at breakfast a letter was brought in to my father. It was from India, and contained news of the death of my brother Tom; which, I need not tell you, who know that he is still alive, was premature. Captain Heneage had been in action, the letter stated, was desperately wounded, and taken up for dead. Tom wrote us word afterwards that it was only when they went to bury him that they discovered he was living. But he is given to joking. Well, we mourned him as dead; and George, in his free, careless manner, told Ethel she had better have engaged herself to him than to me, for that he could make her Lady Heneage, being the heir now, which Harry never could. That George had always admired her, was certain. He had a weakness for pretty women. But for that weakness, and Mrs. Edwin Barley's being pretty, Philip King might be alive now."

Mr. Chandos paused a moment, and then went on in lower tones: "Anne, will you believe that in less than two weeks' time they had gone away together?"

"Who had?"

"George Heneage and Ethel Wynne. They had gone away to be married. When they returned, man and wife, my mother, Lady Heneage, would have refused to receive them, but Sir Thomas, ever lenient to us all, persuaded her to do so. A marriage entered into as theirs had been would bring sufficient punishment in its wake, he observed. The punishment—for Ethel, at any rate—had already begun. She liked me best, far best, but ambition had temporarily blinded her. She married George on the strength of his being heir-apparent to the title, and news had now arrived that my brother

Thomas was alive, and progressing steadily towards health."

"And you—what did you do?" I interrupted.

"I hid my bruised feelings, and rode the high horse of indifference; letting none suppose false Ethel had wounded me. The wound was there, and a pretty sharp one; five fathoms deep, though I strove to bury it." He paused an instant, and then went on. "In six months' time she and George were tired of each other—if appearances might be trusted—and he spent a great deal of his time abroad. Ethel resented it: she said he had no right to go out taking pleasure without her: but George laughed off all complaints in his light way. They made their home at Heneage Grange, and had been married nearly a year when George went on that fatal visit to Mr. Edwin Barley's."

"Then—when that calamity took place he already had a wife!" I exclaimed in surprise: I suppose because I had never heard it at the time.

"Certainly. The shock to Ethel was dreadful. She believed him guilty. Brain-fever attacked her, and she has never been quite bright in intellect since, but is worse at times than at others. Hers is a disappointed life. She had married George in the supposition that he was heir to the baronetcy; she found herself the wife of an exiled man, an accused murderer."

"Has she been aware of the secret visits of her husband?"

"They could not be kept entirely from her. Since the calamity, she has never been cordial with him: acquaintances they have been, but no more; it almost seems as though Ethel had forgotten that other ties once existed between them. She is most anxious to guard his secret; our only fear has been that she might inadvertently betray it. For this we would have concealed from her his presence here as long as might be, but she has always found it out and resented it loudly, reproaching me and my mother with having no confidence in her. You must remember the scene in the corridor when I locked the door of your room; Ethel had just burst into the west wing with reproaches, and they, George and my mother, were bringing her back to her own apartments. She goes there daily now, and reads the Bible to him."

How the things came out—one after the other!

"And now, Anne, I think you know all; and will understand how, with this terrible sword—George's apprehension—ever unsheathed, I could not tell you of my love."

And what if it did? Strike or not strike, it would be all the same to my simple heart, beating now with its weight of happiness. I believe Mr. Chandos could read this in my downcast face, for a smile was parting his lips.

"Is it to be yes in any case, Anne?"

"I—Perhaps," I stammered. "And then you will tell me the truth about yourself. What is it that is really the matter with you?" I took courage to ask, speaking at length of the fear that always lay upon me so heavily, and which I had been forbidden to speak about.

"The matter with me?"

"The illness that Dr. Amos said you would never recover from."

Mr. Chandos laughed. "Why, Anne, don't you see?—it was my brother George he spoke of, not me. I never had anything serious the matter with me in my life; we wiry fellows never have."

Was it so? Could this great dread be, like the other, a myth? In the revulsion of feeling, my wits momentarily deserted me. Pulses were bounding, cheeks were blushing, eyes were thrilling; and I looked up at him asking, was it true—could it be true!

And received my answer for my pains.

"But I do not quite understand yet," I said, when I could free myself from his embrace. "You have looked ill; especially about the time Dr. Amos came."

"And in one sense I was ill; ill with anxiety. We have lived, you see, Anne, with a constant terror upon us; never free from it a moment, by night or by day. When George was not here, there was the ever-constant dread of his coming, the *watching* for him as it were; and now that he is here the dread is awful. When George grew worse, and it became necessary that some medical man should see him, Dr. Amos was summoned to 'Mr. Harry Chandos;' and I had a bed made up in the west wing, and secluded myself for four-and-twenty hours."

"Did Dr. Amos think he came to you?"

"He thought so. Thought that the sickly, worn-out man he saw lying on the sofa in my mother's sitting-room was Mr. Harry Chandos. I being all the time closely shut up from sight in my temporary chamber. Laken, who has been our medical attendant for a great many years, and in our entire confidence, was unfortunately away from home, and we had to resort to a stratagem. It would not do to let the world or the household know that George Heneage was lying concealed at Chandos."

"Then—when Dr. Laken said Lady Chandos was emaciated and obstinate, he really spoke of *him?*"

"He did: because you were within hearing. The obstinacy related to George's persistency in taking his night-walks in the grounds. It has been a grievous confinement for my mother: *she* went out a night or two ago for a stroll at dusk, and was unfortunately seen by Mrs. Penn. Hill was very cross that Mrs. Penn should have gone near the Pine Walk."

"How much does Madame do Mellissie know of this?" I asked.

"She was cognizant of the crime George was accused of having committed, and that he was in exile. She also knew that we always lived in dread of his coming to Chandos; and for that reason did not welcome strangers here."

"And yet she brought, and left, me!"

"But you have not proved a dangerous inmate, my dear one." It was kind of him to say that, but I feared I had. That Mrs. Penn had contrived to give notice to Edwin Barley, or would contrive it, was only too probable. Once the house should be opened in the morning, nothing could prevent her. Troubled and fearful, I had not spoken for some minutes, neither had he, when Madame de Mellissie's voice was heard in the hall, and he left the room.

She came into it, crossing him on the threshold. Just casting an angry and contemptuous glance on me, she withdrew, and shut the door loudly, coming back again in a short time.

"Closeted with my brother as usual!" she began, as if not one minute instead of ten had elapsed since seeing me with Mr. Chandos. "Why do you put yourself continually in his way?"

"Did you speak to me, Madame de Mellissie?" I asked, really doubting if the attack could be meant for me.

"To whom else should I speak?" she returned, in passionate and abrupt tones. "How dare you presume to seek to entangle Mr. Harry Chandos?"

"I do not understand you, Madame de Mellissie. I have never sought to entangle any one."

"You have; you know you have," she answered, giving the reins to her temper. "The letter I received warned me you were doing it, and that brought me over. You and he have dined alone, sat alone, walked alone; together always. Is it seemly that you, a dependent governess, should cast a covetous eye upon a Chandos?"

My heart was beginning to beat painfully. What defence had I to make?

"Why did you leave me here, madam?"

"Leave you here! Because it suited my convenience. But I left you here as a dependent. I did not expect you to make yourself my brother's companion."

"Stay, Madame de Mellissie. I beg you to reflect a little before you reproach me. How could I help being your brother's companion, *when he chose to make himself mine.* This, the oak-parlour, was the general sitting-room; no other was shown to me for my use; was it my fault that Mr. Chandos also made it his? Could I ask to have my breakfast and dinner served in my bed-chamber?"

"I don't care," she intemperately rejoined. "I say that had you not been lost to all sense of the fitness of things, you would have kept yourself beyond the notice of Mr. Harry Chandos. To-morrow morning you will leave."

"To whom are you speaking, Emily?" demanded a quiet voice behind us.

It was his; it was his. I drew back with a shiver.

"I am speaking to Anne Hereford," she defiantly answered. "Giving her a warning of summary ejectment. She has been in the house rather too long!"

"You might have moderated your tone, at any rate, Emily: and perhaps would, had you known to whom you were offering a gratuitous insult," he said, with admirable calmness.

"I spoke to Anne Hereford."

"Yes. And to my future wife."

The crimson flashed into her beautiful face, "Harry!"

"Therefore I must beg of you to treat Miss Hereford accordingly."

"Are you mad, Harry?"

"Perfectly sane, I hope."

"It cannot be your intention to marry *her*? How can you think of so degrading yourself?"

"You are mistaking the case altogether, Emily. I, and my family with me, will be honoured by the alliance."

"What on earth do you mean?"

A half-smile crossed his face at her wondering look, but he gave no explanation: perhaps the time had not come for it. I escaped from the room, and he came after me.

"Anne, I want you to go with me to the west wing. George says he should like to see you."

I went up with him at once. George Heneage—I shall never call him Chandos, and indeed he had never assumed the name—sat in the same easy-chair propped up with pillows. Mr. Chandos put me a seat near, and he took my hands within his wasted ones. They called him better. Better! He, with the white, drawn face, the glassy eyes, the laboured breath!

"My little friend Anne! Have you quite forgotten me?"

"No; I have remembered you always, Mr. Heneage. I am sorry to see you looking so ill."

"Better that I should look so. My life is a burden to me, and to others. I have prayed to God a long while to take it, and I think He has at last heard me. Leave us, Harry, for a few minutes."

I felt half-frightened as Mr. Chandos went out. What could he want with me?—and he looked so near death!

"You have retained a remembrance of those evil days?" he abruptly began, turning on the pillow to face me.

"Every remembrance, I think. I have forgotten nothing."

"Just so: they could but strike forcibly on a child's heart. Well, ever since Harry told me that it was *you* who were in this house, a day or two back now, I have thought I must see you at the last. I should not like to die leaving you to a wrong impression. You have assumed, with the rest of the world, that I murdered Philip King?"

I hesitated, really not knowing what to say.

"But I did not murder him. The shot from my gun killed him, but not intentionally. As Heaven, soon to be my judge, hears me, I tell you the truth. Philip King had angered me very much. As I saw him in the distance smoking a cigar, his back against the tree, I pointed my gun at him, and put my finger on the trigger, saying, 'How I should like to put a shot into you!' Without meaning it—without meaning it, the gun went off, Anne: my elbow caught against the branch of a tree, and it went off and shot him. I had rather—yes, even then—that it had shot myself."

"But why did you not come forward and say so, Mr. Heneage?"

"Because the fact paralyzed me, making me both a fool and a coward, and the moment for avowal passed for ever. I would have given my own life to undo my work and restore that of Philip King. It was too late. All was too late. So I have lived on as I best could, hiding myself from the law, an exile from my country, my wife a stranger; regarded by the world as a murderer, liable to be called upon at any moment to expiate it, and with a man's death upon my soul. Over and over again would I have given myself up, but for the disgrace it would bring to my family."

"I thought it might be an accident, Mr. Heneage—have always thought so," I said, with a sigh of relief.

"Thank God, yes! But the wicked wish had been there, though uttered in reckless sport. Oh, child, don't you see how glad I shall be to go? Christ has washed away sins as red as mine. Not of *my* sins, comparatively speaking, has the care lain heavily upon me night and day; but of another's."

Did he mean Selina's? "Of whose, sir?"

"Philip King's. I gave him no time for prayer. There's a verse in the Bible, Anne, that has brought me comfort at times," he whispered, with feverish eagerness, gazing at me with his earnest, yearning eyes. "When the disciples asked of the Redeemer who then can be saved, there came in answer the loving words, 'With men this is impossible, but with God all things are possible.'"

He might not have said more; I don't know; but Hill came in to announce Dr. Laken. Her face of astonishment when she saw me sitting there was ludicrous to behold. George Heneage wrung my hand as I left him.

"You see, Hill, I am allowed to come even here," I could not help saying, in a sort of triumph, as she held the green-baize door open for me.

Hill returned a defiant grunt by way of answer, and I brushed past Dr. Laken as he came along the gallery with another gentleman, who was dressed in the garb of a clergyman.

# CHAPTER 28

## AN IGNOMINIOUS EXIT

The windows were thrown open to the bright morning air; the late autumn birds were singing, the trees were gently waving; even the gloomy Pine Walk opposite had a ray of sunlight on it. Little thought I as I stood in the oak-parlour with my great happiness, little thought the servants as they went about their work, that one lay dead in the west wing.

Breakfast waited on the table; the postman came with the letters; Hickens looked in to see if he might bring in the urn. He waited on us far more than the rest did, although he was butler, knowing that Mr. Chandos liked it.

A stir in the hall at last: Mrs. Penn's voice speaking to Lizzy Dene. The tones were low, but they reached my ear.

"I cannot think you delivered that letter last evening, Lizzy. I ought to have received an answer long before this."

"Not deliver it, ma'am!" returned Lizzy, with every sound of surprise. "I gave it in to the young man at the door."

"Wait a moment, Lizzy: what a hurry you are in! Are you sure Mr. Edwin Barley was at home?"

"Of course I am not sure," returned Lizzy: and I pictured Mrs. Penn to myself at that moment: her cheeks flushing red, her eyes flashing fire.

"You deceitful woman! You told me last night Mr. Edwin Barley was at home!"

"Ma'am, I told you the young man said he was at home. I can't stay here a minute longer: if Hill finds me gossiping, she'll be fit to pull my ears for me,"

A slight rustling in the portico. I looked from the window and saw Mrs. Penn flying away as speedily as middle-aged, portly women can fly. Mr. Chandos came into the room at the same time.

"How is your brother, Mr. Chandos?"

"Better, I trust, than he has been for many years in this life. It is over, Anne. He died at twelve last night."

The words struck on me as a great shock. Over! Dead!

"He was sensible to the last moment. It was a happy death," continued Mr. Chandos, in low, solemn tones. "Truly may it be said that he has 'come out of great tribulation.' God receive and bless him!"

I sat down. Mr. Chandos turned over the letters in an abstracted sort of manner, but did not really look at them.

When I thought I might venture to speak, I mentioned Mrs. Penn's reproach to Lizzy Dene, and her running off afterwards (there was no doubt about it) to Mr. Edwin Barley.

"Ay, I saw her go," he replied. "The answer she has been waiting for were the police, on their mission to arrest my brother George. They may come now. And presently will do so," he added, "for I have sent for them."

"For the police again! What for?"

He made no answer. Emily came in, looking as he did, rather subdued. She spoke civilly to me: with death in a house people keep down their temper. Mr. Chandos rang the bell for breakfast, and then we all stood at the window.

"Where's Dr. Laken?" asked Emily.

"Gone out," replied Mr. Chandos. "He breakfasted early."

"How unfortunate it is that I should have arrived just now!" she exclaimed, after a pause, during which we were all silent. "The carriages must not go out, I suppose, for the next few days."

"Ill doing is sure to bring its own punishment, Emily," Mr. Chandos said to her, jestingly, with a sad smile. "You should not have run away."

"We shall have Alfred over after me, I expect. His gastric fever will politely vanish when it is necessary that his wife should be looked up. But I am *glad* that I was here, Harry, after all," she added, her voice changing to one of deeper feeling, "for it enabled me to see the last of *him*."

"I am glad that he was here," observed Mr. Chandos, "for it afforded the opportunity of his receiving comforts and attendance in his illness that he could not have had abroad. Now that the dread of his being discovered has passed away, I see how certainly all things were for the best."

"He stayed here a long while this time."

"He was too ill to leave. We could not urge it. The end seemed rapidly and surely approaching."

"Do you call his illness consumption?"

"Not the consumption that attacks most people. If ever man died of a broken heart, George has done so."

"Did he come home to die? I mean, knowing that he was soon about to die?"

"No. He was weak and emaciated when he arrived, worn to a shadow; but he did not become really ill, dangerously ill, until afterwards."

"Do the servants know of it?" she asked, lowering her voice. "Will they be told of it?"

"Certainly not. We hope to keep it private to the end."

"But there must be—"

"Yes, yes," he hastily interrupted, seeing she would have alluded to the funeral. "Laken manages all that. What a bright morning it is!"

Mr. Chandos leaned from the window as if to turn the conversation. Emily, easily swayed, plucked a piece of mignonette.

"I suppose mamma will come downstairs to-day. Well, it's time she did."

"It is," asserted Mr. Chandos.

"For more reasons than one," she tartly added, as a lance-shaft at me.

Hickens came in with the urn. Seeing the letters lying there untouched, he spoke with the familiarity of a privileged servant.

"The Indian mail is in, sir."

Mr. Chandos turned quickly to the table. "I see it is, Hickens." But I don't think he had seen it until then.

"I suppose there's nothing for me from Alfred," said Madame de Mellissie, languidly looking round. "I am not anxious to read it if there is: it would only be full of lamentations and scolding. Or from Tom, either? He never writes to me."

Mr. Chandos shook his head. "There's only one from Tom, and that is to me."

"But I see another Indian letter," she said, slowly approaching the table. "It has a black seal."

"Not from Thomas. It is in a strange handwriting, and is addressed to my mother."

"Any letters for my lady, sir?" asked Hill, entering the room.

"Two. One of them from India, tell her; but not from Sir Thomas."

Hill retreated with the letters. Emily placed herself in my seat at the head of the table, and we began breakfast. It was a silent meal for all of us that morning. Mr. Chandos drank his coffee quickly, and opened his brother's letter.

"They were on the eve of action, Emily," he presently said. "Just going into it when Thomas wrote this. Some local engagement."

"Is it well over?"

"I hope so. But he closed this letter at once. Here is what he says in conclusion: 'I shall drop this into the post now, and if I come out of the turmoil safely, give you a second note to say so. That is, if the post should not have gone: if it has, you must wait another fortnight.' Where's the evening paper?" added Mr. Chandos, seeking out a newspaper which had come with the letters, and opening it. "News of this action, however unimportant it was, ought to have come by telegraph."

He had scarcely said this when Hill came in, speaking and looking like one in alarm. I thought of the police; I fancy Mr. Chandos did.

"Sir—Mr. Harry—my lady wishes you to come to her instantly."

He appeared aroused by the tone—or the looks—and went out at once, opening the newspaper as he did so. Madame de Mellissie demanded of Hill what he was wanted for.

"I hardly know, ma'am. Something very sad, I fear, has happened."

Emily started to her feet. "Hill, that letter never contained bad news from India?—from Sir Thomas?"

"It has bad news of some sort in it, for certain," was Hill's rejoinder. "My lady gave a scream before she had read three lines, and said some confused words about her 'darling son Thomas.' The fear upon me, ma'am, is, that he has been hurt in battle."

Worse than that! It came upon me with a prevision as I thought of the black seal and the strange handwriting. Emily, impulsive in all she did, went running up to the west wing. Whilst I waited alone for them to return with some news, good or bad, I heard Mrs. Penn come in and accost Lizzy Dene, who was rubbing the brasses in the hall.

"Where is the letter I gave you last night?" she curtly demanded, her tones very sharp.

"Why, ma'am, what's the use of asking me?" returned the undaunted Lizzy, after a faint pause. "Mr. Edwin Barley's people must know more about that."

"The letter you delivered was not my letter."

"Not your letter!" repeated Lizzy Dene, evidently affecting the most genuine surprise. "I don't know what you mean, ma'am."

"The letter you left at Mr. Edwin Barley's, instead of being the one I handed to you, was some rubbishing circular of the fashions. How dared you do such a thing?"

"My goodness me!" exclaimed Lizzy. "To think of that! But Mrs. Penn, it's not possible."

"Don't talk to me about its not being possible! You have been wilfully careless. I must have my letter produced."

"I declare to goodness I don't know where it is, or what has become of it, if—as you say, ma'am—it was not the one I gave in to the young man," spoke Lizzy, this time with real earnestness. "I had a letter about the fashions in my basket; but it's odd I could make such a mistake."

"You did make it," Mrs. Penn angrily rejoined. "Where is the letter now?"

"Ma'am, I can't imagine. It must have been spirited away."

"Don't talk nonsense to me about being 'spirited away.' If you gave in the one for the other, you must still have had my letter left in your basket. What did you do with it?"

"If you offered me a thousand pounds to tell, I couldn't," was Lizzy's answer. "Looking upon it as nothing but a letter of the fashions, I thought it was of no moment, else I remember opening my basket after leaving Mr. Barley's, and seeing there was nothing in it. I wondered then what could have gone with the fashions. I'm sure, ma'am, I am very sorry."

Mrs. Penn went upstairs. It was apparently a profitless inquiry. Lizzy Dene rubbed away again at her brasses, and I waited and waited. The servants began to stand about in groups, coming perpetually into the hall; the rumour that something was wrong in India had spread to them. By-and-by the truth was brought down by Hill, with great tears upon her face. Sir Thomas Chandos was dead.

It was not a false report, as had once come, of his death. Ah, no. He had fallen in battle, gallantly leading his men to the charge. The Commander-in-Chief in India had written to Lady Chandos with his own hand: he said how much her son was regretted, and that all the officers who could be spared had attended the funeral. A shot had struck him in the breast. He had but time to say a few words, and died, his mother's name being the last upon his lips.

Hickens entered the oak-parlour and drew down the white blinds. Whilst talking of Sir Thomas he burst into tears. It all proved to me how much Thomas Chandos had been liked by those about him.

The breakfast things were taken away; an hour passed, and the morning was growing weary, when Mr. Chandos came down, traces of emotion on his face. Alas! he was no longer "Mr." but Sir Harry Chandos.

The first person I heard give him his title was Dr. Laken. How strange it was! Had the news arrived only the previous morning, the title must have remained in abeyance. Poor, banned, dying George had been heir to it by right of birth; but I suppose the law would not have given it to him. Dr. Laken called Mr. Chandos "Sir Harry" three or four times in the presence of the servants very pointedly. I thought he wanted to impress upon them the fact that no intervening heir existed. It was all very strange: those blinds that they had not dared to draw down for George, the grief they had not liked to show, the mourning they might have been doubtful whether to assume; all did duty for both brothers now, and might be open and legitimate.

"I think the *shadow* of death had fallen upon Thomas when he wrote," said Mr. Chandos, in low tones. And Dr. Laken echoed the words questioningly.

"The shadow of death?"

"I mean a prevision of it. Throughout his letter to me a vein of sadness runs; and he concludes it, 'Farewell, Harry; God bless you!' He never so wrote before. You shall read the letter, Laken: my mother has it now."

Lady Chandos had been coming down that day, they said; but the news had stopped it, and she would not now be seen until the morrow. The morning went on. Two official-looking persons came, and were taken by Dr. Laken to the west wing. I gathered that it had something to do with identification, in case there should be any doubt afterwards of the death: both of them had known George Heneage in the days gone by.

The blinds were down throughout the house. Every room was gloomy. Madame de Mellissie evidently found it so, and came in listlessly to the oak-parlour. She seemed very cross: perhaps at seeing her brother there; but he had only come to it a minute before.

"Harry, I suppose Chandos will be looking up again, and taking its part in county gaieties after a while—as it never has done yet?"

"Yes," he answered; "after a while."

"It would not be a bad plan for me to reside here occasionally as its mistress. Mamma goes back to the old Heneage homestead: she always intended to do so, if this crisis came in poor George's life, leaving you here to manage the estate for Thomas. And now it is yours, to manage for yourself. What changes!"

"Changes indeed! I wish I could be manager for him still."

"You will want a mistress for it; and I shall be glad to escape at times from home. I grow sick and tired of Paris."

"Many thanks, Emily, but the future mistress of Chandos is already bespoken."

Her fair face flushed; and there was a tart ring in her voice when she spoke again.

"Do you forget that your position is changed? When you gave me that hint last evening, you were, comparatively speaking, an obscure individual; now you are Sir Harry Chandos, powerful, and a wealthy baronet."

What he answered, I know not. There was a smile on his face as I left the room and strolled outside. The sound of approaching footsteps caused me to look down the avenue, and the look sent me running in again. Two of the police who had been there before were approaching on foot.

"I have been waiting for them," said Mr. Chandos, quietly. I cannot get quite at once into the way of calling him anything else. "Emily, will you oblige me by going up to Mrs. Chandos, and make some excuse for taking her into the west wing at once. You can remain here, or go to another room, as you like, Anne."

I went up to my chamber. Madame de Mellissie was already passing along the gallery, her arm linked within that of Mrs. Chandos. Mrs. Penn advanced to the well of the staircase and saw the police. A glow of triumph overspread her whole face.

"Sooner here than I thought for!" she exclaimed. "You will see something now, Anne Hereford."

They came up the stairs, Mr. Chandos with them. Mrs. Penn retreated to the door of the east wing, but she could not resist the temptation of standing at it to look. They went towards her.

"Not here," she said, waving her hand in the direction of the west wing. The person for whom your visit is intended is *there.*"

"Pardon me, madam," interposed Mr. Chandos; "the visit of these officers is to *you.*"

"To me! What do you mean?" she asked, after a pause, her voice rising to a shriek.

Never did I see a change so great come over a human countenance. They all retreated into the east wing, and the door was closed. What took place I learnt later.

In the most courteous manner possible, consistent with the circumstances, Mr. Chandos explained to Mrs. Penn why the police had come for *her.* He had reason to believe that *she* was the person who had been disturbing the tranquillity of Chandos, he said. When she had offered her boxes for search before, he had declined to permit them to be touched: he must, much as he regretted the necessity, order them to be searched now. All this we heard later. Mrs. Penn was taken aback. What she said, never transpired: resistance would have been simply foolish; and she made up for it by insolence. The police quietly did their duty; and found ample proof: a few skeleton keys, that would open any lock in the house. Her own lace was there; Mr. Chandos's memorandum-book. She had come into the house to spy; feverishly hoping to find out the abiding-place of George Heneage.

Her bitter animosity against him had only grown with years. An accidental circumstance had brought to her a suspicion that George Heneage's hiding-place was in England; and she had laid her plans and entered Chandos with the full intention of discovering it. My presence there had somewhat baffled her: she could not go peeping about in my sight; she took Mr. Chandos's private book from his desk in the hope that it might help her to the discovery she had at heart, and then invented the story of losing her lace to divert the scent from herself. Later, she conceived another scheme—that of getting me out of the house; and she stole the money to put it into my box; and arranged the supposed opening of her reticule in my room, and the reading of her sealed letter and abstracted the letter I had put on the hall-table, hoping Mr. Chandos would fall into the trap and send me from Chandos. *Now* could be understood her former anxiety that the police should search her boxes and mine; hers were ready for the inspection, mine had the money in them; and, at that time (as I knew later), also the memorandum-book. Something else was found in her boxes besides skeleton keys—a grey cloak. Putting one thing with another, Mr. Chandos thought he had little need of further speculation as to who had stopped his horse in the avenue that night, and caused his fall from it. And the reason may as well be mentioned here, though it is anticipating our knowledge of it. She had lingered about the private groves of Chandos until dusk that afternoon, hoping to see Mr. Edwin Barley, whose house she was forbidden; in going forth at length, openly, having put her cloak on because she was cold—and how it was Hill had not seen it on her arm when talking with her in the portico, was a mystery, for she had brought it to Chandos, left it in the hall there, and taken it upon her departure—in going down the avenue she met Mr. Chandos riding up it. She had never before seen him, and she took him in the dusk for his brother. She actually thought she was encountering George Heneage; and the noise with which she approached the horse and flung up her arms, was not intended to frighten the animal, but simply to express execration, in her great surprise. At the same moment, even as it escaped her, she discovered her mistake, and that it was not George Heneage.

"Now, madam," said Mr. Chandos, the search over, the proofs in the officers' hands, "what have you to urge as a reason why I should not give you into custody? You have been living in my mother's house under false colours; you have rifled locks; you have taken my money; you have been writing anonymous letters, and carrying tales to Mr. Edwin Barley."

"All that I have done I was justified in doing," she answered, braving it out. "I was at work in your house as a detective: my acts bore but one aim—the discovery of your brother, the murderer. And I have succeeded. In an hour's time from this, perhaps, the tables will be turned. As to your money, Mr. Chandos, it is wrapped up in paper and directed to you. I don't steal money."

"What palliation have you to offer for your conduct?—what excuse to urge against my giving you into custody?" repeated Mr. Chandos.

"If you choose to do it, *do* it," she returned. "Some one of far greater import than I will be shortly taken into custody from this house. I am of the kin of the Barleys: you and they are implacable enemies: all stratagems are fair when the discovery of criminals, hiding from the law, is in question. I have only done my duty; I would do it again. Give me into custody if you like, Mr. Chandos. The tables will soon be turned."

"No, they will not be turned in the sense you would insinuate, and for that reason I can afford to be generous," answered Mr. Chandos. "Had real harm come of this matter, I would have prosecuted you to the utmost rigour of the law. But, as it is beyond your power now, or Mr. Edwin Barley's either, to do us harm, you may go from us scot-free. But I cannot allow you to remain longer at Chandos. Forgive the seeming inhospitality, if I say I would prefer that you should not wait to partake of another meal in the house. Your things shall be sent after you. Or, if you prefer to gather them together, these officers will wait whilst you do it, and then escort you from my house into that of Mr. Edwin Barley."

"I will not be escorted abroad by police-officers," she passionately answered.

"You possess no choice, madam. I have, so far, given you into their charge: and they will take care to undertake it."

A very short time seemed to suffice to put her things together, and Mrs. Penn came forth, attended by the two officers. In some mood of reckless defiance, or perhaps to conceal herself as much as possible from the gaze of the world, she had put on the grey cloak and drawn the hood over her head.

Mr. Chandos recognized her at once, as she had looked that night. He could but be a gentleman, and had gone out to the hall in courtesy when she came down to depart. The sight of her thus startled him for a moment.

"Ah, I should have known you anywhere, Mrs. Penn. What had I or my horse done to you that you should attack us?"

She turned and faced him. It really seemed as though she believed herself in the right in all the past acts, and felt proud to have done so well. All this time, it must be remembered, she supposed George Heneage was alive in the west wing, and would soon be taken from it to a criminal prison. She could afford to make concessions now.

"It was not you or your horse I attacked intentionally. I mistook you for another. For that brother of yours, Mr. Chandos, whose liberty will soon be put beyond jeopardy, and his life after it. Your great likeness to George Heneage, as he looked in those old days at Hallam, is unfortunate. For one thing, it has caused me to hate you; when, to speak candidly, I think in yourself there is not much to hate. You"—turning her flashing eyes on the men—"are seeing me out of the house because I have acted my part effectually in it; a part that Sir Richard Mayne himself would say I was justified in playing; but there is a greater criminal concealed above, for whom a warrant is, as I expect, already in force."

"You are wrong," said Mr. Chandos. "Were the whole establishment of Scotland Yard to make their appearance here, each with a warrant in his hand, they would scarcely execute it. It has been a long, a weary, and a wearing battle: Edwin Barley against George Heneage: but God has shown Himself on the side of mercy."

The words puzzled her a little. "Has he escaped?" she fiercely asked. "Has he left the house?"

"He has not left it, Mrs. Penn; he is in the west wing."

She threw up her head with a glow of triumph, and walked rapidly away down the broad walk, the policemen escorting her.

Standing at the back of the hall in utter amazement, partly at seeing Mrs. Penn go forth at all, partly at the object she presented in the grey cloak, was Lizzy Dene. "Miss," she said to me, as I stood just inside the great dining-room, "I should say she must have been the one to frighten Black Knave that night."

"Perhaps she was, Lizzy. Her cloak is grey."

An impulse came over me that I would ask Lizzy Dene the motive of her suspicious conduct in the past. Now that the culprit had turned out to be Mrs. Penn, Lizzy Dene must have been innocent. Stepping within the large dining-room, I asked her there and then.

"Ah," said she, throwing up her hands, a habit with her when annoyed or in pain, "I don't mind telling now. I was in trouble at that time."

"What do you mean, Lizzy?"

"I have a brother, miss; as steady, well-meaning a man as you'd wish to see," she answered. "He came into this neighbourhood in search of work, he and his wife; and a fine worry he has had with her, on and off. She's wild; if there's a wake or a dance within ten miles, she must be off after it: and at times she has been seen the worse for drink. Not that you'd think it, to look at her; she's a pretty, neat, jaunty young woman; never a pleasanter than she when she chooses. Well, try as he would, he couldn't get work in these parts, except an odd job now and again: and you know, miss, when everything is going out, and nothing's coming in, it doesn't take long for any few pounds that may have been saved in an old stocking, to come to an end."

"That's true enough, Lizzy."

"*Theirs* did. And what should they do when all was gone but come to me to help them. I did it. I helped them till I was tired, till I could help no longer. She, it was, mostly that asked; he'd never have begged a sixpence from me but when driven to it by sheer want. She pestered my very life out, coming here continually, and when I told her I had no more money to give, and it was of no use asking for it, then she prayed for broken victuals. Things had got very low with them. 'Who's that woman that's always creeping here after Lizzy Dene!' the servants said. 'Who's that man that we see her with!' they'd say again. And I did not choose to say who. Both of them had got very shabby then; and he, what with the ill luck and her conduct, had been seen twice in drink. My lady is excessively particular that the servants she has about her shall belong to respectable people; Hill is always on the watch; and what I feared was that I might be turned from my place. It was not a pleasant life for me, miss." I thought it could not have been.

"One afternoon—the same that the accident occurred to Mr. Chandos—Tilda had been up to the house, begging as usual. She vowed, if I would not relieve her with either money or food, to do some damage to the family: but I paid no attention to her, and wouldn't give her anything. After she was gone, I kept thinking over what she had said—that she'd do some damage to the family—and I got right down frightened, lest she should put her threat in force. What if she should fire one of the haystacks, or poison the poultry?—all sorts of horrors I kept on imagining. I begged some cold meat of the cook, inventing a story of a poor sick family, and collected some broken bits of bread, with a pinch of tea, and ran out with it all in a basket, at the dusk hour. They were lodging in one of the lanes close by; and when I got there I found Tilda had not been in. I couldn't stop; I gave the things to John, and told him he must keep Tilda away or I should lose my place; he promised he'd do what he could, but added that I knew as well as he did how little she'd be ruled. In hurrying back through the avenue, with my basket, I came upon Mr. Chandos lying there; you were standing by him. Miss, when I heard what had happened, as true as that we are here, I was afraid that she had done it. I went back and taxed her with it; she had come in then, but was sullen, and would not say yes or no. I was frightened out of my senses for fear it should come out; and I tried to lay it upon the gipsies. But the next day, when her temper came to her, she vowed and protested that she'd had nothing to do with it. I thought then it really was the gipsies, and wished to bring it home to them. That's the whole truth, miss, as I'm here living at this moment."

"And what were you doing in my room that night, Lizzy?"

"What night, miss?"

"When I surprised you, and you appeared so confused. The excuse you made was that you were looking for the ghost."

"And so I was looking for it, miss," she answered: "I was doing nothing else. One of the girls had said the ghost was abroad that night, and I thought I'd look. Between Tilda and the ghost my time was a bad one just then. I'm sure I was thankful when she and John left these parts. He has got work at the malting in a distant town, and they are doing well. I wish the ghost could be got rid of as easily."

If Lizzy Dene had only known how utterly the poor ghost had gone out of the world for ever! Would Chandos ever lose its belief in it?

"I have told you this, miss, because I thought you seemed to suspect me; and I didn't deserve it. I'm true to the family, to the backbone, miss; and so I always will be. My lady has confidence in me; she has known me a long while."

The explanation over, Lizzy Dene left me. I crossed the hall to enter the oak-parlour just in time to see Hickens open the front-door to a visitor, and to hear a colloquy. My heart seemed to shrink within me at the voice, for it was Mr. Edwin Barley's. What could have brought *him* to the house, boldly inquiring for its inmates?

It appeared that Mrs. Penn, on her stealthy visit to his house that morning, had not seen him. Upon inquiring for Mr. Barley, she was told he had gone out betimes, shooting. The information took her aback. Go out shooting, when his enemy, for whom he had been searching night and day these ten years, was close at hand, waiting to be apprehended! And she forthwith accused the footman of not delivering to his master the note left at the house the previous night, upon which she had the pleasure of hearing that the note was duly delivered to Mr. Edwin Barley, and turned out to be a circular about the fashions. All she could do then was to write a few lines, giving him the information about George Heneage, with a charge that it should be put into Mr. Barley's hands the instant he set foot in the house. But Mr. Barley did not return to it quickly. The birds were shy that day.

Later, when he was at length going home, his gun in one hand and a brace of pheasants in the other, he encountered a procession. Turning out at the lodge-gates came Mrs. Penn, one policeman walking by her side, another behind; and, following on, Mrs. Penn's luggage in a truck propelled by a man in the Chandos livery. Mr. Edwin Barley naturally stopped; although he had not been on good terms with Mrs. Penn for some years; and inquired the meaning of what he saw.

"You are the only relative I have left in the world, Mr. Edwin Barley; will you, as such, suffer this indignity to be put upon me?" were the first words she spoke. And he, thus called upon, turned in his haughty, menacing manner on the officers.

"What is the meaning of this? Unhand the lady! Why are you guarding her in that offensive manner?"

"We have orders, sir, to see the lady safely away from Chandos."

"Who gave you the orders?"

"Mr. Chandos."

Mr. Edwin Barley said something about making Mr. Chandos retract his orders before the day was over; but the men were not to be intimidated.

"The lady has not been behaving on the square, sir, and we thought at first she would be given into custody. But Mr. Chandos considered it over; and said, as she had been able to do no great harm, he'd let her go."

Mr. Edwin Barley looked to Mrs. Penn for an explanation. Instead of giving it, she whispered in his ear the information about George Heneage. For the first time for years, Mr. Edwin Barley's face was moved with powerful emotion.

"WHAT do you say?" he asked, in his surprise and bewilderment.

"What I say is sufficiently plain: George Heneage, the murderer of your ward, the indirect murderer of your wife, is in concealment at Chandos," said Mrs. Penn, rather tragically. "The mysteries of that west wing have been cleared to me. Anne Hereford penetrated to it yesterday for some purpose of her own, and saw him: an emaciated being she described him, bearing a striking resemblance to Harry Chandos. Now what do you say to my having entered the house as a detective, Mr. Edwin Barley? And it is for having pursued my investigations that Mr. Chandos has turned me forth in this ignominious manner."

Mr. Edwin Barley drew in his lips. She said not a word, be it understood, of the illegitimate mode in which she had pursued the said investigation. He turned matters rapidly over in his mind, and then addressed the policeman.

"What were you intending to do with this lady?"

"Our orders were to see her into your house, sir. Nothing more."

"My mission in this part of the world is over," interrupted Mrs. Penn; "I shall leave it for London this afternoon. Until then, say for an hour or two, I shall be glad to find a shelter in your house, Mr. Edwin Barley."

"Very good. After that you are at liberty, I presume, to take orders from me?" he added to the officers. And they signified they were, if he had any to give.

"You can then follow me to Chandos. Stay outside the house, and be ready to obey the signal I shall give you. Be prepared to take into custody a criminal who has been evading the law for years, and who will probably make a desperate resistance. What do you say? No warrant? Nonsense. I am in the commission of the peace, and will absolve you of any consequences."

Laying his gun and birds on the luggage, Mr. Edwin Barley turned to Chandos. The policemen, who had not the remotest intention of quitting their prisoner until they had seen her within Mr. Barley's doors, continued their way there. Thus it happened: and the voice of Edwin Barley demanding to see Lady Chandos greeted my dismayed ears as I crossed the hall. Why he should have asked for Lady Chandos, he himself best knew: the demand was an imperative one.

"My lady cannot be seen, sir," was the reply of Hickens. "She is better, I hear; but she is not yet out of her rooms. Sir Harry is within."

"Who do you say is within?" cried Mr. Edwin Barley, probably thinking his ears might deceive him.

"Sir Harry Chandos."

"*Sir* Harry," repeated Mr. Edwin Barley, wondering doubtless whether Hickens had lost his senses. "What do you mean by calling him that?"

"I call him nothing but what's right, sir. He is Sir Harry now, unfortunately: that is unfortunately for poor Sir Thomas. News came this morning, sir, that Sir Thomas has been killed in battle. We have got the house shut up for him."

Mr. Edwin Barley stepped backwards, and looked at the white

blinds, closely drawn behind the windows. The tidings took him by surprise. Having gone out shooting before the letters and papers were delivered, he was in ignorance of the morning's news.

"I am sorry to hear it," he said. "It is an additional blow for Lady Chandos; and she does not need it. Sir Thomas was the best of the three sons: I had no grudge against him. But Mr. Harry Chandos does not take the title, my man."

"Oh yes, he does, sir. He is now Sir Harry Chandos."

"I tell you *no*," returned Mr. Edwin Barley, with a grim smile. "He is just as much Sir Harry Chandos as I am: it is not he who comes into the title. Let it pass, however."

"Did you want him, sir?" inquired Hickens, quitting at once the controversy, like a well-trained servant.

"I do. But I would very much have preferred to see Lady Chandos first."

"That is quite out of the question, sir," concluded Hickens, as he conducted his visitor to the state drawing-room.

As will readily be understood, I have to relate things now that did not at the time come under my personal knowledge: they only reached me later. Mr. Edwin Barley, with those two keen policemen posted outside the house and he within it, considered George Heneage as certainly his prisoner as though he had lain at his feet manacled and fettered. He could not resist the temptation of entering the house that contained his long-sought enemy.

Hickens took his revenge. Returning with his master to the drawing-room, he contrived to let it be known that he maintained his own opinion; giving the announcement with great emphasis:

"Mr. Edwin Barley, Sir Harry."

# CHAPTER 29

## IN THE WEST WING

Mr. Edwin Barley, standing with his back to the door, wheeled round at the words. Sir Harry Chandos waited for him to speak, never inviting him to a seat.

"Good-morning, Mr. Chandos."

"Good-morning," coldly returned Sir Harry. "To what am I indebted for the honour of this visit?"

"I will tell you. One object of it is to demand an explanation of your treatment of Mrs. Penn. She has brought her wrongs to me; her only living relative, as she puts it. I suppose, as such, it lies with me to ask it. Mrs. Penn was engaged by Lady Chandos; engaged as a lady; and you have turned her away as a menial, subjecting her to gross indignity."

Sir Harry stared at the speaker, scarcely crediting his own ears. The exceeding impudence of the proceeding, after Mrs. Penn's treacherous conduct, was something unique.

"You will obtain no explanation from me, sir; you can apply to Mrs. Penn herself; if you require one. I am disgusted at the wickedness, the false deception of the whole affair, and will not condescend to recur to it. You are not welcome in this house, Mr. Edwin Barley, and I must request you to quit it. I cannot conceive how you could have dared to come here."

"The explanation, sir," persisted Mr. Edwin Barley. "Fine words will not enable you to evade it."

He spoke as though he really required the explanation. Sir Harry did not understand, and a few sharp words passed on either side. Both were labouring under a mistake. Sir Harry assumed that all Mrs. Penn had done in the house had been under the express direction of Mr. Edwin Barley. Mr. Edwin Barley, on his side, was not aware that she had done anything wrong. They were at cross-purposes, and at that angry moment did not arrive at an understanding.

"Treachery?" echoed Mr. Edwin Barley, in answer to a word dropped by Sir Harry. "The police will soon be in charge of one, guilty of something worse than treachery. A criminal lying under the ban of the law is not far off."

"You allude to my brother, Mr. Edwin Barley. True, he is lying not far off—very near to us."

The quiet words—for Sir Harry's voice had dropped to a strange calmness—took Edwin Barley by surprise. In this ready avowal, could it be that he saw reason to doubt that George Heneage had already again made his escape? Drawing aside the white blind, he saw one of the police-officers under the trees opposite; the other of course being at the back of the house. And it reassured him. Never more could George Heneage escape him.

"Your brother shall not elude me, Mr. Chandos. I swear it. I have waited for years—for years, Harry Chandos—to catch him upon English ground. That he is on it now, I know. I know that you have him in hiding: here in the west wing of your house. Will you resign him peacefully to the two men I have outside? Revengeful though you may deem me, I would rather spare disturbance to your mother. The fact of his apprehension cannot be concealed from her: that is impossible; but I would spare her as far as I can, and I would have wished to see her to tell her this. If you do not give him up quietly, the police must come in."

"I think—to save you and the police useless trouble—you had better pay a personal visit to my brother," said Sir Harry. "You have rightly said that he has been in hiding in the west wing; he is there still."

"Your brother!—George!" exclaimed Mr. Edwin Barley, quite taken aback by the invitation, and suspecting some trick.

"My brother George," was the quiet answer. "Did you think I was speaking of Sir Thomas? He, poor fellow, is no longer in existence."

"As I hear: and I am sorry for it. Your servant wished to assure me that you had succeeded to the honours; he calls you 'Sir Harry.' I told him better," concluded Mr. Edwin Barley, with a cough that said much.

"I do succeed to them—more's the pity. I wish Thomas had lived to bear them to a green old age."

"Let me advise you not to *assume* them, at any rate, Mr. Harry Chandos: the time has not come for it, and the world might laugh at you. George Chandos, fugitive-criminal though he has been, would succeed until proved guilty. Wait your time."

"You are wasting my time," rejoined Sir Harry. "Will you pay a visit to the west wing?"

"For what purpose? You are fooling me!"

"I told you the purpose—to see my brother George. You shall see him, on my word of honour."

The answer was a gesture of assent, and Sir Harry crossed the hall to ascend the stairs. Mr. Edwin Barley slowly followed him, doubt in his step, defiance in his face. That he was thoroughly perplexed, is saying little; but he came to the conclusion as he walked along the gallery that George Heneage was about to beseech his clemency. His clemency! Hill opened the west wing. Seeing a stranger, she would have barred it again, but Sir Harry put her aside with calm authority, and went straight to one of the rooms. Turning for a moment there, he spoke to his visitor.

"We have not been friends, Mr. Barley; the one has regarded the other as his natural enemy; still I would not allow even you to come in here without a word of warning, lest you should be shocked."

"Lead on, sir," was the imperative answer. And Sir Harry went in without further delay.

On the bed, laid out in his shroud, sleeping the peaceful sleep of death, was the emaciated form of George Heneage Chandos. Mr. Edwin Barley gazed at him, and the perspiration broke out on his forehead.

"By Heaven! he has escaped me!"

"He has escaped all the foes of this world," answered Sir Harry, lowly and reverently. "You perceive now, Mr. Edwin Barley, that were you to bring the whole police force of the county here, they would only have the trouble of going back for their pains. He is at rest from persecution; and we are at rest from suspense and anxiety."

"It has destroyed my life's aim," observed Mr. Edwin Barley.

"And with it your thirst for revenge. When a man pursues another with the persistent hatred that you have pursued him, it can be called nothing less than revenge."

"Revenge! What do you mean? He did commit the murder."

"His hand was the hand that killed Philip King: but it was not intentional murder. He never knew exactly—at the time or since—how he fired the gun, except that his elbow caught against the branch of a tree when the gun was cocked. Some movement of his own undoubtedly caused it; he knew that; but not a wilful one. He asserted this with his dying lips before taking the Sacrament."

"Wilful or not wilful, he murdered Philip King," insisted Mr. Edwin Barley.

"And has paid for it. The banned life he has been obliged to live since was surely an expiation. His punishment was greater than he could bear; it was prolonged and prolonged, and his heart broke."

Mr. Edwin Barley had his eyes fixed on the dead face, possibly tracing the likeness to the handsome young man of nine or ten years ago.

"Of other crime towards you he was innocent," pursued Sir Harry. "He never injured you or yours; there might have been folly in his heart in the heyday of his youth and spirits; there was no sin. You have been unreasonably vindictive."

"I say No," returned Mr. Edwin Barley, striving to suppress an emotion that was rising and would not be suppressed. "Had I ever injured George Heneage, that he should come into my home and make it desolate? What had my wife or my ward done to him that he should take their lives? He killed both of them: the one deliberately, the other indirectly, for her death arose out of the trouble. Charlotte Delves—Mrs. Penn now, of whom you complain—lost her only relative, myself excepted, when she lost Philip King. And for me? I was left in that same desolate home, bereft of all I cared for, left to go through life *alone*. Few men have loved a wife as I loved mine: she was my one little ewe-lamb, Harry Chandos. Vindictive! Think of my wrongs."

Looking there at each other, the dead face lying between them, it might be that both felt there was much to forgive. Certainly Harry Chandos had never until that moment realized the misery it had brought to Edwin Barley.

"I see; we have all alike suffered. But he who caused the suffering is beyond reproach now."

"As things have turned out, the game is yours, Sir Harry," said Mr. Edwin Barley, who was too much a man of the world to persist in denying him the title, now that he found it was his beyond dispute. "For my actions I am accountable to none; and were the time to come over again, I should do as I have done."

He turned to quit the room as he spoke, and Mr. Chandos followed him downstairs. A word exchanged at their foot caused Mr. Barley to inquire what it was Mrs. Penn had done: and then Sir Harry gave him the full particulars, with the additional information that she was assumed to have been acting for him, Edwin Barley.

"She was not," said Mr. Barley, shortly. "I knew nothing of this. Placed in the house by me, Sir Harry? She placed herself in the house, as I conclude; certainly I did not place her there."

"You have met her in secret in the grounds."

"I have met her accidentally, not secretly. Twice, I think; or three times; I am not sure. She chose to repeat things to me; I did not ask for them. Not that they were of any value—as the unmolested retirement of George Heneage here proves." He had been gradually moving to the hall-door. Sir Harry put a sudden question to him, quite upon impulse, as he told me afterwards, just as the thought occurred to him.

"Has your wife's will ever been found?"

"What is that to you?" asked Mr. Edwin Barley, turning to face him.

"Little indeed. I am sorry to have mentioned it: it was not with any wish to add to the discomforts of the day. As I have done so, I will ask you to remember that there are others in the world as capable of error, not to say crime, as was poor George Heneage."

"Do you insinuate that I suppressed the will?" demanded Mr. Edwin Barley.

"No. The will could not disappear without hands; but I should be sorry to give the very faintest opinion as to whose hands they were that took it. With your large fortune, it seems next door to an impossibility that you could have suppressed it: on the other hand, you alone derived benefit from its loss. The thing is a puzzle to me, Mr. Edwin Barley."

"But that you seem to speak honestly in saying so, without sinister insinuation, I would knock you down, Sir Harry Chandos," was Edwin Barley's answer.

"I insinuate nothing; and I say neither more nor less than I have said. It was a paltry sum to run a risk for, whoever might have been guilty of the abstraction. Not only that: no blessing—or luck, as the world would call it—ever yet attende4 one who robbed the orphan."

"You would wish me to make a merit of generosity, and offer Miss Hereford a present of the money," said Mr. Edwin Barley, a ring of mockery in his tones.

"By no means," hastily replied Sir Harry. "Miss Hereford's future position in life will preclude her feeling the want of it. You informed me the last time I had the honour of speaking to you, that you were Miss Hereford's only relative: as such, allow me to acquaint you with the fact that she is to be my wife."

"I expected it would end in that," was Mr. Edwin Barley's answer. "And I tell you honestly that I would have removed her from here in time to prevent it, had it been in my power. I liked the child; my wife loved her; and I had rather she married any one in the world than a Chandos. It is too late now."

"Quite too late. Although I am a Chandos, I shall hope to make her happy, Mr. Edwin Barley. I will do my best to accomplish it."

Hickens went into the hall at that juncture and the colloquy came to a close. Mr. Edwin Barley moved rapidly to the door, which Hickens opened, and went away with a quick step.

"I have no further orders," he said to the policeman who was standing watching the back of the house and part of the avenue. "The prisoner has escaped."

"Escaped, sir! It must have been before we came on then. Shall we search for him?"

"No. He is gone where search would not reach him."

Mr. Edwin Barley strode on with the last words. The man, somewhat mystified, stared after him, and then crossed the lawn to give notice to his fellow that their mission to Chandos seemed to be over.

"Le diable n'est pas si noir que l'on dit," runs the idiomatic saying in France. We have it also in English, as the world of course knows; but it sounds better, that is, less wrong, to give it in the former language. We girls at school there said it often; had one of us ventured on the English sentence at Miss Fenton's, that lady's eyes would have grown round with horror.

It might be applied to Mr. Edwin Barley. Looking back dispassionately, bringing reason to bear on the retrospect, I could not trace one single act or word in him that would justify me in having thought him so bad a man. Taking the colouring from my first view of him, when his dark and certainly ugly face peeped out from the avenue at Hallam, frightening me terribly; and from the dreadful events that followed, in which my childish imagination mixed him up as the worst actor in them, this prejudice had lived and grown in my mind. He had really done nothing to merit it. There was the abstracted will, but it was not proved that he had taken it; probably he had not done so. I had been too young to realize the terrible blow brought upon him through George Heneage. And, as we learned later, the vindictive feeling with which he had pursued him all through these years had its rise in self-defence, as well as in a desire to inflict punishment. The semi-doubt cast, or to himself seeming to be cast, on Mr. Edwin Barley at the time, in the remarks that he had been the only one to profit, and that largely, by Philip King's death, had rankled in his mind, implanting there a burning anxiety, apart from other considerations, to bring to light the real criminal. For his own part, he had never for a moment doubted that it had been intentional, deliberate murder. And I have grown to think that the exaggeration he imparted to Philip King's dying words arose unwittingly in the confusion of the moment; and that he was unconscious that he did so exaggerate. A passive listener hears words more clearly than an actor.

Mr. Edwin Barley went home after quitting Chandos. Seated there, her things off, and a luncheon-tray before her, with no trace of her luggage to be seen, was Charlotte Delves—Mrs. Penn of late years. Was she intending to take up her present quarters at his house? The question mentally occurred to Mr. Edwin Barley, and it did not tend to his gratification. Not if he knew it; he had not been upon cordial terms with Charlotte Delves for years; and what he had now heard of her line of conduct at Chandos vexed him.

There must be a word or two of retrospect. Shortly after Selina's death, Mr. Edwin Barley went abroad. Not a place on the European continent but he visited, one feverish object alone swaying him—the discovery of George Heneage. The detective police were at work in England with the same view: all in vain. At the end of three years he returned home; and almost close upon it there occurred some rupture between him and Charlotte Delves, who had remained at Hallam all that time as the house's mistress. People thought she cherished visions of becoming its master's wife; if so, she was lamentably mistaken. Mr. Edwin Barley was wedded to Selina and her memory; he had no intention whatever of exalting another to her place. Whether Charlotte found out this in too sudden a manner; whether the cause was totally unconnected with this, certain it was that a rupture occurred and Charlotte resigned the housekeeping, and left the house. She took the same sort of service with an old man, a connection also, of the name of Penn. He had married late in life, and had a young daughter, Lottie, who had been named after Charlotte Delves. Very much to the world's surprise—her little world—it was soon announced that Charlotte Delves was going to marry him. Mr. Edwin Barley, hearing of it, wrote to tell her what he thought of it in his own outspoken carelessness: "Old Penn was quite a cripple, and three parts an idiot since he had fallen into his dotage. She would be better without him than with him, and would only make herself a laughing-stock if she married him." The gratuitous advice did not tend to heal the breach. Charlotte Delves did marry Mr. Penn, and very shortly afterwards was called upon to bury him. The young girl, Lottie, by whom her stepmother seemed to have acted a good part, died within a year; and Mrs. Penn, left with a slender income, chose to go out in the world again. She became companion to a lady, and the years passed on.

Time softens most things. Mrs. Penn grew to forget her fleeting marriage and with it the episodes of her middle life; and went back to her old likings and prejudices. Her heart's allegiance to Edwin Barley returned; she was of his kin, and the wrongs inflicted by George Heneage, temporarily forgotten, resumed their sway within her. Whilst she was at Marden (travelling about from place to place with Mrs. Howard) some accidental occurrence caused her to suspect that George Heneage, instead of being abroad, was in concealment in England, and within a drive of Chandos. She at once wrote news of this to Mr. Edwin Barley, with whom she had held no communication since the advent of that letter of his at her marriage. It caused him to remove himself, and four or five of his household, to the vicinity of Chandos. There he took up his abode, and spent his time watching the house and the movements of Mr. Chandos, in the hope of gaining some clue to the retreat of George Heneage. With the exception of this watching, which caused him to stroll at unorthodox hours into the groves and private paths, to peer in at windows by night, his conduct was inoffensive. Mrs. Penn, on her side, seized the opportunity afforded by Mrs. Freeman's illness (it was as though for-tune favoured her), and got into Chandos. My presence in it might have been a serious check to her, only that I did not recognize her. She did not recognize me in the first interview; not until the day when I sent in my name at Mrs. Marden's. Of course Mrs. Penn's object after that was to *keep* me in ignorance of her identity. She had really been to Nulle for a week or two; it was in the autumn I first went there; had seen me at church with the school, and so tried to persuade me it was there I had seen her. Much as she wanted me away from Chandos for the furtherance of her own ends, cruel as were the means she tried to effect it, she had, strange to say, taken a liking for me; and in her dislike to Mr. Chandos had cared little what wild untruths she told me of him, hoping to separate us effectually.

Of her effecting an entrance into Chandos as companion, Edwin Barley knew nothing. After she had settled there she looked out for him, and waylaid him in the grounds. Whilst Mr. Edwin Barley had been ignorant of her life and doings for some years, there was no doubt that she had contrived to keep herself acquainted with his, including his removal to the gates of Chandos. In this interview with him, which I had partially overheard—and I now think it was the first she held with him—she told him what her object was: that of finding out all that could be found out about George Heneage. With the change in Mrs. Penn's person and the remarkable change in her hair, Mr. Edwin Barley had some difficulty in believing it to be Charlotte Delves. The hair was an unhappy calamity. Mrs. Penn, beguiled by fashion and confidential advertisements into wishing to turn her light flaxen hair to golden, had experimented upon it: the result was not gold, but a glowing, permanent scarlet. She told him she was watching at Chandos for his sake. Mr. Edwin Barley, an implacable man when once offended, was cool to her, declining, in a sense, to accept her services. If she made discoveries that could assist in the tracking of George Heneage, well and good; she might bring them to him: and so the interview ended.

Mrs. Penn might have made a discovery to some purpose but for two things. The one was that she was really a coward, and believed the ghost haunting the Pine Walk to be a ghost: the other that she took up a theory of her own in regard to the west wing. She assumed that Lady Chandos had become mad; to this she set down all the mystery enacted in it; and this view she imparted to Mr. Edwin Barley. He neither asked her to bring tales to him, nor encouraged her to do it; if she worked, she worked of her own accord; and his doors remained closed to her. At least, Mrs. Penn did not choose to try whether they would be open. Until this day: and her entering them now could not be said to be of her own seeking.

She sat taking her luncheon. Mr. Barley entered in silence, and stood with a dark expression on his lips. Charlotte knew it of old, and saw that something had not pleased him. Things had very much displeased him; firstly, the escape of the long-sought prisoner; secondly, Madam Charlotte's doings at Chandos. Mr. Edwin Barley might have winked at the peering and prying, might have encouraged the peeping into letters; but to steal things (even though but in appearance) he very much disapproved of, especially as *he* was looked upon as having instigated her.

"What's the matter, Mr. Barley?" asked Charlotte, helping herself to some partridge. "He *is* there, is he not?"

"Who?"

"George Heneage. In the west wing."

"Yes, he's there. I've seen him."

"Ah, I knew it," she said, with a relieved sigh. "Have the police got him?"

"No, the police have gone. I dismissed them."

Charlotte threw down her knife and fork. "Dismissed them! Without taking him! Are you going to show leniency at the eleventh hour, like a weak woman, Mr. Edwin Barley? After what I have done to trace him!"

"You have done a little too much," returned Mr. Edwin Barley. And, abandoning his short and crusty answers, he spoke at length his opinion of her acts at Chandos. He was not in the humour to suppress any bitterness, and said some keen things.

Charlotte went into a terrible passion. Prudence was forgotten; and Mr. Edwin Barley was doomed to listen to the wild ravings of an angry woman. Reproach for the past, for things that she had deemed wrongs in the bygone years, came out all the more freely for having been pent up within her so long. She contrasted her conduct with his: her ever-anxious solicitude for his interests; his neglect and cruel non-recognition of them. As the most forcible means of impressing his ingratitude upon him, she recapitulated the benefits she had wrought one by one; talking fast and furiously. Mr. Edwin Barley, a cool man under petty grievances, listened in silence: he had said his say, said it with stinging coldness, and it was over. Feeling very much inclined to stop his ears was he, when something further said by her caused him to open them, as ears had never perhaps been opened yet. Charlotte had overshot her mark in her reckless rage; and was scarcely aware that she had done so until Mr. Edwin Barley, his face and eyes blazing, seized her wrists.

She had gone too far to retract, and she brazened out her avowal, making a merit of it, rather than taking the shame of it.

It was she who had stolen Mrs. Edwin Barley's will. She, Charlotte Delves. She had taken it as a duty—in her regard for his, Edwin Barley's interests. Who was the child, Anne Hereford, that she should inherit what of right belonged to him? When she had appeared to find the keys in the china basket on the mantel-shelf, it was she who had put them there ready to be found.

There ensued no reproach from Mr. Barley's lips. At first she thought he was going to strike her, staring at her with his white and working face; but the moments passed and he overcame his emotion. Perhaps he feared he might be tempted to strike her if he spoke. It seemed as if a blow had fallen on him—as if the depth of feeling aroused by her confession were, not so much wrath, as a sense of awful injury to himself that could never be repaired.

"What became of the will?" was the only question he put when the silence was growing ominous to her ears.

"I burnt it. It was done for you. Throughout my life I have had regard only to the interests of the Barleys. And this is my recompense—reproach and base ingratitude!"

He quitted the room without speaking another word. This was the worst blow Mr. Edwin Barley had yet received. He knew that the disappearance of the will had been set down by some people to his own hands. Why, had not Sir Harry Chandos hinted as much, only an hour ago? He had treated the past insinuations with contempt, always insisting that there had been no will to abstract—for he fully believed his wife had herself repented of the testament and destroyed it. He knew how capricious Selina was; never keeping in the same mind two days together. And now he had to hear that the world was right and he wrong: the will *had* been abstracted. It did not tend to soothe him, to be told that it was taken out of regard to him and his own interests.

Altogether he deemed it well to cut short his interview with Mrs. Penn. That lady, finding that the house intended to show itself inexorably inhospitable, put her bonnet on and went forth to the railway-station of her own accord, her luggage following her. Whether she should annoy Mr. Edwin Barley by sundry letters of reproach, one of the reproaches being that he had never cared for any living being but his doll of a wife; or whether she should wash her hands of him altogether, and treat him henceforth with silent contempt, she had not determined in her mind. She inclined to the letters. Taking her seat in a first-class carriage, she would have leisure to think of it and decide on her journey to London.

# CHAPTER 30

## THE LAST FRIGHT OF ALL

I saw none of them all the afternoon. After the departure of Mr. Edwin Barley, Sir Harry Chandos went out with Dr. Laken. Mrs. Chandos and Madame de Mellissie were in the east wing, and, I fancied, Lady Chandos with them. Emily had offered to take Mrs. Penn's place for a short time, so far as sitting with Mrs. Chandos went; it was one of the best-natured things I had known her do.

It seemed to me ominous, suffering me to sit there all the afternoon alone, no companion but myself and the oak-parlour, and with death in the house! The few words dropped by Emily to her brother about his changed position were beating their sad refrain on my brain. His position was indeed changed: and I was only a poor governess, although I might be a descendant of the Keppe-Carews, I quite thought that the neglect now cast upon me was an earnest that the family at least would not countenance my entrance into it. Well, I would do what was right, and gave him back his fealty: I could only act honourably, though my heart broke over the separation that might ensue.

It was quite dusk when Mr. Chandos came back—the old name will slip out. Dr. Laken went upstairs at once; he turned into the oak-parlour.

"Alone in the dark, Anne?" he said, drawing up the blind a few inches.

It gave a little more light, and I could see his features. He looked preoccupied; but I thought the occasion had come to speak and ought to be seized upon.

What should I say? How frame the words necessary for my task? With my hands and lips trembling, brain and heart alike beating, I was about to speak incoherently, when some one came into the room.

Emily, as I thought at first; but when she came nearer the window I saw that it was Mrs. Chandos. Being left alone for an instant, she had taken the opportunity to come in search of Sir Harry.

"I have not seen you since the Indian mail came in this morning," she said to him. "Why have you not been near me?"

"The day has been a busy one for me," he answered, speaking with the gentleness that one uses to a child. "Many things have had to be seen to."

"It is sad news."

"Very." And the pain in his voice no one could mistake. "Thomas would have come home now."

"Instead of that, we shall never see him again; and you, they tell me, are Sir Harry Chandos. Who would have thought once that you would ever inherit the title!"

"Strange changes take place," was his reply, spoken altogether in a different tone, as if he did not care to encourage in her any reminiscence of the past.

"It is so singular that they should both die together. At least, die to us. That when we were mourning for the one, news should arrive of the death of the other."

"Very singular. But it enables us to mourn openly, Ethel."

"Shall you live at Chandos?" she resumed, after a pause.

"Certainly."

"But mamma says she shall leave it and take me." She sometimes called Lady Chandos mother. "Would you stay on alone?"

"I shall not be alone for long."

She looked at him questioningly. I could see her lovely blue eyes raised to his in the dim light.

"Perhaps you will be marrying, Harry?"

"Yes. In a short time."

The faint pink on her delicate cheeks deepened to crimson. Could it be that she had ever suffered the old hopes to arise should certain contingencies occur? Surely not! And yet—poor thing!—her intellect was not quite as ours is.

"Have you fixed upon your wife?" she inquired, drawing a deep breath.

"I have asked this young lady to be my wife."

He indicated me, standing as I did back against the window. Mrs. Chandos looked at me, her bright colour varying. The same thought evidently crossed her that I had thought might cross them—my unfitness in point of rank. She spoke to him proudly and coldly.

"Your wife will be Lady Chandos now, you must remember."

"I do not forget it, Ethel."

She sighed imperceptibly, and turned to the door. He went to open it for her.

"Emily and mamma have gone to the west wing. I should not like to go there: I never saw any one dead. I was almost afraid to come down the stairs, and now I am afraid to go up them."

"Do you wish to go up?" asked Sir Harry.

"Yes. I wish to be in my own rooms."

He held out his arm to her, and she took it. I stayed alone, wishing the explanation had been made before he went away. But ere the lapse of a minute Mrs. Chandos was in the east wing, and he back in the room with me.

"Would you please let me speak to you a moment," I said—for he had only returned to take up a small parcel left on the table: and he came up to me, putting it down again.

But I could not speak. No, I could not. Now that the moment was come, every word went out of my mind, power of utterance from my mouth. He stood looking at me—at my evident agitation and whitening lips.

"It is only right that I should speak; I have been waiting all the afternoon to do so, Mr. Chandos—I beg your pardon; I mean Sir Harry," I brought out at last, and the very fact of speaking gave me courage. "I wish—I wish—"

"Why, Anne, what is the matter?" he asked, for I had stopped momentarily in agitation. "What is it that you wish?"

"To tell you that I quite absolve you from anything you have said to me:" and the shame I felt at having betrayed emotion brought to me a sudden and satisfactory coldness of manner. "Please not to think any more about me. It is not your fault, and I shall not think it is. Let it all be forgotten."

A perception of my meaning flashed upon him, badly though I had expressed it. He looked at me steadily.

"Do you mean, not think further of making you my wife?"

"Yes."

"Very well. But now will you tell me why you say this?" I hesitated. I think I was becoming agitated again: all because I knew I was getting through my task so stupidly.

"Circumstances have altered with you."

"Well, yes, in a measure. I am a trifle richer; and my wife—as Ethel remarked just now—will be Lady instead of Mrs. Chandos. Why should you object to that?"

"Oh, Mr. Chandos, you know. It is not I who would object; but your family. And—perhaps—yourself."

"Anne, I vow I have a great mind to punish you for that last word. You silly child!" he continued, putting his arms round my waist and holding me close before him. "But that it would punish me as well as you, I wouldn't speak to you for three days: I would let you think I took you at your word."

"Please don't joke. Don't laugh at me."

"I suppose you think that under the 'altered circumstances,' as you call them, I ought to renew my vows And, by the way, I don't know that I ever did make you a formal offer; one that you could use against me in a suit of breach of promise. Miss Hereford, I lay my heart and hand at your disposal. Will you condescend to be the future Lady Chandos?"

Partly from vexation, partly from a tumult of bliss, I gave no answer. Sir Harry took one for himself.

With my face burning—with my heart thrilling as if touched with the strains of some delightful melody, I ran upstairs, barely in time to change my dress for dinner, and nearly ran against Lady Chandos, who was coming out of the east wing.

"There are twin genii, who, strong and mighty,
Under their guidance mankind retain;
And the name of the lovely one is Pleasure,
And the name of the loathly one is Pain.
Never divided, where one can enter
Ever the other comes close behind;
And he who in pleasure his thoughts would centre,
Surely pain in the search shall find."

The good old words (and I don't at this present moment recollect whose they are) came forcibly to my mind in their impressive truth. The sight of Lady Chandos changed my pleasure to pain: for I had had no assurance from *him* that she would approve of what he had been doing. Hastening into my bedroom, I stood at the open door until she should pass: it would not do to shut it in her face, as though I had not seen her.

But instead of passing, she turned to me. While my head was bowed in silent salutation, she halted, and put her hand upon my shoulder, causing my face to meet hers. With the consciousness of whose it had just met, and very closely, with the consciousness of feeling like a miserable interloper who was to be exalted into the place of her predecessor against her will, no wonder I trembled and bent my shrinking face.

"And so you are to be my daughter-in-law?"

The words were not spoken in pride, but in gentle kindness. I looked up and saw love in her eyes; and she might see the gratitude that shone in mine.

"Harry told me last night in the midst of our great sadness; after you had been into our poor George's room. My dear, I have heard a great deal of you since I have been upstairs in confinement, and I feel sure you will make him a good wife."

In my revulsion of feeling I clasped her hands in mine, thanking her—oh, so earnestly. "There is only one thing," I said, the tears running down my face.

"What is that?"

"I am not good enough for him. And oh, Lady Chandos, I was so afraid you would not think me so. I have been a governess, you know. I would have given him up, I have just told him so, now he is Sir Harry Chandos."

She smiled a little. "One objection arose to me when he first spoke—that you were the niece of Mrs. Edwin Barley. But I have grown to-day to think it may be well to overcome the prejudice. Do you know what Harry says?"

I only shook my head.

"He says, as Mrs. Edwin Barley brought (I must speak freely) a curse into our house, you may be destined to bring to it a blessing as the recompense. My dear child, I think it will be so."

She inclined her head, and gave me a fervent kiss. I could have knelt to receive it. I pressed her hand as if I could never let it go. I watched her along the gallery to the west wing amid my blinding tears. I could hardly help lifting my voice in thanks to Heaven for its great love to me. Hill came up the stairs and broke the charm.

"Why, Miss Hereford, you have no light," she said; and indeed my chamber was in darkness. "Allow me to light the branches, miss."

By the unusual attention—a solitary candle would have been good enough for me before—by the sound of her voice as she offered it, I saw she had heard the news. I could not help putting my hand into hers as she turned round from the lighted branches.

"Hill, I hope you will forget that I used to vex you about that west wing. I did not know what it was, you see. But oh, if you had only told me! I would have been so true to you all."

Old Hill put her candle down, that she might have her other hand at liberty; and she laid it upon mine, making it a prisoner.

"Miss, it is I who have got to ask pardon of you for my ill-temper. We were all living in so much dread, that a stranger in the house brought nothing but extra fear and trouble to it. But I liked you through it all; I liked your face that morning years ago on the Nulle steamer at London Bridge. It is the same nice face still. And, Miss Hereford, I am not sorry to hear that you are to be for good at Chandos."

"We shall be friends, Hill."

"I hope so, miss. I shan't be here; I go with my lady."

She went away with her candle. It gave me a shy feeling to think the news should be known to the household. But I soon found it was not known. Hill, the confidential attendant, it may be said friend, was made acquainted with all things, but she did not carry them to the servants under her.

Emily and Dr. Laken dined with us in the oak-parlour. Lady and Mrs. Chandos dined in the east wing. Except that a subdued air pervaded all, even to the tones of our voices and the servants' tread, the meal and evening were just as usual.

"Why did you never tell me you were a Keppe-Carew?" Emily suddenly asked me when we were alone together.

"But I am not a Keppe-Carew."

"Nonsense. Your mother was: it's all the same."

"As a governess, I did not care to say much about my family."

"You were a little idiot, Anne. The Keppe-Carews are as good as we are—better, some might say; and so I suppose I must reconcile myself to the idea of your becoming my brother's wife."

"Oh, Madame de Mellissie, if you only could!"

"And forget that you were once a governess. Well, child, I never disliked you; and there's the truth. It won't seem right, though, for you to take precedence of us all—as you will when you are Sir Harry's wife."

"I never will; indeed I never will."

She laughed. At my being so simple-minded, she told Dr. Laken, who then came in.

It was chilly that night; and when I went to my room at bedtime, I found a fire blazing in the grate—by Hill's orders, I was sure. Ah me, with all my natural propensity to be simple-minded, my earnest wish to remain so for ever, I did feel a glow of pride at being tacitly recognized as the future mistress of Chandos.

Over this fire—a bright, beautiful fire, as befitted a dull house—I sat late, reading, musing, half dreaming. The clock struck twelve, and still I sat on.

For half-an-hour, or so. It was so delightful to realize my happiness; and I was in no mood for sleep. But of course sleep had to be prepared for, and I took my feet from the fender, wondering what sort of a night it was. There had been indications of frost in the evening, and I drew the heavy window-curtains back to take a view outside. "No fear of seeing a ghost now," I too boastfully whispered.

I thought I should have fainted; I nearly dropped on the floor with startled alarm. Not at a ghost: there was none to be seen; but at something that in that startling moment seemed to me far worse.

Emerging from its progress up the avenue, at a snail's pace, as if it cared not to alarm sleepers with its echoes—advancing, as it seemed, upon me—came a great, black, dismal thing, speaking of the dead. A hearse. A hearse without its plumes, driven by a man in a long black cloak.

For a moment I believed I saw a phantom. I rubbed my eyes, and looked, and rubbed again, doubting what spectral vision was obscuring them. But no, it was too real, too palpable. On it came, on and on; turned round, and halted before the entrance-door.

I sat down to hold my beating heart. Surely never were enacted night alarms like those I had encountered at Chandos. And, whilst I sat, muffled sounds as of measured footsteps bearing a burden, smote upon my ear from the corridor.

I listened till they had passed my door, and then silently drew it an inch open. Do not attribute it to an unjustifiable curiosity: I declare that I was impelled to it by fear. Strange though the assertion may seem, it is true; the real cause of all this did not occur to me. Had I been so absorbed in my own happiness as to forget all else?—or had I grown stupid? I know not—only that it was as I say.

They had gained the head of the stairs, and were stopping there, apparently hesitating how best to get down. Four of them besides Sir

Harry Chandos, and they bore a coffin on their shoulders covered with black cloth—Dr. Laken, Hickens, and two men who looked like carpenters. So! that was it!—the unhappy George Heneage was being removed by night!—and the stairs of the west wing, as I knew later, were too narrow for the burden.

I could not see, for the hearse was right underneath my window, but I heard the sounds as they put in the coffin, after they had got it safely down. And then the great black thing drove away again, with its slow and covert steps, some of them following it. It was going to the railway-station.

Sir Harry and Dr. Laken were away for two or three days. The funeral had taken place from the doctor's house. There was no real reason why he might not have been buried from Chandos, except that it would have created so much noise, and put the place up in arms.

And so ended the life and history of the ill-fated George Heneage Chandos.

# CHAPTER 31

## AT CHANDOS

Once more there was light in the gloomy house of Chandos. The blinds were drawn up; the sunlight was allowed to shine in. He who had been the destroyer of its tranquillity and its fair name—through whom, and for whom, they had lived in dread for so many years, having, as Mrs. Penn aptly expressed it, a sword hanging over their heads, which might fall at any minute—he, the erring man, was laid to rest; and had left rest for them. With him, the fear and the dread were gone—almost the disgrace; there was no further need of secrecy, of retirement, of ghosts, of sleep-walking; there was no longer dread of a night invasion by the police. Chandos could hold up its head now in the face of day.

The deep mourning was supposed, by all save a few, to be worn for Sir Thomas Chandos. When Mrs. Chandos appeared in her widow's garb, people at first treated it as one of her eccentricities, but the truth became known in time. They put me into mourning also; and it was done in this way.

"Would you not like to wear it?" Sir Harry said to me the day he came home. "I think, as you are in the house, one of us, it might be well; also as my future wife. What do you say, Anne? Would you object to it?"

"Indeed I would not object: I should like to wear it. I will order—" And there the state of the case occurred to me, and I sat down in consternation.

I had not a shilling in the world. I had no money, either for mourning or for my wedding clothes. The exceeding incongruity of this order of affairs with my position as the future Lady Chandos, struck on me with shame and dismay. What would they all think of me? What reflections of meanness might even the servants not cast upon me? Tears of mortification filled my eyes.

"What's the matter, Anne?"

"I have no money."

Sir Harry laughed. "Don't cry over that, my darling. You will have so much soon, you won't know what to do with it. Tell my mother of your dilemma."

I did not tell her. Perhaps he did. In the afternoon Hill came to my room with Lady Chandos's dressmaker; and in two days my mourning had come home.

The first visitor we had at the house—and he arrived the day I put my mourning on—was Monsieur de Mellissie, looking very ill. Of course he had come after his wife, having started the instant he was able to travel. A somewhat stormy interview ensued between them; but she spoke as one accustomed to having things her own way, and he appeared rather meek beside her. He had arrived with the view of taking her back to France; she vowed and protested that she was not going home yet—that all the steamers plying between the two countries should not take her there; her mamma was about to spend some time at Brighton or Scarborough, as might be agreed upon, and she purposed accompanying her: she wanted recruiting as well as other people.

Lady Chandos came forward to the rescue, her compassion awakened for the poor, sick, evidently suffering man. The first thing, he must go to bed and be nursed, she said; they would talk of plans afterwards. Monsieur de Mellissie was really too ill to dispute the mandate; neither did he feel inclined to do it: after his hurried journey from Paris, bed seemed as a very haven of rest.

They left the room, followed by Lady Chandos, and the next to appear was the agent, Mr. Dexter. He came in, rubbing his hot face as usual. Not that the weather put him into a heat to-day, but the news he brought.

Mr. Edwin Barley had gone away. Mr. Edwin Barley's servant had called upon him with a cheque for a twelvemonth's rent and taxes, and an intimation that his master would not occupy the house again. Mr. Dexter might make what use he pleased of it. If there were any dilapidations for which Mr. Edwin Barley was legally responsible, they would be paid for on the amount being sent to him at the Oaks.

"Gone away, has he?" cried Sir Harry.

"Gone clean away, sir, bag and baggage," replied Mr. Dexter, who seemed unable to get over the surprising fact. "It's the oddest thing I ever knew. The furniture—it was only hired, as you may remember, Sir Harry—is already being removed from the house. A strange whim, to be red-hot for a place one month, and run away from it the next!"

"Very," said Sir Harry, quietly.

"I suppose the truth is, he found the house so different from his own place, the Oaks, that he couldn't reconcile himself to stopping in it," resumed Mr. Dexter, talking as fast as ever. "A magnificent place that, his servant tells me. He has another, too, close by it, that he keeps up as well. I pressed the question on the servant—a most respectable man, quite superior, Sir Harry—what could be taking his master away; but he said he didn't know, unless it might be that he was disappointed at finding the shooting here so poor. The preserves at the Oaks are hardly to be matched in the kingdom. Any way, Sir Harry, he's *gone*, whatever may have taken him."

As Mr. Dexter went out of the room, unburdened of his news, Sir

Harry came to the window where I sat at work, laid his hand upon my shoulder, and made me look up at him.

"Is that little heart of yours relieved by the tidings?"

"Yes; oh, yes. I have not dreaded Mr. Edwin Barley so much the last few days; but I am glad he is gone. I was always fearing that he might apply for some power that would enable him legally to take me from here."

"In that case I must have got legal power on my side in the shape of a special licence, and married you romantically in the great drawing-room at twelve at night, and so made you secure in that way. I think even now it may be safer, Anne, not to delay the ceremony long."

I looked up in consternation, believing he really thought there might still be danger, and met the expression of his eyes. Mine fell on my work again. I began sewing fast.

"Don't you think Monsieur de Mellissie looks very ill, Sir Harry?"

"I do; but low fever reduces a man greatly. When are you going to abandon ceremony? 'Sir Harry' is worse than 'Mr. Chandos' was."

"But what can I call you?"

"I was christened Harry."

"I shall learn it in time," I answered, shyly, "through hearing the others say it."

"Anne, do you know what poor George said the last night of his life?" he asked, after a pause.

"No. Was it about me?"

"It was about you: when you were the little thing he met at Hallam. He said you were a sweet, lovable child: truthful, honest, and good. I think you are the same still."

I bent my blushing face: praises were so sweet from him. Sir Harry suddenly clasped me to him with a deep sound; and I had to kneel down afterwards and hunt for my needle.

A few mornings subsequent to this, the post brought a packet addressed to Sir Harry Chandos. When I saw it was Mr. Edwin Barley's handwriting, my heart failed me. Sir Harry read it twice over, glanced at me, and put it into his pocket. Monsieur de Mellissie was considerably better; the change of air and scene had almost restored him. He did not yet get up to breakfast. I, Emily, and her brother took it alone. Plans had been under discussion for some days. Sir Harry's marriage was already talked of openly.

"Mamma says it will be Scarborough," observed Emily, following out the train of thought she had been pursuing whilst Sir Harry read his letter. "She shall go there for a month, and get to Heneage Grange for Christmas. Ethel goes with her of course, and so shall I. Alfred also; she has invited him. And you, Anne—where do you go?"

I could not tell. I had neither money nor friends. Except the Miss Barlieus.

"Where are you going, Anne? Don't you hear me?" she cried, with some impatience. "Even if mamma remained at Chandos, *you* could not do so, under the same roof with Harry. It would be out of all precedent, you know. The world *would* talk."

"Wouldn't it?" put in Sir Harry. But I thought he was laughing at her.

"Where are you to be married? I mean, from whose house?" she asked, looking straight at me.

"From—Miss Barlieu's," I suggested, humbly, feeling how very humble my share of everything was altogether.

Emily gave a scream. "From Miss Barlieu's! Sir Harry Chandos take his wife from *them*? Well, you have strange ideas, Anne. You ought to be married from Keppe-Carew."

"There is no one at Keppe-Carew now. Arthur Carew is a boy at school."

"Oh, well, I wash my hands of it," said Emily; "I suppose mamma will have to arrange it all. Listen, Anne; I mean to be a frequent visitor at Chandos, so I give you fair warning."

It was on my lips to say she would be always welcome, when Sir Harry spoke: telling her she might probably find that mamma *had* arranged all that was necessary to be arranged. She flew upstairs to ask, and Sir Harry turned to me.

What wonderful news he had to tell! That old saying I spoke of only a few pages back was nothing to it. I sat and listened as one lost in amazement—and when Sir Harry showed me the letter, I read it twice over, as he had done, before knowing whether or not to believe it.

Mr. Edwin Barley had made over to me the amount of money left by Selina, with the full interest thereon at five percent up to the present date. He frankly stated that the mystery of the lost will had now been cleared up: it had been (contrary to his own opinion) abstracted, and, as he found, burnt. He did not give any hint as to the culprit; with all his sins, he was too much of a gentleman to do that: I could acknowledge it now that my prejudices were partially removed: but we felt sure (and knew it later) that it was Charlotte Delves. This money he had caused to be settled on me to my exclusive use and benefit. He informed Sir Harry that the first instalment of the half-yearly interest was waiting to be drawn by me.

"So you are an heiress, after all," said Sir Harry, laughing. "You can buy your own wedding-dress."

But I did not laugh. I was thinking how I had misjudged Mr. Edwin Barley. I had thought him so hard and unjust a man! Hard, he might be: but strictly just.

"I should like to write and thank him."

"Certainly. Write when you like, and what you like. I shall answer his letter. It contains something more, that I have not shown you."

"Am I not to see it?"

For answer Sir Harry folded back the letter, and placed a post-script before me. It seemed to me more amazing than the other.

"Should my niece, Anne Hereford, find herself less happy as Lady Chandos—your wife—than she expects to be, and wish for a refuge, my house will be open to her. If she enters it, whether in the present year or in those long to come, she will be treated in every way as my own child; and be amply provided for at my death."

"Do you expect that you will need a refuge?"

His eyes were gleaming with merriment as he spoke it—a whole lifetime of affection in their depths. If mine unconsciously looked back at their great and tender trust, it was not my fault. But a vision of sometime meeting Edwin Barley and thanking him for this new kindness; of making some little atonement for my past dislike, so far as words of gratitude could atone, rose within me as a vision.

The following week we quitted Chandos for Scarborough—all of us, except Sir Harry. There were many things to be done to the house, improvements and alterations, and he remained to superintend them. He spent Christmas with us at Heneage Grange: it was a smaller place than Chandos, very open, very pretty, and belonged to Lady Chandos for life. I was to remain and be married from it; Lady Chandos had so decided it.

The winter had passed, the spring had come, before I saw Chandos again. I was then in Harry's carriage: alone with him; his wife of only a day or two. Chandos was very far from Heneage Grange, and we had taken the journey easily, travelling post.

I saw it as we turned from the avenue; and did not know it: so different was it now in its light and gay appearance from the gloomy place of the previous autumn. The trees, some of them cut down, were budding into the fresh green of spring; the flowers were opening; the birds sang joyously; the once closed and barred windows were open to the sunshine. All things spoke of hope for us, as if nature had arrayed herself expressly in her brightest colours.

I saw the servants in their gala clothes, with their happy faces, coming forth to welcome us, Hickens at their head, and Lizzy Dene with her bunches of black curls. The tears rained over my eyes, and Harry turned to me.

"My darling, what is grieving you?"

"Joy, I think. There is a promise of so much happiness that I cannot realize it, can scarcely believe in it. My past life has been nothing but loneliness; can you wonder at my almost doubting the great blessings showered upon me now? Harry!"—and I looked down with a shy whisper—"it seems that I never, never can be sufficiently grateful to God."

"We will try to be so, Anne. Sufficiently, no; but just a little, as He shall give us aid. What has been your life, compared with the suffering of mine?—and He has lifted it from me."

He bent his head, I know in prayer. Prayer never to forget the great mercies given. The carriage stopped at the door, and he helped me out.

Once more in the old hall; but it had light now, and bright painted windows, and all sorts of beautiful things. Hill came forward. It was a surprise. Lady Chandos had despatched her there, to superintend our reception, lending her to Chandos for a week.

"Welcome, my lady; welcome home."

My lady! I think it was the first time I had been so addressed, and glanced at Harry. He had me on his arm, and was leading me into the oak-parlour! The dear oak-parlour! We might have to keep state at times, but that would ever be his favourite room and mine.

"Harry, how beautiful it all is! Do you know who I should like to ask to come and see us first of all?"

"Well!" he said, smiling.

"Miss Annette Barlieu."

"And so we will."

Harry came into my dressing-room that night, with an open Bible in his hand. He made me sit down by him while he read a chapter aloud; and I found it was to be his usual custom morning and evening. It was that chapter in Deuteronomy where the following verses occur; and I knew why he had chosen it:

"And it shall be, when the Lord thy God shall have brought thee into the land which He sware unto thy fathers, to Abraham, to Isaac, and to Jacob, to give thee great and goodly cities, which thou buildedst not,

"And houses full of all good things, which thou filledst not, and wells digged, which thou diggedst not, vineyards and olive-trees, which thou plantedst not; when thou shalt have eaten and be full;

"Then beware lest thou forget the Lord, which brought thee forth out of the land of Egypt, from the house of bondage.

"Thou shalt fear the Lord thy God, and serve Him . . . And thou shalt do that which is right and good in the sight of the Lord: that it may be well with thee.

"And it shall be our righteousness, if we observe to do all these commandments before the Lord our God, as He hath commanded us."

"Amen!" said Harry, softly, as he closed the book, carrying it with him from the room.

And I knelt alone to say my prayers, my heart overflowing with a sense of its great blessings, and lifted up in thankfulness to Heaven.

THE END

Printed in the United Kingdom
by Lightning Source UK Ltd.
118915UK00001B/120